MA[illegible]

Lost and Found

Fontana
An Imprint of HarperCollins*Publishers*

Fontana
An Imprint of HarperCollins*Publishers*,
77–85 Fulham Palace Road,
Hammersmith, London W6 8JB

A Fontana Original 1992
9 8 7 6 5 4 3 2 1

First published in 1991 by Crown Publishers, Inc., USA

A catalogue record for this book is
available from the British Library

ISBN 0 00 647136 6
Set in Meridien

Printed in Great Britain by
Clays Ltd, St Ives plc

For Judge who never loses faith and
for Katie, Justin, Emma, and Clare
for their gifts of joy

I believe that we are lost here in America,
but I believe we shall be found . . .

THOMAS WOLFE

Part One

December 24, 1930
Tulsa, Oklahoma

Someone told her to squat for as long as she could and let her legs absorb the pain. But a searing agony cut down from her breasts across her abdomen and exploded in her groin, and she couldn't sustain the position. The baby was shifting inside her.

A comforting hand reached out to stroke her shoulder. 'What can I do? Is this your first?'

She tried to answer, but the upheaval pushed her onto her knees in a curious attitude of prayer and left her fiercely whispering, 'God,' over and over again, not praying, but more like a persistent child in need of attention.

'Go on, make all the noise you want. No one can hear you down here.'

Someone was in the room with her. Who? She didn't know and couldn't take the time to look. The pain was coming at her again, causing her to roll onto her side, both hands clutching at her swollen belly.

In the corner of the shadowy room she saw dim distortions, a stack of boxes on the verge of collapsing, a strange line of mops and brooms like pencil-thin soldiers waiting for battle.

Her shoulders contracted in an attempt to accommodate new agony, the shifting weight in her stomach struggling as she was struggling, both longing to be free of each other.

She ground her head backward on the floor and bit her lip in an effort to keep from screaming.

'How can I help? Please, tell – '

Someone was hovering over her, a useless someone who could do nothing but watch, and she was sorry for the sounds she was making, sorry for the hot water now gushing between her legs, the circle spreading beneath her hips, her knees raised in a futile attempt to ease the pain. Somewhere inside her head she heard terrified breathing. Was this a death place or a life place?

Then the agony was at large again, and she arched her body upward as far as humanly possible. The distortion exhausted her, though the pain was as fresh and lively as ever, the struggle itself just one more stage of the strange liberating process that was taking place.

Nearby someone was praying. She stared upward at the distortion of shadows with unblinking eyes. She knew she was helpless, knew she might die here. The acceptance of death wrapped itself around her like a small victory, and she was just beginning to relax when the final assault jarred her system, the baby inside pushing downward. She was screaming nonsense now, her hands grasping at air while the baby with sly intelligence forced its way out in a continuous stream of warm, quivering life.

The light in the room was fading. The ordeal was over. She tried to raise up and couldn't. Someone cried out, a sound of exuberance, a certain gleam of something alive . . .

December 24, 1930
Tulsa, Oklahoma
Salvation Army Mission

'Where's Martha?'

Captain Meeks shouted out the question above the din of human voices swirling about him. Beyond the counter he saw the second wave of hungry men surge forward, their eyes as hollow as their bellies.

'Skipper? Where's Martha?'

'Don't know, sir. Stand back. Hot soup coming through.'

Quickly Captain Meeks moved to one side as Skipper and Bobby Tucker lugged the big black cast-iron kettle to the serving counter and hoisted it up, spilling some in the process, causing them to jump back while the men on the other side gasped at the waste.

Meeks glanced beyond the solid wall of cadaverous human bodies into the vast Salvation Army Mission hall, chill and dark save for a line of bare bulbs flickering on the ceiling. The red-brick walls were unadorned and blackened by years of neglect. Since the stock market crash last year, his usual number of drunks and derelicts had been joined by men who had lost everything.

'More at the back, sir.'

The frantic voice jarred him into movement. He hurried toward the front door and jerked it open. The sudden cold cut through him despite his jacket and warm woolen trousers. He stood in the open doorway, trying not to breathe in the frigid air, and searched up and down the deserted night street, seeing nothing but piles of dirty snow and stiff strewn garbage where hungry men had scavenged for something to eat.

Martha. Missing all day. It wasn't like her.

Hurriedly he drew his jacket about him. Even with the door closed he still could feel the cold. He saw his lieutenant, Bobby Tucker, hurrying toward him, his face creased with worry.

'There's about twenty-five more at the back door, sir. But there's no more room. What shall we do?'

'Have you seen Martha?' Captain Meeks asked, answering a question with a question.

'No, Captain. What about the men?'

'Let them in,' Meeks ordered.

'But, sir, there's no more – '

'I said let them in,' Captain Meeks repeated, and regretted the harshness in his voice. 'And tell Skipper to start serving,' he added. 'We'll do the best we can.' He felt a new blast of cold air on the back of his neck and thought the door must have blown open. He was just turning to close it when he saw her.

'Martha . . .' He smiled, relieved at first; then he grew suddenly angry that she'd deserted her duties.

It seemed she stood forever in the open doorway, her great gray cloak blowing about her, her normally neatly

braided blond hair mussed and loose about her face. She clung to the door with one hand while with the other she clutched at what appeared to be a boot box just visible beneath her cloak.

Captain Meeks started to scold her, to remind her of his generosity when she had first appeared at his mission door about six months ago, a large strapping farm girl named Martha Drusso from west Texas, about eighteen, down on her luck, in search of a home and a calling. Then she'd seemed the picture of health, with rosy cheeks and a warm ready smile and a way with the lost and lonely.

Softened by his thoughts, he dismissed the scolding and concentrated instead on the young woman who, having made it to the door, seemed incapable of going a step farther.

'Where have you been?'

'There was a woman,' she said. The light from the bare bulb overhead illuminated her face, which seemed without color. 'She was pregnant, on the verge of labor – '

'Where?' Captain Meeks interrupted.

'In the basement of the Mayo Hotel. I sat with her. I wanted to take her to the hospital. But she had no money. I was going to bring her here, but there was no time. She – delivered so quickly.'

Martha reached backward for support as though she had lost her balance. 'She died.'

Captain Meeks closed his eyes and said a brief prayer. 'The infant?'

'Dead, too.'

'Did you call someone in authority?'

'Oh, yes, sir. The hotel manager came. He said he would tell the policeman about it. I waited with her until they came and took her away. She was alone, just . . .'

Her words drifted off. She shook her head as though trying to clear it. 'Sir, may I go to my room for a minute? Then I'll be ready for work.'

'Yes, of course,' Captain Meeks said. 'We can manage here.'

'Is R. C. – '

'Asleep.'

'Thank you, sir. I'll only be a minute.'

With effort she pushed away from the door, seemed to renew her grasp on the boot box beneath her cloak, and started around the shadowy edges of the large room.

Captain Meeks watched her and started to call out other questions, then changed his mind. For now he was just grateful she'd returned. The little boy, R. C., had questioned him all day as to her whereabouts. Not the least of Captain Meeks's worries had been what he'd do with the boy if Martha hadn't returned.

About three months ago Martha had found the child tied to the lamppost outside the kitchen door with a simple note pinned to his jacket.

Please take good care of R. C.

Attached to the note was an envelope containing a certificate of birth for Roland Clarke and a history of the boy. The son of Scottish immigrants, his father, a teacher, had died of influenza in 1926, shortly after R. C. had been born. His mother had died of pneumonia in 1929. As the authorities had been unable to locate any living relatives, the boy had been taken to an orphanage in Albany. A few months later he was placed on an orphan train heading west. The people who had contracted for him had failed to claim him at the Tulsa station. With funds exhausted, the officials had apparently depended on the Christian charity of the mission.

Against his better judgment, Meeks had allowed Martha to keep the boy.

Now he turned his attention back to his crowded mission hall.

'Come along, men,' he called out in a voice that cut through the chill of the room. 'I know you're hungry, and we'll fill your bellies. Then we'll try to fill your hearts with the certain knowledge that God loves you.'

As the ambitious promise echoed about the room, the men stirred. The odors of unwashed bodies and soiled linens joined the food odors of cabbage and coffee coming from

the kitchen. Captain Meeks moved down the line, patting a ragged shoulder, shaking a trembling hand, calling a few of the men by name.

As they started to file past, he grew careless and allowed his faith to falter. *Did* God love these men?

There was no answer to the question, but in the process of asking it, Captain Meeks did enormous damage to himself and felt the night grow colder.

Martha closed the door behind her and in the dark felt for the light cord overhead. She pulled it and set the bare bulb into a gentle swinging motion, the skittering light illuminating first one side of the room, then the other.

She saw R. C. soundly sleeping on his pallet against the wall. Slowly she knelt before her bed and withdrew the boot box. She removed the lid of the box and, using both hands, reached in and lifted out the baby, birth blood still on her body.

She nuzzled the small chest, the beautifully formed head with its soft downy covering of hair. Then she observed a small birthmark on the side of her throat in the shape of a perfect little bell. She smiled and kissed the birthmark.

'Belle. You'll be Belle. Belle Drusso.'

December 25, 1930
Tulsa, Oklahoma

A few minutes before five, shivering in the predawn darkness, Captain Meeks banked the coals in the kitchen cookstove. Christmas morning, always a promising day. The ladies from the Methodist church would be here soon with their baskets of turkeys and great black kettles filled with potatoes and baking pans of dressing.

As the black coals turned red gray around the edges, he stood up and slammed the grate, hoping he'd not awakened Martha sleeping in the next room.

Thinking on Martha, he stared backward through the

passageway that led through the pantry to her room beyond the kitchen. The corridor was pitch black except for the slit of light coming from beneath her door.

He approached the door and knocked quietly. All movement ceased. 'Martha?' he whispered.

There was no answer. He thought he heard something, a faint cry or perhaps a drawer squeaking. Then he heard the doorknob creak and saw the door opening.

He smiled in relief. She was dressed in her dark blue woolen skirt and shirt, her hair drawn back from her face in braids and then a knot. There was a good smell of soap about her and something reassuring in her pleasant and honest face.

'I was concerned,' he began, standing back from the open door. On the corner of her bed, he saw a very sleepy R. C. The little boy looked at him and yawned.

'Be about it, young man,' Captain Meeks said. 'There are trash bins to be emptied and – '

Then he heard a baby's fretful cry. He looked from Martha to the bed and back to Martha.

She moved around him without a word, lifted the bundle, and drew back the corner of the blanket.

'Where did that come from?' he demanded, looking down on the pink face of a newborn infant.

Martha took a minute to find the truth. 'I – I lied, Captain Meeks. Forgive me. I've already asked God for forgiveness. The baby at the hotel – she didn't die.'

'Why didn't you turn her over to the authorities?'

'What would they have done with her?'

'Placed her in the orphanage.'

'Which is already filled, as we both know.'

Yes, he did know that. Almost every day he got requests to feed unwanted and wandering children. And every day he said no. His Salvation Army was not equipped to handle children.

'She can't stay,' he pronounced flatly.

'Then where will she go?'

'You already have one – '

'Then how will another hurt?'

'You're just a girl yourself – '

At that, Martha sat slowly on the bed and drew R. C. under one arm and cradled the infant close in the other. 'Look at me, Captain Meeks,' she said with impressive directness. 'I'm plain, I'm unpolished. No man will ever give me children. God has seen fit to give me two. Please, I beg you, don't take them from me.'

Before such a plea, Captain Meeks faltered. 'What if they interfere with your work?' he challenged.

'They won't. I promise.'

Captain Meeks bowed his head. He was getting old. Everything seemed to wear him out.

'Look at her,' Martha invited, and he glanced down on the baby and saw her newness, her beauty.

'It's Christmas,' he said, with no thought to continuity. Defeated, he warned, 'On a trial basis,' and backed his way to the door.

'Yes, Captain Meeks.' Martha beamed, the light and color newly restored to her face. 'Her name is Belle.'

'And hurry. The Methodist ladies will be here soon.'

He closed the door and stood in the darkened passageway, listening. He heard Skipper in the kitchen, banging the coffeepot about. Outside he heard the crunch of tires on snow. The Ladies Guild had arrived. A hectic day was beginning, the world celebrating another Christmas with one new soul to contribute to the hope for peace on Earth and a better tomorrow.

Belle?

He shrugged in pleasant despair and wondered how in God's name he could prevent Martha from turning his Salvation Army Mission into a haven for lost children . . .

May 3, 1933
Tulsa, Oklahoma

Blue was her color. No doubt about it. It caught the unique blue sparkle in her eyes and highlighted her curly blond hair, which lay in ringlets upon her brow.

Nothing in the world gave Martha greater pleasure, purpose, or hope for the future than her two children. Here she was, coming from nothing, on her way to nothing, and God had sent her two reasons to live, two goals to strive for, and two reasons to forget the grief of the past. Daily she vowed to protect them with her life, sustain them with her efforts, and provide them with all the love they required in order to reach adulthood and know for themselves how important it was to serve something other than oneself.

'Stand still, Belle,' Martha scolded, and at last managed to tie the bow on the blue cotton dress and was rewarded with a smile.

'I go find R. C.,' Belle pronounced with childish seriousness, and started away from Martha through the busy kitchen.

'No, wait,' Martha called, snared the child by the hand, and drew her back to the low stool.

'No,' she repeated. 'You are not to go and *find* R. C.,' she corrected. 'You are to sit on the front steps and *wait* for R. C. He'll be home from school in about ten minutes. Then the both of you are to come back in here to me. Do you understand?'

Belle nodded solemnly and pulled at the blue ribbon that Martha had just tied.

'You're a monkey,' Martha said, and hugged Belle to her. Then she heard Belle whisper close to her ear, 'You monkey, too.'

As Martha laughed aloud, she looked up and saw Skipper grinning at them.

As soon as Belle was out of the door, Martha moved quickly to the serving line so that she could watch her the length of the mission hall. Strange, but that one small splash of blue dress and blond hair seemed to be the only color in the gray brown black of the mission hall.

There were three checker games going on at various points along Belle's route to the front door, and as she passed, all three games were brought to a halt as the men spoke to her, one reaching out to touch her.

'She's got Shirley Temple beat a mile if you ask me,' Skipper commented, and turned hurriedly back to his big black cookstove, where the fried potato hash for the evening meal was on the verge of burning.

'I'll get my apron,' Martha called back to Skipper. As she started toward her room she glanced toward the sunlight beyond the back door. From where she stood she could see the lilacs on the bush beside the steps. Drawn by the warmth of the sun and fragrance of the flowers, she pushed open the back screen door, lifted her face to the sun, and thought of Charlie Groveton.

The past was a burden. She'd have to put it down one day. The truth was, she was doing all right now. She had a job and a sense that she was helping someone. She had R. C. and Belle. Still, she missed her mother, and she missed Charlie.

'Martha, we need help.'

'Coming, sir.'

About fifteen minutes later, her blue denim apron pulled tight across her midsection, Martha plunged her hands into a pail of hot water and lye soap suds, splashed the cloth around, and scrubbed the table surface with all her strength. Only twenty-nine more to go.

Then she heard R. C.'s familiar voice. 'I'm home. I have homework. Can I ask Skipper for a piece of bread?'

Martha raised up and saw him making his way through the tables, his dark hair and dark eyes accenting his pale skin. He was bright, of that Martha was certain. Hadn't his teacher at Lincoln Elementary School told her so, very bright for a seven-, almost eight-year-old.

'Wait,' Martha called, and lovingly indicated he was to take a detour toward her in his steady trek toward the kitchen. 'A hug and a kiss,' she requested, 'and that will do for starters.'

R. C. ducked his head to one side and presented himself for whatever affection Martha needed. She drew him close and smelled that lovely smell of a little boy's hair, damp with perspiration. A strap had torn loose on his overalls. She'd have to mend it, again.

Then Martha remembered. 'Where's Belle?'

At the kitchen door, R. C. shrugged and immediately disappeared. For a moment Martha was lost in the sudden vacuum. 'R. C.?' she called, louder this time, and felt a small panic.

Belle had gone out to the front steps less than fifteen minutes ago. Quite probably R. C. had walked right past her. Martha placed the bucket of water on the floor and started at top speed through the tables.

'Belle?' she called out even before she had pushed open the front door.

She looked down the steps and saw nothing. 'Oh, God,' she murmured, and ran back through the mission hall.

Inside the kitchen she saw R. C. perched on a high stool, gnawing hungrily on the hard heel of a loaf of bread.

'Please, R. C.,' she gasped, strangely out of breath for such a short sprint. 'Belle was to wait for you on the front steps. She's not there. Did you see – '

Before he could answer, Martha turned and ran back through the mission hall. She was aware of footsteps behind her, but all she knew was that Belle wasn't where she was supposed to be, tiny Belle, trusting of everyone, attracting everyone like a magnet.

As she reached the front steps, the panic was fully developed, causing her heart to accelerate. She glanced to her right toward busy Elgin Avenue with its constant rattle of automobiles and streetcars, then beyond Elgin to the train station.

She started off at a dead run, still aware of footsteps behind her but unable to alter her focus from the busy intersection ahead. As she drew near to the corner she saw a shower of blue sparks coming from beneath the wheels of the streetcar. Blue, the color of –

'Dear God, please,' she prayed aloud, and turned toward the left. At that moment she felt a tug at her skirt and looked down to find R. C., his big dark eyes larger than ever.

'Martha?'

'It's all right,' she soothed, seeing his fear. She cupped her hand around his head and drew him close. 'Come on, we must find Belle. She can't have gone far.'

Ahead now she saw a large crowd gathering on the sidewalk, something at the center holding their attention. Encouraged with every step, she pushed through the crowd as politely as possible until at last she was close enough to see that it was an organ grinder, a tattered fellow, half-starved in appearance, his red coat with gold braid hanging on what once had been broader shoulders.

He wore a smart black waxed mustache, and his thin olive face beamed at the little monkey who was turning around and around on top of the hand organ. The monkey in his perky red cap looked better fed than the man, and he danced as the grinder piped out 'Pop Goes the Weasel.'

Approaching the heart of the circle, Martha saw several people on the opposite side smiling at something closer to the ground. Her panic subsided when she saw Belle staring absolutely transfixed at the dancing monkey.

'There she is,' R. C. squealed.

Martha shushed him, not wanting to interrupt the act, not wanting to disturb Belle's enjoyment, despite the fact that now, having found her, she knew very well that the rest of the afternoon would have to be spent in teaching the child to obey without question and always to stay exactly where she was told by those who loved her . . .

October 10, 1933
Tulsa, Oklahoma

Captain Meeks had given her the letter out of the morning mail. Martha had seen the postmark – Hitchings, Texas – and had taken the letter to her room, placed it on her nightstand, closed the door, and then forgotten about it.

Neither time nor inclination had permitted her to touch it again until now, after eleven o'clock at night.

Moving quietly, not wanting to disturb the children, she

tiptoed to her bed, reached down, and switched on her bed lamp. Sitting on the edge of the bed, she bent over to loosen the laces on her shoes, and as she did so, her eyes fell on the letter from Mr Clarence Reader, Hitchings's only lawyer.

Slowly she raised up, feeling new fatigue as she always did when confronted by her past. Why had Mr Reader sent the letter? Why not her mother? Her mama had written to her several times since she had been at the Salvation Army, brief, sad, exhausted letters, the result of forty years of living with 'the man.'

That was what Martha's mother called her father, had always called him:

'Best get the porch swept. The man will be home soon.' 'The man doesn't like soup that's too hot. Stir it a dozen times before serving him.'

The man.

God forgive her, but she hated him. She shouldn't. She knew that, and she'd tried so hard to understand him, his needs, his disappointment with her.

There had been a son, a god of a son. She'd never known him. He had died of smallpox the year before she was born. She was to have been the replacement, the one who eased the grief, the hope of the future, an exact duplicate of Matthew, tall, strong, all things that any man would ever want in a son.

Then out of her mother's womb had come – Martha, small, sickly, and most unforgivable of all – female. Somehow she had been born knowing that her father hated her. And every minute of every hour of every day of every year had proved her correct. She was capable of offending him simply by drawing breath.

Finally there had been that terrible night when he had told her to get out of his house.

The memory caused a renewal of hate that welled up in her throat like undigested food, and for her own sake she killed the memory. Now with new determination, as though hate were a source of energy, she reached for the letter and opened it to read.

Dear Martha,

Your father asked me to write to you. Your mother is ill, near to dying. He wanted you to know, and if possible, would you return home?

Sincerely yours,
Clarence Reader

Martha read the brief message twice, then bent over, covered her face with her hands, and saw clear as day the thin, gray-haired woman, her hair braided and drawn back in a coiled knot.

'Mama, what does being in love mean?'
'Not much unless – '
'What, Mama?'
'Shhh. The man will hear.'

She raised up and faced an insoluble problem: R. C. and Belle. She couldn't take them home. Her father wouldn't tolerate the needs of a child. She should know. And if Mama *was* dying, it was no place for children. Then what?

Of course the trip home needn't be long. At most three days. If her mother died, there was nothing to keep her there. The children were comfortable here. If only she could enlist the aid of Captain Meeks and perhaps Skipper to keep their eyes on them. R. C. was almost eight and very responsible. He in turn could take care of three-year-old Belle.

No, she dismissed the idea immediately, more on selfish grounds than anything else. She doubted if she could survive without R. C. and Belle for three days. As she lay back on her pillow, she took Clarence Reader's letter with her and stared up at the low plaster ceiling.

If she went back to Hitchings, there was the outside possibility that she could see Charlie Groveton. She had something to tell him.

Charlie . . . How she missed him. She closed her eyes and found him effortlessly in her memory, tall, blond, his skin bronzed by the Texas sun, dark blue eyes the exact color of the heart of a larkspur, a smile that was oddly off balance but was capable of dispelling the gloom of a rainy Sunday. He walked ramrod straight yet with the grace of an Indian, and he loved everything that grew on the earth. Sometimes they would sit silently on his porch and watch the two old barn cats deep in conversation. Charlie always liked to try and guess what they were saying. He had taught her to think things and see things that she had never thought or seen before, and when he came into her view after even a short absence, her heart would behave in a peculiar manner, beating too fast at first, then refusing for a second or two to beat at all. And his touch –

Where was he now? She had no idea. When she'd left Hitchings he had been working in the oilfields, trying to earn enough to pay the back taxes on his farm. Hitchings's farmers were going under right and left these days, victims of the three D's, as they were called back home – drought, debt, and dust.

She missed him. They'd grown up together. Since the age of four they had shared every secret, every fear, every triumph, though there hadn't been many triumphs in the hard life of Hitchings.

Still, she remembered clearly the night Charlie had won the high school poetry contest. He had written the words for his German shepherd dog. Sue had died of old age. Martha had helped him to bury her and had sat with him on the back of his old pickup and had held him while he'd cried.

The next day during American Lit. Charlie had slipped her a smudged piece of paper, the beginning of his poem for Sue: 'Death leaves such an empty space that I would rather choose to lie within that darkened place than be the one to lose . . .'

Martha closed her eyes in an attempt to prolong the remembrance, which was as fresh as though it had happened yesterday. Charlie had finished his poem at Martha's urging and had submitted it to the poetry contest. He had won first prize, a slim dark blue volume of verse by a lady named Miss Emily Dickinson from somewhere back east. They had read the poems all summer long until the pages of the book were dog-eared and worn, the volume itself sweat-stained from where Charlie had tucked it inside his shirt while he drove the tractor for summer planting.

The night of graduation he had given it to her, and she still had it in her small tin box beneath this very bed.

Softly she heard Belle whimper and turn in her sleep. Martha sat up and peered over at the sleeping child. Within a few minutes Belle was quiet again, one tiny arm resting above her head, the other outstretched as though beckoning someone to share her dreams.

For several moments Martha fed on Belle's beauty. It was amazing how often it sustained her. Now as Martha shifted on the edge of her bed, the letter from Hitchings fell onto the floor, reminding her of her dilemma.

Mama ill and near to dying. It seemed impossible. Her mother had always been 'the strong one,' the one who caught no illness and nursed everyone else. If it hadn't been for her mother's love, for her constant nurturing and reassurance, Martha doubted seriously if she could have survived childhood.

Mama . . .

She didn't want to think anymore. Where was the sleep that would blot out all pain of the past? She stretched out again on her bed and turned her face to the wall. White paint was peeling in a graceful curve that reminded her of the bloom of a calla lily, the flower of death.

'Mama . . .'

She whispered the name and knew somehow that her mother would die and she must go home.

'Death leaves such an empty space . . .'

Charlie –

Then sleep came, and she found him in her dream.

'Come on, Martha, race you to the Indian cemetery.'

'Charlie, wait – '

And she raced after him . . .

October 11, 1933
Houston Harbor

In the black-green depths of Houston Harbor, in the reflection of his own face, Charlie Groveton found the dream of Martha, the one person in his world who always made everything else make sense.

Lord, she was pretty – not store-bought pretty, but pretty by God's definition, fresh, scrubbed. In summer the sun turned her hair golden blond. She wore it in a long braid down her back, and when she unbraided it Charlie loved to place his hand on the soft ripples of hair. She looked good in anything from worn blue jeans to patched summer shorts. The firm yet placid mouth, the clear, knowing green eyes, all this was a permanent part of Charlie's heart. She was the bright gleam that soothed his dark moods, and in her eyes he found all the love a man would ever need, like that night so long ago . . .

'Come on, Martha, race you to the Indian cemetery.'

'Charlie, wait – '

They'd just come from their high school graduation, 1929. The night was cool, and soft moss damp from the spring nearby grew like green velvet on the sacred ground. He was still wearing his new suit, and she was so pretty in her white dress with puffy sleeves. The sky was star-filled, and the moon was as bright as a sun.

'What are you looking at, Charlie?'

'You.'

'I know . . .'

He moved closer, barely brushing her breasts with his arm. It was the first time he'd ever felt such a sensation. And before he knew it, their school finery lay in a heap on the moss and they were all tangled up in each other, feeling things they'd never felt before, doing things they'd never done before but doing them anyway because Charlie had known since he was a boy that Martha was his and he was Martha's and that's just the way it had to be.

Then why had she gone off with someone else?

The shrill whistle of the nearby freighter startled him and brought him back to the present. No matter. The dream had turned sour anyway. He shook his head in an attempt to move away from the past. The ship's whistle had signaled the first call for boarding, and he gazed up at the battered old *Isabelle Marie* where she lay moored to Pier 1, taking on a cargo of oilfield equipment bound for Venezuela. He too was part of that equipment, having signed on for a job as an oil driller in the Lake Maracaibo fields.

'You look like you were a thousand miles away.'

The voice belonged to Reed Spence, Charlie's best friend, who was now sitting on a packing crate rolling a cigarette.

'Sorry. I guess I was woolgathering.'

'You sure weren't anyplace in this neighborhood.'

Charlie smiled and thought how much he would miss this good friend. They had a lot in common. Both had grown up on farms. Both had left home to work in the oilfields, and both had sent money home when crops and markets had failed. About the only thing they didn't have in common was the fact that Reed had a good wife and Charlie had nothing but a dream. The realization hurt.

'You got any more of that bootleg whiskey on you?'

Reed finished rolling his cigarette, pulled the string on his tobacco pouch with his teeth, and at last reached into his back pocket and passed Charlie the bottle along with a question.

'You want to tell me why you're doing this?'

'Money, pure and simple. You heard that recruiter. They need experienced drillers down in Venezuela, and they're paying top dollar.'

'Fat lot of good it's gonna do you if you're dead.'

Charlie took a deep swallow of whiskey. 'What's going to get me down there that won't get me here?'

'Snakes, cannibal fish, bugs big enough to throw a saddle on – '

'Well, I'm going anyway.'

For a few minutes they passed the bottle back and forth and sat in silence. But a second blast on the ship's whistle reminded Charlie that time was short and he owed Reed an explanation.

'Look, Reed, some things happened back in Hitchings that you don't know about. I've lost the farm, couldn't raise the money to pay the back taxes. When my father passed away four years ago he had two crop failures in a row. Then the dust came and the Depression. Hell, you know most of it.'

'I have a little money.'

'You also have a wife. Besides, it's too late. The farm went on the county auction block and somebody's already bought it.'

'Who?'

'I didn't stick around to find out. I drove by the old place. It's pretty run-down.' He paused. Here was the hard part. 'I found out Martha was gone.'

Reed blinked. 'I thought you two were going to get married.'

'That's what I thought. But I stopped by the Drusso place and her old man told me she'd married an insurance salesman from Dallas.'

'I'll be damned. I'm sorry.'

The whistle blasted a third time. Charlie wanted to say something else, but Reed beat him to it. 'I've got a little going-away present.' He reached into his jacket and produced a fresh bottle of bootleg whiskey. 'Here's a little Texas white lightning. It'll inoculate you against all them diseases. I don't want anything to happen to you.'

'Reed, I –

'Go on. Get up that gangplank. We all do what we have to do. I'm going to miss you, though.'

It was the moment Charlie had looked forward to for weeks. Yet something was pulling him back as hard as something else was pushing him forward. He shook Reed's hand, tucked the bottle into his back pocket, and at last took the gangplank running.

A short time later he stood on the deck and watched the Texas shoreline disappear, like everything else in his life had disappeared, his mother dead, his father dead, the farm gone, Martha gone –

My God, when would it stop hurting, the memory, the sound of her voice inside his head?

'Charlie, listen to this poem: "We shut a door and Fate following behind us bolts it and –"'

He rested his arms on the railing and covered his ears with his hands and stared down at the churning white foam caused by the wake of the ship.

But he couldn't shut her out. Even with his eyes closed, she clung to his consciousness and filled his memory with the music of her voice, the sweetness of her smile, the love in her eyes . . .

October 11, 1933
Tulsa, Oklahoma

The fall rains were commencing, which always meant a crowded mission. On this overcast day Captain Meeks stood at the back door and sniffed at the rain.

'Good morning, sir.'

The voice startled him, and he turned to see Martha looking strangely weary for seven o'clock in the morning.

'Martha,' he said stiffly, and heard the children giggling from where she had left the door open to her room.

'I was hoping for a moment with you,' she began, and he noticed a letter in her hand.

'What is it?'

'News, sir, from home.'

'Not bad, I hope.'

'My mother is ill, according to the letter near to death.'

'Then you must return home,' he said. Assuming the matter closed, Captain Meeks started around her.

'Sir?'

He turned back.

'My father,' she began, 'is a – hard man – '

'Good for him.'

'– who doesn't understand the needs of a child.'

He looked up, wary of where she was leading.

'I was wondering, sir, if, while I'm gone, I might leave R. C. and Belle in your care.'

'No!' His rejection was swift and strong.

'Captain Meeks, all I'm asking is that you allow them to stay in our room as they have always done, that Skipper gives them their meals, as he has always done, that you allow them to play on the steps until dark, as you have always done, and allow them to go to sleep in their own beds.'

She shook her head. 'R. C. is almost eight, quite responsible. Nothing would be required of you except your Christian generosity.'

Her pleading embarrassed him. He was not by nature an emotional man. Life was hard, therefore those who passed through it were required to be hard as well. Still, she *was* the best worker he had ever seen. He would hate to lose her.

'Very well,' he said at last in a weary voice that lacked enthusiasm or conviction. 'But I must make it clear to you that I absolutely refuse to take ultimate responsibility. You must set the rules and make it clear to them that they are to obey.'

He'd just started to walk away when he heard, 'And, sir, one more thing?'

'What now?' His patience really had been tested.

'The children, sir. Give them a chance. They really are most rewarding.'

Lacking a response, he turned about. The rain overhead was a downpour now. He could hear it striking the old roof of the mission. Leaks everywhere.

'Skipper, get out the buckets. The storm is upon us.'

In more ways than one, he brooded, and went to perform his duties in his flawed and leaky kingdom . . .

* * *

It was perhaps the most difficult thing she had ever done.

'Belle, sit still, right there beside R. C. I want you both to listen to me as you have never listened before.'

She positioned the children on the edge of her bed, knelt before them, and tried to organize her thoughts. She would keep R. C. out of school until she returned. She needed him here. There was a noon train to Amarillo, and she'd thumb a ride from there. With luck she would be in Hitchings by late that night.

'Now,' she began. 'What I want to tell you is this. I've received a letter from a man who is a friend of my father, and he writes to tell me that my mother is ill. I must go home for a few days.'

'This is home,' R. C. interrupted, wise at almost eight.

'No,' Martha corrected gently. 'Not my real home. My real home is in a place called Texas.'

'Texas,' Belle repeated, clearly pleased with the feel of the word on her lips.

'Are you leaving us?' R. C. asked.

She looked up to see apprehension in R. C.'s face. 'Oh, my dearest,' she soothed, and took both his hands in hers.

'Now, listen, both of you, I have spoken with Captain Meeks. He has promised me that you can stay here in this room, that Skipper will see to your meals, and that both he and Skipper will keep a close eye on you. Now I must ask something of you, R. C., please. You must take care of Belle.'

'Me Belle.' The little girl smiled, recognizing her name.

'Yes, you're Belle,' Martha said, finding it easier to deal with Belle's blissful ignorance than with R. C.'s knowing eyes.

'How long will you be gone?' he asked, his face already mirroring his fear.

'I'm not sure,' she replied honestly. 'No more than three days. Two, I hope. Not very long, is it? Two short days.'

R. C. studied the scuffed toes of his shoes. The laces were loosened. Normally she would have instructed him to tie them.

Instead she bent over and did the job for him, all the time talking. 'R. C., I'm expecting a lot from you. You're the oldest. You are never to leave Belle. Stay close beside her, and if she needs a strong hand, I expect yours to be the one. Do you understand?'

'Will your mother die?'

'I don't know, R. C. But you'll be fine.'

'R. C. fine,' Belle parroted.

Laughing, Martha reached out and effortlessly captured the imp, clasping both children to her as though they were the lifeline and she was drowning . . .

October 14, 1933
Tulsa, Oklahoma

R. C.'s first memory was of his mother's coffin.

His second memory was of rain. It had been raining the day they had put his mother's coffin into the ground and the big hole was filled with water, and he didn't like his mother being put into a hole filled with water. He tried to get the men to lift his mother up, but they wouldn't do it, and a man had turned him around and taken him away.

After that, some things he remembered were very clear, others not so clear. The man had taken him to a big building in Albany where there were lots of other children and there was always noise and cold air coming in through the windows and some people were nice to him and others weren't nice. Then one day he and a lot of the other children were put on a big train. The train ride was fun. The train kept stopping at places, and every time it stopped some of the children would get off.

When they came to this place called Tulsa, the man had stood with him on the platform for a long time, and when no one came the man took him by the hand and led him up the hill to the Salvation Army Mission, tied him to the lamppost with a piece of rope, and pinned a note to his jacket. Then he'd gone off and left him.

He had been frightened and he was hungry and cold, but he had not cried, not once. The door to the mission had opened and R. C. had looked up and seen Martha. Of course he hadn't known her name then, but somehow when he had looked up into her face, he had known that from then on he was going to be safe.

'Don't cry, Belle,' he whispered, and pushed closer to her in the narrow space beneath the staircase.

Poor Belle. She had cried all night for the last two days. It had started that first night when Captain Meeks had made them get out of Martha's room so that he could 'sleep a dozen men' on the floor there. At first they had been permitted to spread their blankets in front of Skipper's big cookstove in the kitchen, and it had at least been warm there.

But on that first night, R. C. had seen a rat looking at them. Belle had seen it as well and had screamed her head off. Then Captain Meeks had moved them out of the kitchen to beneath the staircase in the back hall.

So far they hadn't seen any more rats. They hadn't seen anything, it was so dark. R. C. had tried to clear out the spiderwebs and comfort Belle as best he could, but she was scared. There was nothing he could do.

'R. C.?' Belle gasped between sobs. 'I'm hungry.'

'So am I.'

'Can we get some – '

'Come on,' R. C. said quickly.

Quietly they tiptoed into the kitchen. Belle, in her eagerness, climbed up onto the counter and was just reaching into the big breadbox when her arm struck a stack of cups. They clattered endlessly about on the counter, some of them crashing to the floor, all breaking in the process, causing an awful racket.

R. C. started to scold her, but then he saw the light come on at the far end of the hall and heard Captain Meeks shout, 'Who is there?'

R. C. tried to grab Belle, hoping to hide someplace in the kitchen, but there was no time. Before he could get her down off the counter, the kitchen was flooded with light and Captain Meeks was before them, clad in his bathrobe, his face red with anger.

Belle, unmindful of anything except her hunger, was still perched on the counter happily munching on the heel of a loaf of bread.

'I warned you,' Captain Meeks began, his voice strangely calm compared to the red in his cheeks. 'I warned Martha. I will not have food stolen from my mission, is that clear?'

'She was hungry,' R. C. began.

'A large portion of the world is hungry,' Meeks countered. 'That does not give everyone license to steal, now, does it?'

'No, sir.'

'No, sir indeed. I won't have it. I'm afraid you have forced me to phone the orphanage tomorrow. They will find good homes for both of you. You'll be all right. Now put that bread back and get to your beds. A decision has been made, the right one, the one that should have been made long ago.'

Without hesitation R. C. lifted Belle down from the counter. In the process she dropped her bread. As she stooped to retrieve it, Captain Meeks stepped forward, scooped it up, and replaced it on the counter beyond her reach.

R. C. had never heard such cries. Even after they were back beneath the steps, nothing he said could comfort her or stop the tears.

Still echoing inside his head were Captain Meeks's words, 'I'm afraid you have forced me to phone the orphanage tomorrow . . .'

No! They would never see Martha again. No –

'Belle,' he whispered. 'Do you want to come with me and find Martha?'

Instantly the sobs ceased, though the spasms remained. 'Yes.'

R. C. thought furiously for a moment. They couldn't leave now at night. But come morning the men would leave Martha's room. R. C. had seen her put the letter from Texas into the drawer in her night-stand. If he could find that letter, he could find the name of the town where she had gone. Then he would take out her money box and get enough to buy two tickets on the train, and once they got on the train they'd be all right because he'd been on a train before and knew very well how it was done.

'Not tonight,' he said beneath the blanket. 'First thing in the morning, though, I promise. Right now, you need to close your eyes so you won't be sleepy tomorrow, 'cause it'll be a long trip to find Martha.'

'I go to sleep,' Belle promised, and pushed close to R. C. He felt her hand on his jacket.

'Go to sleep, Belle,' he soothed. He liked the feeling of someone needing him . . .

At first light of dawn R. C. rolled out from beneath the stairs, taking Belle with him. They ran toward Martha's room and found it empty, all the men having been drawn into the mission hall by the smell of breakfast. He drew open the drawer on her nightstand and found the letter, turned it over, and read, 'Mr Clarence Reader, Hitchings, Texas.'

Where was Hitchings, Texas? He had no idea, but the man at the train station would know.

On his stomach now, he reached beneath Martha's bed and pulled out the box, pushed open the lid, and saw a scattering of one dollar bills, about ten, and some coins.

He took it all and shoved the box back under Martha's bed.

'Belle,' he whispered. 'Hurry, let's go.'

Ahead was the front door, and R. C. took it running, with Belle struggling to keep up. He was doing the right thing, of that he was certain. They'd find Martha, then everything would be all right.

Looking both ways, as Martha had taught him, he tightened his grip on Belle's hand and led her across the busy intersection and into the train station. Just inside the doors, he stopped. There were people everywhere, and all of them seemed to be in a hurry.

To one side he saw the ticket windows. Behind them was a man with a green eyeshade counting something. He didn't look up as R. C. stood on tiptoe, the top of his eyes barely even with the bottom of the window.

'Sir?' R. C. called out, which finally got the attention of the man, who peered out and over thick glasses. 'We want to go – here.' R. C. placed Martha's letter on the counter where it said *Hitchings, Texas*, on the envelope.

He reached into his pocket and withdrew some crumpled one dollar bills and put them on the counter, then grabbed Belle's hand again as she started to wander off in search of a cinnamon bun.

'Here you go,' the man said, and shoved a white ticket back across the counter along with some change. 'The little girl's under five. She rides for free.'

'Come on, Belle,' R. C. said, grabbed her hand, and led her away from the ticket window toward the crush of people heading down into the big tunnel that led up on the other side to the train.

He felt ever so big walking along, having just done a man's job, buying a train ticket that would take him and Belle to Martha.

'Hungry,' Belle said again, more softly this time.

'It's all right,' R. C. comforted her. 'I'll put you on the train, then I'll go and get us a cinnamon bun.'

He felt into the bottom of his pocket past the ticket for the change, two quarters, a dime, and four pennies. It meant breakfast for both of them.

Still feeling proud of himself and certain that Martha would be proud of him as well, he guided Belle down through the tunnel, climbed the big ramp to daylight, and saw an immense black shiny train sitting on the track in front of them.

He led her into an empty coach, selected the third row down from the vestibule, guided her into the row, and boosted her up on the seat by the window. She was so small that she disappeared from view.

'Now,' he said, 'you stay right here. Promise me, Belle, right here!' he repeated for emphasis.

He waited at the end of the coach to see if she peered out or over or around the seat, thus breaking her promise.

She didn't.

Then he was running back through the tunnel, dodging foot traffic and hurrying back into the station where the food vendors were just beginning to line up.

He must hurry. With the coins clutched at the ready in his hand, he bought one big red apple and then looked up and down in search of a cinnamon bun.

Overhead, the man on the loudspeaker announced the departure of a train. A group of people surged forward, running. The swirl and turmoil about him increased, and still he searched everywhere for the bun man.

Then he spied him.

R. C. hurried toward him, plopped down a dime, and politely requested, 'Two buns, please, sir.'

Now ladened with his apple and buns, R. C. turned about, again feeling proud of himself. He grinned, took the tunnel ramp running, and emerged into the bright light of the crisp October morning, looking eagerly ahead for the coach in which he'd placed Belle.

And saw nothing.

He stopped, thinking perhaps he'd taken the wrong tunnel. Was there more than one tunnel? There had to be because he'd left a train here and now it was gone and Belle was on it.

He walked closer to the tracks, still clutching the apple in one hand, the two buns in the other, so close he could peer over and see the tracks cluttered with blowing papers, an old grapette bottle, and a wine bottle with a broken neck.

'You there – boy! What the hell do you think you're doing?'

He swirled around at the sound of the harsh voice and saw a man in a dark blue uniform.

'Sir?'

'I said what in the hell do you think you're doing?'

'L-looking for a train, sir. There was one going to Texas.'

'Well, you're on the wrong track,' the man said, pushing his hat back. 'You see that stairway, boy?' He jerked R. C. around until he was facing a metal staircase that led to the walkway over the track.

'Yes, sir.'

'Well, that is where you belong, and you best hurry 'cause the Amarillo train, she's loading now, and she'll be gone in' – he withdrew a big gold pocket watch – 'less than five minutes.'

'Sir, could you tell – '

'Git, now. I mean it. You oughtn't to hang around these tracks. It's dangerous. One tumble and your people would sue the hell out of the company.'

'The t-train that was here, sir,' R. C. stammered, panic increasing.

'Gone!'

'Where?'

'LA. Where do you think? Now are you gonna git or do I have to pick you up and – '

Then R. C. was running, dropping his apple in the process. As he started up the metal stairs he saw the man stroll forward, pick up his apple, and polish it on the seat of his pants. He smiled up at R. C. and took a big juicy bite.

R. C. turned about and half ran, half stumbled up the steps.

LA? What was LA? And where was Belle? And why hadn't she gotten off the train when it started to move and he wasn't on it?

Because he had ordered her not to move.

He hurried down the other side of the stairs to the long train that was filling with people. He reached into his pocket and withdrew his ticket.

'Here, sir,' he said to the man standing beside the low step.

'Amarillo, right on board.' The man smiled. 'Put the ticket back in your pocket. I'll come for it later.'

'Sir, could you tell me about the other train that – '

'Move along, sonny, people behind you waiting.'

The man lifted R. C. by the elbow to the top step. Dazed and terrified, R. C. made his way to the back of the coach, where he found an empty seat. It looked just like the one where he'd put Belle.

He sat and stared at the cinnamon buns in his hand. Crushed now.

He thought of Belle, all by herself on the train, hungry, not knowing anyone, not knowing where she was going, probably not even knowing where she'd come from. What would Martha say? He turned his face to the window so no one would see him crying . . .

October 15, 1933
Hitchings, Texas

Martha stood in the blowing wind atop the hill above her father's farmhouse and tried not to look into her mother's grave, tried not to hear Preacher Wills's droning voice saying nothing but preacher things, and tried not to see the tall skinny old man in dirty overalls who stood about fifty feet away.

She closed her eyes and replaced her father's face with images of Belle and R. C. How she missed them. Well, she was leaving tomorrow. Nothing more to stay for. She was still hoping to see Charlie Groveton if he was back from the oilfields.

She shifted from one foot to the other and looked out at the hard landscape dotted here and there with farms, dust covering the good wheat land.

So few families lived around here anymore. Hitchings was fast becoming a ghost town. Even in good times Hitchings had been on the poor side, surrounded by farms where it was necessary to work from can-see to can't-see, and even then there was little to show for it at the end of the day except blisters, bruises, and empty bellies.

'Amen.'

At the sound of the voice she looked straight up into Preacher Wills's puzzled eyes.

'I'm finished, Martha,' he said sheepishly as though he knew she hadn't been listening, and closed his Bible.

'Thank you for coming,' Martha said, and wondered why he was still looking at her as though there were something else to be done. Then all of a sudden she saw the pine coffin and realized someone had to put her mother into the ground.

'Oh,' she said weakly, and looked from Preacher Wills to the coffin and back to Preacher Wills.

'Who dug the hole?' Preacher Wills asked as though they were tracing a culprit.

'He did,' Martha said, and indicated her father, who was still keeping his distance.

They both looked at the old man in soiled overalls, who didn't budge an inch, though surely he knew the nature of their dilemma.

'I'll help,' Martha offered, and moved toward the coffin. 'You grab one end, Preacher. I'll take the other. We can manage.'

For a moment a stricken look crossed Preacher Wills's face as though he were unaccustomed to dealing with the dirty end of death.

'Heave-ho.' Martha smiled, still unable to feel anything but relief for her mother, who at last was freed from her earthly prison.

Reluctantly at first, then getting into the spirit of the occasion, Preacher Wills put down his Bible, lifted up his end of the coffin, and with considerable effort helped lower the pine box into the deep hole. It fell the last few feet of the way.

'Bye, Mama,' Martha whispered. She turned around,

picked a late blooming black-eyed Susan, and tossed it down into the grave.

'Thank you for coming, Preacher Wills,' she said. 'I can give you a cup of coffee and a piece of cornbread, but I'm afraid that's all.'

Preacher Wills smiled. 'How did you know that was my fee?'

As Martha started back down the hill, she saw a car coming fast, leaving in its wake a dust trail.

'That's Doc Tremble's car,' Preacher Wills mused, lifting his hand to his eyes against the glare of morning sun and swirling dust.

What would Doc Tremble be coming back for? He'd been out last night to pronounce her mother dead.

'Maybe he forgot something,' Martha muttered, and inched down the incline, feeling gravel slide inside her shoes.

'Did you forget something, Doc?' Martha asked, at last on the road and level with the car.

'No. Did you lose something?' Doc Tremble asked.

'I – don't – '

'They found him wandering about the train station asking for you. Ned Hadley called me to come in and pick him up.'

All the time he talked, he gestured toward his car. Martha frowned, not understanding a word he was saying. Then all at once the car door on the passenger side opened and she saw the top of a child's head.

But it was enough. She'd scrubbed the back of that neck as well as washed that black wavy hair. 'R. C.!' She grinned, then met him in front of the car and lifted him into her arms, a growing weight that reminded her that her days of lifting this child were limited.

At first she was so glad to see him that it didn't occur to her that somehow he'd wandered into the wrong world. 'R. C., I can't believe – how in the – '

As she sputtered out her confusion, she lowered him and in the process caught sight of the fear in his eyes.

'R. C.? What happened?'

'Belle was hungry and Captain Meeks said he was going to phone the orphanage, said they'd find us homes.'

Anger as raw and urgent as any Martha had ever felt fought its way through her system. How dare he? What right? But anger would not serve her now. Or Belle. 'Go on, R. C.,' she ordered, still struggling for control.

'So Belle and me ran away,' the boy said solemnly. Then his eyes betrayed him. Up close Martha saw fresh tears.

'Where is Belle?' Martha asked. She left R. C. and hurried around the car, peering in through the dust-covered windows to the backseat, hoping Belle was there, sleeping.

Then all at once R. C. buried his face in his hands and cried as Martha had never heard him cry before, hot, inconsolable tears that racked his shoulders and prevented him from speaking at all.

'Come on,' she begged, kneeling before him, wiping at his face with her big white handkerchief. 'R. C., look at me. You must tell me what happened. I'm sure it's not as bad as – '

'B-Belle's gone,' R. C. spluttered.

'What do you mean?' Martha demanded.

'I – put her on the train and told her to wait and I went to get her a cinnamon bun and when I got back the train was gone.'

As fresh spasms jarred his small frame, Martha was tempted to shake him into coherence. 'Listen, R. C., I need to – I must hear everything. Will you try?'

Martha listened with held breath throughout the whole recital. She didn't interrupt until R. C. got to the part where he put Belle on the train. 'Did you ask where the train was going?'

He shook his head and studied the toes of his shoes.

'Why not?'

'There was nobody around. I just put her in the seat and – '

'Was there anyone else on the coach?'

'No.'

'And when you came back from fetching the cinnamon buns, it was gone.'

'Yes.'

Martha looked straight up to heaven, closed her eyes, and tried to discourage the fearful thing that was taking root inside her.

'I found out later where the train was going,' R. C. volunteered.

'Where?'

'The man said LA.'

'Los Angeles?'

'No,' R. C. corrected. 'He said LA.'

Movement was necessary, and she walked a few steps away and tried to stay calm.

'Martha?'

The voice was Doc Tremble's. 'Look, I don't think you have much of a problem here. I'll take you and the boy back to the station in Amarillo. Surely the dispatcher there can tell you what you want to know, the number of the train, the places it stopped, that sort of thing.'

'I appreciate it,' Martha said. 'R. C., you get back into the car and wait there.' To Doc Tremble she said, 'I'll get my things. I'll only be a minute.'

Then she ran up the front steps and onto the porch and felt torn between R. C.'s bleak account and Doc Tremble's confident solution. Of course they'd find her, she was certain of that.

What frightened her was the thought of how scared Belle must be, alone, among strangers, barely able to tell them her name, waiting and looking for a familiar face.

Inside the living room she looked through to the kitchen and saw her father sitting at the table. She walked into the room and started to speak, then realized she had nothing to say.

He apparently did. 'Who'll take care of me now?' he asked in a toneless voice.

'You'll have to take care of yourself,' she said, going on

through to the bedroom to where her mother had been sleeping before she died.

The pillow on the bed still bore the indentation of her mother's head. She caressed the pillow, then folded her sweater. She grabbed her brush, comb, and toothbrush wrapped in waxed paper that she'd brought from the mission.

In the kitchen she saw her father still sitting at the table, unmoving.

'I'm leaving now, Papa,' she said.

'It's your place to stay and take care of me,' he announced in that cold, brittle way of his.

Martha almost laughed. 'Don't you remember, Papa? You sent me away.'

'You were godless.'

'I was in love.'

'A lot of good it did you. Charlie Groveton's gone off with some fancy lady from Amarillo, or hadn't you heard that?'

The despair started at the base of her spine and spiraled upward.

Charlie gone – some fancy woman from Amarillo.

She let the screen door slam behind her.

'You okay?' Doc Tremble asked.

She said nothing and started into the car, then stopped. 'Preacher Wills, thanks again for coming. If you care to, you might go in and sit a few minutes with my father.'

'I will, Martha, and I want you to know I'll be praying for the little girl.'

Martha closed the door behind her and turned around in the seat to see R. C. staring at her with wide eyes.

'Come on up,' she invited, and helped him settle beside her.

'I'm – sorry.'

'No need,' she scolded lovingly. 'You heard what Preacher Wills said. He will be praying for her. We'll find her. Close your eyes, R. C., if you wish. Doc Tremble will run us into Amarillo. You got forty-five minutes ahead of you. Might as well nap.'

R. C. relaxed against her, and Doc Tremble slid into the driver's seat, grinning at Martha. 'For an unmarried lady, you managed to find yourself quite a brood.'

Martha said nothing, laid her head back against the seat, closed her eyes, and saw Belle, surrounded by strangers, all asking questions she couldn't answer.

October 17, 1933
San Bernardino, California

Though Mr Moses had retired from the railroad three years ago, he was still called to duty from time to time when one of the company boys wanted to take off fishing. It was the least he could do.

He didn't mind. It made him feel good, needed. He was just leaning up to pour himself a cup of coffee when he heard a knock at his door. Through the wavy glass he could see a figure.

When he opened the door, he saw a grim-faced woman on the other side, middle-aged, plump, a red feather sticking out of her black hat like an Indian, which gave her a funny look. But she wasn't looking very funny now.

'You'd better come, sir,' the woman said.

He got his company hat and invited, 'Lead the way.'

As the lady started down the platform, Moses saw the last of the passengers who had just gotten off the train to LA. Smart bunch in Moses's opinion. He hated what had become of LA. When he was a kid one of them clear blue ocean breezes would breathe on the valleys and you could pick up the perfume of orange groves all the way to the train station.

It had been heaven, that's all, just heaven.

'Here, sir, this is the coach.'

'What are we – '

'A child, sir,' the woman contributed. 'A darling thing, but I'm afraid quite lost and very much alone.'

Moses blinked. A kid? Kids rode the trains all the time

now. Parents brought more than they could handle into this world and put the leftovers on a train, fairly certain that someone would find them and take care of them.

As Miss Red Feather pushed past him, he saw her walk to the third seat and stop. 'Here she is. Look for yourself.'

Cautiously Moses approached the spot. Red Feather was right. There she was, a little girl, tiny, blond hair, and big blue eyes, looking a little worse for wear.

'I don't know where she came from,' the woman said.

'When did you first notice her?' Moses asked, trying to think of important-sounding questions to ask that ultimately wouldn't make a bit of difference.

'Well, sir,' the woman said, 'I first noticed her when I got on in El Paso. I have a granddaughter about her age, and I saw . . .'

Lord, the woman was a talker, but then most were.

At last Moses held up a staying hand and turned his attention to the child herself.

'Hello.' He smiled and pushed his company hat back onto his head.

The child started to smile back, then seemed to change her mind. Miss Red Feather was right on one matter. The little girl was filthy. Everything she'd eaten in God knew how long was there on the front of her blouse. Worst of all was the odor of dirty underpants. Apparently she'd had several accidents along the way.

'Do you know your name?' Moses asked, trying the direct approach.

The woman interrupted. 'She told me her name is Belle. I couldn't make out the last name. It seems that someone named Arcie put her in this seat and ordered her not to move. And she hasn't.'

Moses knew it. Suspicion confirmed. Someone had dumped the kid on the company. 'What a world,' he muttered, shaking his head.

All right, then, what was needed here was a decision.

'Do you want her?' Moses asked bluntly, and got Miss Red Feather's attention quick enough.

'You can't do that, just go around giving children – '

'Now listen, lady,' Moses said, always keeping politeness uppermost in his mind. 'Ain't no one coming for this kid. I've seen it happen time and again.'

The lady was shaking her head even as he spoke. 'Why is it my responsibility?'

'It isn't. It's just that you're the one making the fuss.'

'I – have a family.'

'Don't we all?'

Outside the window he saw the conductor about to signal that the train was ready to move. 'Now look, lady, we could just leave her here and let her take her chances in LA, though frankly I don't think much of those chances.'

'Or?'

'Or I can get her off and try to find a family that will take care of her. Or I can take her across town to the Catholics. They never turn away any kid that they can convert into a fish eater.'

Slowly the woman stood and looked sadly down on the little girl. 'Oh, dear,' she sighed. 'How could anyone just – abandon her?'

Unable to face the answer to her own question, she withdrew a handkerchief from her pocket, pressed it against her face, and disappeared into the car ahead.

At the opposite end of the coach, Moses saw a few passengers climbing on board. 'Come on, honey,' he said to the little girl, and held out his hand. He thought for a moment of where he would go. Probably over to the Melvilles. Brother Melville was a preacher, and Florence Melville had a good heart.

'Come on,' he said again to the child, who had yet to move.

'Can't,' the little girl said, and looked up at him with fearful eyes.

'Oh, yes, you can, little darling,' and he scooped her up in his arms and tried not to breathe too deeply the odor of wet bloomers.

When she started to object with a wail, he quickly plopped

his company hat down on her tousled head. Instantly the wail was canceled as she tried to examine what now sat atop her head.

On the platform Moses walked slowly in the event anyone wanted to claim the child. But no one, not one person on the crowded platform, even glanced his way.

'Easy on the hat, little darling,' he muttered, and cursed the bastard who had brought such a treasure into this world, then abandoned it . . .

Florence Melville stayed on her knees a moment longer, as she always did after praying. Just in case God chose to answer her in a direct and intelligible manner, she'd be there to catch it. At times she really got tired of 'His mysterious ways.'

She looked up now from her kneeling position at Stanley's face, so pale on his pillow, his lips still blue from his recent attack. Doctor Rule had pronounced it a bad heart, and there wasn't a thing on earth that could be done about it except rest and relaxation.

Now how in the world was a Methodist preacher with a growing flock going to get rest and relaxation?

Florence repeated her recent prayer. 'Dear Heavenly Father, whatever task you ask me to undertake next, I promise I'll do so with a happy heart and a joyful spirit. Just let Stanley get well.'

All at once the doorbell rang. Hurriedly she tiptoed out of the room and closed the door behind her. Through the curtain she saw a man with a child in his arms. Closer up she saw that it was Mr Moses from the train station.

'Good day,' she said as she drew open the door.

'Good day to you, Mrs Melville.' Old man Moses smiled.

'What's that you got?' Florence asked, crossing her arms and at the same time looking down the road for the school bus that would bring her three home from school. She wanted to head them off before they hit the house like a tribe of wild Indians.

'– and there she was, just sittin' looking for all the world like – '

Belatedly Florence realized that old Moses had been talking all the time she had been woolgathering.

'Where'd you say you found her?' Florence asked, not really interested, but as a Methodist preacher's wife she had to mind her P's and Q's with all the townspeople.

'On the train,' Mr Moses said, sounding a bit short of patience.

'Can she speak?'

'Some.'

Florence stepped back from the door, prepared to close it. The child was a pretty little thing, but enough was enough. 'Well, Mr Moses. I suggest you cart her right over to the east side and let the nuns have a go at her. I'm afraid we just can't manage another mouth here, we just – '

Dear Heavenly Father, whatever task you ask me to undertake next, I promise I'll do so. Just let Stanley get well.'

She looked at the little girl in Moses's arms. Was this the task that God was asking her to do next?

'How – old is she?' Florence asked, eyeing the child as she would a Sunday chicken.

Moses shook his head. 'No idea. Young.'

Florence saw tears in the child's eyes, as though she were trying hard not to cry.

'What's her name?'

'She calls herself Belle.'

'What do you think?' Florence asked, still not sure if this was the task that God wanted her to do.

Moses shook his head. 'Best bet is she got on the train with someone and that someone got off without telling her.'

Florence looked up to heaven, hoping for a more direct sign from God. But she saw nothing but the cobwebbed ceiling of the old front porch with peeling paint and dead flies waiting to be spider dinners.

She closed her eyes. 'I'll take her,' she said at last, weary, somehow serving notice on God that He'd better remember this act of generosity.

'You will?' Moses grinned and immediately held the child out as if she were a sack of potatoes.

Florence took her and smelled potty accidents, saw dried food all over the front of her blouse. Now she had a question for God. How come He let people bring children into His world, knowing full well they hadn't one notion on how to take care of that new life?

No answer, but then she really hadn't expected one. Twenty-two years of being a preacher's wife had taught her just one sure thing, that God sometimes wasn't paying as close attention as He ought to be.

'Now, you keep your eyes and ears open in case someone comes looking for her, you hear?' Florence called after Mr Moses, who seemed to be departing on the wings of relief. He didn't even answer, just gave a backward wave, then took off toward his old car.

Florence looked at the child, feeling trapped somehow. Another mouth to feed when there wasn't enough to feed her own. How in the name of –

Then she heard something, a faint shuffling coming from behind her, and she looked over her shoulder and saw Stanley, clad only in his pajamas and house slippers, his thinning hair tousled, his cheeks as pink as she had ever seen them, not a sign of blue about his lips.

'What's that you got in your arms, Mother?' he asked in that kind soft voice of his that made all his church ladies fall a little in love with him.

'It's a child, Stanley,' Florence replied, stunned to see him up and walking. 'Are you – should you – are you feeling – '

'Fine, Florence.' He smiled and tightened the drawstring of his pajamas around his mound of a belly. 'In fact, I have never felt so fine, and what's more, I'm starved. Now bring that little darling to me and tell me how we came to be so lucky.'

Florence watched, amazed, as Stanley walked across the living room with an erect and even gait, his hands outreaching to the child even before he got close enough to take her.

Dear Heavenly Father, whatever task you ask me to undertake next –

'Now, what's your name?' Stanley cooed to the child, and kissed her on both cheeks.

'Belle,' the child responded, her voice low but clear.

'Belle. What a lovely name. Isn't that a lovely name, Florence? Belle. Belle. Belle.'

Each time he said it he lifted his face heavenward, and Florence swore she had never seen him look as well or as happy.

'She got left on the train, Mr Moses said,' Florence explained.

'No-o-o-o,' Stanley said as though shocked by the news. 'Surely not. Who in their right mind would abandon Belle?'

'That's just what Mr Moses said.'

'And she's ours now?'

'If we want her.'

'Want her? Of course we want her.' And tenderly, Stanley enclosed the little girl in his arms and rocked with her. 'Little Belle, you're now with people who love you, and there's no need to be afraid any longer, do you understand?'

Florence saw a tiny white arm creep up around his neck and return the embrace, and she dabbed at her eyes because apparently for the first time in her forty-seven years, God had seen fit to answer her prayers in a direct and tangible way.

Off in the distance she heard the rattle of the school bus. Her own brood was returning.

Stanley had heard the bus as well. 'Won't Esther be pleased?' He smiled over the little girl's shoulder. 'She's always wanted a sister.'

He looked straight at Florence, a soft sweet look in his eyes. 'You're a good woman, Mrs Melville.' He beamed. 'I couldn't have asked for a better partner.'

Florence saw Stanley push off of the sofa with vigor and energy. 'Where are you going?' she asked.

'To the church office. I have to do some work on Sunday's sermon.' He stared thoughtfully at the floor. 'I believe I'll change the text. I'm not in the mood for Job. I'm in a definite resurrection mood.'

Smiling, he disappeared into the bedroom, leaving Florence to gape.

Sometimes she felt there was just too much mystery to God, too much for His own good . . .

November 2, 1933

As the train was approaching San Bernardino, Martha relaxed against the seat. R. C. was sleeping beside her, his head on her lap.

She'd never been so tired in her life. With her eyes closed, the last two weeks blurred into an indistinguishable parade of faces, names, voices, false hopes, false leads, despair, heartbreak, and grief.

Had it only been two weeks? Sometimes it seemed more like two years or two lifetimes. She'd called Captain Meeks and told him what had happened, had asked if he had threatened to send the children to an orphanage. He'd admitted to making the threat but claimed he hadn't meant it, had said it to frighten the children into obedience. Then Doc Tremble had deposited her in the dispatcher's office in Amarillo, and she had learned with a sinking heart that the coach that R. C. had put Belle on had detached in Oklahoma City and been reattached to the Santa Fe train heading for Fort Worth. There it was changed to the Texas-Pacific heading for El Paso, San Bernardino, Los Angeles, and about fourteen smaller towns in between.

The dispatcher, a courteous man with one eye missing, had given her a schedule of stops along the way with times of arrival. Further, he had arranged with the permission of the railroad to give her two courtesy passes that would see them all the way to LA and back to Tulsa.

Martha opened her eyes and stared out at the passing scenery. Desert for the most part.

Belle.

The name caused a pain that almost took her breath away. She still couldn't believe what had happened. R. C. was suffering, too. Twice during their stop in Fort Worth he thought he had seen her and had gone racing across the terminal only to return red-faced and embarrassed.

'Dear God, help us,' Martha prayed. 'You gave her to me. Don't take her away from me like this.'

She looked ahead at the empty seat opposite her. Everyone had asked for her picture, a few had even scolded her for not having a picture. Where in her world would she have found a camera or money to buy film?

'San Bernardino, ten minutes. Los Angeles next stop.'

The muddled voice of the conductor startled R. C.

'It's all right,' Martha soothed. 'Why don't you run to the lavatory and throw some cold water on your face and wash your hands?'

He was starting up to his feet when Martha altered her instruction. 'Wait. I'll come with you.'

They could disappear so quickly, children could, grown-ups, too. Best keep them in sight at all times.

As she struggled down the narrow aisle after R. C., she saw the conductor coming toward them from the opposite direction. 'Excuse me, sir, but do you know the name of the stationmaster in San Bernardino?'

'Oh, yes, ma'am, that would be Jerry Watson, though I warn you he likes to be called Jerome.' The man winked at her. 'I warn you further that he's something of a ladies' man, so I'd be right careful if I was you.'

'Thank you,' Martha said, and followed R. C. down the aisle.

'Don't need no cold water,' R. C. said, staring out at the farmhouses and dirt roads.

'Don't need *any*,' Martha corrected, and guided him on down to the vestibule, where a fragrant breeze met them along with a good smell of earth and growing things.

She stood on the open vestibule, watched the little settlements go by, and saw hard times even here. Everywhere she looked was an old broken-down car or silent, wide-eyed children.

Despite the grimness of her vision, she experienced a curious feeling of excitement. 'I think she's here, R. C.,' she murmured, and tightened her grip on his hand lest he too get separated from her.

When the train stopped, she stepped down the high steps, then reached back for R. C. 'Come along,' she said. 'Mr Jerome Watson, that's who we're looking for . . .'

Jerry Watson kept a five-by-seven mirror from the dime store in his top desk drawer. When the day was slow he liked to open the top drawer, angle the mirror forward, and study himself in the glass.

In the mirror, he caught a glimpse of the black armband. They all had to wear them for at least two weeks when a company man died.

Now he looked at his face. Many people had told him that he bore a striking resemblance to Douglas Fairbanks.

He lifted his face to the mirror and found himself staring straight at a woman and a little boy, who stared back at him from his open doorway.

Damn. The bitch hadn't even bothered to knock.

'What is it?' he asked, and returned the mirror to the top drawer, straightened his black armband, and wondered how long she'd been standing there.

'Are you – Mr Watson?' she asked timidly.

'Who else would I be?' he said, still embarrassed.

'I need to talk with you for a few minutes,' she began.

'About what?'

'A lost child,' she replied.

'When?'

'About two weeks ago?'

'Two weeks,' he parroted. 'What took you so long to get started?'

The little boy was staring at him with unwavering dark eyes. It was an unsettling stare, and Jerry Watson wished he wouldn't do it.

He shoved a form across the desk with terse instructions. 'Fill it out and bring it back to me along with a photograph of the lost child, and we'll put both on the bulletin board and – '

'I don't have a photograph,' the woman said.

'Well, I'm not certain that I can help you.' A quick glance at his watch told him it was four-fifteen. Fifteen more minutes and he could leave. Hopefully Ramona would be waiting for him at Smithys.

When he looked up the woman was still there, a new look of sadness on her face.

'Oh, come on,' Jerry Watson said, and offered her a chair. 'Now tell me the trouble and we'll see what we can do.'

A few moments later, when she reached the end of her story, she looked up at Jerry expectantly.

He shrugged helplessly. 'I'm afraid I can't help you, and frankly I haven't heard of a lost child. Old Moses was on for a day a couple of weeks ago, but he didn't file a report and I'm afraid this here is for him.' He slapped the black armband. 'He departed this world two days ago. But if a lost kid did come through here and was brought to our attention, I'm pretty sure I can tell you where it would be now.'

'Where? Please tell me.'

'The Catholic orphanage. They take most of our strays, certainly the ones that we pick off the trains.'

'Could you tell me how – '

He stood up, the better to point the way to the big red-brick building about eight blocks away. Even as he talked, the woman reached for the boy's hand and started out the door.

Jerry Watson watched her until she was out of sight, making certain she wouldn't sneak back on him like she had done the first time. He locked his office and stepped out onto the platform and started walking toward Rivera Street.

Strange. A woman like that losing a child. She looked like an Okie, sounded like one, too.

At that moment he saw a dusty truck, brim full of Okies,

with gaunt farm faces, come out to mess up this pretty valley of his.

As far as he was concerned, he wished they would just go back where they came from . . .

She knew it.

She'd had the feeling on the train that it was here they'd catch up with Belle.

'Hurry, R. C.,' Martha urged, aware that he was struggling to keep up.

If the child got this far, she'll be in the orphanage.

A few blocks later they approached the front door, a massive archway with a crucified Christ done in stone over the portal. She spied a smaller door, human-size, in the large door and saw, at the same time, a bell chain. She gave it one good yank, then stood back and waited.

A new stillness had fallen over R. C.

She looked up at the bell as though somehow it had failed to do its duty and was on the verge of pulling again when suddenly she heard movement on the other side of the door, a latch being thrown, then a bolt, then a chain.

Martha saw the door pulled open and saw a tall thin nun, her sharp features appearing even sharper within the tight white band that encircled her face.

'Yes?' she said, and made the word a question.

'I beg your pardon,' Martha murmured, momentarily undone by this stern female.

'Did you want to leave the child?' the nun asked, and reached one hand toward R. C., who in turn ran behind Martha and clung to her skirt.

Shocked and fearful, Martha said, 'No,' indignant that this woman would simply reach out for any child as though it were rightfully hers.

'Then how may I help you?' the nun asked, and in the shadows beyond the opened door, Martha saw faint ghostly movement, nuns floating by, and she thought, What a fearful place for a child.

'I've lost a child, a little girl,' Martha began with as much directness as she could muster.

'When?'

'Two weeks ago. Apparently she was put on the wrong train, and – '

'How careless.'

'Yes.'

'She isn't here,' the nun said, and continued on with a cold sermon. 'God does not entrust precious human life to us so that we might abuse or misplace it. Perhaps Our Heavenly Father meant this as a lesson to you.'

'I'm sure He did.'

'Then you must repent and ask His forgiveness.'

Martha dared not speak. Tears were too close, and she didn't want to give the woman the satisfaction. She felt R. C. pressing close behind her and without a word took his hand and started down the steps.

She'd taken no more than three steps when she heard the nun call out, 'I'll pray for you, I'll pray for the child. Remember we love a forgiving God.'

Whether it was the unexpected kindness or the words themselves, Martha didn't know. All she knew for certain was that she was crying and couldn't stop it. Fear, hopelessness, fatigue, and hunger conspired against her, and she grasped R. C.'s hand and walked as rapidly as possible down the walk.

A few minutes later she saw a small park at the end of one of the main streets that led out from the business district. As she settled on a bench, she heard music in the distance, a hymn familiar to her childhood: 'I Come to the Garden Alone.' She looked about and saw a small white frame church on the far side of the park. It was Wednesday night prayer service. She closed her eyes, the better to listen to the music.

'Hear that, R. C.?'

'Are you crying?'

'No.'

'Do you love me anymore?'

'Of course I love you. My goodness, what a question! What on earth would – '

'Because I was the one who – '

Martha drew him close in her arms and, resting her chin atop his head, tried to think of what she could say to reassure him. 'You mustn't blame yourself, R. C.,' she began.

'Well, if I hadn't – '

'You were trying to do what you thought was best. That's all. No one, not even God, can fault us for that.'

'But what if we don't find her?'

'We'll find her,' Martha said, and heard a fierceness in her tone.

The singing had stopped. Obviously the preaching had started. She looked up to see the sun setting. Dark soon. They'd better get back to the station and check on the next train coming through for Los Angeles.

'Come on, R. C.,' she said, and gathered him to her and kissed his eyes, still salty with tears.

'I'll never leave you, Martha,' he promised.

'Nor I you . . .'

When the hymn was over, Preacher Melville's voice sailed out over the small congregation, as firm and clear and steady as Florence had ever heard it.

She settled in the front row pew, her brood at her side, exactly where Stanley liked them to sit so that they could set a good example for the rest of the congregation. And she was proud of her brood today, except for the little girl who was struggling to get off Esther's lap.

Annoyance increasing, Florence indicated that Esther was to release her. The instant Florence got her hands on that small arm, she carried her kicking and screaming down the central aisle and into the dusk where their car was waiting.

Angrily she put the child in the backseat, climbed in beside her, closed and locked the door. Then she reached beneath the seat where she kept a leather belt, ready for any child who misbehaved away from home.

Without a word of explanation – the explaining would come later – she forced the child down over her knees onto her belly, pulled down her underpants, and held her steady.

The first stinging blow drew a shrill, high-pitched cry from the child. The second another, accompanied by tears now, the third a wail for Florence to quit, the fourth a pitiful groan, the fifth nothing.

Five was enough, anyway.

The child was sobbing, her tiny hands clenched into fists. There were welts on her behind, but Florence hadn't broken the skin, and now was the time for words.

'Belle, you must listen,' she began, and sat the girl in the seat beside her.

'I – w-want Martha,' the child sobbed.

'Well,' Florence said, miffed, 'whoever this Martha is, she clearly didn't want you, or she wouldn't have left you. We're not going to leave you. Pastor Melville and myself, we've given you a place in our hearts and in our home. But we expect certain things of you in return. Do you understand?'

The little girl nodded.

'Well, I tell you what. You can sit here in the car until services are over and think on how naughty you were.'

'It's . . . dark – '

'The dark won't hurt you. Ask God to sit with you.'

'No – don't . . .'

Florence was rather pleased with the child's fear of being left alone in the car at night, a residual punishment. Before she slipped out of the backseat, she locked all the doors and looked back to see the child crying through the back window.

High-strung, that one was, and spoiled. Well, God had sent her to the right hands. Florence would care for her, love her, punish her as she would her own in everlasting gratitude for having spared Stanley's life.

And the next time she asked the little girl to sit quietly in church, it was Florence's educated guess that she would sit quietly . . .

When the Los Angeles train pulled into the crowded Union Station, Martha warned R. C. not to let go of her hand in the rush and crush of foot traffic.

Overhead on boards were red flashing arrows pointing to tracks leading in all directions. Above the din of voices she knew she couldn't make herself heard, let alone understood. Then she noticed an interesting sign about fifty feet down from the women's room, a single gold cross on a white wooden rectangle and below the cross one word – *Chapel.*

'Come on, R. C., let's see if we can't find us a place to sit and think.'

She opened the door onto a small room. There were two candles burning on the altar, which appeared to be a packing crate turned on its side. Flanking the center aisle were four wooden benches, two on either side. There were three dead roses in a Mason jar atop the altar, and then Martha noticed something else, a pair of heavily hosed legs, someone on hands and knees backing out from between the benches and into the center aisle.

'Hello,' Martha said, bewildered by the sight.

A colored woman raised up. 'We closed,' she said, her round black face glistening with perspiration. She plopped her scrub cloth into a pail of water, swished it around, wrung it dry with powerful hands, and disappeared again between the benches.

'Come on, R. C.,' Martha murmured, and was just starting out of the door when she heard the voice again.

'Wait there,' the woman called. 'Go ahead. Sit yourself. The kid, too,' she ordered. 'Suppose you want to pray?'

Bewildered, Martha sat on the back bench and shook her head no, then said, 'Yes.'

The woman grinned. 'The Jesus puzzle got you,' she said, and dropped her scrub cloth into the bucket of water, wiped her hands on the front of her soiled apron, and sat at the end of the front bench, knees spread.

Once settled, she demanded, 'Ain't that right? Ain't it the Jesus puzzle that's got you?'

'I . . . don't know.'

''Course you do. You got yourself a great big cross that's pressing down on your shoulders, making your skin to bleed.'

'I don't understand what – '

'You *is* a mess,' the woman said now, frowning at Martha. 'You wanna tell Bridy what is this cross pressing against you?'

R. C. muttered, 'Let's go,' and Martha sensed the boy's apprehension. But the invitation to speak was too great a temptation, and she settled on the wooden bench and began at the beginning.

When she had finished, she saw the woman fixed before her. 'Lord have mercy,' she breathed, and shook her head. 'Looks to me like you can't afford the Jesus puzzle.'

'What is the Jesus puzzle?'

'It's when we wonder if we believe or not, believe in Jesus.'

She got up from the end of the bench and lifted her arms into the air. 'You see, if you haven't crossed through your valley yet, it's easy to say, "I don't believe." But after you've been through your valley all alone and after you've lost everything you've ever loved and after you've shivered in the cold, you're likely to hear yourself saying, "Come on, sweet Jesus, warm me, come on, sweet Jesus."'

As the woman spoke she rocked back and forth on her heels, her face still lifted to the ceiling.

Then the room was silent. 'You know what I'm thinkin',' the woman said in a different tone of voice. 'I'm thinkin' if I was you, I'd hightail it back to Tulsa, 'cause just as I was praying it occurred to me that your little girl might not be the one who's lost, that maybe you're the lost one and she's back at home this very minute waitin' for you to come home.' The woman concluded with a smile.

Martha gaped. 'How would – '

'Simple,' the woman explained. 'She just up and told

someone where she come from, and they set her down on the train going that direction, and presto! She's home while you're out here gallivantin' around.'

Why hadn't Martha thought of that? And if it had happened that way, Captain Meeks didn't even know where she was. How could he call her and give her the news?

'There! See?' The woman pointed at Martha. 'Problem done solved. Jesus puzzle solved as well. You're on your way.'

'Yes,' Martha said, feeling remarkably well.

For a moment each woman held the other in her gaze.

'I hope you find your young 'un,' the woman said.

'Thanks,' Martha replied, and pushed her way out of the door.

The woman had given her hope, and what a wonderful gift it was. She was fairly dragging R. C. across the crowded terminal, heading toward the tracks, when suddenly she stopped.

'R. C., do you know if Belle could say Tulsa?'

'Don't know – '

'Did you ever *hear* her say it?'

He shook his head. 'But then I never asked her to say it,' he concluded wisely.

'Of course. Well, come on, let's find our way home. I think someone asked her where she was from and she told them and they put her on the right train and she got off the train in Tulsa and ran up the street to the mission and there she is now, sitting on those old crumbling steps, just waiting for us.'

Her vision was contagious, for R. C. broke into a smile.

A short time later they were seated in the rear of a crowded coach. As the rhythmic metal lullaby of moving wheels started, she saw R. C. succumb instantly. Then she too felt a kind of intoxication caused by the vibrations and the curious noise the wheels made as they rolled over the tracks.

Going home going home going home going home, they seemed to be saying.

'Yes,' Martha breathed, then closed her eyes and saw in

perfect sequence two faces, first Belle's, whom she had lost and would shortly find, and second Charlie Groveton, whom she had lost and would never find . . .

November 5, 1933
Tulsa, Oklahoma

The cold rain did little to dampen Martha's feeling of hope, which had been nurtured and encouraged at every stop along the way back from Los Angeles Union Station. The dispatcher at Fort Worth had been especially kind.

'Makes sense to me,' he'd said.

'Look, Martha, there she is.'

At R. C.'s excited cry and use of 'she,' Martha felt her heart accelerate as she looked out of the rainswept window, half expecting to see Belle standing on the platform. But then she saw that R. C. had been referring to Tulsa, the familiar train station.

'Will we be staying at the mission?' R. C. asked, standing up while the train was still moving.

'Of course, where else would we go?' Martha asked. 'If Belle isn't there, we must wait for her and keep on looking. Do you understand?'

The boy looked out of the window at the ragged edge of town, the shanties and salvage lots, a brown-and-gray and despairing landscape that caused Martha to remember the lush green of San Bernardino, the one place where her hope had seemed so strong and right.

'Train's stopped,' R. C. announced, excitement growing. Martha felt sorry for him. During these past two weeks he had shared all her hopes and disappointments. He'd been dragged from station to station, office to office, and all the time she'd observed something different about him, the quiet knowledge that if it hadn't been for him, Belle would –

No!

She must never allow herself to think that. It wasn't fair to any of them.

'Come on.' She sighed and reached for his hand. 'We're going to have to run for it or we'll drown. Are you ready?'

Martha didn't look up until they were approaching the mission. The treacherous footing didn't permit it. She was soaked through and muddy, as was R. C. Then she took the front steps running and pushed open the heavy door and held it for R. C. She let it slam behind her and turned to confront at least fifty men relaxing on their cots, a few smoking in the corner over a game of chess, others standing against the wall, one foot raised like a species of rare bird.

'Come on,' she whispered to R. C., and moved toward the kitchen, eager to retreat to the warm privacy of her room, where she and R. C. might change out of their filthy wet clothes into dry clean ones.

Carefully she led R. C. through the dark passageway and pushed open her door, longing to see something familiar. Instead she saw her room filled with cots, scarcely an aisle between, and at each cot was a man who looked up sleepily at the intruder, then turned over and went back to sleep.

'See, I told you,' R. C. whispered close beside her.

She felt anger rising steadily as she looked about for her things. Then she saw Captain Meeks just coming up the steps, shaking rain off his black umbrella before he drew open the door.

He looked up. Recognition and guilt covered his gaunt face. 'It's you,' he said.

'Yes.'

'Did you find what you were looking for?'

'No. Has anyone asked about – I mean, has Belle – come home?'

'No.'

More disappointment. False hope. Always false hope. She looked up in search of relief.

'I wish you hadn't threatened the children,' she said.

'You left me in charge. I did what I thought was best. They were stealing food.'

'They were hungry.'

'They were not my responsibility.'

She fought back anger. It would serve no purpose. She needed this man. Where else could they go?

'Captain Meeks, I was wondering, where are my things?' she asked, shivering from her wet clothes, eager to get R. C. into dry ones as well.

'I moved them,' he said.

'I can see that. Could you tell me where you – '

'We needed the space,' he went on. 'It's been very busy around here since you took off. I moved your things to the basement.'

'But the basement isn't suitable for – '

'Take it or leave it,' Captain Meeks said.

The basement. It was big and warm near the boiler. But it was dark and dirty.

Apparently Captain Meeks saw something on her face. 'I'm sorry, Martha. Please consider it temporary. I'll move the men out as soon as possible.'

This kindness, so unexpected, almost proved her undoing. She reached back for R. C.'s hand.

'Are his clothes down there as well?' she asked.

'Yes.'

'And Belle's?'

'Yes.'

She started down the corridor toward the cellar steps at the far end.

'Martha?'

She looked back.

'I'm sorry about the little girl,' he said. 'I feel confident she'll turn up.'

Turn up! Bad pennies turned up, lost slippers, misplaced gloves. Small children did not.

'Thank you, Captain Meeks. Give me a few minutes to get into something dry and I'll be right up.'

'I'm glad you're back.'

'Thanks.'

She was certain that he watched her all the way down

the corridor. Yet when she reached the basement stairs and looked back, he was gone. If she remembered correctly, there was a light switch on the wall. As her hands went groping, she found it and flipped it on.

Below she saw two cots. On top of one were several boxes with certain familiar items visible. To the right of the cots was an enormous boiler. She could feel its warmth from where she stood. R. C. had already gravitated to its sides.

At first Martha thought she could deal with her sinking spirits. After all, she was an expert with a broom and a mop, and she had a rag rug that would look nice in front of the two cots. Packing cases made wonderful makeshift drawers, and surely Captain Meeks would let her have her dressing table. What need did the men have for a dressing table?

So even as all of these plans were settling comfortably in impoverished parts of her mind, there was a deeper, more significant despair that could not be assuaged by thoughts of a rag rug or dressing table.

Belle was probably lost to her forever.

No!

Without warning she sank to the bottom step, aware of the fear and guilt in R. C.'s eyes and at the moment unable to do anything about it . . .

May 15, 1935
Tulsa, Oklahoma
Salvation Army Mission

Was the world coming to an end?

Martha sat on the front mission steps and read the headlines of the *Tulsa Tribune,* and even as she read she felt the dust swirl about her and bite into her cheeks.

Only last month the town of Stratford, Texas, had been buried by what the papers were calling 'the Black Sunday Dust Storm.' She had read the death lists every day of the people who had died of suffocation.

'You're gonna get buried, Martha,' a man yelled as he ran up the steps, holding on to his hat, and into the mission.

As the door slammed behind him, she thought he was probably right. But she only intended to sit here long enough to meet R. C. coming home from school. She squinted down the street and considered walking to the corner to meet him, but she was trying hard now not to hold him too close.

Since Belle had been lost her impulse was to keep R. C. in sight at all times. But that wasn't good for him. Or her. So he walked to school every morning, and if her duties permitted, she was always waiting to meet him. Few things brought her greater pleasure than her first glimpse of R. C., grown tall and darkly handsome at nine, rounding the corner, lifting his hand in greeting, then breaking into a run.

For several moments her eyes locked on the newsprint, but she saw nothing.

Belle.

The pain had not eased with the passage of time. If anything, it had grown worse. Captain Meeks's advice was sound and stupid all at the same time.

Try to think of her as happily living with a new family.

The only things that really helped were the weekly letters she sent out to dispatchers and station managers and police stations in every town between Tulsa and Los Angeles.

God, why?

This was her nightly prayer. Why had He taken Belle from her?

'Martha?'

The familiar cry blended with the wind.

She looked and saw R. C. running up the hill, his knickers blowing with the gusts, making him look like a little Dutch boy. As he drew nearer she saw his cheeks were flushed, his dark hair tousled. In his arms were books. He loved books, was an excellent student, very bright according to all his teachers.

'How was school?' she asked as she hugged him and pushed his hair back from his brow.

'Do you know all of the capitals of all of the states?' he asked, breathless from his sprint up the hill.

'My no.' Martha smiled. 'Do you?'

'I have to know them by tomorrow.'

'Then we have our work cut out for us tonight.'

'Will you help me?'

'Of course,' she promised. 'Come along, we'll get an early start on our chores so we can have a clear shot at them.'

As they reached the door, Martha heard a car pull up at the curb. She looked back and saw a police car, a familiar face peering up at her. She knew most of the police department, all of them at one time or another having dropped off a homeless man or woman in need of food.

'You go on in,' Martha instructed R. C. 'Get the big blue pail in the kitchen and wet down all the cloths at the windows. Change your clothes first. I'll be right in.'

'You're not going anyplace, are you?'

'No, no, of course not. I'll be right there.'

Now she hurried to the bottom of the steps.

'Sorry to bother you,' said the officer on the passenger side, 'but we had a letter from San Antonio. They found a dead kid out there. The chief said that he had recently received word from you, telling him about your lost kid. He was just wondering – '

The wind felt like a hand trying to knock her down.

'We have photographs. Do you want to – '

'May I?' she asked, indicating the backseat of the police car. She couldn't fight everything at once, including the wind.

As the officer in front stretched backward to unlock the door for her, she drew it open and stepped into the backseat.

'We're sorry to – '

'No, no, I appreciate that,' she said.

'How long has it been now, Martha?'

'A year and a half.'

'Of course you know with every year the trail becomes more difficult to follow. The child grows and changes, if, that is, she's still alive.'

As he said this, the officer behind the wheel handed over a large manila envelope, and she saw an apology in his eyes even as she took it.

'This kid is about six,' he said. 'They found her near the city dump. She's been cut up pretty bad, but her face is – '

Her hands trembled as she unwound the red tie that held the envelope flap secure. She withdrew 3 eight-by-ten photos. The first was a facial close-up revealing a little girl's face with swollen eyes. The second was of the dump itself, a distant shot of irregular shapes and forms. Martha had to look closely to see the naked child lying at a distorted angle among the old mattresses and cardboard cartons.

She looked at the third photograph of the child lying naked on a metal table. There were open slash marks on her legs, her stomach, her chest, her throat.

'Is it – '

'No. No,' Martha said quickly, and returned the photos to the envelope and rewrapped the red twine on the flap as though to seal forever the horror within.

'Well, we had to ask,' the officer said, and took the envelope from her. 'I'm sorry if – '

'No, I'm glad you came,' she said, and reached for the door. 'And there may be other photos, news, letters, anything. Please let me know. I can't tell you how – '

'I have three of my own,' the police officer said. 'I understand.'

'Thanks again,' Martha called back, and climbed out of the patrol car on shaky knees. She waved the policemen down the hill and, reaching into her pocket, found some coins. Then she ran down the street toward the busy intersection and the row of shops facing the train station. She had seen it the day before and considered buying it then.

Now it was the only possible way she could dispel the image of the dead child tossed on the dump.

As she pushed open the shop door, a bell rang overhead, summoning Mr Prince from the back room of his nickel-and-dime store.

'Martha, you back again?'

With only a glance, Martha went directly to the table at the back and picked up a book of Shirley Temple paper dolls with five dresses, five coats, three hats, and three pairs of shoes. 'This one,' she said, and placed the book on the counter, then fished through her pockets for the dime and put the coin on top of the book.

Mr Prince looked up at her over the top of his specs. 'Is – have you found – is Belle –?'

'No,' she replied to his stammering. 'But she'll be home any day now, and we must have a toy for her. She'd like this, I know.'

'Of course, what little girl wouldn't?'

He slipped the book into a brown bag along with a cherry lollipop. 'For R. C.' He winked.

'Thank you.'

'Now you best get on back up to the mission. Look at that sky.'

She clasped the bag and pushed open the door to see the sky yellow with dust, people scurrying in all directions, all holding their hands over their noses to keep from breathing the swirling particles.

As she started up the mission steps, she grasped the railing and tried to prepare herself for the duties yet ahead of her this night, serving the meal, cleaning up, seeing that everyone had a blanket, helping R. C. to learn all the state capitals, trying not to think on the dead child.

If only she had someone to talk to, like Charlie. What good talks they'd had on his parents' front porch or walking down the road.

At the door she stopped to gather strength, to make herself a clean slate for the needs of others, to empty her heart of all vanity.

Then she was ready and shifted the Shirley Temple book to the other hand, opened the mission door, and went in . . .

September 10, 1935
San Bernardino, California

Florence put the pot of Saturday beans in front of Stanley and started back into the kitchen for the cornbread when she heard a peculiar sound, like someone holding his breath and not letting it out.

She looked back and saw Stanley fall face forward.

Esther screamed and reached for Belle. The two boys sat transfixed as though they had never seen their father behave in this manner.

For that matter, neither had Florence.

'Stanley?' she said, and saw his hands limp in his lap. She started to ask him if he was all right, but she touched his arm, then the back of his neck, and knew he was not all right, knew he was dead.

'Mama, is Papa – '

Florence shook her head as though trying to shake sense into it. Grief arrived quickly, as did anger. But both had to be postponed. 'Your father has – passed on,' she whispered, and reached for him, wanting to help him, wanting to get his hair out of the bean pot. But her hands were shaking too badly, and Esther and the boys were crying openly. The only dry eyes about the table were the big blue ones belonging to Belle. The imposter. She was no more a gift from God than the man in the moon.

'Esther, take all the children onto the front porch for me.'

She encircled Stanley once, thinking there was something she could do to make him more comfortable and realizing belatedly that comfort was not a big issue with him anymore.

At last she felt tears and let them come.

She went down on her knees at Stanley's side and cried hard for about two minutes. That was all she needed. Then her tears were dry and she looked up at Stanley's face, distorted at the angle in which he had fallen onto the table. As he'd fallen, he'd dropped a ladle of beans. The mess was running down the sides of the oilcloth. It was strange to see the beans moving while Stanley was so still.

She had to call someone. It wasn't often that she admitted to it, but she needed help.

'Seth, I want you to run down the road and fetch Harold Shoda. Tell him your papa has – died.'

Harold Shoda would know what to do. Poor man had lost both his parents a few months ago.

What in the name of God would she do now?

She couldn't very well stay here. The church couldn't support her and her family forever. Oh, they'd be charitable for a few weeks, bringing in food, condolences, and prayers – but sooner or later the bishop would assign the church a new pastor. Florence and her brood would be out on their ears in the middle of the road, and what then?

A short time later she heard Harold Shoda's familiar old pickup rattling to a stop before the house.

'Mrs Melville, is it true?' he called out.

Florence answered yes. She saw the passenger side of the truck open, saw Kim Shoda slip out from where she had been holding Seth on her lap.

While Kim huddled with the children in the porch swing, Florence led Harold into the house. She waited while Harold felt the back of Stanley's neck.

'I'm – so sorry, Mrs Melville.'

Florence had grown to like the Shodas immensely. They were childless and had more or less adopted Florence's brood, were always bringing them little gifts. They were good people, 'third-generation Japanese all-American,' as Harold Shoda was fond of saying.

'May I use your phone?' Harold asked with characteristic politeness.

'Of course.'

'We'll call the coroner's office. They will do the death certificate, then we must notify a funeral home.'

'Florence?'

It was Kim who came into the living room and put her arm about Florence's shoulder. 'I know that the next few hours will be difficult. I was wondering. I left a pan of fresh gingerbread in the oven. Could I – would it be all right with you if I put all the children in the truck and took them back to the farm for some cold milk and hot gingerbread?'

It sounded like a lovely idea, and Florence only wished that she could join them. Behind her she heard Harold on the phone, talking low. In front of her, she saw Kim gathering up the children, reaching out for Belle in particular and enclosing her in her arms with all the need of a childless woman.

Four mouths. Five counting Belle. A dead husband and no future. Still staring into the patch of sun beyond the open door, Florence wondered if it would help if she wrote to Mr Roosevelt. The local papers were always filled with letters from people all over the country who had written to the president about their specific problems and had received personal assistance in one form or another.

'Florence?'

It was Harold Shoda coming up behind her. 'The coroner will be right out.'

But Florence found she was unable to get her mind off the great fearful question mark of the future. 'What will I do, Harold?' She sighed and sat in her rocker, then motioned for him to have a seat as well.

'I don't understand.'

'I'm a widow with four children, no savings, and no skills beyond scrambling an egg, scrubbing a toilet, and making a bed.'

'You have friends here.'

'Who can barely take care of their own.'

'Kim and I – '

'Have enough to do without adopting a family of five. There's my problem, Harold. All those children. Well, I think it's clear that the little one will have to go to the Catholics. Certainly my first obligation is to my own flesh and blood. Don't you agree?'

'You – would do that?' he asked, sitting up on the edge of his chair.

'Do what?'

'Put Belle in the orphanage?'

'If I can't feed her, yes.'

About twenty minutes later they heard a car pull up on the gravel in front of the house. Florence was on her feet immediately, ready to do whatever had to be done to get this day over with.

She looked back to see Harold Shoda still staring at her as though suddenly she'd grown another head. 'Are you coming?'

'Why, yes,' he muttered, and took his troubled expression all the way to the door, where he extended a hand to the county coroner, a rail-thin man with a small black bag.

'Mr Dixon,' he said, and introduced him to Florence, who assumed the pose and posture of the grieving widow and thrust her handkerchief to her lips, though truth be known she was thinking less about poor Stanley and more about poor Florence . . .

Kim lay perfectly still in the bed next to Harold and thought back to the beginning.

Sacramento 1910, the date and place of her birth. Her father, Akimo Takura, had been a lawyer. He had wanted terribly for Kim to follow in his footsteps. Once she had planned to do that, but when she was ten years old, her parents had taken her to San Bernardino to visit the Shoda family, and there she had met a little boy named Harold, who was twelve and had dirty fingernails from working in his fields but the kindest eyes she had ever seen. She'd fallen in love with the pretty white farmhouse, the rich black soil, the orange groves, the beautiful vegetables, and the little boy with dirty fingernails.

In 1928 she had married Harold Shoda before a justice

of the peace and had moved into the big white farmhouse with Harold's formidable father and mother. That was seven years ago, and in all that time Kim had suffered only one heartbreak, when Dr Anderson had told her that children would not be coming along, that due to an obstruction she would never be able to conceive.

For the first time since she'd launched this journey into the past, she turned carefully onto her side, facing away from Harold, and saw Rosie, her favorite mongrel dog, fast asleep on the floor beside her. She reached down and rubbed her neck.

With one hand caressing soft animal fur, she found the courage to face what she knew was keeping her awake.

Belle.

After dinner, Harold had driven Florence Melville and the children home. He had returned and had told her what Florence Melville had said. She was going to give Belle to the Catholics, as she could no longer feed the child.

Kim closed her eyes, still unable to comprehend such a threat. The child had been a part of the Melville family for two years. You didn't just give away a part of your family.

Then Harold had made a singularly stunning suggestion.

'Why don't we take her? We have plenty.'

'Harold?' She nudged him lightly. 'Do you really think Florence will let us have her?'

His first response was a sleepy groan. Then: 'I don't know why not.'

'Do you suppose she has already spoken to the orphanage?'

'I doubt it. Her husband just died, remember?'

'Could we go first thing tomorrow and find out?'

He drew her close. 'Yes. I promise.' He kissed her on the forehead. 'So you want a little blond-haired blue-eyed daughter?'

'Yes. Oh, yes.'

'Belle Shoda?'

'Yes.'

'Go to sleep now. You need your rest if you're to become a mother tomorrow.'

She waited a few moments longer, not wanting to disturb him a second time, then slipped carefully out of bed, avoiding Rosie in the process, and padded barefoot out of their room and down the hall toward the large bedroom his parents had occupied, the best room, really, with a lovely little balcony overlooking the verdant fields in three directions.

She pushed open the door, turned on the light, and noticed the heavy dark mahogany furniture that had belonged to her parents-in-law.

She sat in the near rocker and studied the room. She could see in her mind's eye pale pink walls, with a pleasant arrangement of white wicker, a pretty pink floral carpet underneath, white organdy at the window, and a beautiful brass four-poster right over there, canopied, of course, in the palest pink dotted Swiss, her ivory cachepots filled with pink begonias and lining the balcony, a little girl's paradise. And filling her closets, exquisite dresses, made by Kim on the new sewing machine that Harold had given her two years ago, and –

Suddenly she felt movement about her ankles and looked down to see Powderpuff, her white Persian, brushing against her.

'Puff, come here,' she whispered, and scooped up two handfuls of soft white Persian cat.

As she stroked Puff's whiskers, the cat's purr increased. In a spasm of pure contentment, Kim pressed her head back against the rocker, closed her eyes, and saw with perfect clarity the daughter she'd never had and always wanted . . .

October 2, 1935

Florence knew it. The new pastor and his family were already in town, just waiting for her to leave.

Well, they could just cool their heels in that fancy hotel. She would leave when she was good and ready.

As she tied cord around the last box of kitchen utensils, she brushed her hair back and looked at the chaos in which they'd been living for the past two weeks.

A letter had come from the bishop's office, kindly informing her that there was a Methodist home outside Los Angeles where widows and families of deceased Methodist pastors could go while they tried to sort through their lives and put them back together, 'for the benefit of Christ.'

That's how the bishop had put it, 'for the benefit of Christ.' And although she really hadn't had Christ's benefit in mind, she had been grateful.

'Esther,' she called sharply, 'we're leaving here in five minutes. I want that box hauled out to the car, and I want Belle's suitcase placed out by the mailbox so she'll be ready when the Shodas come.'

'But why do we have to leave her, Mama?' Esther sobbed. 'She's part of our family.'

'No, she isn't, and you know she isn't.'

Now Florence physically separated Esther and Belle with a stern tone that sent Esther running out the front door carrying the box while Belle stared at Florence with those calm blue eyes.

'Now, you listen,' Florence began. 'I'm certain you understand what is happening. With Pastor Melville's passing, the children and myself are forced to find another life. I've made arrangements for Harold and Kim Shoda to come for you. Do you understand what I'm saying?'

Still no response on that pale face.

Without warning, the child stepped forward and put her arms around Florence and hugged her.

'Come along,' Florence said, swallowing hard. 'I'll show you where to stand, and I promise the Shodas will be along.' She led Belle to the road where the boys had placed her cardboard suitcase.

'Now you stand right here by the mailbox, Belle, do you understand? Mr and Mrs Shoda will be along any minute now.'

She glanced at her watch. Three o'clock had been the

meeting time, but Florence had always planned to leave early. She had said her good-byes to Harold and Kim, and the first time had been hard enough. She had no intention of going through it a second time.

'Be good, and love God,' Florence whispered, and patted Belle on the head, then ran back to the car, slid behind the wheel, and took off with such speed that she raised a cloud of dust, briefly obscuring the spectacle of the child waiting beside the mailbox.

October 2, 1935
San Bernardino, California

While Harold changed the flat tire on the truck, Kim ran upstairs for a final look at Belle's room. They were going to be late. But she was certain that Florence would wait with the child until they came.

Now, as she took the stairs two at a time, she could smell her beef stew simmering on the stove. It would be Belle's first dinner with them. Also on the kitchen table was Belle's favorite, chocolate cake.

'We mustn't spoil her,' Harold had warned.

Why not? The child needed a lifetime of love and security, and she intended to see that Belle got it.

Now, as she pushed open the door to Belle's bedroom, the sight brought a smile of pleasure, as it had done every day since they had finished the redecorating. She looked out onto the balcony and saw the row of white cachepots filled with pink-and-white begonias and beyond the begonias the beautiful vista of the farm, the perfectly aligned rows of vegetables, and to one side the orchards for as far as the eye could see.

If there was a paradise, it would have to resemble this.

Then she heard the horn blaring, Harold's signal that the tire had been changed.

She hurried back to the room, stopping to straighten

Raggedy Ann and Andy where they'd flopped over onto Shirley Temple's lap atop the old trunk, now painted white. Inside the trunk were books, games, and more toys, all suitable for a five-, almost six-year-old. Florence had told her that they had no idea of the child's actual birthday but had assigned her Christmas Eve.

Kim wasn't so certain about that, but it could all be worked out later. For now they must go and fetch her, bring her back to her new home, and try to convince her that while she might have a real mother and father somewhere in this world, no one was prepared to love her more than Harold and Kim Shoda . . .

A short time later Harold spotted her, standing alone beside the Melville mailbox, a cardboard suitcase at her feet.

'She's alone,' he said, and looked about for a sign of life as he guided the pickup close to where the child was waiting.

Simultaneously he saw the excitement on Kim's face and the fear on Belle's. 'Move carefully,' he suggested as Kim threw open the car door and made a mad dash around the pickup. At the same time the child bolted, ran through the front gate, up the steps, around the porch, and disappeared from sight.

'Kim, wait,' Harold called out, and caught up with her. 'She's frightened,' he advised, and saw the hurt and confusion in Kim's eyes. 'Let's just sit here on the steps. She couldn't have gone far. Maybe she'll come out from hiding and join us.'

But Kim obviously didn't approve of the idea. 'No, we have to find her and tell her she doesn't need to be afraid. She knows us, she knows – '

'Only that her family has left her,' Harold broke in.

But Kim ignored him and started slowly up the steps as though she were playing a game of hide-and-seek.

'Belle?' she called out. 'Can you hear me? Wouldn't you like to come and stay at our house? Rosie wants to see you, as does Puff.'

But there was no response, and Harold watched as Kim

made her way around to the side of the porch where Belle had disappeared.

'She's gone,' she called out full-voiced, as there was apparently no longer any need for games.

Harold joined her, followed the direction of her gaze, and saw a small dot of a child running as fast as she could through the field behind the parsonage.

Harold and Kim exchanged a weary glance. 'I suspected that it wouldn't be easy,' Harold murmured.

'I didn't,' Kim said, and sounded on the verge of tears. 'What do we do now?'

'We can pick her up at the section line. Come on.'

Back in the pickup he saw Kim slump on the seat, an expression of defeat on her face. 'Don't worry,' he soothed. 'It'll take time.' How much time, he didn't know.

About ten minutes later they were waiting at the section line when they saw a very red faced and scratched up little girl emerge from the high weeds. When she saw the pickup, she started to dart back into the fields.

But Harold ran after her and grabbed her hand, expecting to speak calmly, civilly, to her. Instead, at first contact the child started flailing at anything that got in the path of her fists. It was with a distinct lack of ceremony that Harold brought her back to the pickup, where almost angrily he wedged her onto the front seat between them.

All the way home he was forced to endure not only the child's tears, but Kim's as well . . .

During the next three weeks Belle ran away five times, and each time Kim and Harold got into the pickup and cruised up and down the farm roads and section lines, always finding her and bringing her back.

Once, when her grief seemed to know no bounds, Kim thought she'd heard the child cry out for someone named Martha. But that was the only word she'd spoken since the Melvilles had left. Meal-times were nightmares of silence. Harold was gone most of the day in the fields, so it was Kim who was left to fathom the mystery of the child.

On this chill November morning, she was forced to admit that perhaps they had made a mistake. Maybe she'd be happier with the nuns across town. Maybe –

Kim stopped kneading the bread dough and glanced across the kitchen. Belle sat on a straight-backed chair before the window, hands folded in her lap, watching the rain. She'd sat like that for over an hour, though Kim had placed an inviting arrangement of books, puzzles, and paper dolls within easy reach on the table.

Kim had invited her to help make bread.

No response.

She had asked her if she'd like to go into town with Harold.

No response. And Harold had left without her, a look of relief on his face.

What were they doing wrong?

Outside she heard Harold's pickup. He'd gone into town for winter seed and fertilizer. When the rain stopped it was time to plant the winter crops.

'Harold's here,' she said, and received no answer. Hurriedly she slapped the dough into a smooth round ball, dusted it with flour, and covered it with a cool cloth.

She'd just wiped her hands on her apron when she heard his step. Then the door burst open and a very wet and dripping Harold appeared, holding his yellow slicker close to his body in a peculiar pressure as though he had –

Kim heard it, and even before he drew back his slicker, she smiled and knew that he'd returned from town with more than fertilizer and winter seed.

Then there it was, a small brown ball of wet fur, wriggling in Harold's hands and trying to lick them all at the same time.

'Let me.' Kim grinned, took the puppy from him, cradled it, determined it was female, then kissed it and checked it for wounds.

The puppy was whole and remarkably well fed. They knelt before the fire, wrapped her in the towel, and rubbed until the soft brown fur was dry and fluffy.

'A new baby for Rosie to mother,' Kim said. Her older Rosie always adopted every new stray as though it were her own.

So engrossed were they in this new fascination that they failed to hear a slight movement coming from the chair at the window.

Though it took every ounce of Kim's self-control, not once did she look up but continued to stroke and fondle the puppy, and Harold did the same even when they were aware of Belle standing right behind them, drawn to the abandoned puppy as though by a magnet, homeless, as lost and without love as Belle fancied herself to be.

Slowly she knelt, her eyes wide with interest and curiosity. At last there were words. 'May I hold her?'

'Of course.' Kim smiled and drew the towel away from the puppy, placing the brown ball of fur in Belle's arms.

For a few moments there was a mutual inspection as Belle studied all aspects of the pup and the pup in turn sniffed the newness of someone else. Then, as though by mutual consent and need, Belle wrapped the puppy in her arms and buried her face in the fur, while the puppy wriggled up into the small hollow of Belle's neck and settled peacefully, as though at last she had found her rightful home.

'May I have her?' Belle asked.

'Of course,' Kim said. 'I most definitely think that she's your dog.'

'She needs a name,' Harold suggested.

Without hesitation, Belle answered in a clear tone. 'Belle.'

Kim and Harold exchanged a glance. 'You . . . want her to have your name?'

'She's like me.'

'How about Little Belle,' Harold suggested. 'That way when we want the puppy to come we'll call out Little Belle. And when we want you, we'll call Belle.'

About thirty minutes later, with Little Belle fed and sound asleep in a basket by the fire, Kim finished her bread, put it in the oven, and started to peel potatoes for the evening meal. She moved more slowly than usual, occupied as she was by the sight of Harold and Belle at the big oak table, piecing together a jigsaw puzzle of the Statue of Liberty, Belle squealing, 'Here's the torch!' and Harold sliding it into place, then hugging the child, praising her, and looking up at Kim with a very satisfied grin . . .

May 14, 1937
Oklahoma City, Oklahoma

Charlie Groveton had never heard so much union talk. Here he was, sitting at the dinner table of Rita and Reed Spence on Northeast Twenty-third, when what he'd been sent all the way from Lake Maracaibo to learn about was the new flat-bottomed rock bit being used extensively in the capital oilfields of Oklahoma City.

But so far he'd been here two days and had done nothing but sweat, eat, and listen to Reed Spence talk foolishly about forming a union.

'More pie, Charlie?' asked Rita, a plump, pleasant woman who always had a smile on her face and a willingness to pack up and follow her driller husband anywhere. She was a good oilfield wife.

'No, thank you, Rita. I've had plenty.'

'So what do you think, Charlie?' Reed asked, settling back in a rocker and putting his feet up on a low table.

'About what?'

'About the union. Good God, man, haven't you heard anything I've said tonight?'

'I've heard everything, Reed, and I think it's the dumbest notion you've ever come up with.'

Charlie knew he'd been blunt, but the heat was awful, and he wanted to take a look at the drill bit in action, maybe place an order for his field superintendent at Maracaibo, then get on back to Caracas where he felt safe from his memories.

'You're gonna have to explain yourself,' Reed said, and Charlie heard the hurt and anger in his voice.

'All right.' Charlie was trying to choose his words more carefully. He hated to destroy any man's dream. 'You see those fireflies out there?' he asked, pointing to the darting specks of light dancing all over the front lawn. 'You have about as much chance of unionizing those bugs as you have of unionizing roughnecks. My God, Reed, you know who we are. We're not men to be tied down to anything. We're not men content to just clerk in a store or be unionized or regimented in any way. We're happy only when we feel free to get full of quit. Independence is our way of staying free. Hell, if you don't like what the man's paying you, go find another job.'

'Unions *are* coming,' Reed insisted, mind unchanged.

'Not to the oilfields. Now what I want to know is when in the hell are you gonna show me that flat-bottomed bit? I got me a field superintendent on the lake eager to see how it works.'

He saw Reed shake his head. 'You've gone native on us,' he mourned.

'No.' Charlie grinned. 'It's just that there's gonna be a whole lot of head bashing on account of this union talk, and I don't want it to be my head or yours. When John L. Lewis meets US Steel, you're gonna see a blowout bigger'n Spindletop. Hell, life's too short, Reed. Don't go lookin' for losin' battles.'

Reed stretched. 'You give up too easy, Charlie, always have.'

Charlie started to protest and wasn't given a chance.

'What was that girl's name from Hitchings?' Rita asked quietly from the door. Charlie looked back and saw her shaking Jergens lotion onto her hands after doing the dishes. 'It was Martha, wasn't it, Charlie? Whatever happened to her?'

'Her pa told me she'd gone off to Dallas with some insurance man. Now come on, Reed, you gonna take me to the rig or do I have to walk?'

'I'll take you,' Reed said. He kissed Rita in passing, told her not to wait up. Charlie thanked her again for the home cooking and hoped she didn't say anything else. He didn't like talking about himself, certainly not the part that hurt as much as Martha Drusso.

A short time later, Reed drove over the curb into the area around the well, and Charlie saw lots of activity on the rig floor. Most of the roughnecks and drillers were hanging back, while two men were going hard and fast in some sort of heated debate.

'Damn,' Reed muttered, turning off the ignition and peering up through the windshield. 'The company man. Come on, let's see what all the ruckus is about.'

As they started toward the derrick steps, Charlie held back to observe the drill in motion, the rhythmic sound of an old clock turning, a sound that was as familiar as the beat of his own pulse.

Reed scrambled up the steps ahead of him, and from Charlie's position at the bottom of the stairs, he saw Reed listening to the men arguing, something about the test flow.

The company man in his white shirt and tie stood out like a sore thumb among the dirty rig workers. Clearly the one giving him all the trouble was the rig foreman.

'But you gotta close the pipe,' the foreman shouted.

'No, you lose on production. Keep it open.'

'But I tell you, man, it ain't safe.'

Charlie stepped back from the rig stairs and paced slowly in the soft dirt around the base of the steps. Why was it that the idiots were always in charge? The process they were talking about was a simple one designed to eliminate the fire hazards, a very present danger, as live oil was just as volatile as gasoline.

Charlie saw that Reed had now joined in, a peacemaker, taking the rig foreman aside and trying to calm him, then talking to the company man, trying to diffuse his anger as well.

Reed offered to pull a few stands of pipe just to see how it went.

Charlie gaped along with everyone else as Reed pulled a stand, wrapped the mud box around the break, broke the joint, and then picked up the stand. Oil gushed out onto the derrick floor.

To a full chorus of shouted obscenities, the men jumped back. Only Reed, covered with oil, held his position. The company man's white shirt was not so white anymore as he ran all the way back to the driller's station.

Charlie shook his head at the shenanigans. Would he ever get to see the new bit he'd come all this way to see?

Exasperated, he looked upward and saw the naked one-hundred-watt bulbs strung around the rig floor and up the derrick leg, where Reed was standing dripping oil. If a light bulb blew, every man on the rig floor was a dead man.

'Reed – '

Just as Charlie yelled, the gas trapped in the drill pipe with the live oil belched and sprayed Reed again.

'Reed, get the hell – '

For several seconds pieces of gravel exploded all over the place, striking the light bulbs less than two feet overhead from where Reed was standing. Then there was a pop, only a small noise considering the conflagration that followed, converting Reed Spence within the instant into a human torch.

'God!' Charlie shouted, and as all the other men ran backward, Charlie scrambled up the narrow rig steps, his feet slipping, a nightmare movement in which it felt as if something were holding him back. And all the while he kept his eyes on the man inside the fireball, writhing, his hands flailing uselessly against the pain, his legs lifting and falling in a macabre dance of agony, the flames curiously limited to Reed and the floor around him.

As Charlie clawed his way to the top of the stairs, someone appeared with a fire extinguisher, covering the flames with white foam, and at last Reed fell.

Charlie dropped to his knees, hands extended, ready to help, though he knew that Reed was beyond help, far beyond his efforts to do anything but stare helplessly down at this contorted, charred disfigurement that now resembled a smoldering log more than a human being.

No one else was approaching. He was aware of that and recognized it from past accidents. The impulse of survivors was to maintain a safe distance lest the bad luck spill over onto them. Even the man wielding the fire extinguisher had retreated, leaving a coating of slippery wet, white foam everywhere and the still smoldering contortion of a log that once had been a good man.

When would somebody come forward and take charge, make it right, find the culprit –

At last Charlie looked toward the driller's station.

Then he was moving, with great deliberation at first, through the slippery white foam, at last finding sure footing, then running toward the driller's station and the bland face of the company man who at sixty-plus just didn't want anything bad to mess up his retirement. Well, something really bad had messed up Reed Spence's retirement, had messed up his life, had messed up Rita's life, had now messed up Charlie's life. If the company man hadn't insisted, if Reed had been firm in his judgment based on fifteen years' experience instead of trying to be diplomatic, if Charlie hadn't insisted on seeing the new drilling bit tonight . . .

As guilt joined grief, Charlie kicked in the door of the driller's station. He saw the man pressed against the far wall, his face mirroring the tragedy he'd just caused.

'You bastard,' Charlie muttered, and the last thing he clearly remembered was lunging for the man and finding his throat, feeling soft rolls of flesh beneath his fingers as he brought the man to ground.

It wouldn't bring Reed back, but it helped to ease the grief of the moment.

He'd have to settle for that . . .

August 20, 1937
San Bernardino, California

'What's a movie, Kim?'

Kim shook the bedsheet that Belle had handed her, pinned it to the clothesline, took the opposite end, then bent over and kissed Belle on the side of her neck where that tiny birthmark in the shape of a bell was just visible. 'You'll just have to wait and see.'

This morning at breakfast Harold had promised them that tonight they'd go into town to the Palace Theater and see a movie called *Snow White and the Seven Dwarfs.*

Belle had looked puzzled at the promise but had said nothing. Very much like her. For the last year Kim had noticed that there were moments when certain words and certain mysteries left the child silent and unresponsive. Thank God those moments were rare. For the most part Belle was a joyous child who loved kisses, hugs, pretty dresses, and her dog, Lil. The name had been shortened from Little Belle, which had become too cumbersome by the end of that first week. Now Lil and Belle were inseparable.

'Hand me the towels,' Kim now directed, and grabbed another handful of clothespins. Every time she looked at Belle, she thought of a flower opening wider each day, revealing different colors, different shapes, different patterns. It was as if her eyes seemed to search out and investigate everything as though confident of finding a clue to the mystery that still haunted her.

Her voice was enchanting and utterly irresistible. Her long blond hair framed a face that was becoming more and more radiant, as though whatever light was shining from within could not be dimmed. Kim knew that Belle would grow inevitably into a great natural beauty, and she frequently caught herself marveling at this jewel of a child who had entered her life on the wings of a miracle.

And matching her physical beauty was an internal beauty equally as stunning. She could not abide seeing others hurt, and she had a generous and loving heart.

They'd started her in first grade last year, but the teachers had quickly determined that she was bright and had moved her immediately into second. Even there she was working far ahead of her class.

'Have you ever been to a movie?' Belle persisted, clearly excited over the treat for the evening.

'Oh, my, yes.' Kim laughed. 'I adore movies. I used to go all the time. I had my favorite movie star. I wanted so much to look like Jean Harlow.'

'What did she look like?'

'She had blond hair like yours and big blue eyes like yours.'

'You're prettier,' Belle said, and dipped into the basket again for a pair of Harold's overalls.

The compliment took Kim by surprise. She dropped Harold's overalls, reached for Belle, and after only a moment they both were laughing and hugging with such force that they fell into the grass where Lil was sleeping.

The tumble left them winded, lying on their backs looking up into the cobalt blue summer sky graced here and there with fluffy white cloud formations. They played their favorite game.

'I see,' Belle began, 'a horse.'

'Where?'

'There, right there, see? And there's a monkey riding on his back.'

'I don't see any such thing.'

'Well, what do you see?'

'I see . . . a ship with a big sail.'

'Kim?'

'Yes?'

'Promise me something.'

'Anything.'

'That no matter what, you'll never leave me.'

Kim stared up at the high blue sky. 'I promise.'

'Kim?'

'Yes?'

'I love you.'

The laundry would have to wait, dinner would have to wait, the whole world would have to wait while Kim drew Belle into her arms and savored this moment she'd waited for all her life . . .

November 26, 1938
Salvation Army Mission
Tulsa, Oklahoma

Martha looked about at the pleasant apartment, a dream come true after the basement beneath the old mission. Last month Captain Meeks had given them this small apartment on the second floor. They each had a room plus a small kitchen and living room. It was heaven. Of course he'd put her in charge of all bill paying, yet another job. But she didn't mind. Now she was aware of R. C. watching her in the reflection of the mirror. She finished brushing her hair, pulled it back, fastened it with her mother's shell clip, and studied the results in the mirror along with R. C.

'You're beautiful,' R. C. murmured, his homework on the desk before him clearly forgotten.

Martha felt the heat of a blush on her cheeks. 'We need to have your eyes checked,' she joked. 'But I thank you,' she added, and treated herself to a long, satisfying look at this very handsome young man.

At twelve, R. C. had grown tall and lean. His dark eyes seemed to search constantly for something. Lindy Marcher said that R. C. always reminded him of a bird dog that couldn't quite pick up the scent.

'Are you going to see him tonight?' R. C. asked, as though capable of reading Martha's mind.

'You mean Lindy Marcher?' Martha asked, torn between R. C.'s needs and her own.

He didn't answer but turned on his radio. His favorite, *Fibber McGee*, would start in a minute. For now he had to make do with Billie Holliday singing 'Harbor Lights.'

The song, the moment, Martha's own sad confusion, left her without words, and she smoothed down her best purple crepe dress and wished her hands weren't so rough.

She wasn't quite sure what she felt for Lindy Marcher. There was something about him that reminded her of Charlie Groveton. They were both tall men. But the resemblance stopped with the physical. Charlie was such a quiet, gentle man, sometimes not even aware of his own strength, and certainly a man who had little or no use for boasting or bravado.

'Harbor Lights' came to a sweet conclusion. Martha looked over to see R. C. staring out of the window. Then the door burst open and there was Lindy, grinning from ear to ear, a small bouquet of chrysanthemums in his hand.

'Don't you look bee-yootiful,' he marveled, and encircled Martha, at last handing her the flowers. She was fairly certain he had stolen them from someplace. Still, she thanked him and was on the verge of leading him out into the hall when suddenly he started 'acting' again.

'Who is that lurking in far shadows? I do believe it is the young Hamlet. Come, sire, bid your cousin fair greeting lest his heart break – '

'Leave me alone. You've come for Martha. There she is.' R. C. turned his back on both of them and left an embarrassed silence in the room.

Lindy shrugged and led the way out of the door.

'Good night, R. C.' Martha called back.

'Good night,' he replied, but did not turn to look at her.

Briefly she held her position in the doorway, wondering how she could tell R. C. that she was twenty-six, that she liked it when Lindy held her hand, and she'd even liked it when he had kissed her last night, that it didn't mean she loved R. C. less, that it just meant – what?

A moment later she pushed open the front door and

there he was standing curbside, holding open the door of a taxicab.

'Madam.' He grinned when he saw her surprised expression.

Martha had never ridden in a taxicab in her life.

As she approached the opened door, Lindy bowed low at the waist. 'Aren't you looking pretty tonight? You'll be the belle of the ball.'

Martha felt the heat of a blush on her face. By the time she settled herself on the backseat, Lindy was beside her.

'Is anything – did I say anything wrong?'

She felt foolish and apologetic. 'No, of course not. I'm sorry. You said belle of the ball. I knew a Belle once.'

He slapped his forehead with the palm of his hand and slumped on the seat. 'Of course, I *am* sorry – the child you found,' he murmured, 'and lost.'

'How did you know?'

'Oh, the men talk at the mission. They told me everything.' There was a pause, during which time he examined his hands. 'You know, I've been meaning to talk to you about her, about the little girl. I have a good friend who happens to be a private detective, *the* best, I might add. He's been known to track down missing persons like a human bloodhound. If you wish, I could have him come around to the mission and you could just talk to him.'

Martha succumbed to a moment of dreaded hope. Then good sense intervened. 'I don't have any money.'

'Who mentioned money?' Lindy exclaimed.

'I'm sure your friend wouldn't work for nothing.'

'No, but he owes me a favor. Several, as a matter of fact. How would it hurt just to talk to him?'

He was sitting very close to her, his hand resting on her shoulder. 'We'll see,' she said as she looked out of the window and noticed that they were passing through downtown Tulsa, heading toward the river.

'Where are we going?' she asked, wanting to change the subject.

'To a Thanksgiving dance.'

She laughed. 'I know that, but – '

Before she could finish, he took her in his arms and kissed her. She could feel his tongue pushing inside her mouth, a sensation she didn't like, and struggled to push him away. At last he released her, and in an attempt to hide her embarrassment she slid to the far side of the car and concentrated on the passing scenery.

'I'm sorry,' Lindy said. 'I didn't mean to – it was just that you looked so . . . pretty.'

'Here 'tis,' the cabdriver announced full-voiced, and pulled into a parking lot in front of a low stucco building that faced the river.

While Lindy paid the driver Martha struggled to negotiate the gravel in her high heels. She clung to the fender of a near car and noticed the parking lot was full, over thirty cars. The front of the building was completely dark, the windows on either side of the door boarded up. The whole area looked deserted, except for the cars.

Then she felt Lindy's hand on her elbow and heard a sweet apology. 'Would you please forgive me? I would do nothing in the world to hurt or offend you.'

He sounded like a small child wanting parental approval.

They were at the front door, in the dark, not another living soul in sight.

'I thought you said this was a party.'

'It is. Be patient.'

He stepped up to the closed door, knocked three times, then paused, then knocked twice again.

She heard a noise beyond the door and looked up to see a small square panel in the upper part of the door swing open.

'Identify!' demanded the male voice on the other side of the door.

'Herr Marcher,' Lindy said, suddenly sober.

'Good evening, Herr Marcher. Do you have a companion this evening?'

'I have. Her name is Martha Drusso.'

During this exchange, Martha noticed that Lindy was

standing ramrod straight as though he were under review of some sort.

'Come along,' Lindy said, and took her arm as together they stood before the door while she heard bolts on the other side being slid.

Then it opened and Lindy led the way into a large room filled with people, the men all dressed exactly like Lindy, black trousers and brown shirts, black ties, all wearing red armbands with a curious insignia, a black crooked cross, a running cross, or so it appeared to Martha.

There were a few women scattered here and there, all plainly dressed.

'Good evening, Herr Marcher, glad you could come.'

A portly man approached. He had a kind face and rosy cheeks and deep blue eyes. Martha smiled under his close inspection, and as Lindy introduced him, she caught the name, Joe Stockton, and blushed when he lightly kissed her hand before moving on to another couple.

'Will you excuse me for just a minute?' Lindy asked.

And with that he disappeared into the crowd, and she lost sight of him but took advantage of the moment to study the curious room and the people in it.

It was a large room shaped like a meeting hall, with a small platform down front, an arrangement of chairs on the platform, and others arranged facing the platform. Behind on the wall hung a big American flag flanked on either side by banners bearing black crooked crosses. Beyond the crosses on one side was an immense picture of George Washington. On the other side was an equally large picture of a man with black hair smoothed down over his forehead and a neatly trimmed black mustache. She heard polka music coming from a scratchy phonograph record. Everyone seemed to be chatting easily. Several of the women smiled at her, though no one approached directly to speak.

Then she saw Lindy near the platform. He was talking with the man who had greeted them, Joe Stockton. Suddenly Lindy pointed directly at her. The man followed his gaze, and Martha felt embarrassed.

Then all at once Joe Stockton reached into his pocket and handed something to Lindy. Martha was left to survey the people who now had organized a small polka. She retreated back as far as she could and noticed a few familiar faces. There was one of the young officers from the police station, Rodney was his name. He looked right at her and never acknowledged her.

Now, as he danced near, she smiled and called out his name. But there was no response, though he looked right at her.

'Shall we try it?'

The near voice was Lindy. She had not seen him approach.

'I . . . don't know, I've never – '

'It's not hard' – he grinned – 'just hang on tight and follow me.'

Before she could protest, he locked one arm around her waist, clasped the other high in the air, and plunged them both into the polka circle.

At first she did little more than stumble after him, holding on for dear life. But with Lindy's laughing encouragement and with a good solid beat of the polka, Martha at last closed her eyes and felt the freedom of movement like an intoxicant, a glorious explosion of noise, voices, song, and abandonment that she hoped would never end.

But it did, with shouts of approval as partners clung together, and Martha felt sweat on her forehead.

'Your attention,' someone called from the platform. 'Your attention, fellow Bundists, come along, bring your ladies and take a seat. We've business to attend to.'

She looked up to see Joe Stockton standing on the platform, his right arm stiff and raised in the air. Within the moment she heard the scuffling of chairs as all assumed the same position, including Lindy. Then she heard him shout, 'Heil Hitler,' quickly followed by all the others, who shouted back, 'Heil Hitler.'

They made this curious exchange three times, each louder than the time before.

'Our beloved president,' he began, 'Fritz Kuhn, recently

made the statement that the Nazi salute is the coming salute for the whole United States of America.'

This statement prompted a roar of approval, quickly followed by a rapid-fire series of Heil Hitlers, so many that Martha lost count. Finally the fervor died down and everyone took their seats, all staring toward Joe Stockton on the platform as though scarcely able to wait for his next word.

'Welcome to the German–American Bund,' he said, his voice normal, his manner kindly. 'To the old members, we thank you for your continuing loyalty and support. To the new members, we thank you for the wisdom of your choice. And to our visitors, all we ask is that you listen closely and see if you don't hear something that makes a great deal of sense, not just for your life, but for our beloved country that now is struggling for its very survival.'

Martha listened as Joe Stockton had asked her to do and saw everyone else following suit.

'Now as we all know,' Joe Stockton began in the manner of a kind teacher, 'everyone is searching for a remedy to the country's problems. Most of them err on one principle, and that is the foolish notion that you can build something good on the foundation of something rotten. It cannot be done. It simply cannot be done, and what that means, in essence, is that the government in Washington must be overthrown.'

This won shouts of approval all around. Martha glanced at Lindy. He appeared transfixed.

'The Nazi party, as you all know, takes its inspiration from Berlin, from the genius of Adolf Hitler. Other messiahs of all stripes will come and go. They are a dime a dozen, but when the hands of time write large the history of the world, the name of Adolf Hitler will be engraved in bold script for all of posterity to see. Hitler sees clearly the need for a pure race. Hitler sees clearly that the pollution of niggers and Jews cannot be tolerated. It is Hitler who reminds us that George Washington, the father of our country, was the first fascist and now we must find our way back to Washington's true path – and in the process we must lead all of our citizens to the true light of world fascism, world purity, under the leadership of Adolf Hitler and the Aryan race.'

Again the people were on their feet, their right arms raised in the chanting repetitive salute of, 'Heil Hitler, Heil Hitler, Heil Hitler!'

Joe Stockton talked for the better part of an hour, and though Martha listened carefully she didn't understand half of what he said. Her main problem was that she didn't know exactly what the word *fascism* meant. She'd never really thought that people like Benny, the Negro cook at the mission, or Dr Levine, who stopped every day and treated the sick for free, were bad people.

So, all in all, the hour-long harangue was lost on her.

Then there was music coming from somewhere, a stately rendition of something that brought everyone to their feet, a song Martha had never heard before, something about Dutch-Land, or at least that's what it sounded like to her.

At the end of the song there was a moment's quiet, as though everyone were reflecting on what had been sung and said.

'Did you enjoy it?' Lindy asked, placing his arm around the chair.

'I must confess I didn't always understand.'

'It's simple,' Lindy said with dispatch. 'See that man?' and he pointed toward the large photograph of the man with the small black mustache. 'Well, that's Adolf Hitler, and he's going to be the savior of the world.'

Martha heard music again, very soft, sweet dance music, one of her favorites, 'Love Walked In.'

'Would you like to dance?' Lindy asked.

'Yes.' She smiled and allowed him to lead her to the dance floor.

It was approaching midnight when her feet began to feel like bloody stumps. She noticed that the crowd had dwindled, less than a dozen left dancing.

'We'd better go,' she suggested. 'Morning comes early, and my feet are – '

Lindy agreed. 'Come back here with me. I need to get something in the office. Then we'll go.'

'No, I'll wait here.'

'Come on, I want to show you something.'

Reluctantly Martha agreed and hobbled after him.

'In here.' He smiled and stood back after he had unlocked the door and pushed it open. 'Joe Stockton's office,' he explained. 'He left some books in here for me. Come on in.'

Martha hesitated, then was drawn forward into one of the prettiest rooms she'd ever seen. Everything was cream-colored and pale blue, a cream-colored carpet that made her feel as if she were walking on clouds, pale blue walls made to look like marble, ahead a magnificent bed with a pale blue satin comforter, and in front a mammoth white fur rug, while all about were calla lilies in big brass urns.

'It's something, isn't it?' Lindy grinned.

'This – is an office?' Martha marveled, and followed Lindy's pointed finger to a small white desk with gold trim in the corner.

While she was still admiring the room, she heard the door close behind her, thought she heard the click of a lock, and looked back to see Lindy busily engaged with a champagne bottle, pouring the amber liquid into two crystal glasses.

'My lady.' He smiled as he presented her with one.

'Lindy, I must – '

'Drink. No questions.'

He led off, draining his glass as if to show her how it was done.

She took a sip, then placed her glass on the near table. He sat on the end of the bed, begging her just to come and see how soft it really was.

'Then we'll go?' she asked.

'I promise.'

She walked to the foot of the bed, felt the heavy blue satin comforter, sat beside him, and agreed the bed was perfect in all ways.

'Are all good fascists going to get a bed like this?' she asked.

She hadn't meant to be funny, but apparently she was, for Lindy laughed heartily, lay back across the bed, and before she could protest grabbed her by the wrist and pulled her down beside him.

'Lindy, don't – '

'A kiss. How would it hurt?'

'No.'

'Please – '

Even as he begged, she felt his leg atop her, felt his hands on her breasts, and as she struggled, his tone and manner changed.

'Lie still,' he ordered.

He had both her wrists pinned over her head now and with one hand tore open the front of her dress, sending buttons flying every which way. In the next moment, moving with alarming speed, he freed her breasts from her brassiere, and as his teeth bit into her flesh, pain, pure and precise, gave her the strength she needed to free one hand and push against him.

But no sooner had she regained one hand than she lost it again; all his strength channeled down on her arms while his legs pushed hers apart, and at that moment she found the strength to bring one knee up as fast and as hard as she could, a stunning blow to his groin that sent him reeling backward with a cry of agony. Martha reached for the heavy brass calla lily urn on the near table and delivered a sound blow to the back of his head that caused him to flatten like a pancake on the white fur rug, which rapidly turned red from his bleeding head wound.

She stayed only long enough to determine that she had not killed him. Then she smoothed her clothes, reattached the few buttons that were left, found the key to the door in the pocket of his jacket, lifted her head, straightened her shoulders, and walked out into the meeting hall.

She had hoped that it would be empty. But it wasn't. Joe Stockton sat on the edge of the platform talking with two other men. They looked up, surprised, as Martha walked past. Despite her sore feet, she tried to walk without limping and called back, 'Thanks for the interesting evening. Mr Marcher may require medical attention. Good night to you.'

She was afraid someone would try to stop her. But they didn't, and she pushed open the front door, stepped out into the chilled dark night, and continued to walk across the street to the bank of the river with all the dignity of a woman who knew precisely where she was going.

Of course she didn't, and the damage done to her dress was nothing compared to the damage done to her heart and soul. But she continued walking along the river for several blocks, in pain until at last the tears started. She stopped walking and bent over a large boulder, clinging to it as though she were a survivor adrift at sea.

It was a good feeling, a release that, curiously, was followed by anger. Martha gave in to this anger for possibly the first time in her life. She picked up a small rock at her feet and began systematically to strike the large boulder. Her rage soon acquired a rhythm as with each blow the tears diminished. Somehow she was beating them out in the dead of this night.

The objects of her outrage were numerous and varied; most recently Lindy Marcher and his crazy friends who saluted a crooked cross and spoke confidently of taking over the world. Then the list jumped back to Hitchings, to her father, then to her mother for patiently enduring her father, then dying, then Charlie Groveton for running off with some woman from Amarillo and leaving her, then to Captain Meeks, who had given her enough jobs to keep at least four people busy, then to R. C. for allowing Belle to –

All at once, with the stone raised over her head, she stopped. She didn't hate R. C. She loved him. But something had happened in this awful night, some recognition that left her drained. She dropped to her knees beside the boulder, pressed her face against its cool roughness, and felt baffled, defeated, triumphant, lonely, and lost.

She stayed there all night, not sleeping, just newly aware of the incredible amount of luck and guts it took to make one's way through this treacherous world. At the first streaks of dawn, she stood, and using the smaller rock she'd spent all her anger on, she broke off the stupid heels of her shoes, pulled out the nails, and slipped them back on. Then, enjoying a modest degree of comfort, which was probably all any human being had a right to expect, she started off across the early morning Tulsa streets, hoping to get to the mission before R. C. woke up. She planned to cleanse herself of the night and be there ready to take R. C. in her arms, kiss him, tell him how much she loved him, and promise him as she always did every morning before he left for school that they *would* find Belle.

He had her word on it . . .

September 2, 1939
San Bernardino, California

She liked *Major Bowes' Original Amateur Hour*, though the thought of getting up in front of all those people and singing terrified her.

'How do they do it, Kim?' Belle asked as she settled on Harold's big chair by the radio for her favorite program.

Kim laughed. 'My Lord, they *want* to do it. In many cases it's what they've practiced and trained for all their lives. I think some of them consider it their big break.'

Belle shook her head in astonishment and drew her feet up, knees under her chin, and listened to the familiar voice of Major Bowes as he shouted out, '– aspinning goes our weekly wheel of fortune, around and around she goes, and where she stops nobody knows – '

Belle listened for the front door, Harold returning from taking down the flag. He'd be in soon, Belle would relinquish his chair, Kim would come in from the kitchen, and they'd all pick their favorites from among the contestants, then see who won.

'Rain is coming.' This announcement came from Harold,

who placed his carefully folded American flag to the right side of the kitchen hutch.

'Now, who's been on so far?' he asked, sinking into his comfortable chair and bending low to deliver a kiss to the top of Belle's head.

'Only a coal miner from Virginia who played music with his ears,' Belle said.

Harold laughed. 'Not much call for that, I wouldn't imagine.'

'Rain, did you say?' Kim asked, threading her needle.

'I'm sure of it. I can smell it.'

'What does rain smell like, Harold?' Belle asked.

'It smells wet.'

'Shhh – listen,' Kim whispered as Major Bowes was announcing the next contestant, a female singer from Stockton, California, named Faye Something-or-Other who was going to sing 'Jeepers Creepers,' a silly song that Kim went around singing for the better part of the day.

Belle grinned and leaned back against Harold's chair and stared at the big Zenith radio on the opposite wall. On top she saw a framed picture of herself taken by Kim last summer in front of the rose trellis in the back garden. She'd been eight then and very thin and bony compared with now.

Belle looked back and forth between these two whom she had come to love so much. At first she remembered she'd been frightened of them. But all of her apprehension had quickly faded, only to be replaced by a new worry, that these loving people who let her share their home would not want her any more one day. Once again she'd be left beside the road, alone and waiting.

'Belle, what is it?'

It was Kim, who apparently had seen something in her face.

'Sometimes I get afraid.'

Quickly Harold lowered his newspaper. Kim put down her sewing and knelt where Belle was seated on the floor.

'Of what, my darling?' Kim asked.

'That you'll go off one day like Mrs Melville did – '

But she never had a chance to finish. Kim reached out for her at the same time Harold did, and all at once Belle was caught up in a double embrace.

'You're a silly goose, you know that, don't you?' Kim scolded.

'Look at me, Belle, and listen. No one will ever take you from us. Do you hear? Do you believe me?'

Belle was impressed by the tone in Kim's voice, the expression on her face. And Harold's was the same.

'Belle, listen,' he said, clasping both her hands in his. 'I know you're tired of us asking, but could you, could we – try again? If only we knew where to look for your birth certificate. We need to know so much more before we can adopt you. And until we can do that . . .'

He never finished, but Belle knew the answer. It meant that she really didn't belong to Harold and Kim, that she was just staying with them, and that at any time –

'All right, Belle, let's try again,' Kim suggested, sitting flat on the floor before Belle, smoothing back her hair. 'You do remember the Melvilles?'

'Yes.'

'Do you remember who took you to the Melvilles?'

Belle closed her eyes. Her first vivid memory was being in the backseat of an old car with Mrs Melville, who was spanking her with a strap of some sort. She remembered that it hurt, and she remembered that she was afraid. No one had ever hurt her before.

'Belle?'

In the distance she heard the whistle of a train.

'A – train,' she whispered, looking up, amazed. Someplace inside her head there was the memory of a big train.

Kim got up on her knees. 'Go on. Where was this train?'

'There was a big seat,' Belle said, seeing it clearly now, 'and someone told me not to move.'

She paused, aware of the intensity of Harold's and Kim's attention. She was remembering things she'd never remembered before, or was she just making them up to please Harold and Kim?

'Anything else?' Harold urged, and shifted positions on the hardwood floor. 'Do you remember where this train was?'

'No . . .'

'Do you remember who was with you, who it was who told you not to move?'

Belle looked up. For just a split second she did. Then the memory was gone.

'It's all right,' Kim soothed.

Belle heard scratching at the back door, scrambled out to the kitchen, and pushed open the door for Lil, who was ready to go to bed for the night.

While Lil lapped water from her bowl, Belle heard the radio announcer interrupt the amateur hour.

'And now we bring you a special news bulletin.'

Belle stood still in the darkened kitchen, listening.

'At five-twenty A.M. a German bombing plane dropped a projectile on Puch, a Polish fishing village and air base near Hel Peninsula. At five forty-five A.M., the German training ship *Schleswig-Holstein* lying off Danzig fired what was believed to be the first shell, a direct hit on the Polish ammunition dump at Westerplatte.'

'What is it?' Belle asked.

'Not good,' Harold muttered.

'War in Europe, I'm afraid,' Kim explained.

The news announcement came to an end and left Harold bent over the radio listening to the closing theme of the amateur hour.

'We missed it.' Belle sighed. 'We won't ever know who won.'

'Do you want to practice your jitterbug?' Harold asked slyly as though he knew full well what Belle's reaction would be.

She started to squeal, but Harold put his fingers to his lips, turned off the radio, and lifted the arm of the phonograph next to it. Belle loved to jitterbug, and with the first hard beat of Duke Ellington's 'It Don't Mean a Thing,' she forgot all about her mysterious past, who won the amateur hour, or the German bombing of the Polish fishing village.

Then she saw the wildly gyrating Harold opposite her, his hands extended to her, his voice singing along with the magical music.

Oh, it don't mean a thing if it ain't got that swing,
Do-op, do-op

Belle laughed and took his hands and let him pull her into the pulsing rhythm.

'Turn your hips,' Harold shouted, 'hips one way, feet the other, round in a circle. "Oh, it don't mean a thing" – '

And it didn't. Nothing mattered but the loud pulsing music, the room swirling as Harold turned her around and around. Lil was barking at them from the kitchen door and Kim was shaking her head in loving indulgence.

'You two,' she shouted, and watched with what Belle thought was admiration. She was getting good. Harold's smile told her that much.

Belle closed her eyes and felt the beat of the music going faster than her pulse, then she grinned up at the ceiling as she heard Harold shout:

'You're a shiner! . . .'

December 7, 1941
Tulsa, Oklahoma

Sometimes R. C. felt as though his insides were being torn in half by the memory of what he had done. He had lost Belle, and that awareness went with him everywhere. No matter how involved or preoccupied he was with any given subject, sooner or later that awful day came back unchanged by the passage of time. He could remember everything, the way she looked up at him from the train seat, the seriousness in her eyes when she had promised faithfully not to move.

Abruptly he bent over his desk, unable for the moment to accommodate the memory. He'd thought more than once about running away, but always common sense had intervened. What would be accomplished? Martha would be devastated, Belle would still be lost, and he would still be responsible.

He covered his eyes with his hands and wished with all his heart that it would stop hurting for just a minute, just long enough for him to catch his breath and find the courage to go on with the morning.

Quickly he spread out the Sunday *Tulsa World* on his desk, looking forward to a quiet afternoon. No homework, no mission work. These afternoons were his, and he liked to start them by reading the paper, though the news was never very good anymore. US troops were moving to Iceland, US ships were being sunk by Nazi torpedoes, US aid was going to both Russia and Britain, and US industry was tooling up for defense.

He pushed aside the newspaper, saving the comics until he felt better. These awful moods always left him feeling restless and dissatisfied.

Now he switched on his radio and heard dreary organ music coming from some church service. No matter where he turned the dial, he got organ music or some preacher shouting about the devil and hell.

He pushed back in his chair, opened his top desk drawer, and found his drawing pad and pencil. He liked to draw and had one picture that he kept at the very back of his drawing pad. He looked at it almost every day and had yet to show it to anyone.

It was a little girl with curly blond hair and bright blue eyes, a small birthmark on the side of her throat, and she was smiling up from a train seat.

R. C. stared at it, transfixed. He closed his eyes and rested his forehead in his cupped hands. The picture on the page lived permanently in his mind. He saw her every day as he had last seen her.

What did she look like now? Why had they never been able to find her? They'd searched so hard.

Caught between the awful mood and all the talk of the devil on the radio, R. C. pushed back from his desk with such force that the chair fell over. Maybe it would be better downstairs with the smell of cabbage and the men laughing at his cracking voice.

He had just reached the door when he heard the preacher's sermon stop and then the announcer's voice:

'We interrupt this program to bring you a special news bulletin.'

He looked back at the radio as though it had spoken to him. There was the sound of static crackling for several moments, then the announcer's voice, strained, as though he were having trouble with the words he was speaking.

'At seven fifty-five this morning, December 7, 1941, the Japanese attacked Pearl Harbor by air. Over one hundred planes, possibly more, attacked in the morning mist while Pearl Harbor slept. Later – '

R. C. frowned at the radio, then inched closer.

Pearl Harbor. He tried to place it. Maybe someone downstairs would know.

'The attack came in three waves,' the announcer said now. 'Of ninety-six vessels at Pearl, one lone destroyer was under way.'

R. C. heard someone coming up the stairs at the end of the hall, coming fast.

The door burst open and he saw Martha, still wiping her hands on her apron. 'Have you heard?' she gasped.

Behind her was Captain Meeks, moving more slowly, struggling for breath after the fast sprint up the stairs.

'We let the others listen to the radio in Captain Meeks's office. There was no more room,' Martha tried to explain, but she too was out of breath and excited.

For several moments they all stood at various positions about the room listening to the announcer as he struggled for something to say. 'At this point it is difficult to assess the total damage. Due to the nature of the attack, there was a complete lack of preparedness, but we have just been handed a first casualty list – two thousand four hundred men killed and – '

Martha sat on the straight-backed chair by the table

and bowed her head. R. C. went to her side. Captain Meeks looked sad. 'If you'll excuse me.' He stood up and straightened his blue jacket. 'I'll go back down and see if – '

'I'll come, too.' Martha sighed.

'No, you stay here with the boy. We're almost finished downstairs. You take the afternoon off.'

Martha thanked him, closed the door, and stared at R. C.

'You okay?' he asked.

'Not really. So many dead, and I'm afraid it's only the start.'

'War?'

'What else? Mr Roosevelt won't sit still for this, nor should he. Listen – '

She shushed herself and heard the announcer say that they would now return to the program in progress, promising to come back on the air as soon as there were more details.

As the somber church music started up again, Martha sat on the sofa and slipped off her flat brown shoes.

'You know,' she said, 'if there is a war, and if it goes on long enough, you could be called.'

That hadn't occurred to him. He was so accustomed to being referred to as 'the kid' around the mission that he had never dreamed he might one day be old enough to fight in a real war.

As his face brightened, he saw Martha's still shadowed by doubt and fear. 'I couldn't bear to lose you both,' she said.

He sat beside her on the sofa and wished they would play some music other than church music.

From the vacant lot below the window came the sound of voices raised in excitement. Curious, R. C. went to his desk and looked down to see a dozen or so men from the mission erecting some sort of straw figure. He saw two filled pillowcases tied together to form a lumpy shape, a partially deflated basketball painted yellow with two elongated slits for eyes, and the whole grim figure placed in the middle of the vacant lot.

He started to call out for Martha, but then he heard her come up directly behind him. Together they watched as one man doused the image in gasoline, then another struck a match. In a few minutes, the effigy burst into flames.

In a way R. C. didn't blame them. The Japanese were clearly the enemy now, even more so than the Germans. Still, it seemed a silly thing to do.

As he looked back, curious at Martha's silence, he discovered that she hadn't even seen the activity beyond the window. Instead she was now sitting on R. C.'s desk chair, her eyes focused in one clear direction, on R. C.'s sketch of Belle as he'd last seen her. He started to speak, but something about Martha's position suggested that now was not the time for words.

He waited forever, or so it seemed, for her to look her fill. Then he knelt beside her. 'I didn't mean to make you sad.'

Quickly she shook her head. 'You didn't. It's Belle.'

'I didn't want to forget her.'

Still she studied the picture, once touching the curls on the forehead as though they were real.

They sat for the better part of the afternoon by the radio, waiting for bulletins, each grimmer than the one before, but news of any sort was welcomed. The men played in the vacant lot for the rest of the afternoon. Someone had found a carton of rotten oranges, and they had painted a Japanese face on each orange, then used them like baseballs, splattering orange pulp every which way.

By evening prayer services, someone announced that they had 'killed' close to sixty-five Japs that afternoon in the vacant lot behind the mission. R. C. had never seen the men's faces so alive, their cheeks so red. Everyone talked of joining up, even the very old.

It was as if with the promise of war, they had found a direction and purpose for their lives and were now eager to get on with it. With some difficulty, Captain Meeks summoned their attention long enough to thank God for His various blessings and to have mercy on them all in the difficult days ahead.

But R. C. saw nothing grateful or repentant in all those men's faces. He saw only relief, eagerness, and joy that a door had at last been opened for them. They could wear a uniform now and be a part of this country.

Somehow R. C. had the feeling that the Depression was over . . .

Part Two

January 1, 1942
McAlester State Prison
McAlester, Oklahoma

Charlie took the brown envelope filled with all his worldly possessions: his wallet with twenty-seven dollars in it, his driver's license, now expired, a faded photo of his parents, and one of Martha Drusso taken the night of their high school prom.

There was some other junk in there, none of which meant a damn to Charlie now. He'd spent four years in this hellhole, arrested and convicted of accidental manslaughter in the death of the company man that night in Oklahoma City when Reed Spence had burned to death.

'Anything else, Warden?' Charlie asked now, looking out at freedom for the first time in four years. It was pouring rain, a cold January Oklahoma rain, the sky looking like the bottom of a dirty toilet. But to him it was beautiful.

'Okay, Charlie, here's your ten spot. You've been a good prisoner. Probably shouldn't have been here in the first place. But now you've done your time, and if you ain't got hard plans, let me make a suggestion. Why don't you get yourself to the first recruiting office and join up? Your country needs you now.'

'I'll think about that, Warden. But I'm not sure I want to start killing again so soon.'

The warden looked at him as if he were seeing him for the first time.

'Is that about it, Warden?'

'Do you have friends coming to pick you up?'

'No.'

'Hell, it's pouring, man, don't you even have a raincoat?'

'Don't need one.'

'Okay if you say so. Open up, Bobby Joe. Got one coming through.'

The man inside the guardhouse waved him through, and he stood there while the heavy barred gate clanged down behind him.

Then this part of his life was over. He looked right and then left down the two-lane highway. Not a car in sight. He whispered, 'Eeny meany miny mo,' and chose the right, then started off down the center of the highway, hands shoved into his pockets, teeth chattering.

Here he was almost thirty, and he'd not done much of anything to make anyone proud of him, least of all himself. He'd have to work on that.

Behind him, coming up out of the rain, he heard the squeak of an old horn. He looked back to see a pickup truck keeping pace with him. He moved to one side and waved for the pickup to go past him. But it merely pulled up even with him, and someone rolled down the window on the passenger side.

'You like wet?' a voice called out, and Charlie saw the biggest Indian he'd ever seen behind the wheel. The man was wearing a faded blue shirt ripped under the arm and work pants that once perhaps had been brown. Now it was hard to tell. His long black hair was braided and hung down his back. His eyes were black and heavy, and when he grinned Charlie saw one gold tooth and a few white ones. The rest were missing.

'You deaf?' the Indian now demanded.

'No, I – '

'You like wet?'

'No.'

'Where are you going?'

'Where are *you* going?'

'Headed up toward Tulsa.'

'Me too,' Charlie said with a grin, though he didn't know a living soul in Tulsa.

'Then git in,' the Indian shouted, and Charlie did. 'They just let you out?' the Indian shouted over the rattle of the old truck. The gears screamed as he shifted.

'Yeah.'

'Well, you survived the bastards. That's all that counts. What's your name?'

'Charlie Groveton.'

'Skinny Half Moon,' the man announced, and extended his hand. Charlie took it, then took the can of beer that Skinny offered him, drained it in one gulp, and felt resurrected.

There was just one problem. What in the hell was he going to do in Tulsa? . . .

February 10, 1942
Hominy, Oklahoma
Osage Nation

Charlie Groveton was forever indebted to Skinny Half Moon and his wife, Twila Mae, and their brood of six.

They'd taken Charlie in when he had no place to go. They had given him a bedroll and his own corner in their already crowded cabin. Skinny had even taken Charlie out to Grey Bull Creek, about fifteen miles northeast of Hominy, and had gotten him hired on at the Cities Service Osage Field.

So no doubt about it, Charlie was grateful to Skinny. But there was a problem. Skinny liked to steal. He would steal anything, anywhere, off anyone. He could even have a fresh wad of bills in his back pocket, money enough to buy anything he wanted, but if he passed a hardware store with bailing wire out front, he'd pull over, bide his time, then, despite its size, creep up, toss a roll or two of bailing wire into the back of his pickup, and take off shrieking.

Every time he stole something, he'd do his war cry, giggle, spit on his finger, make an invisible mark on the air, and proclaim with pride, 'Mark one for Skinny Half Moon.' Once he'd told Charlie that the white man had stolen this land from the Indian and now Skinny was gonna steal it back piece by piece.

Well, as far as Charlie could see, he was off to a good start. There were three old sheds about fifty feet behind the Half Moons' cabin, and all three were chock full of stolen goods of every size, shape, and description – tires, small appliances, bailing wire, good lumber, bricks, buckets of paint, tools of all sorts, and other items too numerous to mention. Of course Skinny stole food, too. Tons of it, but that all ended up on Skinny's table, and if they had more than they could use, Skinny always shared it with other tribal members.

It made Charlie nervous. So when Skinny announced one night that his son Raymond, age twenty-eight, was coming home from McAlester Prison where he'd served twelve years for armed robbery, Charlie began to think in terms of moving on. What he wanted to do with his life, where he wanted to go, he had no idea. All he knew for certain was that he wanted nothing more to do with prison. Yet here he was, sitting in the middle of a hotbed of crazy Indians who stole because it was 'the most fun they ever had in this life.'

The Osage fields were shutting down anyway because oil exploration was shifting to the West Coast. There was very little for him here. But where would he go? Maybe Tulsa?

One place he knew he wouldn't go. Back to Hitchings. He'd have to choose another destination.

So it was on this cold bitter February 10, 1942, that Charlie Groveton packed up his bedroll. He left a note of thanks to Skinny and Twila Mae as well as a ten-dollar bill out of his earnings on the Osage field for some new shoes for all the kids. Skinny was having trouble stealing shoes. Then Charlie slipped out of the cabin after midnight, braced himself for the first slap of freezing wind, and headed toward Hominy's main street, hoping to hitch a ride into Tulsa and from there – where?

As he trudged down the rutted frozen road, Charlie wondered how long he'd have to wander before he could find a place where he felt comfortable . . .

February 15, 1942
San Bernardino, California

Belle knew that something was wrong. No matter how hard she tried to concentrate on her studies, the feeling of uneasiness persisted. She looked around at the empty kitchen, usually filled with Kim's cheerful voice and good smells of baking.

Now Kim was out in the field helping Harold. In the last month since the bombing of Pearl Harbor, Harold had lost so many of his helpers, most of them chased off by townspeople calling them names like 'slanty-eyed Jap' and 'yellow devil.'

Belle pushed back in her chair and started to the icebox for a drink of cold water, then changed her mind and returned to the table. She encircled it once and finally made herself sit down and stare at the page in her history book: 'Causes for the Civil War.'

But she really wasn't interested in the Civil War right now. There seemed to be a more urgent one raging all around her, not the least of which was the terror that went with her every day, that something would happen to Kim and Harold and she would be left alone again, lost, not knowing where she had come from or where she was going.

This fear was so real that now she saw her hands trembling and quickly clenched them together, closed her eyes, and tried to remember all of Kim's reassurances.

'My goodness, we're third-generation Japanese, both of us much more American than Japanese, and everyone knows that. Please don't worry. Nothing will happen, I swear it.'

Oh, how Belle wanted to believe her, and she did.

Gradually she relaxed on her chair. Her fists unclenched and became hands again, and she leaned back and listened to the quiet, the lovely peaceful sound that always filled a home made of love. And there was so much love here, Kim and Harold's love for each other, their love for her, and her absolutely limitless love for them. Her daily prayer was, 'Let nothing change, please, God.'

The pleasant thoughts helped to dispel the ugly ones, and she bowed her head over the history book and again tried to focus her concentration.

'Causes for the Civil War . . .'

On the rim of her hearing was the sound of a car rattling down the farm road outside the house, coming closer.

'The first cause was – '

It wasn't a car, it sounded more like a truck, a pickup truck.

Belle sat still, certain the truck would pass by. But she had just leaned up to turn the page when she heard the bumping of tires bouncing over the grate that led into the courtyard outside the kitchen door.

She held still for a moment, then slowly moved to the kitchen window. At first she saw nothing. Apparently the truck had stopped just inside the gate. She leaned farther out and at last saw three boys, high school age was her guess, crawling down out of the high seat. She didn't recognize them, but perhaps they had come in answer to Harold's advertisement for help with the winter crops. Of course, that was it. Then she'd speak to them and direct them out to the field where Harold was working.

She paused a moment to tuck her blouse into her skirt, and then she pulled open the back door and saw an odd thing. One of the boys was at Harold's flagpole, lowering the American Flag.

'Hey,' she called out. 'What are you – '

But all three boys merely looked up at her and continued what they were doing. Harold loved the flag, raised it with respect every morning and lowered it every evening, never permitted it to fly in the rain, and always glanced up at it every time he passed.

'No, wait,' she called out again as she saw the flag in their hands, saw them take it off the standard and drop it on the ground.

'No, you mustn't,' she protested, anger increasing, and

started down the steps at a run. 'You have no right, what do you – '

But as she started to pick up the flag, one of the boys beat her to it and whipped it up over his shoulder and again dropped it to the ground behind him.

Then she saw in their faces a desire to hurt.

'My, ain't she a pretty thing,' one said, grinning.

'Come on, we didn't come out to see her,' another scolded.

'Maybe we should have.'

'You got the other flag. Give it to me.'

Belle held her position, afraid to move backward or forward. She saw one of the boys run back to the truck and take out a large white square of material. Someone had torn a bedsheet into quarters and painted right in the center of the white material a big red circle.

'Now you folks will have the right flag flying over you. You're Japs, and this here is a Jap flag, and we Americans can take back our flag so as it won't get polluted, you hear?'

'No!' Belle screamed, and started forward. 'No, that's Harold's flag. You have no right!'

As she approached the boy by the flagpole, she felt strong arms grab her and pull her back and down. With nothing to break her fall, she landed flat on her back with such force that the wind was knocked out of her. For several seconds all she could do was flail at the air and gasp for breath.

'Jap-loving bitch,' someone cursed down on her.

Then she heard another voice. 'Got any more of that yellow paint?'

'Sure do.'

'Well, what do you say? I for one think she's got the wrong color skin.'

She was just beginning to regain her breath when all at once she felt someone straddling her, someone behind her holding her head rigid. She looked up and saw fingers smeared with shiny yellow paint coming toward her face. She closed her eyes and mouth as she felt the hand smear the paint up and down and from side to side.

At some point she started screaming, a nonstop cry for help, but no matter how hard she struggled she was no match for their strength or hatred.

'You missed an ear,' someone said, giggling.

'Should we do her whole body?'

'Might be fun.'

'What do you – '

As she struggled against this new threat, she heard Lil in the distance, barking as she had never heard her barking before. She saw the three boys look up from their fun.

'Son of a – '

'Let's get the hell out of here!'

Through one eye watering from burning paint, Belle saw Lil round the corner of the house running low to the ground, her fangs bared, now chasing the truck, which spun about in the drive and headed back toward town, leaving a cloud of dust.

Belle tried to sit up but couldn't. Paint filled her mouth and nostrils, and she felt as if she were suffocating . . .

Kim knew something was wrong when she heard Lil barking. She'd never heard her bark like that, and without a word to Harold she took off after the dog down the long row of lettuce.

Then she heard Belle's screams and bowed her head into the wind and ran, reaching the courtyard in time to see the pickup speed off down the road, the American flag on the ground, and that ridiculous white one hoisted halfway up the flagpole, and –

'Belle! Oh, my God, Belle – '

She knelt beside her and lifted Belle into her arms, held her and rocked her, all the time trying desperately to cleanse her face of the slick yellow paint.

'Oh, my darling, I'm so sorry. I – '

Then she started to cry, although she knew it wouldn't help a thing.

'Who – were they, Kim? Why did they – '

'I don't know, my darling. Come on, let's get you cleaned up.'

Just as she was helping Belle to her feet, she saw Harold, breathless from his run, his eyes trying to take in everything at once.

'See?' Kim said with a sad degree of satisfaction. She had warned him that they would be exempt from nothing. 'I told you. They don't consider us Americans at all. Look, look at Belle.'

She saw the pain in his eyes and was sorry for it, but there was nothing she could do about it. He shook his head and turned toward his flag. Damn his flag. Couldn't he see that the worst was yet to come, that Belle might be taken from them?

No!

Now, as she saw Harold lovingly lift the flag in his arms, she led Belle up the steps, still trying to cleanse the paint from her face. At the top of the steps she paused, an idea dawning. She looked at Belle. And smiled. The idea was fully developed. And it would work. Kim would see to it. If worse came to worst, Kim had a plan . . .

March 20, 1942
San Bernardino, California

Harold Shoda bowed his head and prayed that what was going on upstairs in Belle's bedroom would be successful. Otherwise he didn't know what they would do.

Lil sat beside him on the step. The dog sensed something going on. She'd stayed close. Baldwin, his friend at the feed and seed store, had promised to come and get her and give her a good home. Now Harold hoped that Baldwin arrived before the army bus did. It would break Belle's heart to leave the dog sitting on the steps.

Briefly Harold gave in to a moment of despair that he'd fought so successfully for the last several weeks. He had tried to explain to both Kim and Belle what had happened. With the bombing of Pearl Harbor, all Japanese-Americans were on shaky ground.

The timetable for tragedy had moved with terrifying swiftness. The day after Pearl Harbor, banks had frozen all Japanese funds. The entire West Coast press spewed forth daily racial malice against all Japanese.

Whether alien or native born, they had now been branded as 'Japs,' 'Nips,' and 'mad yellow dogs.'

Harold scuffed at the gravel with the toe of his shoe. Lil pressed closer. He petted her head and rubbed her ears and realized how much he would miss her. Even as he had tried to explain to Kim and Belle, he had on occasion foundered himself. He knew all too well that Japan's military operations in the Pacific had given rise to fears that an invasion of the United States mainland might take place. Hit-and-run Japanese carrier strikes against the West Coast were also considered a serious threat. Nearly half of all military aircraft were built in the Los Angeles area. In addition, the fleet depended heavily on oil pumped from California's coastal fields. This vulnerability worried the United States government, which now saw spies in every Japanese face and had suggested that Japanese civilians might take hostile action against military targets.

Harold looked up, having lost count of how many times he had tried to explain this to all of them. Of course they hadn't understood, and down deep neither had he. He was not Japanese. He was an American. His grandparents had been Japanese, and they were dead, but if they'd wanted to stay in Japan, they would have. Truth was they had wanted more than anything to come to America. Fresh start, like new field, his father had said.

On February 19, President Roosevelt had signed an order that authorized the secretary of war to establish military areas for the confinement of all Japanese and Japanese-Americans.

Harold and Kim had received notification four days ago

to be ready on March 20, each carrying one suitcase. They would be taken to the fairgrounds outside San Bernardino, where they would be reassigned to an internment camp. They were further informed that Manzanar in California was filled, and they would be taken by train to another camp in the hinterlands of the United States.

He stood and stretched a tightness out of the small of his back. Belle. She had been a problem that they had almost never solved. Apparently she wasn't even listed on the military police bulletin. She certainly wouldn't be permitted to go with them, and Kim had refused to leave unless Belle went with her.

But there had remained two seemingly insurmountable barriers.

One – Belle's long blond hair.

Two – Belle's deep, bottomless blue eyes.

Kim had said not to worry, that she would fix both. As he glanced at his watch, he called back over his shoulder, 'Hurry, you two. They'll be here soon.'

Dear God –

He prayed briefly to a confusion of gods, part old, part new, all clearly absent during this travesty of justice.

Then he heard steps behind him and saw Kim first, with that drawn expression that had inhabited her face since the seventh of December. She looked down on him expectantly, then stood back in a curious manner as though making way for someone.

Now she stood on the porch beside a bizarre creature who wore one of Kim's brown housedresses over her small frame. Her eyes were covered by dark sunglasses. Her hair was short, bobbed, and coal black, and her face was covered with red dots that extended from her forehead down the side of her face and disappeared into the neckline of the brown dress.

'This is our daughter, Harold,' Kim said quietly. 'I'm afraid she's ill, measles, but I'm certain that won't stop the United States government.'

'It's me, Harold. Belle.'

Suddenly Harold burst out laughing. She looked so funny, not a trace of the real Belle left. And yet, how perfect.

'It's good, Kim,' Harold praised at the end of his laugh. He drew near and put his arm around Kim's shoulders, and they both stared at the child they loved so much.

He heard something then, the clatter of a bus, and saw a dust cloud a distance away. 'Hurry now,' he urged, seeing the terror in their faces. 'Belle, help Kim with the bags. When we get – where we are going, I'll tell them who you are. They'll leave us alone, I'm certain.'

'If you're certain of anything, you're a bigger fool than I thought,' Kim said, and disappeared back into the house, leaving Harold to gape after her. She'd never spoken to him like that before. It was almost as if she hated him.

'She's just afraid,' Belle said, and followed Kim, leaving Harold alone to face the rapidly approaching military bus.

Damn Baldwin. He'd promised to be here early. Lil –

He looked back to see the bus carefully angling its way into the courtyard. Now he hurried down the sidewalk in time to greet the military policeman as he stepped down from the bus.

'Harold Shoda?' the MP called out, clipboard in hand.

'Yes, sir. Coming, sir,' Harold replied cordially, and noticed Lil get up and climb the steps of the house to a position of safety.

'Kim Shoda?' he heard the soldier reading now.

'Be right along,' Harold said, and started up the steps to see what was keeping them. In a sideward glance, he saw faces at every window, the bus filled beyond capacity.

Then he heard footsteps and saw Kim and Belle on the other side of the screen door, suitcases in hand. Kim had draped a dark silk scarf over Belle's head and now appeared to be supporting her through the door.

Harold met their eyes in an effort to convey courage, but Kim had caught sight of the filled bus, the faces staring, and for a woman with a great need for privacy, the public exhibition that had now become her life took a dreadful toll. Quickly she bowed her head and renewed her grasp on Belle's shoulders. With heads touching, the two made their way slowly down the steps until Belle saw Lil and pulled away.

'Lil,' she whispered, and dropped to her knees beside the dog. She looked at Harold, who stood at the bottom of the steps only a few feet away from the soldier. 'I thought you said that Mr Baldwin would come for her.'

'Who is this?' the soldier demanded, clipboard still grasped in his hand.

'This is our daughter,' Harold claimed, and rushed right on. 'Come along, Belle. Mr Baldwin will be here soon.'

'I see no name for her,' the soldier said, scanning down the list of names.

'Oh, it's there, I'm sure,' Harold said offhandedly.

'No, you're wrong. I don't see it. Here is Shoda – Harold – Kim, that's it. Whoever that person is, we can't take her.'

Harold blinked at the impasse, heart accelerating. What in the name of God now?

But Kim flew to admirable life, dropped her luggage on the gravel, marched back to the steps, climbed to the top, and sat.

'Then I stay, too,' she pronounced flatly, 'and any soldier who would physically force a mother to abandon her ill child would certainly have to be reported to the authorities.'

The soldier stared at her. 'Ill?'

'Of course, can't you see? Belle, show him.'

Cooperative at least in this matter, Belle lifted her face to reveal the red dots, all the while keeping one protective arm around Lil.

The soldier was impressed. Harold could even see a reaction from the people on the bus.

'How – sick is she?' the soldier asked, taking a couple of steps backward.

'You can see for yourself,' Kim snapped. 'Measles, though the fever has broken. I doubt if she's contagious, but I know as well as I know my own name that I will not abandon her.'

'Then why don't I have her name on this list?'

'I cannot be held accountable for your inefficiency.'

'Kim!'

Harold tried to signal her to be polite and patient. But clearly she had exhausted her supply of both.

'Well?' she demanded.

'Go on, get on the bus, all of you,' the soldier said. 'I'll let someone else sort it out down the line. Come on, hurry. We've wasted enough time as it is.'

'Thank you, sir.' And with that brief expression of gratitude, Harold grabbed Kim by one hand, who in turn grabbed Belle, and without giving anyone much of a chance to protest, he half led, half dragged them to the opened door of the bus.

'Lil!' Belle cried.

'Lil will be picked up by Baldwin. Now hurry in, both of you, and I mean it.'

As Harold ran back for the luggage, he stopped to pat Lil's silky head and whispered, 'Be a good girl.' Then he ran back to the bus, lifted up the luggage, and pulled himself on board.

They sat quickly on the long backseat, pushed the luggage beneath, and looked back at all those staring eyes.

Harold didn't recognize one face. Clearly they were not from around San Bernardino. Then he heard the bus door close, heard the motor turn over, the soldier at the front still looking back at them.

A child started to cry somewhere near the front. The bus turned out of the courtyard and headed toward town. Harold was aware of Belle turning sideways in the seat.

'Lil.' She started to cry.

'Don't,' Kim begged.

Harold looked backward, though he vowed not to. Dear God, he'd forgotten to take down the flag. It mustn't fly at night. It was a sign of disrespect.

'The flag,' Harold whispered to Kim's questioning look. 'I forgot to – '

'Damn the flag,' Kim muttered, and hid her face by looking out of the opposite window.

Maybe he'd have a chance to use a telephone. He'd call Baldwin and remind him to pick up Lil and take down the flag.

The big white farmhouse was out of sight now. Belle looked back. Kim kept a silent vigil on the opposite window. And Harold brooded about the flag that he'd left flying, worried that night would fall before Baldwin would come . . .

The only way that Kim could survive was to let something die within her, nothing vital to her drawing breath, but something more significant, an impulse, an inclination toward hope.

There was no hope. And she'd fallen a little out of love with Harold for his refusal to see that.

This was not a busload of Japanese–American evacuees. This was a busload of the damned. She knew, if Harold didn't, that they were driving down this road for the last time, that they had seen their home for the last time.

This wasn't their country any longer. A country did not do this to its citizens. They were not in Nazi Germany, although how did this differ, confiscation of property, uprooting and separation of families, labels, long, crowded inhumane train rides to – what?

And there was the greatest fear of all. Where were they being taken? And what would happen to them after they got there? And Belle? Kim couldn't keep boot black on her hair forever, and if they figured out that she was not Japanese, what would they do then?

For now this moment was all they had. The past was past, the future was an uncertain nightmare. This crowded, hot, smelly bus was all they had, that and each other. Kim reached over and found Belle's hand.

'Mr Baldwin will come,' she whispered, 'I'm certain of it.'

'What if he doesn't?'

'He will, I promise,' Kim said, making a promise she had no right to make, but making it anyway.

A short time later the bus slowed and drove through the

gates of the county fairgrounds and onto a concrete parking lot that was already filled with buses identical with theirs, all waiting in obedient rows, the only movement that of soldiers, a few carrying clipboards like the one on their bus. The others were carrying rifles.

As they pulled into the parking lot, a military policeman on the ground waved them forward into a slot between two other buses.

'May I have your attention?'

Kim looked toward the front and saw the soldier, clipboard still in hand, his face flushed with embarrassment or the heat of the day.

'I must ask you to remain quiet and in your seats. We'll only be here for a short time, then we'll leave for the trains.'

After having spoken his short speech, he was in the process of heading toward the door when a woman seated on the aisle caught his arm.

Kim noticed all the other passengers watching and listening as closely as she was, curious as to what the woman wanted.

The soldier shook his head once, but the woman grew more insistent and started down the narrow aisle after him. She cried out clear enough for all to hear, 'But my mother is old. We've been on the bus since early morning. She must have a rest stop, I beg you – '

'I'm sorry. There are no accommodations.'

'But there have to be. There are young children on board. They too must – '

But quickly the officer signaled for the driver to open the bus door. He stepped out, and the driver closed it after him.

Outside the window, Kim saw the soldier in a close huddle with another man. The second made some comment, then burst out laughing. Kim felt anger deep inside her. There were ample accommodations in the main building of the fairgrounds. Why were they not being permitted to use them now?

Outside the bus, Kim saw a soldier carrying a galvanized bucket, which he gave to the soldier from their bus, who in turn took it, laughed, and shrugged.

Seconds before he got there the driver opened the door, and without a word the soldier stepped up and placed the bucket in the center of the aisle. He winked at the driver, then stepped down again, and the door was closed.

For a moment all eyes remained fixed on the bucket. No, prayed Kim. Leave it alone. But apparently the needs of the old woman were great, and at last she reached for the bucket.

Then Kim had had enough. She stood quickly and said, 'No! Leave it alone!'

At the sound of her voice, all heads swiveled backward.

'Leave it alone,' Kim repeated, softening her voice, slipping past Belle and out into the aisle. She was vaguely aware of Harold calling her name, but she ignored him.

'Tell your mother to use the floor,' Kim suggested. 'All of you who have been confined and are in need, use the floor.'

For a moment her suggestion hung unreceived on the shocked air. Every face frowned at the idea, finding it repugnant and unacceptable.

Then Kim took another step forward and added with emphasis, 'It's their bus.'

That's all she had to say. A young family about midpoint on the bus led the way. The father stood and blocked the view as his wife lifted her skirt. The sound of relief was clear for all to hear.

There were a few giggles, then the entire bus was alive with movement, the children being allowed to go first, the sound of water striking the floor repeated and amplified. Kim felt Belle standing behind her and turned to see a smile on her face. Only poor old Harold looked stricken. 'You're going to get us all into trouble,' he said, and sank deeper into his seat as though disclaiming knowledge of everything.

As far as Kim was concerned, let him be. There was life, movement, and on occasion even laughter on the bus. The

United States Army bucket was sitting totally ignored. In the act of emptying their bladders, talk had sprung up. Introductions were being offered and returned. The one small simple act of rebellion had given them back a degree of their spirit and in a curious way their dignity.

Of course there was the sweetish smell of urine. But they could live with that. And there was the outraged face of the driver, who had taken all that he could and now fled the bus on tiptoe to report the rebellion to the soldiers laughing and joking outside in the fresh air.

Kim watched carefully to see what action would be taken now. Apparently the bus driver was having trouble making himself understood. Now he pantomimed in a humorous fashion to his own genitals, then stood as though he were urinating. A broad arm gesture following that apparently meant 'all over the bus.' At last the soldier looked toward the bus and headed their way at a run.

Kim was not the only one who'd been watching. By the time the soldier reached the bus door, all of the passengers had resumed their seats in an attitude of compliance and obedience.

'Damn,' the soldier muttered, and lifted his foot off the step of the bus where the urine river had run downhill.

'Goddammit,' he said again, louder this time. 'Whose bright idea was this?'

No one said a word. Kim knew they wouldn't.

'I should make the lot of you clean this mess up,' he muttered, still searching frantically for a dry place to stand.

Someone called to him from the parking lot. Kim heard a whistle blow, and she saw the buses near the front start to pull out.

'I'll just let you-sit in it,' the soldier shouted finally, 'all the way to the train station.' He bent forward in an attempt to reach the empty bucket. 'The United States Army was trying to be decent and humane. Fat lot of thanks this is.'

At last he grasped the edge of the bucket and drew it rapidly toward him. Apparently someone up front *had* used the bucket, and now urine sloshed out over his hand and arm, sending him backward down the steps, bucket abandoned, as he wiped furiously at his urine-soaked shirt.

Not one person on the bus moved, spoke, or even breathed until the door was pulled shut, both driver and soldier standing outside. Then as if on cue everyone in the bus burst out laughing, the most marvelous sound Kim had ever heard, a sound of hope and courage to face the difficult days ahead. She was fairly certain of one thing, that whatever discomfort and inconvenience they had suffered on this one bus was nothing compared to what was ahead of them . . .

March 23, 1942
Fort Smith, Arkansas

At four o'clock on the afternoon of the third day in a driving rainstorm, the train that had left San Bernardino on a warm early spring day reached Arkansas.

The jolt of the stopping train awakened Belle. At first there was that awful feeling of not knowing where she was.

Then all at once the soldiers stirred them into action. 'On your feet,' one shouted. 'We've reached our destination. Gather your things, form a line, and follow the officer at the rear of the coach to the buses. Come on, look lively!'

About thirty minutes later, Belle saw the buses pull through a large gate. Fences of barbed wire stretched out on either side as far as she could see. The fence was interrupted about every hundred yards with a high wooden guard tower.

The caravan of buses filed into a large field opposite a low squat building. On the porch beneath a broad overhang, she saw a row of desks, and behind these desks were more soldiers.

As their bus made a wide turn, Belle caught a glimpse of a long broad street, lined on either side with barracks, and this double row of barracks stretched as far as she could see.

Then a soldier was standing before them. 'I'm afraid I must

ask you to follow me. We had hoped the rain would stop, but it hasn't, so . . .' He gave a helpless shrug.

With the officer dry under his slicker, the others followed him out into the rain, using whatever was at their disposal to keep dry. A few hoisted their suitcases up onto their heads. Others rebuttoned their coats over their heads and looked like turtles, while most simply concentrated on keeping their shoes on, for the field in which the buses had stopped was now a mudhole. With every step Belle felt herself slipping and saw others doing the same. In this manner, they made their way slowly toward the broad covered front porch.

When they were less than twenty feet from the first desk and the promise of shelter, Kim straightened up and looked back at Belle.

'No. Oh, God – no!' she gasped, attracting everyone's attention and causing the armed soldiers to step forward.

Harold tried to wave them away but couldn't, and they focused all their attention on Belle.

'Hey, Sarge, lookee here,' one of them shouted, attracting the attention of the officers on the porch.

Black dye now ran in solid streams down Belle's face. It seeped into one eye and momentarily blinded her. As she struggled to wipe it away, she saw Harold and Kim being led up onto the porch, then felt a hand on her arm, leading her after them.

Their presence attracted a good deal of attention. Soldiers came the length of the porch, the last one arriving with a broad grin and a white towel.

'Who in the hell would be dumb enough to try to sneak into this place?' He laughed and tossed the towel to the soldier who'd escorted Belle onto the porch.

'Please, sir, let us explain – '

'You keep quiet.'

Harold tried to speak, to no avail. Belle shivered in a way that had nothing to do with the rain, and before she knew what had happened, the towel had been draped over her head and strong hands wiped at her scalp.

'Good Lord, it's a blond. Lookee there.'

For too long everyone did just that, stared at her, walked around her. One at last exclaimed, 'She's just an American kid with blond hair and blue eyes.'

'Please, sir, let me speak.'

It was Harold again.

'Go ahead, Jap,' one officer said, perching on the edge of the desk, his arms folded across his chest.

'My name is Harold Shoda. This is my wife, Kim, and this is our daughter, Belle.'

'How in the world can that be?' the officer asked.

'Not our real daughter.'

'You better believe it.'

The soldier looked about the porch, then looked back at Belle. 'Now what in the hell are we going to do?'

A quick conference took place, four officers whispering together, pointing back to Belle, who finally had had enough of standing alone and went to Kim.

'Well, we can't process her through, no way,' one soldier said.

'She ain't Japanese. This here is a Japanese War Relocation Center. We can't process someone through who ain't Japanese.'

All four agreed to this wisdom, and for a moment they stared at Harold and Kim as though they resented them for presenting the problem.

'Well, I guess you better call the colonel. We can't solve this one. Go on, Corporal, go get him.'

'You keep an eye on them,' the officer instructed. Two soldiers with rifles and fixed bayonets stepped forward. 'Come on,' he shouted at the long line of waiting and soaked evacuees. 'Let's get it moving again.'

Belle huddled against the wall of the building, Kim on one side, Harold on the other. What really scared her, more than the fixed bayonets pointing at them, more than the ugly scene in front of her, more than anything else in this world, was the sight of Harold's hand on her arm, trembling as though he were an old man . . .

* * *

Colonel Raymond Collier stood in his office, staring out at the driving rain, and wondered as he'd wondered every day for the past two weeks who in hell he had pissed off to draw this god-awful duty. There were good solid shooting wars all over the world, and here he was, bedding down almost ten thousand Japanese.

Had General DeWitt lost his mind?

He heard a knock at the door. 'Come,' he called out.

The door opened and a young corporal appeared. 'Yes, sir, you're wanted at the processing tables. There's a young girl, American, who is posing as a Jap.'

'What?' Colonel Collier repeated incredulously.

'Yes, sir, hair dyed, the whole bit. They – don't know what to do.'

Colonel Collier started to ask further questions but changed his mind. 'I'll be right there.'

An American posing as a Jap? A spy? He'd heard of such things, Intelligence officers infiltrating Jap enclaves in an attempt to uncover saboteurs.

He grabbed his raincoat and shook it on, then adjusted his cap and hurried out of the door toward the problem. If it was Intelligence, you'd think they'd have the decency to tell him. How could he protect an infiltrator if he didn't even know he was there?

Hell, it was to be expected in a fly-by-night procedure such as this. Americans weren't expert at the wholesale rounding up of peoples and shipping them off to prisons. And make no mistake. That's exactly what these places were. The government liked to call them by different names, relocation centers, detachment compounds, loyalty control administrations – but the long and short of it was they were prisons.

If anyone didn't believe him, they could check the miles of high, sturdy barbed-wire fence, the guard towers, the searchlights, the desolate areas in which all were located.

His thoughts carried him past the three secretaries working in his outer office to the porch.

'Here, Colonel,' someone called out.

He made his way through the clutter of chairs, heading toward the table at the end where he saw Sergeant Drury and two corporals standing guard over three Japanese, one man and two women.

But as he drew closer, Colonel Collier saw something different about the younger woman, a girl, really, her face streaked with black.

'Problem, sir,' Sergeant Drury called out bluntly. 'This here? She ain't Jap. Look for yourself.'

Colonel Collier did, stepping closer to the adolescent girl, twelve, possibly thirteen. The sergeant was right. The black streaks on her face were caused by the running dye in her hair, and behind the sunglasses were sky blue eyes and a look of terror.

'Who are you?' he asked, and belatedly realized his manner was doing nothing to ease her terror.

'Belle,' the girl said, her voice little more than a whisper.

'Belle what?'

But before the girl could answer, the man stepped forward, his manner polite, his hands rough, obviously a farmer. 'Sir, my name is Harold Shoda. If I may – '

'What's she doing with you?'

'She is our daughter, our – '

This provoked a laugh from the soldiers standing nearest to the desk. Colonel Collier silenced them with a look and turned his attention back to the Jap, who appeared to be wilting before his eyes.

'Wait here,' he said wearily. 'I'll go call civilian authorities. Perhaps they will know what – '

He never finished his sentence for the simple reason he had no idea what they would do. All he knew for certain was that the girl couldn't stay here. If the press ever got hold of the fact that he'd locked up a young American girl with about ten thousand Japs, good God –

Who to call? The local sheriff? A local preacher? No, no preacher. Better the civilian law. Let them figure it out.

Thus resolved, he closed his office door, went into his lavatory, ran the basin full of hot soapy water, and washed his hands for five minutes. Some Japs carried diseases, and he'd been standing close to one . . .

According to the watch on the sergeant's arm, they'd been waiting on the porch for one hour and forty-seven minutes. Several times the sergeant had grinned and told them, 'Go ahead and just sit flat down.'

But Kim had refused to do this and had not allowed Belle to do it, either, and now she stood holding her in a quiet embrace. Harold stood beside them looking bewildered and tired.

Kim closed her eyes against the reality of her own physical discomfort, which was nothing compared to her emotional pain. She'd seen a look in the colonel's eye, a certain condemnation.

But for now all she was concerned with was keeping Belle locked tightly in her arms and with *on*, a uniquely Japanese frame of mind taught to her by her old mother-in-law, a stoic stance in which you tell yourself:

I will do what I have to do with grace and dignity.

'Do you suppose that Lil is okay?' Belle whispered, her head resting on Kim's shoulder, the treasonous bootblack smeared all over both of them like some unorthodox mark of disgrace.

'Oh, I'm sure,' Kim said quietly, though with conviction. 'I'm sure she's been picked up by now. You know Lil. She likes nothing better than meeting new people.'

'She was a good dog.'

'Is a good dog,' Kim said with emphasis.

I will do what I have to do with dignity and grace. I will do –

She looked up and saw the colonel returning. He appeared warm and dry, his tongue playing with a piece of food caught in his teeth. Clearly he'd just finished supper. He seemed to look beyond them toward the front gate.

Kim looked up along with everyone else at the sound of a car. She glanced toward the camp entrance, saw the military police run out into the rain and open the gates for a squat black Ford that drove directly up to the porch.

In the front seat she saw two policemen and in the back a woman, quite portly, dressed in a black suit.

I will do what I have to do with grace and dignity and –

'Shoda, come here,' Colonel Collier called out, and when Harold refused, more out of confusion than disobedience, the men walked directly to a position in front of Kim.

'This is Sheriff Louis,' Colonel Collier said. 'He has come to take the little girl to a – '

'No!'

Kim spoke only one word, but it seemed to resound over the camp as though amplified.

'Look, lady,' Colonel Collier tried again, 'she can't stay here. Now I suggest this as a temporary measure. You will be informed as to where she has been taken, and as soon as – '

'No,' Kim said again, this time her voice calm, carefully measured.

I will do what I have to do –

'Run, Belle,' Kim whispered, and grabbed Belle by the hand. They were halfway to the opened gates when she heard the colonel shout behind her.

'Go get them, stop them – '

And they were stopped, one MP catching up to Kim and pushing her down into the mud, then placing his boot on her back while the two civilian police officers caught Belle, one on each arm, and dragged her backward through the mud to the waiting car, where the portly woman held open the back door.

'Kim!'

The cry resounded in Kim's ears. 'Belle, don't be afraid. I love you. *Belle!*'

Twice she tried to get up, and twice the military policeman pushed her back down into the mud. From this trapped position, crying openly, not giving a damn about grace and dignity, she watched, clawing at the mud as Belle was forced into the backseat of the car, the door closed and locked behind her, the two men jumping into the front seat as fast as possible and turning in a wide circle toward the gate.

Kim caught a last glimpse of Belle, who apparently had engaged the woman in open warfare. Through a tangle of arms and shoulders she saw a pale white face, streaked with bootblack, tearing at the closed window, her mouth open in a continuous and silent scream.

Kim watched as the car sped through the gates and disappeared into the rain. Only then did she feel the pressure of the boot leave her back, though now she had no desire to rise. What was the point? Where would she go? To fresh brutality and new humiliation? To a husband who still loved this country? To Belle? Belle was gone. No more laughter, no more beauty, no more humor.

No reason for life . . .

April 21, 1942
Fort Smith, Arkansas

The Baptist Orphanage was a two-storey red-brick building, overcrowded, dilapidated, and on the outskirts of town. When Belle had been brought here a month ago, she'd been bathed and scrubbed in a big bathtub by a woman named Wilma Hardcastle, the same woman who'd been her captor on the ride from the internment camp.

Belle's butchered hair had been washed free of all bootblack. She'd been given a shapeless dark blue dress and house slippers. Then she'd been presented to Brother Carmichael Bledsoe, a large man with a pig nose, a ruddy face, and a fixed smile.

He'd made her get down on her knees and thank God for having been saved from the godless Japanese. Then he had turned her back over to Wilma Hardcastle, who had taken her to a large dormitory filled with girls, all staring at her from their bunk beds.

She had run away that very first night, though at dawn the police had caught her in front of Walgreen's Drug Store where she was trying to get a ride out to the internment camp.

They'd brought her back. Wilma Hardcastle had looked sternly at her and had told her she would not tell Brother Bledsoe this time, but if it ever happened again . . .

Belle had bided her time, had observed and listened carefully. She planned to run away again, but she also planned not to get caught this time.

After eavesdropping on the kitchen help, she learned that the garbage truck that came every Friday went directly out to the internment camp.

Unfortunately the garbage truck did not go to the internment camp on this Friday. Instead it went to the city dump, and as the rear of the truck had been raised to excrete the garbage, Belle had come tumbling out as well. One of the garbage men saw her, tied her hands and feet so that she wouldn't run again, and placed her in the back of the empty garbage truck because she was too smelly to ride in the front with the men.

Now it was almost midnight. Wilma Hardcastle had bathed her – again. She'd said nothing to Belle this time, not one word, though once she'd looked at her with an expression of sadness. After the bath, she gave Belle a short cotton robe, told her to dry herself, put the robe on, and wait.

Dried now, Belle slipped on the robe and noticed a rip beneath the left sleeve. Kim would never let her wear anything with a rip in it. The length barely covered her knees, and she felt silly in it and wished that Miss Hardcastle had given her a clean dress. She couldn't very well run away in this.

Then it dawned on her. Of course she couldn't run away in this. That was why they had –

She heard the bathroom door open, saw Miss Hardcastle, a folded blanket in her arms. 'You're a very stupid girl, you know that, don't you?'

Belle said nothing.

'Brother Bledsoe is a forgiving man, but he can only forgive so many times. I hope you understand this.'

Miss Hardcastle shifted the blanket to her other arm, revealing a book she had hidden beneath the blanket.

'Here,' she said, and thrust the book at Belle. 'Take it. It's a Bible. You'll have need of it during the next few days, I assure you.'

Belle took the Bible and turned it over once in her hands. It reminded her of the Melvilles. Pastor Melville always carried his Bible with him.

Now she saw Miss Hardcastle lift a large key ring from her pocket. 'Come on,' she said at last, and briskly led the way out of the bathroom. Belle had to move fast to catch up. All the while she tried to keep the skimpy robe together and at the same time tried not to drop the Bible.

As bad luck would have it, halfway down the stairs they encountered a group of children coming up, led by a teacher whom Belle did not know. The woman herded the children to one side of the stairs.

After Belle had passed them by, she heard the teacher say in a whisper but loud enough to be heard, 'You see, take a close look, children. That's what disobedience will earn for you.'

Belle kept her eyes front and padded barefoot across the cold concrete after Miss Hardcastle. Now the woman turned left down a dark corridor where Belle had never been before. She smelled dampness, and from the slight slope beneath her feet she knew they were going deeper.

Miss Hardcastle made two more turns, one to the right, one to the left, leaving all light behind except that provided by the bulb overhead. At last she stopped before a low closed door. She glanced briefly at Belle, then fumbled with the big key ring, inserted the skeleton key into a rusty lock that grated once, then swung open. Miss Hardcastle turned on a switch outside the door, and a bright light flooded the room.

Inside, Belle saw a small cell, low-ceilinged, like the corridor. To one side she saw two low wooden stools, saw a mussed couch on the other side and a large pot of some sort sitting beneath a three-legged table.

Miss Hardcastle stepped back to the door and out of it, and even before Belle could protest, she saw the door close, heard the key grate again in the lock, and felt her heart accelerate.

'Miss Hardcastle?' she called out, certain the woman was still on the other side of the door. She hadn't planned to apologize for running away twice, but if it got her out of this awful place, she'd be willing to try.

Then she heard retreating footsteps and wondered what she was supposed to do and how long she would have to stay.

Well, she certainly wasn't going to give them the satisfaction of crying. Carefully she dragged one of the wooden stools to a position by the door, wrapped the robe about her as tightly as possible, sat on the stool, and opened the Bible to page one.

She'd read only two pages when she heard footsteps in the hall outside the door. She was hungry and thirsty and hoped that whoever had come had brought food.

'Miss Hardcastle? Is that you?' Belle called out.

But the face that appeared as the door was unlocked was not Miss Hardcastle. It was Brother Bledsoe.

'How is the naughty girl?' he asked, coming all the way into the room, closing and locking the door behind him, then standing directly beneath the glare of the bare bulb.

As Belle backed away from him, she noticed that he too was wearing a robe, much fancier than hers.

'Good,' Brother Bledsoe exclaimed, and pointed to the Bible in Belle's hands. 'I see you're reading the word of God. Perfect. I'm so pleased.'

Belle watched him carefully as he paced off a limited inspection of the room.

He was fat. His robe was pulled tightly over his protruding belly and made him look like a red plaid ball on toothpick legs. His hair was straight, gray and thinning, and he'd brushed it back over his bald head until now, in this light, it resembled cuts on his skull.

'You know why you are here, don't you?' he asked, his hands behind his back.

'N-no, I'm not – '

'Well, let me help you. Punishment is useless in the eyes of God unless the one who is being punished understands her transgression. Here, hand me that stool and you take this one, and let us sit down, heart to heart, and work all of this out so that we might redirect your life along a more positive and godly route. What would you say to that?'

Belle said nothing.

He waited until she was settled, then he arranged his stool, their knees touching, a closeness she didn't like but had no idea how to avoid.

'Now, let's begin,' he said, and planted his hands on his knees, looking directly at her. 'This will be our classroom for as long as it takes. Do you understand?'

No, she didn't understand but still said nothing.

'Now, why did you run away, Belle?'

'I – wanted to be with Kim and Harold,' she replied.

'The Japs?'

'Why do you keep calling them that?'

'Because that's what they are. Why do you keep denying it?'

'I love them.'

'You've been misguided.'

'No.'

'And you ran away twice?'

'Yes,' Belle snapped, growing angry.

'And will you do it again?'

'When I get the chance,' Belle said, and realized too late that she'd said the wrong thing. 'I mean – '

'I know very well what you mean,' Pastor Bledsoe said, his manner changed.

Belle started to get up from the uncomfortable stool. But she had no sooner made a move than he reached out and dragged her back down.

'Take off your robe,' he ordered in a low voice.

She looked up, certain that she'd not heard him correctly.

'Take off your robe,' he repeated. 'It's time for lessons. Anatomy lessons. Have you ever had an anatomy lesson?'

'N-no.'

'A detailed study of how our bodies are made, the function of each and every part. Do you know what I'm speaking of?'

'No – '

'Then let me show you. It's time you learned at twelve years. Perhaps past time. Better a gentle teacher like me than some godless Jap.'

'Please don't say that,' she whispered, her hands grasping the robe tightly together.

'Take off the robe,' he repeated yet a third time, and now reached forward and drew her hands down, pushed the robe from her shoulders, and let it fall in a circle about the stool.

She felt a blush on her cheeks as she stared down at her body.

'Now it's time for me to shed my robe, the better to continue with our demonstration.'

All at once he stood up and untied the cord about his waist, slipping the robe off his shoulders.

Belle had never seen a naked man, and as he stood before her he seemed to take pride in her close scrutiny.

'Study it all,' he invited, 'for God created it, and what is of God is good.'

She only half heard his words, so stunned was she by the mountain of pale pink flesh that stood directly in front of her. There was a fine covering of white curly hair on his chest, then the rolls of flesh started, three large ones with smaller ones developing about his waist and hips, on down until the hair turned black and curly. Out of this protruded something brown and wrinkled, like a small tube, and hanging behind it was what looked like a pouch.

Just as she was about to turn away, she heard a noise at the door and saw Wilma Hardcastle appear, her face flushed as though she were angry. 'You're wanted, Brother Bledsoe. Upstairs.'

For a moment he seemed equally angry. Then, abruptly, he retied his robe and brushed past Miss Hardcastle, muttering something about God frowning on those who don't mind their own business. Miss Hardcastle said nothing and waited – until the sound of his footsteps had faded in the cold underground corridor.

Frightened, Belle also listened to the fading footsteps as she closed her eyes and thought of Kim and Harold and the safe warm world that once had been her own. Then, she looked up at the ceiling and started searching for objects that made sense in that world – there, a teddy bear, and there, a ball like Lil used to play with, and there, Kim's mother-of-pearl comb and brush, which Harold had brought to her after a trip to San Francisco. And there –

April 28, 1942
Baptist Orphanage, Fort Smith, Arkansas

Wilma Hardcastle considered it the most significant action in her lackluster life, her rescue of the young girl named Belle.

For a few moments Pastor Bledsoe had looked at her as though she were the world's greatest annoyance, but then something – Wilma wasn't quite sure what – had flickered across his face. Conscience? Perhaps.

She felt almost giddy. She'd never gone to bat for anyone before. But this child was different.

'Come along, Belle, I've come to fetch you. You can come back up to the dormitory now.'

'I don't want to go back to the dormitory.'

Astonished, Wilma asked, 'Well, where do you want to go?'

'Back to Kim and Harold.'

'You know as well as I that that is out of the question.'

'Why?' she murmured.

'You – don't belong there,' Wilma replied.

'I love them. They love me.'

'Apparently that's not enough for the United States government.'

'I'll find a way.'

'I would not advise you to run away again,' Wilma said sternly. 'I doubt if Pastor Bledsoe would listen to me a second time.'

For several moments Belle stared at her. Wilma took advantage of the interval to study the child. Something unique about the little girl, like she'd come from good people originally, not, of course, the Japanese, but before them.

Then Belle was off the couch and heading toward the door.

'Wait,' Wilma called after her, now more fascinated than ever by this mystery child.

She caught up with her at the top of the second-floor landing and made an instantaneous decision that she knew she might live to regret.

'No, not that way,' she called out as the little girl headed toward the dormitory and the communal bath. 'This way.' She motioned Belle in the opposite direction, toward her own private quarters.

Belle looked puzzled at first, then followed Wilma to her apartment and once inside went instantly to a bouquet of lilacs that Wilma had cut just that morning.

'Can I stay here?' Belle asked. 'With you? I wouldn't be any trouble.'

Wilma caught her breath. Her thoughts exactly. How nice to have the child here with her, like the child she never had.

'Bath time,' she called back to Belle, who was still standing at the table, her face buried in the lilacs.

'I don't think Kim had lilacs,' she said, coming into the bathroom, where steam was already beginning to rise in the big white tub.

'All right, hop in,' Wilma said, and emptied a portion of lavender bubblebath into the hot, steaming water. At once fluffy mountains of bubbles filled the tub, and Belle grinned, then shook off the robe.

Wilma held her hand as she stepped into the tub and sank down pleasurably into the fragrant water. For the first time

Wilma noticed a small birthmark on the side of her neck in the shape of a bell. Normally it was hidden by her collar.

'Take your time,' Wilma said, placing the towel nearby. She was just pulling the door closed when she heard a soft voice.

'What – do I call you?'

'I'd like Wilma, but perhaps Miss Hardcastle would be best.'

As Wilma turned away for the second time, she heard, 'Thank you, Wilma.'

She considered a response but decided none was needed. What had come over her? Had she 'befriended' the child? Pastor Bledsoe was always advising the staff not to 'befriend' the orphans. The ultimate goal of a good orphanage was to farm out the children into good Christian homes. A friendship would just make things more difficult. No matter.

She went to her linen closet and withdrew two clean sheets and a blanket. With dispatch she shook a sheet free and sailed it out and over the couch and had just bent low to secure the corners when she heard a curious sound, like humming at first, then at last words evolving.

She raised up, a corner of the sheet still in her hand. The child was singing, a curious song, a popular dance number that the children liked to play on the radio in the dining room. But whereas normally the song was played very fast, Belle was singing it slow like a hymn, or a lullaby, though each ridiculous word was crystal clear:

Dancin' to swingeroo quickies,
Juke Box Saturday Night

Amazed, not at the song, but at the singer, Wilma marveled at the special voice. As choir mistress she was trained to recognize talent. The child's pitch was perfect, her tone clear as crystal, high notes or low.

Wilma stood listening until the song was over. Dropping the sheet, she stuck her head around the corner of the door. 'You sing well,' she said, and saw Belle relaxing in the tub.

'Kim and I used to sing along with the radio.'

'Was Kim a good singer?'

Belle laughed, the first that Wilma had heard. 'No, Harold used to say she sounded like a bag full of cats.'

'Would you sing another song for me?'

Belle looked up at her. 'I will if you don't look at me.'

'All right,' Wilma agreed, stepped away from the door, returned to the couch, and started to shake on the sheet again.

She'd almost completed the bed when she heard the voice once more, a lovely rendition of 'Silent Night.' At some point she sat on the edge of her chair, folded her hands in her lap, and gave herself completely to the beautiful music, the splendid natural voice – a gift from God, and perhaps its owner was not yet even aware of its value.

Long before Wilma was ready, the hymn was over.

'Did you like it?' came a call from the bathroom.

'Very much,' Wilma called back. 'We have a choir here at the orphanage, Belle,' she went on, content to talk through the crack in the door. 'Would you be interested in joining? We have lots of fun. And come Christmas we get to travel all over town singing for different churches.'

'Would we sing for the people in the internment camp?'

Wilma opened her eyes, newly alert. 'I don't know,' she answered truthfully. 'Possibly.'

'Then I'll sing,' came the reply, followed by a simple statement of fact. 'I don't have any pajamas.'

She appeared, dripping wet, the towel wrapped tightly around her as though embarrassed by her own body.

Wilma laughed. 'Wait right there. I'll find something.'

The last sight she saw as she hurried into her bedroom in search of suitable nightwear was Belle clutching the towel, dripping water on the floor, her face buried in the bowl of lilacs.

And what she heard in an echo of memory was that perfect

voice, touching her in a way she'd never been touched in her life . . .

May 15, 1942
Fort Smith, Arkansas

Malcolm Burgess sat in his oak paneled study on the first floor of his Georgian estate and looked out through leaded glass at the vast expanse of green and rolling lawn. At the bottom of the drive he saw Emmanuel working on the prize roses. On the opposite side the azaleas were just past their prime. They'd been beautiful two weeks ago, the day of the funeral, when he had buried his only daughter, Lenora, dead at the age of twelve.

Overcome, he rested his head in his hands and hoped he'd remembered to lock the door. He didn't like Billie Rose to see him like this. She had her hands full with Charlotte.

Now he leaned back in his chair and prayed to God for strength just to get through this hour. Then he'd concern himself with the next hour when the time came.

Someone – he couldn't remember who – had counseled him that his work just might be his salvation.

Before him was the oversize yellow legal pad on which he always scribbled the first draft of his editorials. Now he straightened the pad, reached for his trusted fountain pen, placed it on the top line – and waited.

The internment camp outside of town. That was the subject, and one about which he felt strongly for the disgrace that it was, not just for Arkansas, but for the entire country. FDR had been wrong. Again.

Still the pen sat unmoving, despite the thoughts in his head. The presses would wait until six-thirty. Herb said he'd come for the editorial around five.

Two hours away.

Again he positioned the pen at the top of the page and wrote in his broad scrawl: 'The Shame of the Camps . . .'

And the pen stopped, as did his thoughts. He heard footsteps on the stairs and hurried to his door, unlocked it, and saw Doctor Benjamin Murdoch just descending from the third floor and his recent visit with Charlotte.

'Ben?' Malcolm called out to the man he'd known all his life. 'How is she?'

'She's fine, Malcolm. She's always been fine. Her problem is not physical.'

'I know, I know,' Malcolm cut in.

'She still thinks Lenora is alive,' Ben said with cruel directness that sent Malcolm edging back toward his study. 'And you too need to face it in a way you never have,' he persisted, something in his tone resembling anger. 'I'm amazed at you, Malcolm. Charlotte thinks Lenora is still alive, and you don't quite believe she's dead.'

Dear God, make him stop saying those words. 'I have work to do, Ben,' Malcolm struggled. 'We'll talk later.'

'No, we'll talk now. Come on.'

And with that, Ben took him by the arm and forcibly led him back into his study, closed the door, and sat him down on his big leather chair.

'Now,' Ben began, placing his black case on the floor. 'Look at me.' He stood directly over Malcolm, forcing his attention. 'Lenora is dead,' he said with terrifying directness. 'She died last Thursday after a week of complications from polio, though I swear we did everything within our power to save her. You and I both wept over her. You kissed her and promised you'd love her to your grave. Are you remembering all this, Malcolm? Because somehow between that day and this one, a form of madness has taken over this house, and I fear that you're not helping Charlotte so much as she's winning you over to her point of view, that Lenora is not dead, did not die, and is waiting in another hospital for both of you to come and get her.'

The words cut down on Malcolm. Lenora, age twelve, his only daughter, his only child, blond, beautiful, intelligent, the best of a long line of Burgesses and Hawthornes, had caught a cold, a nasty spring cold that had turned to something worse, with a raging fever and a stiffness in her neck and legs. On Tuesday at Doctor Murdoch's urging they had put her in Mercy Hospital in Fort Smith, and on Thursday she was dead.

Still, Malcolm couldn't think about it and breathe, couldn't do anything at all but weep as he was weeping now, openly, in front of this man who had forced this catharsis and who now bent over him trying to comfort the very grief he'd worked so hard to provoke. After a lost number of minutes, Malcolm saw a white handkerchief appear before his blurred vision. He took it, wiped his eyes, and tried to find something in his world strong enough to cling to.

His work, he had the editorial yet to write. If only he could get his mind engaged on that, perhaps it would ease the pain of memory.

'Better?'

He looked up to see Ben seated before him, truly a good friend. 'Malcolm, I said these things to Charlotte not fifteen minutes ago. And you know what her response was? Outrage, aimed at me. She said I was lying, that you had sent Lenora to a hospital in Colorado. Then she changed that to a hospital in Texas. She said further that you both were going to pick her up this very weekend. Then I'd be sorry I had said all those bad things about her.'

Ben paused. 'I know a psychiatrist,' he said quietly. 'In Kansas City. He's the very best as far as I'm concerned. Let me call him.'

'Do what you think is best,' Malcolm agreed wearily, hating the word *psychiatry* and having even less faith in it.

'Malcolm, it will take time. I know you're tired of hearing that. I was too when Ben junior died. I thought, If one more person says that to me, I'll punch him in the nose.'

Malcolm looked back from the window, at last vaguely interested. Ben junior, a young naval officer, had died at Pearl Harbor on December 7, 1941. He'd been trying to pull his commanding officer from a fire on the bridge and had become engulfed himself.

Peggy Murdoch had been a primary voice in bringing the

internment camp here. It helped somehow to think of 'those people behind barbed wire.'

'Did Peggy go through what Charlotte's going through?'

'No, she always accepted the fact of Ben's death. Oh, she drank a bit too much and still does, and of course you know her role in the . . . camp.'

'Yes.' A sore point. Malcolm had editorialized against it, was ready to do so again.

'Well, I have to go now.' Ben sighed and pushed up out of his chair as though he were a man of eighty instead of forty-five.

He walked in a shuffling manner to the door, then looked back. 'It's the hardest thing in the world, Malcolm, to lose a child. But Ben junior and Lenora are gone now. You can question and challenge their deaths all you like, but I promise you you won't get any answers, not any satisfying ones.'

He stepped through the door and had almost closed it behind him. 'May I call Doctor Lingstrum?'

'Go ahead.'

'Thanks.'

Then the door was closed, Ben was gone, and Malcolm was alone by the window.

All right, enough, a puritanical voice said inside him, and on a rush of energy and purpose he returned to his desk, sat, and straightened the legal pad, then picked up his fountain pen.

'The Shame of the Camps.'

He closed his eyes and saw a young girl's face, with wide-set blue eyes and –

Slowly he pulled open the top left drawer and reached in for the photograph, taken last Christmas. He placed the picture in front of him on top of his legal pad and saw the sweetness of her face, Lenora Elaine Christina Burgess. Her face was framed by golden curls, her eyes dancing under the lights of the camera, like sun on blue water. There was a lift to her chin as though she knew how promising she was.

'Oh, my dearest,' Malcolm mourned, and placed the

photograph flat on his desk, then bent over and rested his forehead against it and prayed that the pain would end soon, that Charlotte would find a way out of her madness, and that their good and quiet life would resume.

He prayed earnestly with the conviction of a young man who believed in faith and prayer, yet with the skepticism of an old man who prayed by rote because it comforted him to do so even though he knew in the end it wouldn't change a damn thing . . .

June 1, 1942
Internment Camp
Fort Smith, Arkansas

Doctor Frank Kiyami had been chief surgeon at one of the largest hospitals in the San Francisco Bay area. Now he was in charge of the camp hospital, a facility not much larger than his conference room back home.

Since March, when they had arrived, he had presided over seven births and seven deaths. The manner in which nature kept score always amazed him. Now, as he slipped into his white coat for 'morning rounds,' he thought with a degree of pride, *I am enduring the unendurable. I am doing the best I can.*

'Good morning, doctor.'

He looked up at the sound of Lee's voice. Lee Harata was his night nurse, a good woman who left her three children with her husband every night so that she could come and help with the sick.

Now he saw a particularly worried look on her face.

'What is it, Lee?'

'It's Kim Shoda. Her breathing is not good.'

Dr Kiyami had been expecting it. Mrs Shoda had caught a cold that first day of arrival. The cold had refused to go away, and now she was in the hospital with double pneumonia.

'Let me see her,' he said, and glanced into the ward, where

out of twelve beds only two were filled, one with Kim Shoda, the other with an old man who didn't know where he was and wouldn't eat.

'Has Helen come on yet?' Helen Kobayashi was the day nurse and one of the best nurses Dr Kiyami had ever worked with.

'No, doctor, though I expect her any moment. I'll go with you.'

Leading the way, Dr Kiyami started down the center aisle. He could hear the rattle in Mrs Shoda's lungs from several feet away.

'I tried all night to break the fever, doctor,' Lee said. 'We need more medicines.'

Aspirin. That's what the camp authorities had given him. Aspirin, Mercurochrome, and Band-Aids. He had asked for some of the new sulfa-based drugs, but to no avail. Now, as he stood over Kim Shoda, he saw her mouth open in an effort to draw enough air into her lungs.

Dr Kiyami placed great faith in the so-called will to live. Other doctors didn't. But he'd seen it too often, a patient giving up on himself, finding nothing in this world worth staying for and thus moving on to see what was ahead.

Repeatedly he'd asked the husband to speak to her of better times. But when he had, there was no response.

'Good morning, all.' The cheery voice belonged to Helen Kobayashi, who marched energetically down the center aisle, then stopped short of Kim Shoda's bed.

Sobered by what she saw, she whispered, 'The husband is outside. I told him he could come help me give her breakfast.'

For several seconds the three of them stared down on the ill woman as though confronting their own failure to make her well. It was obvious the woman would not be eating breakfast this morning, though Dr Kiyami gave gentle orders to bring her husband in while there was still time.

He heard footsteps and looked up to see Lee escorting a very frightened man, small in stature with the slightly bent posture of someone who had worked the earth all his life.

'Mr Shoda,' Dr Kiyami said, extending his hand and noticing that the man was already focused on his wife.

'How is – '

'Not good.'

For the first time in several weeks of constant vigil, Dr Kiyami heard the man make a sound of grief. Then he was in control again, bending over his wife, holding her hand.

'We'll leave you,' Dr Kiyami said.

'Doctor? Did you remember to ask – '

Dr Kiyami nodded before the man completed his question. 'Yes, I'm afraid I couldn't get in to see the colonel, but his aide told me that it was out of the question. He said the child was settled into another life now and it would serve no purpose.'

All at once he saw Mr Shoda rise, his face taut with anger. 'It would have served a purpose. To see Belle is the one thing that my wife would respond to. She is dying because she thinks she's lost her. Can't you see that? Can't anyone see that?'

The raspy breathing stopped. Dr Kiyami hurried back to the bed and saw telltale blue around her lips. Quickly he lifted her to a sitting position. Supporting her with his own body, he commenced to massage and alternately pound her back in an attempt to dislodge some of the fluid, at least enough to permit the passage of air.

'Hold her up straight,' Dr Kiyami ordered Helen, still massaging, still trying to force that first intake of air before it was too late.

He established a rhythm to his work, four broad circles, then a sharp rap, four broad circles, then a sharp rap, four broad –

He lost count of the number of times he performed this movement. At one point he felt almost machinelike, which was fine, anything to keep the feeling part of himself occupied.

It was Nurse Helen who took his arm in an attempt to stop his futile efforts. 'Doctor, please, it's no use.'

Those words caused an agony of regret. His mentor in San Francisco had once told him he would never be a top-flight doctor until he disciplined himself to stop feeling the death of every patient.

Then he would never be a top-flight doctor. At last he found the courage to look up at Mr Shoda while at the same time gently lowering Kim Shoda back onto her pillow.

'I'm so – '

He couldn't say 'sorry.' It seemed a mean word. Mr Shoda stood at his wife's bed, hands limp at his side, tears streaming, though he was making not a sound.

'Mr Shoda, we did everything we could do.'

To his amazement Mr Shoda looked up, thanked him, and asked to be left alone with his wife.

Dr Kiyami hurried down the aisle toward the privacy of his office, where he shut and locked the door. He dropped to his knees before a straight-backed chair and tried to summon the Buddhist gods of his parents but could not, then tried to summon the Christian God of his youth but could not, and was left facing a void too deep for human understanding . . .

December 15, 1942
Baptist Orphanage
Fort Smith, Arkansas

Belle brushed her hair, stared into the mirror, and wondered why she couldn't remember.

In many ways, life in the orphanage reminded her of something she'd known before. Some place in her memory was a scene of another big room where people slept together and ate together.

'Hurry, Belle. We're leaving in fifteen minutes. Don't keep the bus waiting.'

'I'm coming,' she called back, and hurriedly secured her long blond hair – it had grown out again – with a red ribbon and adjusted her white blouse and black skirt, the uniform of the Baptist Orphanage Children's Choir. Then she grabbed her coat and caught up with Miss Hardcastle just outside the door of their apartment.

'Well, don't you look nice,' Miss Hardcastle said on half a grin.

'Thanks,' Belle murmured self-consciously, and skipped along beside Miss Hardcastle, always excited when they got to venture out from the orphanage.

'Where tonight, Miss Hardcastle?' she asked.

'St Michael's Episcopal Church,' Miss Hardcastle said, 'a very important church where very important people go.'

'Who are these important people?'

'You'll see. Just sing your prettiest. But then you always do.'

'I get so nervous' – Belle laughed – 'that my knees shake.'

'Of course you do, but there is no need. You have a lovely God-given voice, and you're a very sweet young girl.'

Belle blushed. 'Thank you.'

About a half an hour later, they pulled into the parking lot of a church, the sides of the building lined with big stained-glass windows and on the front door the biggest Christmas wreath that Belle had ever seen. She stared out of the bus window, wiped a place clean of fog, and gazed at the arriving families, a father, clearly a father, and always a mother.

'Come along, children. Now when we enter the church, do so as quietly and as respectfully as possible and leave your coats on the large table, then follow me down the side aisle.'

A latecomer arrived, a tall man with partially graying hair in a black overcoat and white silk scarf. He looked straight at them for a long moment as though he were angry with them. Then he went to the head of the aisle, made some kind of sign on his forehead and chest, and started down toward a front pew.

'All right, children,' Miss Hardcastle said in a loud whisper. 'Sing your prettiest and maybe they will invite us back. And remember, watch me at all times. Do you understand?'

As they started down the aisle, the choir launched forth into 'Silent Night.' Belle noticed the latecomer again, the gentleman seated on the front row. He hadn't even bothered to take off his black overcoat and white scarf, and next to him were two empty places.

They sang their entire concert, nine selections, and then it was time for Belle to sing 'Ave Maria' a cappella. Miss Hardcastle had taught it to her. Now she closed her eyes, the better to hear the perfect tone in her head.

As she started to sing she kept her eyes closed, hands folded, face lifted, and let the music wash over her and spread over the congregation. As she brought the song to a close, she heard nothing. It was as though she were standing in the church alone.

Then the priest, a thin man with sad eyes and a rim of white hair, thanked her for the music and thanked God for giving her such a gift.

Belle followed the choir into the row of chairs arranged on one side of the altar and felt Miss Hardcastle squeeze her arm lightly. Although she said nothing, Belle knew that she was pleased. As the priest prayed, she settled back onto her chair and saw the entire congregation go down on their knees. Except for one.

The gentleman in the first row did not bow his head, did not go down on his knees. He sat up and stared straight at her . . .

Malcolm Burgess had not intended to come in for the Christmas service. In fact, since Lenora's death, he'd not attended church at all. Father Whalen had been out to the house several times, urging his return.

But Malcolm wasn't here now because of Father Whalen. Malcolm was sitting in St Michael's Church simply because he could not stand being at home any longer.

Charlotte was growing worse. After two sessions the psychiatrist had said that her delusion about her daughter still being alive was too deeply rooted. She had no desire to give it up, and therefore she never would. The man had suggested with a perfectly straight face that they have another child. Then he'd gone back to Kansas City.

Malcolm had practiced massive self-control to keep from laughing in his face. He, Malcolm Burgess, was close to fifty, Charlotte already in the change at forty-seven. Lenora had been a late miracle child. There would be no more.

Belatedly Malcolm slipped to his knees and from that position continued to watch the young girl who had sung so beautifully.

'I believe in God the Father Almighty, maker of heaven and earth, and in Jesus Christ His only son our Lord, who . . .'

As Malcolm chanted by rote the words he'd learned as a child in this very pew, his mind was free to return to the house where Charlotte was decorating a massive tree, hanging Lenora's stocking on the mantel and arranging dozens of gifts, all for Lenora.

He'd tried to join in the festivities but couldn't and had at last excused himself, called for his car to be brought around, and driven himself into town without the slightest idea of a destination until he'd passed St Michael's, seen the lights, and gone in.

He had of late denied all knowledge of a faith in Lord Jesus Christ and in His Heavenly Father. If Lenora's death had been whimsical, it was in bad taste. If it had been 'part of His plan,' it was in worse taste. Even God must have a code of behavior.

Prayer over, Malcolm sat back in the pew, free to focus again on the children from the orphanage, all ages, all sizes, many of mixed blood, except for –

Again his eyes returned to the delicate little blond girl who had completely entranced the congregation with her singing. She was different from the others, her splendid voice aside. The way she sat, so erect, head held high, though slightly tilted to the left, like –

His breath stopped with the thought.

Like . . . Lenora –

As Father Whalen droned on about the greatest gift the world had ever known, Malcolm relaxed into his pew, fascinated by this game of comparison.

Lenora was slightly heavier, more filled out, her face not as thin. But the cheekbones were almost the same and the color of the hair exactly the same and the age – Malcolm guessed this child to be eleven, perhaps twelve, Lenora was eleven, almost twelve when she –

This thought held at bay by a vigilant and practical heart crept up and attacked him before he could stop it.

When she died –

Malcolm must have made a noise because he was aware of Father Whalen in the pulpit gazing down on him, was aware as well of the little girl staring at him.

'You should have another child . . .'

His head lifted. He stared straight at the child, who was staring back at him.

'Let us pray.'

On their knees again, he kept his eyes on the child, the idea still taking root, still growing.

What if – what harm? If Charlotte didn't want her, he could always take her back to the orphanage. Of course she could never be a replacement for Lenora.

Still, this child would be a living, breathing presence in that house of death. And as for Charlotte, who knew what she would do? Since she'd never accepted Lenora's death anyway, and was convinced that it was only a matter of time until she was returned to them, maybe – oh, God, who knew, who in the hell knew?

In growing desperation and increasing need, Malcolm continued to entertain the bizarre notion. Civilized people did not substitute a live child for a dead one.

Still, the psychiatrist had suggested, 'Have another child.' What if the child was already spoken for? Clearly she was the cream of the crop. The choir director seemed to pay special attention to her. Perhaps the child was hers.

And what in the hell did Malcolm know about her except

that there was a vague resemblance to his Lenora and that she sang like an angel?

Was that enough? Was anything enough?

For the rest of the service, Malcolm followed along the prayers by rote, always keeping his eye on the young girl, as though convinced at some point she would give him a sign. Then just before the choir rose to sing the last carol, she looked directly at him and gave him the sweetest, most direct smile he'd ever seen.

He sat more quietly in the pew, more at ease than he'd been in a long time.

He stared down at his left hand, which in his mind represented the girl. He gazed at his right hand, which stood for Charlotte and himself. If the left hand represented need and the right hand represented need and if by putting the two hands together in a position of prayer you eliminated both needs, then what in the world was he waiting for? . . .

December 24, 1942
Tulsa, Oklahoma

Christmas was the hardest. This Christmas was particularly difficult, what with the world falling apart: the Japanese conquering the Philippines, the Nazis knocking on Moscow's front door. Sometimes it seemed to Martha that chaos was the order of the day.

The number of men in the mission was diminishing. A lot of them were joining up, at last finding a point and purpose to their lives. If the numbers continued to shrink, the mission itself might have to close.

Now she shut her eyes and tried to find the spirit of Christmas somewhere deep within her. Unable to do so, she opened her eyes and glanced at R. C. He was reading *Time* magazine. He loved to read about the war. Good heavens, but he had grown, a young man in almost all respects.

Take good care of R. C.

She smiled at that distant beginning and remembered the time that someone had tied a German shepherd dog to Charlie Groveton's mailbox. There had been no note then, just the trusting brown eyes of the dog, who had been Charlie's constant companion for the next nine years, at last dying peacefully in Charlie's arms of old age.

Charlie –

'Martha, when are we going to decorate the tree?'

R. C. brought her back from the past in the nick of time. 'Now,' she said, and sat up, leaving the hard memories in the squashed pillow of the sofa where they belonged.

'Do you know where the boxes are?'

'Sure.'

'Then go and fetch them.'

As R. C. sped into the dark hallway, Martha studied the poor specimen of a tree that the man on the corner of Peoria had given to her. The tree, about three feet tall, tilted to the left, a flaw she remedied by sliding three Salvation Army booklets beneath the stand.

'Hey, that looks good,' R. C. said, confirming her own opinion. 'Here, you take one box and I'll take the other.'

She opened her box of Christmas decorations and released a flood of memories.

A bell. A small golden bell. She had bought it years ago, the first Christmas after Belle had –

'Look what I found.'

'I remember when we bought it,' R. C. said. 'It cost ten cents at the five and dime.'

'Right you are.' Martha smiled, trying to lighten the moment. They both had expended so much energy on remorse and sorrow. Surely tonight they could shake free of it.

But somehow she knew they couldn't, and for the next few moments they hung the ornaments on the tree in silence. The only sound was that of distant carolers.

'There,' Martha said at last, and stood back to admire their handiwork, deciding that it *was* a beautiful tree, albeit a small one.

'Where shall we put this?' R. C. asked, and Martha turned to see him studying the gold bell.

'Where do you suggest?'

'I know.' He stepped up to the tree and placed the bell at the top, the spot usually reserved for the angel.

Martha smiled. 'Perfect.'

Now there was so much she had to do. She and R. C. were going to have their own private Christmas dinner tomorrow after they had helped to feed the men downstairs. She had stuffing to make and cornbread and a pumpkin pie, but for the time being she was quite content to sit on the sofa with R. C. and stare at the pretty tree with the shining gold bell at the top.

The carolers out on the street were coming closer. She could hear the refrain of 'Silent Night.'

If only there was a constancy to life. But there wasn't. So she'd have to make do like everyone else . . .

December 24, 1942
Tulsa, Oklahoma

Charlie Groveton had Christmas Eve dinner at the Black Moon Café on Archer Street in downtown Tulsa. He had a chicken-fried steak, cream gravy, mashed spuds, and black coffee. He ate fast because both Vera and the old Mexican cook were clearly eager to get home.

'Pie, Charlie? Ain't much, I'm afraid. Last of the chocolate.'

Charlie shook his head and remembered his mother's golden pumpkin pie that smelled of cinnamon and cloves.

'You know what, Charlie?' Vera said, clearing his plate and draining the Silex into his coffee cup. 'You oughta go out and find yourself a woman. A good-looking fellow like you ain't got no business running loose on a holiday or any day. You know what I mean?'

Charlie smiled and looked away. Vera knew she could talk to him like that because she'd served him breakfast, lunch, and dinner every day since he'd left Skinny's place out in Hominy.

He had hitchhiked back into Tulsa and taken a walk-up apartment over Judd's Garage about half a block from the Black Moon Café. He'd worked for an oilfield equipment company until they had closed, and now he was living on the last of his savings and wondering what to do next.

'I had a woman once,' he said, embarrassed to hear himself talking like that.

'Your wife?' Vera asked, suspending the dirty cloth above the counter where she was taking broad swipes.

'No, not my wife, though we were thinking about getting married.'

'What happened?'

'She found someone else.'

He could see the understanding pain in Vera's face. 'Oh, Charlie, I'm so sorry. Bad things like that shouldn't happen to a decent fellow like you.'

In the kitchen he saw the old Mexican cook turn off the light. 'See you, Vera,' he called out in the dark. 'Merry Christmas.'

'Same to you, old man,' she called back. 'Be sure and thank your wife for the candy. It's great.'

Charlie heard the back door slam, then felt a rush of cold air about his ankles. He drained his coffee, made a face at it, and slipped off the stool. He dreaded going out into the cold night and back to the empty walk-up apartment. And what in the hell was he going to do in the morning, Christmas? Nothing would be open. He couldn't even look for a job.

'Hey, Vera,' he called out as he laid a dollar and seventy-five cents on the counter to pay for his meal.

'Hey, that's too much, Charlie.'

'No, take the buck and buy something special for your kids.'

'You don't have to.'

'I know I don't have to. I want to.'

'Listen, Charlie,' Vera said, coming around the counter

and confronting him by the door. 'You know what? The Salvation Army puts on a real good Christmas Eve social for their men. You know, music, and all the church ladies bring fancy food. It's just down the street. Why don't you stop in?'

Charlie said nothing. He patted Vera on the shoulder, stepped out into the freezing night, pulled his coat up around his neck, and plunged his hands into his pockets, where his left hand just kept right on going through a hole in the fabric.

Turtlelike, he started down the street, heading toward the Salvation Army Mission, getting colder with each step.

The Salvation Army. His pa once told him that only bums went there.

When he reached the intersection he looked up the hill toward the mission. In the distance he could hear a group of carolers singing 'Silent Night.' There'd be people at the mission and warmth and perhaps a good cup of hot coffee. How would it hurt?

But then he heard his pa again – *'men who can't take care of themselves'* – and he turned to the left toward the train station.

He was freezing. He'd just slip into the station to get warm before he started back to his apartment. Then tomorrow maybe the sun would be out and he could think more clearly.

He pushed open the heavy doors and felt the first good blast of a working furnace. The terminal was practically empty. Somewhere he heard a loudspeaker playing Christmas carols. He wandered around for a bit, then sat in the middle of a long row of seats, stretched out his long legs, and looked squarely into a big color poster of Uncle Sam pointing a pencil-sharp finger straight at him.

Uncle Sam Wants You.

It was good to know someone wanted him. He rested his head on the rear of the seat and studied the high ceiling above. There had been one Christmas – he'd never forget it – when he and Martha had taken his dad's old Ford pickup into Hitchings to a silent movie starring Rudolph Valentino. Neither he nor Martha had been able to figure out what all the fuss was about. Then they'd gone to Rosie's Ice Cream Parlor and had bought a double-dip chocolate cone and sat on the front seat of the pickup and licked it 'til they like to froze to death. Then he'd kissed her, for the first time . . .

He sat up, breathing hard and hating like hell the things he was remembering. Somewhere on the loudspeaker he heard 'White Christmas.' There was too much music in this place.

Uncle Sam Wants You.

He stared at the scowling face with stringy white hair. Why not? He was strong, there was nothing for him here. At least he'd be doing some good for someone and serving his country in the bargain.

Uncle Sam Wants You.

'You got me,' he muttered, and turned up his collar again, walking rapidly out of the warm terminal and into the bitter cold night.

Cold was better, he decided as he hurried back to his apartment. Cold kept you busy, didn't let you think, or worse, didn't let you remember like warm did . . .

December 27, 1942
Baptist Orphanage
Fort Smith, Arkansas

Wilma Hardcastle had never heard of such a thing and now said as much despite Pastor Bledsoe's pained expression, despite the high-and-mighty Mr Malcolm Burgess, and even despite Belle, whom she knew was listening to every word that was being said from the next room.

'I've never heard of such an arrangement,' Wilma repeated. 'What are we doing here? Loaning children out on a trial run? Pastor Bledsoe, I implore you,' she begged. 'Put a stop to this ridiculous meeting. There is no longer any – '

'Miss Hardcastle, if I may remind you, Mr Burgess has been ever so generous.'

This was news. So! Money had changed hands. Now they were selling children.

'Whose interests are we considering here?' Wilma went on, knowing she was out of line but speaking anyway.

For a moment neither man spoke. Then finally Mr Burgess said, 'Miss Hardcastle, why don't we leave the matter up to the child? Let her decide. You're right. I have no business coming in here with problems of my own and looking for a child to solve them. But you see, we recently lost our daughter, to polio. She was about Belle's age, her same build, her coloring. My wife is . . . distraught with grief. I just thought – '

All the time he spoke he stood before her like a repentant child, this powerful and wealthy man who could give Belle the moon with a fence around it. Totally disarmed by Mr Burgess's moving speech, Wilma foundered. She had no knowledge that the Burgesses had lost a child. How sad to have all the money in the world and lack the one thing you want.

'There is absolutely no need to leave such an important decision up to a child,' Pastor Bledsoe protested, clearly afraid that the check in whatever amount was slipping through his fingers.

Wilma ignored them both and turned away for a moment's privacy at the narrow window that gave an imperfect view of the bleak December Arkansas landscape.

Defeated. That was how Wilma felt as she turned back to face the two men. 'Only on a trial basis,' she said, a tinge of anger in her voice. 'At the first sign that she wants to come back, she can come back, is that clear?'

Wilma was amazed that she was talking like this and even more amazed that they were listening, apparently more than ready to follow her every instruction.

'I'll go get her,' she said at last, feeling a peculiar weariness at midmorning.

'Miss Hardcastle, Pastor Bledsoe, my thanks to both of

you. Let me warn you of one more possible complication. If my wife refuses to let her stay, if she will not and cannot accept her as Lenora, of course I'll bring her right back.'

'Of course,' Miss Hardcastle said, and did nothing to alter the sarcasm in her voice.

'Belle?' she called out, and just hoped that they would go soon, without hanging around a minute longer, just go and get out of this orphanage and her life so that she wouldn't have to feel the pain of loss a moment longer . . .

Belle sat on the passenger side of the great black car, whose motor purred like a cat. The air inside the car was warm and smelled of flowers even though it was snowing outside.

'I heard you sing at St Michael's,' Mr Burgess said, though never taking his eyes off the road. 'You have a lovely voice.'

'Thank you. I saw you in the front row.'

'Yes. Not two weeks ago, was it? Such a short time.'

'Yes.'

Silence then as Mr Burgess maneuvered the car through traffic at a busy intersection. 'You know why you're here, Belle?' he asked, relaxing after traffic.

'Here, in this car?'

'Yes, going home with me to meet my wife, hopefully to become a part of our family.'

'I'm afraid I can't become a part of your family. Harold and Kim are my family.'

'Yes, but they are in the camp, and as long as you can't be with them, then maybe you could be happy with us.'

'Maybe.'

'We had a daughter, very much like you. She died recently.'

'I'm sorry.'

Mr Burgess said nothing more for several minutes, then he spoke in a husky voice, 'My daughter's name was Lenora.'

'Lenora,' Belle repeated, lightly stroking the soft gray velvet of the upholstery with her fingertips. It was a pleasant sensation.

'Yes, we both still miss her so.'

Again there was that awkward silence, which Belle could understand because she still missed Harold and Kim so much that it hurt. Late at night was the worst. When she tried to go to sleep she'd see their faces in the dark, so close, yet she couldn't reach them.

'Belle?'

'Yes, sir?'

'And please don't call me "sir."'

'What should I call you?'

'I want us to be friends.'

They were leaving downtown now and heading out on a broad avenue with a row of winter dead trees down the middle. Hanging from every street lamp, Belle could see big Christmas wreaths with red bows. There were houses on either side, with Christmas wreaths on the doors. Everything was very pretty, and she thought of the families she'd seen at St Michael's that night, the father and the mother and the children. She imagined those families lived in houses like these, where the father and mother had a room and each child had a room and they all ate breakfast together and talked about what they were going to do that day.

'Belle?'

'Yes, sir?'

'I want to warn you . . .'

'Of what?'

'My wife – her name is Charlotte. She may not call you Belle. She may call you Lenora.'

'That's the name of your daughter.'

'Yes.'

Silence.

'Would you mind terribly?'

'My name is Belle.'

'Yes, I know, but if Charlotte wants to call you – '

'I like my name. It's all I have.'

'Of course. Don't worry. Let's just take it a step at a time.'

That seemed to satisfy him, and it certainly satisfied her

because at least she hadn't agreed to being called Lenora, which was a pretty dumb name in her opinion.

'Here we are.' Mr Burgess turned the corner and guided the car carefully up to a tall gate. A man came out of a little house, unlocked the gate, and waved them through.

Then her attention was summoned forward to the low, rounding driveway that led straight up to the biggest house she'd ever seen, almost as big as the orphanage but much prettier, with a row of tall white columns in front and high arch windows with tiny panes of glass.

Mr Burgess brought the car to a halt in front of the red-brick stairs that led up to big doors on which hung two Christmas wreaths. 'Are you ready?' he asked politely. 'Come on. You must be freezing in that thin coat.'

She went with him up the steps, and no sooner had he reached out a hand to the front door than it opened all by itself. On the other side Belle found herself staring up at a dazzling bright light, suspended on a chain from the center of the ceiling. She heard the door close behind her and was vaguely aware of someone else in the hall with them. At last turning away from the brilliant lights she saw a Negro woman, slim, pretty, in a black uniform with white lacy apron. She stared back at Belle now with a stern expression as though somehow Belle had angered her.

'Belle, I would like you to meet Billie Rose. She runs this house, make no mistake.'

'Hello.'

The Negro woman said nothing and continued to stand before her, staring down on her with that unhappy expression, her dark eyes fixed critically on Belle.

'Here, let's have your coat.' Mr Burgess said.

As Belle slipped out of the coat, Mr Burgess took it and handed it to Billie Rose, who now looked at the coat in the same manner in which she'd recently looked at Belle.

'Billie Rose, could you tell me where Mrs – '

'In her room, resting – again.'

'I see,' Mr Burgess said, and rubbed the back of his neck as though trying to make an important decision.

'I'd go on up if I were you,' Billie Rose said, making the decision for him. 'Might as well see right off what's going to happen.'

Ahead was a large staircase that fanned out at the bottom and at the top like a wishbone.

'Are you ready?'

It was Mr Burgess again.

'Yes, sir.'

Then Mr Burgess started up the staircase, leaning heavily on the banister. Belle waited until he had gotten a few steps ahead, then she followed after him. Suddenly she felt an uncontrollable urge to turn around and look back down into the hallway. She did so and saw Billie Rose standing right where they'd left her, holding Belle's coat out at arm's length, still watching Belle.

Then all at once Billie Rose winked at her. There was a smile on her face. Belle smiled back, then hurried to catch up with Mr Burgess, who had turned a corner and started up yet another flight of stairs. Stopping before double doors, he stood a moment, his head bowed as though he were at prayer.

'Charlotte? It's me. I have someone here to see you. May we come in?'

He opened the door and motioned for Belle to follow as he led the way into a darkened room, a fire burning to one side, a big chair in front of the fire, and one hand lazing gracefully over the arm of the chair.

'Charlotte? Are you awake? You'd better look and see who is here.'

Mr Burgess drew Belle forward until she was standing directly in front of the chair staring at a woman who looked thin, her neck bones visible above the collar of her robe. She turned her head slowly as though it hurt and brushed at her mussed hair to get it out of her eyes.

'Malcolm, is it – '

Mr Burgess smiled. 'Look for yourself.'

Then all at once the woman started to cry and reached

out one thin hand to Belle, who took it because the woman looked so sad.

'Lenora?' the woman whispered. 'Lenora, is it really you?'

Then the woman was laboriously pushing her way up out of the chair and approaching Belle with her arms open. Belle stepped into the embrace and heard the woman whispering that name over and over again.

'Are you feeling better?' the woman asked, peering close in concern. But before Belle could answer, the woman caught sight of her plain blue dress. 'Those clothes, Lenora, are those hospital clothes? Well, no matter. You must go to your room and pick something pretty and special. Tonight will be our Christmas, won't it, Malcolm? I have all of your presents wrapped and waiting, Lenora.'

Belle felt self-conscious. The woman kept calling her Lenora, and every time the woman called her that, something inside Belle objected. Her name was all she had, and she couldn't give it up.

'I've chosen a new name,' she announced, and let the shocked silence fall where it may. 'I have,' she repeated, walking with the woman a few steps closer to the fire. 'It came to me in a dream, my new name.'

'A . . . new – I don't understand,' the woman faltered.

'In this dream,' Belle began, 'someone came to me and said, "Belle, that's your name now. Belle." And I liked it and I hope you like it, too.'

For several tense moments it was impossible to tell if the woman liked it or not.

'Belle,' the woman repeated, and continued to focus on Belle as though hoping she would change her mind.

But she didn't, and at last the woman drew a deep breath. 'Belle, it's pretty. Yes, you're Belle now. Oh, thank God you're back,' she whispered, and hugged Belle, who now hugged her in return. Everything was going to be all right now, Belle thought. She had her own name, plus a woman she could play like was her mother and a man she could play like was her father and a nice house and she would ask Mr Burgess if he'd try to take her out to see Kim and Harold.

There she would explain to them that she was going to stay with the Burgesses only until they got out of that camp. Then the three of them would go back to San Bernardino and move back into the white farmhouse and Lil could come home as well and everything would be exactly as it was before.

'Why don't you go to your room now, Len–Belle,' the woman said, making a valiant effort to get things right. 'Billie Rose will draw you a hot bath. Then you pick out something as pretty as your new name to wear for dinner tonight, and Spoons will fix all of your favorites. Your father and I will be waiting for you in the dining room in one hour. Is that enough time?'

'Yes.'

'Come, my dearest, give me a kiss. How I've waited for this day. See, Malcolm, I told you. God would not let her die. Not our special child. I told you, didn't I, that she'd be returned to us. And here she is.'

The woman's face was dazzling to see. Mr Burgess was grinning as though he too were very pleased.

In the hallway another problem presented itself. Where was this room she was supposed to go to? Not wanting to go back into the woman's bedroom, Belle made her way quietly down the staircase to the second-floor corridor.

Then she heard a faint, 'Pssst.'

She looked toward the right and saw Billie Rose at the end of the corridor, leaning against an open door, holding a stack of clean towels in her arms.

'I told Spoons if that little girl knows where Lenora's room is, I'm gonna get down on my knees and praise God.'

Belle started toward her. 'Who is Spoons?'

'Cook. Boy, you have a lot to learn. You called her that when you were a baby because she'd always give you spoons to play with in the kitchen. But don't worry. Billie Rose is going to be right at your side the whole way. You hear? And I'll be frank to say I didn't like this idea at first. You just don't get a replacement for another human, now do you? Of course not, but if you ask me, you have single-handedly turned this old house back from being a grave into being a home again, and for that we are all very grateful.'

Belle listened carefully, still having difficulty sorting it all out.

'Who won?' Billie Rose asked, stopping just short of the double doors at the end of the hall.

'Who won what?'

'The name. Are you Lenora or are you Belle?'

'My name is Belle.'

Billie Rose's face split into a wide grin. 'Good,' she said. 'Good for you. You see, we have to consider you in all this as well as the white folks. Where's your real ma?'

It would have been a difficult question at best, but now it was an impossible one because at the moment Billie Rose asked it, she pushed open the double doors, and Belle gaped forward and forgot everything she'd ever known as she caught sight of the room before her.

It resembled more than anything else a cloud, one of those big white fleecy clouds you see on a high hot summer afternoon. There was white carpet on the floor, white walls, a big white bed with four posters and soft ruffled white material floating over it. There were two white soft chairs before a warm fire, and the only color was in the arrangement of dolls and stuffed animals on the right wall.

'You've never seen a room like this, have you, child?'

Belle shook her head.

'And we haven't even started yet,' Billie Rose said. As though she were part little girl herself, she hurried to the mirrored wall and pushed something on the side, and suddenly the mirror started to slide open, revealing a closet at least half the length of the wall itself and filled with clothes.

'Well, pick out something and I'll go draw your bath. Lenora loved pretty clothes.' She disappeared in the opposite direction, and a moment later Belle heard water running.

Now she turned in a slow circle to survey the room once

again. All she could think of was how much she wished that Kim could see it.

A few minutes later, 'You ready?' Billie Rose called from the other room, and at that instant reappeared in the doorway. 'Have you picked out a dress?'

'No.'

'Need some help?'

'Yes.'

'All right, let's see. Come on, give me your hand.'

As Billie Rose motioned her forward, Belle joined her in a slow inspection of what surely was at least a hundred dresses.

'How about this one?' Billie Rose asked, and drew forth a pink velvet dress with white lace collar and white lace cuffs.

Still Belle was not functioning too well, and fortunately Billie Rose didn't wait around for an answer. Instead she hung the dress on a separate hook and led Belle into the bathroom, a room as big as Kim's kitchen at home.

Hurriedly she unbuttoned her dress, slipped out of it, removed her shoes, slid down her underslip and panties, and stepped quickly into the mountain of bubbles.

'Now, let's attack this together, shall we?' Billie Rose smiled and got down on her knees beside the tub. Belle found her a very pretty lady. She acted as though she were in charge of almost everything. Belle felt her strong soapy hands massaging and washing her back all at the same time.

'Well, look at this,' Billie Rose said, and Belle felt her hands examining the small birthmark on the side of her neck.

'Who named you?' Billie Rose asked.

Self-conscious as always when her past was discussed, Belle scooped up two handfuls of bubbles and said to the bubbles, 'I don't know.'

'All right, tilt your head back,' Billie Rose instructed, and cupped her hand beneath Belle's head and began to shampoo her hair. Ten minutes later Belle stood on the bath mat, dripping water, her scalp still tingling from Billie Rose's strong fingers.

She felt a soft towel go around her shoulders. Billie Rose sat on the edge of the tub and turned her around and around, drying her and studying her. Then she did a very unexpected thing. She put her arms around her and drew her close and just held her for a moment, and it felt good.

Almost a half an hour later, Belle caught a glimpse of someone in the mirror she'd never seen before, a girl, about her age, in a pink velvet dress. She was wearing white hose and shiny black patent-leather shoes with tiny black bows on the toes.

Billie Rose had dried her hair, then brushed it back into a ponytail and secured it high on the back of her head with a pale pink satin ribbon. Around her forehead she had pulled a few curls loose, then had stood back to admire her handiwork.

'You are a picture,' she said at last.

'Thank you,' Belle said to Billie Rose's reflection.

'Then here we come, ready or not.' And Billie Rose led the way down the hall . . .

Malcolm Burgess stood by the bar in the downstairs study, sipping a sherry, amazed at the transformation that had come over Charlotte. She looked radiant and alive for the first time since Lenora's death. Her hair was combed back into a French knot, and she wore Malcolm's favorite white lace dress with the diamond necklace he had given her on their tenth wedding anniversary. Now she was wholly involved with the Christmas tree in front of the window, rearranging the ornaments and presents beneath.

Then the study doors opened and he saw a vision, a young girl with long blond hair wearing a pink velvet dress. Charlotte stirred first while he was in a state of very pleasant shock.

'Oh . . .' She smiled and went to Belle's side and kissed her on the cheek. 'You look beautiful, so very beautiful. Look at her, Malcolm. Come and look at our – Belle.'

And he did, grinning all the way as Charlotte was doing, as Billie Rose was doing, as Belle herself was doing . . .

Belle looked about the study and saw more books than she'd ever seen before.

'Did you find everything you needed, Belle?' Mr Burgess asked, coming up alongside her.

'Yes, sir, everything. Billie Rose helped me.'

Mr Burgess laughed. 'See? I told you. No one functions in this house without Billie Rose's help.'

'Dinner,' Billie Rose announced, 'and Spoons is waiting to say hello to Belle. If you don't mind.'

'No, of course not,' Charlotte said, and taking Belle's hand led the way through the door and down the hall until at last they entered the kitchen.

'Spoons, here they are,' Billie Rose called out, attracting the attention of another black woman, though one most unlike Billie Rose. This woman was plump with no waist and a round pleasant moon face that sat directly on top of her shoulders. At the sound of Billie Rose's voice, she raised up and fanned at her face with a hot pad.

'Oh, Lord.' She smiled and approached Belle where she stood between Mr and Mrs Burgess. 'Look at you, just look at you,' the woman said, grinning. 'We have done drove that old polio plumb out, now, ain't we?'

At first Belle didn't understand. Then she remembered. The other girl had died of polio.

'Yes,' she said, growing self-conscious under the woman's affectionate, though relentless, gaze.

'I just can't believe that's the same little baby that used to come crawling in here. I hope you're hungry, child,' Spoons said, and pointed toward pots bubbling on the stove.

'We're all hungry, Spoons,' Mrs Burgess said. 'We'll be in the dining room when you're ready.'

Then Mrs Burgess led Belle back out of the kitchen to the dining room. There was a long table with candles and Christmas flowers, and Mrs Burgess escorted her to the end, where three places had been put close together.

Billie Rose reappeared, pushing a cart filled with covered bowls and platters. For the next hour Belle ate more food than she'd ever eaten before at one time in her life, including things she'd never tasted before.

At the end of the meal all agreed that the chocolate cake would have to wait, and Mr Burgess guided Belle into the study, where he invited her to take a chair by the fire.

'Where's Mrs Burgess?'

'She'll be along.'

There was an awkward silence. Belle watched the flames dancing in the fireplace.

'Well?' Mr Burgess asked. 'What do you think?'

'About what?'

'Us. Do you think you could be happy here? I promised Miss Hardcastle I would call her as soon as – '

Belle didn't even hear the rest of his words. 'Yes,' she said simply, and hoped it would suffice. Apparently it did, for Mr Burgess smiled down on her, drew deeply on his pipe, warmed his hands by the fire, and looked very pleased.

'Mr Burgess?'

'Yes?'

'I do have a favor.'

'Name it.'

'Do you remember when I asked you if I could see Harold and Kim? I would like so very much to tell them where I am so that they won't be worried and that when they get out – '

'Of course. Give me a day or two. Let me see what I can arrange. I think we can manage it.'

Now it was Belle's turn to smile. A day or two. Then she'd see Kim and Harold. It had been so long.

'Are we ready?' This cheery voice belonged to Mrs Burgess, who entered the study ladened with gifts.

'All right, come, my darling,' Mrs Burgess urged, sitting close to the Christmas tree. 'Most of these have your name on them, so you'd better get to work . . .'

* * *

The big clock at the end of the study was striking midnight when Billie Rose suggested that everyone might be getting tired and that perhaps it was time to call it a night.

'Yes indeed,' Mrs Burgess agreed. She apologized for the mess of wrapping paper they'd left and approached Belle where she stood near the fire.

'We're so glad you're home,' Mrs Burgess went on.

'I am, too.'

Then all at once she hugged Belle, and Belle hugged her back. In a way she felt sorry for this woman who had lost her daughter.

'Come along, now' – Billie Rose smiled – 'or you'll be a real sleepy-head come morning.'

At the door Belle looked back at Mr and Mrs Burgess. 'Thank you for everything.'

A short time later, she was in the process of crawling sleepily into the inviting bed where Billie Rose had just turned down the white satin comforter and sheets.

'Oh, no, you don't. Just hold on there,' Billie Rose scolded. 'Aren't you forgetting something?'

'I . . . don't – '

'Your prayers,' Billie exclaimed. 'We never forget our prayers in this house.'

Belle gaped up at her, one knee raised on the bed, the other foot on the floor.

An expression of curiosity crossed Billie Rose's face. 'Don't tell me you've never talked to God before.'

To hide her embarrassment, Belle fidgeted with the lace on the sleeve of her nightgown.

'What about your Japanese friends?' Billie Rose persisted. 'Didn't they ever teach you how to talk to God?'

Belle shook her head, mildly defensive. 'They didn't have to. They were good all by themselves.'

At this declaration Billie Rose's eyebrows slid all the way up into her hairline. 'Well, no one is good all by themselves. We all need to get on our knees every day and talk to God and tell Him where we've failed and what we're working on and thank Him for everything. Do you understand?'

At last a soft look of sympathy crossed Billie Rose's face, and she knelt beside the bed and indicated that Belle was to follow suit. 'Now, do your hands like this,' she instructed, and Belle clasped her hands together exactly as Billie Rose was doing. 'I'll start and you listen.'

Fascinated, Belle saw Billie Rose lift her face and look straight up at the ceiling. For a moment there was an expression of extreme concentration, and at last she started to speak.

'Our dearest Jesus, I want to thank you for sending us Belle. She's right here beside me and we have a lot of work to do, but I think she's going to be one of your good ones. She's eased the burden of grief in this house in just a few hours, and for that we're grateful.'

Belle listened closely to what Billie Rose was saying and the manner in which she was saying it. She perceived a difference between the way Pastor Melville had prayed and the way Billie Rose was praying. Pastor Melville always seemed to be afraid of his God. He kept his head bowed and was always beseeching Him this and beseeching Him that.

But Billie Rose met Him head on, face front, eyes open, as if they were equals.

Billie Rose prayed some more and then suddenly said, 'Amen,' and turned to Belle with a blunt announcement. 'It's your turn.'

'I couldn't – I have no idea of what to say.'

''Course you do.'

'No – '

'Look around. You think every twelve-year-old girl in America lives like this?'

'No-no . . .'

'Of course not. Then what do you call what happened to you today?'

Belle shook her head.

'A blessing, and God is the one who sends down blessings, and so who do you think ought to be thanked?'

'God.'

'And who is in your life that you love the most?'

'Harold and Kim,' Belle said without hesitation.

'Then thank God for Harold and Kim.'

Belle resumed the position of prayer and tried to remember what Billie Rose had called Him and couldn't and so just addressed Him straight on.

'God,' she began, her eyes pinched tight in concentration. 'Thank you for your blessings and for helping me get out of the orphanage.' She opened one eye to see how she was doing.

'Go on,' Billie Rose urged.

'And please bless Harold and Kim because they need it more than I do.'

'You might ask Him to bless Mr and Mrs Burgess,' Billie Rose coached in a massive whisper.

'And bless Mr and Mrs Burgess. They're nice and very sad because – '

'He knows why they're sad. Anyone else to bless?'

'Bless Miss Hardcastle.'

'Good. Anyone else?'

Belle thought and thought and couldn't think of a soul. 'No.'

'Are you sure?'

'Yes. Who?'

'Your real mother,' she suggested softly. 'I bet she's someplace missing you terribly.'

Belle bowed her head deeper. Kim had told her once that her real mother probably was dead. Now here was Billie Rose suggesting that she was still alive and missing her.

With the realization that she might not be dead, Belle decided that she didn't want to pray anymore, not to a God who would take her away from her real mother and leave her with strangers.

Belle climbed into bed and felt the cool sheets on her bare legs and the pleasant weight of the fluffy comforter. Billie Rose tucked the sheet in around her shoulders, sat on the edge of the bed, and smiled down on her.

'You're special, Belle, and never forget it. But at the same time you must never forget those less fortunate. Do you understand what I'm saying to you?'

Then Billie Rose kissed her. Belle started to put her arms around her neck but felt awkward, so she just gave her a polite kiss.

'Sleep tight now.' Billie Rose smiled. 'Every night you and I will have these talks with God.'

'Where do you sleep, Billie Rose?'

'Oh, I've got the nicest apartment up over the big garage. I'll show it to you tomorrow so that you'll always know where to find me if you need me.'

Then she was gone, closing the door behind her.

'. . . so you'll always know where to find me if you need me.'

Belle liked that, being able to go and get someone if she needed them.

She snuggled deeper into the bed and thought on all that had happened this day. She'd walked smack into another world.

'I bet your real mother is someplace missing you terribly.'

Her last conscious thought was of Billie Rose and how much she looked forward to seeing her tomorrow . . .

January 2, 1943
Internment Camp
Fort Smith, Arkansas

Harold had just returned from visiting Kim's grave when he saw a soldier standing in the snow on his dormitory steps, waving to him.

'You Shoda?' the soldier yelled down through the snow flurries.

'Yes, sir,' Harold replied.

The soldier pointed toward the administration building. 'Visitors. You'd better hurry. The colonel's bending the rules as it is.'

'Who is it?'

'Some man from town and a girl.'

Then Harold was running, losing his footing on the ice.

Belle –

The face accompanied the name, and he saw her so clearly, her long blond hair and that smile that could melt the hardest heart, at least that's what Kim had –

Kim. Dead.

Belle didn't know. For the first time he faltered. What should he do? What should he say? And why was Belle here?

A few seconds later he found himself inside a small smoke-filled office. On the floor was the orange glow of a portable heater. He stood at attention before the empty desk, keeping his eyes on the partially opened door to the right, through which he heard voices.

Then he saw the top of her head where she sat on a straight chair against the wall. He felt his heart accelerate and stepped farther toward the door, mustering all his self-control to keep from calling out her name.

She looked so . . . so grown-up, so pretty.

Then she saw him, called out his name and was in his arms, clinging to him.

He was not faring so well. The sight of her had been painful enough. But to hold her in his arms was unbearable, and yet he knew there were more difficult moments ahead.

At last he felt her arms relax. Her first words were, 'Where's Kim? Is she coming soon? Can we go and get her? I've so much to tell her.'

It was while Harold was struggling for a response that he saw a gentleman step forward, a pleasant, dignified-looking man, hand extended in greeting.

'I'm Malcolm Burgess,' he said. 'Belle is staying with us. Better than the orphanage.'

'My name is Harold Shoda,' he replied, shaking the man's hand, grateful for any diversion that postponed the inevitable.

'Harold, where's Kim?' Belle persisted, looking past him toward the front door where the snow seemed to be letting up.

'Would it be all right if I had a few moments alone

with Belle?' Harold requested. Somehow the presence of an audience promised to make a difficult task impossible.

'It wouldn't hurt, Colonel, would it?' Mr Burgess asked. 'I think the snow has slacked off, and I'd like to see the rest of your facility. Why don't we say half an hour? Back here?'

'Well, considering the nature of Mr Shoda's message,' Colonel Collier said.

No, Harold begged silently. *Please, no –*

'You see, Mr Shoda has news for the child.'

'I don't understand,' Mr Burgess said.

'It's about the woman.'

'Kim?' Belle asked eagerly, at last paying attention to what the adults were saying.

'What about her?' Mr Burgess asked.

'She died several months ago,' Colonel Collier said.

'Died?' Mr Burgess repeated, and all at once the confusion on his face turned to anger.

But Harold's only concern now was for Belle, who was looking from one adult to the other as though wanting someone to refute the words that had just been spoken.

'Belle?' he said softly, taking her hand. 'She was sick. She caught a cold that first day in the rain. The cold got worse, and a doctor here took care of her. I visited her in the hospital every day. Then the doctor said there was nothing more he could do.'

Harold rubbed her hands, which suddenly had become very cold.

Still no response. She seemed content to stand before him, eyes down, saying nothing.

'I'm . . . so sorry,' he heard Mr Burgess say. 'Why wasn't Belle notified at the time?' he demanded.

'I made the request,' Harold said, still focusing on Belle. 'But it was denied.'

'Why?' Burgess demanded angrily.

Colonel Collier, always a man to stand his ground, said simply, 'Rules. It was our judgment that – '

'Damn your judgment,' Mr Burgess said with admirable courage, and joined Harold, clearly concerned for Belle.

'Belle? I'm so sorry.' He stayed bent over her, then an idea occurred. 'Is there a grave? Might she – '

'Yes, of course, if she wishes.'

A few moments later they were walking in a silent parade back down the avenue that ran between the two rows of dormitories to the very end, where a few of the men had fenced off a small camp cemetery. Kim had been the eighth person to be buried in the graveyard. Now there were over fifty, narrow plots marked in whatever fashion served the mourners, some with wooden crosses, others with painted rocks, others with growing plants.

The snow had stopped, though the sky was still overcast and threatening. The north wind had increased, and Harold knew that both Mr Burgess and Belle must be freezing. But he led the way to Kim's grave near the end of the front row, which he'd marked with a wooden cross.

Mr Burgess stood a distance to one side, his hands clasped before him.

Belle assumed a position directly in front of the grave. She stood there for several minutes. Her only movement was when she knelt beside the cross and reached one hand out to touch it.

Finally she stood. As far as Harold could tell she had not shed a tear. She looked very composed, very grown up in her red coat, her hair drawn back. Then at last she looked directly at Harold.

'I'll stay with you now,' she announced. 'I want to stay here with you and Kim.'

This was said so matter-of-factly. Harold and Mr Burgess exchanged a worried glance.

'No, Belle,' Harold countered gently, and led her away from the grave.

'Why not?' she protested. 'Kim would want me to.'

'But I'm not going to be here.'

'Where will you be? Are you going back home to California?'

'No, no. I'm – going into the army, Belle,' he said. 'There are several of us here who want to serve our country, to show our loyalty. We expect President Roosevelt will sign the new policy soon, as early as next month.'

He paused in an attempt to read her expression. 'Please try to understand, Belle,' he begged, drawing closer. 'Being an American is a matter of the mind and heart, not a matter of race or ancestry. All we want is a chance to prove ourselves good Americans.'

He paused to see if she was going to say anything. She didn't. She glanced back down on Kim's grave, then looked once again up at Harold. He might have been mistaken, but he thought he saw anger there.

'Belle, please try to – '

Without a word she turned about, passed Mr Burgess without stopping, increased her pace, and, even as Harold called out for her to come back, broke into a run until at last she appeared as no more than a small lone figure clad in red running head down for the big black Packard.

Harold glanced down on Kim's grave. 'I handled it badly.'

'No,' Mr Burgess said. 'You did your best at an impossible task.'

'If only I could make her see . . .'

'She will. In time. May I shake your hand?'

Puzzled, Harold extended his hand and felt Mr Burgess take it in a moment of warm and genuine respect.

'Are you certain you want to do this?' Burgess asked. 'Roosevelt hasn't signed – '

'He will. And soon,' Harold said. 'We can be of invaluable service to our country.'

'I'd say that your country has treated you rather shabbily.'

Harold smiled. 'It has, but it's frightened, and I understand that. I'm only sorry that Kim didn't.' He cleared his throat. 'Will you look after Belle for me? And may I write to her? It may sound strange, but she's all my family now.'

'Of course.'

'I wish I could tell you more about her. She came to us through the Methodist minister in San Bernardino, and they had no idea where she had come from before that. But they found her unique, as did we. She has a rare heart and a great need to love and be loved. Please take good care of her.'

The men walked in silence. Harold kept his eye on the closed car door, hoping, praying, that Belle would step out and tell him good-bye.

When they were about twenty yards from the car, he stopped. 'Thank you for coming,' he said to Mr Burgess. 'Thank you for bringing Belle. Tell her I'll write. Tell her – I love her.'

Mr Burgess reached quickly into his pocket and withdrew a small white card. 'Here, you can reach her here any time you wish. I promise she will be loved and cared for.'

Briefly the two men clasped hands again. 'I wish you all the best,' Mr Burgess said, and with that he was gone, walking back up the slight incline to where his car was parked.

Harold held his position in the middle of the road, keeping his eye focused on the blond bowed head in the passenger seat. Would she come and tell him good-bye? Please, God . . .

Malcolm took a backward look as he opened his car door. Mr Shoda was still waiting.

At last he slipped into the car, keenly aware of the brooding Belle seated beside him. He started to speak but could think of nothing to say worthy of her silence. Instead he turned the key in the ignition, put the Packard in gear, and took another look in his rearview mirror. Shoda was still standing there.

He eased the car forward, heading toward the front gate. He turned on the heater, certain that both of them needed warmth, and was in the process of turning on the radio when all at once Belle said, 'Stop.' Even before he'd brought the car to a steady halt, she was out of the door and running back toward the waiting man. When she arrived his arms were open, and Malcolm watched it all in the rearview mirror, an embrace that was at once a greeting and a farewell.

They stood together for about fifteen minutes. Malcolm had no idea what they said. He sensed that a peace of sorts had been made between them, and for that he was grateful.

Then at last she was coming back toward the car, head bowed, hands shoved into her pockets. When she reached the door, she turned back for a final wave, and Harold waved back. Then Belle got into the car and sat perfectly still, hands folded on her lap.

'I'm to stay with you and mind you, though I'll never forget Harold and Kim.'

That was all she said, but it was enough to build on, and for that Malcolm was grateful.

'Shall we go home?' he asked.

'Yes,' she replied, and never once looked back . . .

July 5, 1943
Tulsa, Oklahoma

They had seen the advertisement in the *Tulsa World* for three days running:

Nestor Croft, world's best private detective, guaranteed to find anyone regardless how long they have been missing alive or dead.

There had followed a phone number and an initial payment due of one hundred dollars.

The one hundred dollars had stopped them dead, even though Martha had one hundred thirty-eight dollars and fifty-five cents in her savings. But it was earmarked for R. C.'s college next year. He had been awarded a full scholarship from the navy on the V-5 program. Still, there would be expenses.

But R. C. had been excited over the ad, and ultimately Martha had caught that excitement, made the call, and Mr Nestor Croft was to meet them at six-thirty in the Colonial Cafeteria on Franklin Street in downtown Tulsa.

'Do you have everything?' R. C. asked.

'Everything,' she said.

Mr Croft had asked that they bring an article of the missing person's clothing. In an act of considerable pain, Martha had brought down from the top shelf in the closet all of Belle's baby clothes.

'We will get this sweater back, won't we?' she asked, newly concerned.

'Of course, I'm sure we will. And I have my sketch, here . . .'

He lifted the small portrait of Belle he'd done several years before, a likeness executed from memory of what Belle had looked like when he'd last seen her at age three.

'Come on. We're going to be late.'

R. C. led the way out of the sweltering second-floor apartment into the stuffy corridor and down the steps and out the back door.

They paused on the curb near the sidewalk. Martha caught a glimpse of the big kitchen clock in passing. Six-twenty. They had plenty of time if they walked briskly.

She set the pace and did not slow down until she saw the green neon sign of the Colonial Cafeteria.

'What does he look like, you suppose?' R. C. asked, lowering his voice as they pushed open the double doors of the cafeteria.

Martha hadn't considered that. She shifted her handbag, moved slowly through the rush of people, and was just about to turn and search the opposite direction when she felt a hand on her shoulder. Glancing to her left, she saw a man who resembled an Old Testament prophet or Santa Claus. Either one was promising.

'Miss Drusso?' he said in a deep voice. 'My name is Nestor Croft, and you are Martha Drusso and this lad would be R. C. Drusso.'

Martha glanced at R. C., saw the surprised smile on his face, and at last rescued her hand from where the man had pumped it continuously since his first words.

'I'm so glad you could come,' he went on. 'This way, if you will. I arrived a few minutes ahead of time and reserved a table for us out of the ebb and flow of humanity. I hope that suits you.'

'Why, yes, that's fine.'

He took them into what appeared to be a private dining room. 'I've taken the liberty of ordering us coffee.' He smiled and held a chair for Martha. 'Unless of course you're hungry and choose to go through the line.'

'No. No, thank you,' Martha said quickly. 'We've already eaten.'

'Well, then, let's talk,' he said with admirable directness.

As he filled coffee cups around, Martha studied him and tried to read his character. She was good at that, having dealt with men all of her adult life. Now she found herself baffled by Mr Croft. His black suit was worn but clean. His nails were long and filthy. The string tie around his neck was held in place by an immense piece of uncut turquoise that had been crudely fashioned into a tie clasp. He was plump, yet his face was lean and angular, at least what she could see of it around and through the thick uncut white beard.

'Now,' he began, having stirred four spoonfuls of sugar into his coffee. 'We are meeting here tonight on behalf of . . .'

Martha didn't have the slightest idea what he wanted her to say.

'The missing one,' he said with emphasis.

'Yes, her name is Belle,' Martha replied.

'Missing since when?' Mr Croft asked, writing in a small black notebook with a black-and-white fountain pen whose top he still held between his teeth.

'Since 1933.'

'Last seen?' he asked.

'The train station.'

'Where?'

'Here in Tulsa.'

'How old?'

'Three.'

The eyebrows slid up in surprise and stayed there. 'You let a three-year-old go alone to – '

'She wasn't alone,' R. C. interrupted. 'I was with her. We got on the wrong train. I left to get us food, and when I came back – '

'Yes, the train was gone. You'd be surprised how often it happens.'

'Does it really?' Martha asked, finding this news encouraging.

'Oh, my, yes. All the time.'

'And do you – '

'Always, always.' He turned a page in the black leather notebook, drained his coffee in one gulp, poured another, and looked directly at her.

'Did you launch a search?'

'Of course. R. C. and I traveled the length of the train line to Los Angeles.'

'And?'

'Nothing. We talked to so many people. They all promised to – '

'And delivered nothing.'

'No.'

'Well, you see, that's the difference. Nestor Croft *will* deliver, I give you my word. I have found – oh, my, well over a thousand people in the course of my career. The smartest phone call you ever made was to Nestor Croft because – '

Suddenly he closed his eyes and pressed the palms of both hands against his temples. 'Because it's Nestor Croft's guess that I'll find Belle Drusso – within the week.'

'Then please get to work,' Martha urged, 'and if indeed you do find her, we'll be forever in your debt.'

'Not so fast,' Mr Croft protested, holding up one hand in the manner of a traffic policeman. 'I need certain things.'

'Oh, yes,' Martha said, and reached into her handbag and withdrew the pink sweater, which she'd wrapped carefully in tissue paper.

'Pretty, very pretty,' Nestor Croft said, lifting the sweater free of the paper, sniffing at it, and at last burying his face in it.

'Mr Croft, when you are . . . finished, may we have the sweater back? I have so few things that actually – '

'My dearest lady, when I'm finished with my job, you will not have need of this one small sweater. You will have the person herself to embrace.'

Martha saw R. C. grin.

'Now one more thing,' Mr Croft said, and studied his notebook. 'Expenses, if you will, in the amount we discussed on the telephone.'

'Yes,' Martha said, reaching into her handbag and withdrawing the envelope filled with five twenties as Mr Croft had requested. No checks. No large bills. Just then she heard a female voice calling to Mr Croft.

'Mr Croft, is that you?'

The woman was attractive and middle-aged. She broke free of the cafeteria line and headed toward their table.

'Oh, Mr Croft, I thought I'd never see you again, you dear, dear man.'

All at once the woman broke off and looked embarrassed at Martha and R. C. 'Oh, my, I've interrupted, haven't I? I am sorry, but in a way I'm glad, because if you are seeing Mr Croft about finding someone who is lost, you couldn't have chosen a better man.'

'Please, Mrs Hill,' Mr Croft protested modestly.

'No, they must be told about my poor mother, missing over four years, wandered off, just like that, and the police said, give her up, she couldn't survive, not at her age. But – '

She raised her hand in tribute to Mr Croft. 'This dedicated man found her in less than a week, wandering about the bus station in Wichita Falls, Texas. How she got there, who knows? How she managed to live all that time, who knows? This talented man brought her back to us.'

Martha listened closely, amazed at the testimonial, as was R. C.

'Well, now I have taken up enough of your time,' Mrs Hill said. 'I just wanted you to know about this man who is well known for reuniting families and mending broken hearts.'

She kissed him on the cheek and quickly disappeared around the corner. Mr Croft looked embarrassed and tried to apologize.

But Martha handed over the envelope filled with 5 twenty-dollar bills. 'Please, Mr Croft, do as well for us as you have done for her.'

Mr Croft took the money immediately, placed it inside his pocket, stroked his beard once, and stood. 'You may hear from me on Friday.' He smiled. 'I have a very good feeling about this case. I think I'm going to solve it rather rapidly.'

'Why?' Martha asked.

'Because God wants it solved. I sense this urgency. I've felt this feeling before. It's a good feeling. It means that everything is going to end very well. Now one last thing. Your phone number. Where you can be reached. Night or day.'

Relieved that they hadn't overlooked anything major, Martha took a piece of paper from her handbag, accepted a pen from Mr Croft, and jotted down the mission phone number. 'Here. Friday, then.' She smiled.

'Yes, Friday.' Mr Croft nodded. He shook her hand, then turned about and disappeared into the crowded cafeteria.

'What do you think?' R. C. asked.

She shrugged. 'I don't know.'

Martha followed him out of the private dining room and into the cafeteria, where the crowd was beginning to diminish.

'Oh, ma'am,' the girl called out from the cash register, 'that will be fifty cents.'

Surprised, Martha looked up. 'For what?'

'For the pot of coffee.'

'But I didn't order it.'

'No, but the gentleman did, and he said you would pay.'

Martha reached into her coin purse and placed a quarter, one dime, and three nickels on the rubber pad.

'Thanks,' the girl said, and scooped up the coins.

Outside it was dark, though the absence of sun did nothing to alter the heat. They walked slowly down the street crowded with people, soldiers and sailors mixed in, some home on leave, others passing through. A few blocks later they turned the corner into their part of town, kept alive now mainly by the train station. Most of the small shops had closed, their owners involved in the war effort in some way. Things were changing, and she didn't like it.

'Read to me, R. C., when we get home. Will you do that?'

'Of course, I love reading to you. What?'

'You pick. I just want to lie back, close my eyes, and listen to your voice.'

'Come on, then.'

They increased their pace almost as if they had a real destination . . .

Three Fridays later when the phone never rang, R. C. and Martha went to the police station and told a sympathetic detective named Mortimer the whole story.

He listened, with his feet up on his desk, his chin resting in his hands, his mouth pursed. He started shaking his head when they were only halfway through their story.

At the end he said nothing, just burped, tasted something unpleasant from lunch, and went to a large filing cabinet against the wall, jerked open the top drawer, rifled through the brown folders, and finally withdrew one.

'This him?' he asked, making the toothpick dance in the side of his mouth.

Martha had only to glance at the folder, then she closed her eyes. 'Yes.'

'But that's not his name,' R. C. exclaimed, looking over her shoulder. 'Donald Steptoe, that wasn't his name at all. And he seemed – '

'What? Younger?' the detective interrupted. 'This here picture is about five years old. We've been trying for that long to catch the son of a bitch.'

Martha gave him a look that suggested he watch his language. He sat back down on his chair and flipped through the file behind the photo. 'Let's see, he has called himself

Arnold Ditsman, Leroy Block, Sam Jones . . . What did he call himself for you?'

Martha glanced up to see if R. C. would answer the question. When he didn't, she did. 'Nestor Croft.' She still saw that bearded face and thick white hair. He had seemed so sincere, so eager to help.

Suddenly a thought occurred. 'The woman,' she said, punishing herself with new hope, 'there was a woman who came over to our table and claimed that – '

Again the detective started nodding even as she spoke. He went to the filing cabinet, pulled out a file, slapped it on the table, and there she was, Hill, Mrs Hill, in league with the con man.

'It's an act' – Detective Mortimer smiled – 'and a damn good one. They prey on the misfortunes of others. What with the war on and all, there's plenty of families lost, misplaced, separated. I'd love to nail his hide for you, Martha, but they're slippery. My bet is they're in Mexico by now.' He paused, and back went his feet on the desk, hands laced behind his neck. 'Must say, I'm surprised he caught a smart fish like you. Who was it you wanted him to find?'

Embarrassed, and only now beginning to realize that she'd lost her hard-earned one hundred dollars, to say nothing of Belle's pink sweater and R. C.'s sketch, Martha wasn't faring so well. 'Belle,' she said.

Mortimer frowned at her. 'You still hoping – '

'Yes, we are,' Martha replied with conviction and a touch of anger.

'Good Lord, it's been – what, over ten years.'

'Ten,' R. C. confirmed.

'Even if you found her, how in the world would you recognize her?'

'I'd know her,' Martha said. 'Come on, R. C., let's go.'

'But, Martha – '

'There's nothing more that Mr Mortimer can do. He has confirmed for us that we are fools.'

Mortimer stared at her a moment longer. 'Let me check

missing persons on the wire. We'll see what we can come up with.'

Martha appreciated what he was doing, which was trying to make her feel less like a fool. 'Thanks,' she said.

As R. C. pushed open the door, the August sun struck both of them like a blast from an open furnace. Briefly Martha closed her eyes and walked blindly down the street in the direction of the mission a few blocks away.

There were no savings now, less than twenty dollars in the checking account. R. C. started college in September. How she'd buy him the new suit he needed, she didn't know. How she'd be able to give him pocket money for those inevitable small expenses, she had no idea.

'Martha, I'm sorry – '

'Don't be,' she soothed, and took his arm as she stepped off the curb.

'It was my notion to hire the man.'

'Mine, too. We both thought it was a good one.'

'But we've lost the money, Belle's sweater, and the sketch. How can a man like that live with himself?'

For several moments they walked in silence, combatting the heat and their loss of faith.

Cynicism solved nothing. Martha had lived long enough to know that. 'Hey, look,' she said with a smile. 'This isn't the end of the world. You start college in a few weeks, tuition paid, and we've got a roof over our heads. I have a job, we can eat three meals a day, and believe me, R. C., in every sense of the word, we are rich.'

As always she fell for her own line and felt her spirits lift. Perhaps it wasn't so bad after all. 'Come on,' she urged. 'Maybe I can talk you into drawing a new sketch of Belle. How you think she might look now. Would you try to do that for me, if you have the time, that is?'

R. C. looked sideways at her and at long last smiled. 'I love you, Martha,' he said with disarming simplicity.

A short time later they were settled in their apartment

above the mission, the oscillating fan on the floor going full tilt. Martha kicked off her shoes, rolled down her hose, and stretched on the sofa, a tall glass of iced tea in hand. 'For some reason, if my feet are cool, the rest of me is cool.'

R. C. grunted in acknowledgment, already at his desk working on Belle's new sketch.

The fan made an odd lullaby. The heat helped in its own way. Within minutes Martha felt that good ease that comes with imminent sleep. So they had made a mistake, a costly one. Still, they had each other, this apartment, this security –

A knock at the door brought her back forcibly.

'I'll get it,' R. C. volunteered, and pushed away from his desk, pen still in hand.

Martha wondered who it could be. She had an hour before the evening meal. No one needed –

'It's Captain Meeks,' R. C. called back.

Quickly she sat up and tried to smooth her hair.

'Martha,' he said apologetically, and only then did she notice that he was holding a letter.

'Might I come in?' he asked.

'Of course,' Martha said.

'I received this, and I felt that you should see it.'

'What is it?' she asked, taking the letter over the back of the couch.

He said nothing, stepped back, folded his hands before him, and waited.

Good Lord, he was acting as though he had delivered a death message.

'Is it from Mr Croft?' R. C. asked hesitantly, clearly still vacillating between hope and despair.

Martha tilted the letter toward the late afternoon light and read the letterhead: 'National Office of the Salvation Army.'

My Dear Captain Meeks,

We regret to inform you that starting September 28,

1943, we are closing the mission in downtown Tulsa and consolidating our efforts in our larger facilities in Oklahoma City. There will be a place for you, but unfortunately the rest of your staff will have to be given notice.

This is not a step we take lightly and do so only after close studies have indicated we can no longer support two missions in the area.

Martha read the rest of the letter but comprehended little.

'Martha?'

It was R. C., curious.

'I'm so sorry, Martha.'

It was Captain Meeks, sympathetic.

For the moment she could not respond to either one. Dear God, what would they do now?

September 21, 1943
Fort Smith, Arkansas

Hillcoat was a private girl's school, established at the end of the last century for the daughters of professional men who had come from the East to settle the southwestern territories. It sat on fifty acres of prime land west of Fort Smith and catered both to boarding students as well as town girls. The only requirements were intelligence and money, not necessarily in that order. It had been determined that Mr Burgess would drop Belle off every morning at eight-thirty and Billie Rose would pick her up every afternoon at three.

Now as Malcolm pulled into the rounded driveway that led to the administration building, he could see the uncertainty and apprehension on Belle's face.

'Scared?'

She indicated that she was and clutched her book satchel to her as though it were a shield. The headmaster, a stern, granite-faced Englishman named Dr Priestly, had assured both Malcolm and Charlotte that 'the girl will be treated as everyone else, with justice and great expectations.'

Malcolm brought the car to a halt. 'Now go directly to Dr Priestly's office. Remember? He said he would show you around.'

'What grade am I?'

'Dr Priestly said you would start in the seventh and we would just see how it goes.'

When she was half-in, half-out of the car, Belle stopped and looked back at him. 'May I call you Mac?'

Only one person in his life, his adored father, had called him Mac. Surprised, Malcolm gave one short laugh. 'If you wish.'

'I wish.' And with that she leaned across the seat and kissed him on the cheek.

'Bye, Mac. Tell Billie Rose not to be late.'

Then she was gone, running up the stairs, her long blond ponytail keeping a counterrhythm to the movement of her body.

Malcolm thought she might turn back and wave from the door. She didn't.

But she had kissed him! For the first time. He put the car into gear, drove into town, and smiled all the way to his office . . .

Belle paused inside the door and looked down the long polished hall.

'May I help you?'

She turned back toward the voice and saw a reed-slender woman, her graying hair pulled back in a bun. 'Yes, I'm looking for Dr Priestly.'

'Shouldn't you be in class?'

'Dr Priestly said he'd take me there.'

'And you are . . .'

Before Belle could reply she heard Dr Priestly's deep English voice. 'That's the child living with the Burgesses, Miss Hepplewhite. Remember, I spoke to you about her.'

Clearly he'd told Miss Hepplewhite something of interest. 'Oh!' she exclaimed. 'That one.'

'Yes,' Dr Priestly confirmed, and placed his hand on Belle's arm, inviting her to, 'Come along. I believe we agreed to start you in Seven B, and if that proves too difficult, we can always initiate a remedial program. I'm going to assign a guide to you, one of our older girls. She will meet with you after each class, show you to your next one, take you to the cafeteria, and answer any and all of your questions. Is that agreeable?'

'Yes.'

'Ah, there she is.'

Belle looked ahead and saw a girl waiting at the end of the hall. She was tall and very pretty with curly red hair and pale skin.

'Belle, this is Mandy Foster, one of our best senior students. Mandy, this is Belle Burgess. We spoke of her, remember?'

Mandy smiled. 'Yes.'

'Now, enough time wasted,' Dr Priestly said with dispatch. 'Here is her schedule.' He withdrew a piece of paper from inside his jacket. 'Check with each teacher at the end of every period. We need to know immediately if she's working ahead or behind her capabilities.'

'I will, Dr Priestly.'

'Then it's off to class with you,' Dr Priestly said, and made a funny motion with his hands as though he were shooing chickens.

Without a word Mandy led the way into a corridor to the right. 'English lit. first,' she read from the schedule. 'There you are. That's the door. Tell the teacher who you are as you go in and take a seat.'

Belle pushed open the door.

The teacher, a plump, gray-haired lady whose spectacles sat on the end of her nose defying gravity, asked bluntly, 'And who are you?'

Belle swallowed hard. 'My name is Belle.' And because she'd recently heard Dr Priestly say it, she said it as well, 'I'm Belle Burgess, and I was told that – '

All at once the plump lady became agitated. 'No. Oh, my, no,' she protested. 'Headmaster knows better. I'm afraid I have a full house here. Headmaster is just going to have to make other arrangements.'

Stunned and embarrassed, Belle was fully prepared to back out into the hall and close the door.

'No, no, you wait here, little girl,' the woman said at last. 'Wait right here,' she repeated as though Belle were dim-witted.

'And the rest of you' – she pointed a finger in the direction of the group of girls – 'read quietly among yourselves, chapter ten. Someone be able to tell me precisely why Silas Marner wanted to keep Little Eppie. He had a good reason. Now see if you can find it.'

And with that she was gone, leaving Belle facing twelve girls who clearly hadn't the slightest intention of reading the books before them. Of far greater interest was Belle.

For several moments she stood near the door, clasping her book satchel to her. She felt the intensity of their gaze like a fire on her face.

'Are you the orphan?'

The voice came from the girl in the middle of the semicircle, a dark-haired girl with black eyes.

'I . . . don't know,' Belle replied.

'Did Lenora Burgess die?' came yet another question.

Belle looked up. 'Yes.'

'And you are taking her place?'

'Yes.'

'Mama says that's evil. Mama says you oughtn't go about replacing one human being with another human being.'

There was a soft murmur as apparently they found it necessary to consult with one another on this matter.

'Did you live out at the orphanage?'

'Yes.'

'Was it awful?'

Belle heard a new quiet in the room and sensed interest in this subject about which she was an expert.

'Awful,' she repeated.

'Well? Tell us what – '

Belle stirred for the first time, walked to the teacher's desk, placed her book satchel on top of it, and looked out of the window at distant trees just turning into autumn reds and yellows.

'Well, there's this basement room,' she began, keeping her eyes on the trees of the far horizon, 'and if you misbehave' – she swallowed hard, realizing the truth would never do – 'they put you down there, chain you to the wall, turn off all the lights, and go away and leave you.'

There. She'd safely made it past the truth. Of course she'd never never tell anyone what had really happened.

She looked around at her audience and swore that no one was even breathing.

'All right, young ladies, I believe we have it all settled now.' The voice of the teacher broke the spell. 'Belle will stay with us for a while until we can find a more perfect place for her. Now, Belle, I see you've settled in. My name is Miss Hutsell. I teach English literature, and we are at the moment studying *Silas Marner*. Here is a text for you, and try to have it read by the end of the week. Now I – '

'I've read it, Miss Hutsell,' Belle said, taking the small red book anyway.

Miss Hutsell looked surprised over the rims of her glasses. 'You've read it?' she repeated, clearly disbelieving. 'When?'

'Last year in San Bernardino.'

There still was a look of disbelief on Miss Hutsell's face. 'But you said you were only in the sixth grade.'

'I was, but Mrs Putnam let us read anything from her special library, and she said that I was reading four grades ahead of my level so she thought I might enjoy *Silas Marner*. I did. The book is one of George Eliot's best, a good example of domestic realism in the nineteenth century, and in answer to your question, Silas wants to keep Eppie as a substitute for the money that has been stolen from him. Also, Eppie gives Silas a reason to live and a hope for the future, and in her love he finds his way back into the arms of humanity.'

When Miss Hutsell spoke again, her voice was quite high and she had to clear her throat in order to bring it down to the proper level. 'Miss Burgess, would you be so kind as to make out a list of all the books you have read. I think that would be most helpful.'

'Of course, Miss Hutsell.'

'Thank you. Now as Belle works on her project, the rest of you girls continue with your reading. There will be a quiz on Friday.'

Thus having set everyone to work, Miss Hutsell took another look at Belle over the rim of her glasses, opened a green notebook, and started to write.

Belle brought forth a tablet from her satchel and a pencil and wrote carefully at the top of a clean page:

'Books I Have Read.'

And remembered the long lazy summer afternoons with Harold and Kim sitting on the porch, Lil at her feet, the creak of the porch swing sounding for all the world like *heretostayheretostay* . . .

But nothing had stayed, neither Kim nor Harold nor Lil, and not even Belle. Now here she was in another borrowed family, and nothing would last here either.

As she stared at the blank sheet of paper, she saw a small white folded note come into view beneath her left arm. She took it and read, 'Will you eat with us today in the cafeteria?'

It wasn't signed, but Belle had the feeling that the invitation had come from all of them.

She smiled yes and tried to ease from her mind all those who were dead or missing and replace them with those who were alive and present.

It seemed the wisest thing to do . . .

October 24, 1943

By the end of October, Billie Rose was spending every afternoon driving Belle about to various places. She now was taking piano lessons, voice lessons, ballet lessons, and speech lessons and, according to her various instructors, excelling in every one.

And when there were no lessons, Billie Rose picked her up at Hillcoat, where she was always surrounded by giggling girls who hung on her every word and would have willingly followed her off a cliff if she had requested it. Her magic was undeniable and increasing. In a way it alarmed Billie Rose.

Still, she was the first to agree that there was no sight prettier than a group of Belle's friends, after they'd shed their Hillcoat uniforms and slipped into rolled-up blue jeans, their fathers' long white shirts, and penny loafers, lounging on the patio by the pool, supposedly doing their homework but in reality playing endless Frank Sinatra records.

In fact, Billie Rose had to fight old Spoons for the privilege of carrying out the trays of Coca-Cola and lemon cake. Even Mrs Burgess put in appearances from time to time, inquiring after certain girls' parents, listening to the latest music hits, stretching out on the chaise next to Belle and holding her hand.

On this autumn afternoon a week before Halloween, Billie Rose picked up Belle after school along with Fanny Allbright and Stacy Whiteside, two of her best friends, who wanted to go shopping for Halloween decorations for a class party.

Now, as Billie Rose saw the three dashing toward the car, she enjoyed a final moment's silence, then turned up the volume on the radio the way they liked it and let the song greet them as they flung open the doors.

There was a communal squeal as they heard the bouncy refrain of 'Don't Sit Under the Apple Tree.'

They were all singing along now, Stacy and Fanny in the backseat, Belle in the front seat beside Billie Rose, where she delivered a quick kiss to the side of Billie Rose's face. It was a habit that neither one thought anything about, but in the rearview mirror Billie Rose could tell that Fanny and Stacy thought something about it.

'What's the matter?' Belle demanded.

'You . . . kissed her,' they said, giggling.

'So? I always kiss her. See?' And as though for demonstration Belle leaned across and delivered another kiss to Billie Rose's cheek.

Billie Rose shook her head lightly and made a mental note to have a talk with Belle. Most upper-crust people were born knowing that servants had their place and were expected to stay in it. Belle clearly lacked such knowledge.

'Okay, you three, where to?' Billie Rose asked.

'The dime store,' Fanny called out, 'the one on Commerce. It's the best. Did you bring the list, Belle?'

Still humming, Belle fished through the pocket of her sweater and held up a folded piece of paper.

'Dr Priestly said boys could come,' Fanny announced, and that summoned everybody's attention.

'He didn't,' Belle challenged, hanging over the back of the car seat.

'He did,' Fanny repeated, giggling, 'as long as they are your father or your brother.'

Both Belle and Stacy looked toward heaven, while Fanny dissolved into helpless laughter.

'I'm thirsty,' Belle announced. On the right side of the street about a block ahead was the Juke Box, a favorite hangout of the high school kids.

'May we stop, Billie Rose?' Belle asked. 'Just for a cherry Coke, please?'

'All right, but I'm not paying.'

'We have money,' came the chorus from the backseat as Billie Rose broke speed, searching the crowded drive-in for a parking slot. At last she found one near the order window, where carhops on roller skates picked up burgers and shakes for the waiting cars.

'Come on,' Belle called out, 'let's go inside. Come on, Billie Rose, you too.'

Billie Rose thought she was joking. But clearly the two in the backseat did not. Quickly they scrambled out onto the pavement and tugged at Belle's arm. 'Are you crazy?' Fanny asked in a massive stage whisper.

But their alarm was lost on Belle. 'No, why? Come on, Billie Rose. We'll just get something to drink, then – '

All at once she heard a man's voice coming from behind the glass enclosure of the drive-in window. 'Hey, you! No niggers allowed here. You know better.'

Billie Rose closed her eyes. It had been years since she'd heard that. Working for the Burgesses kept her safe.

'Look,' she said to Belle. 'I'll go around the block and pick you up on the corner. You hear?'

But Belle wasn't listening. Instead she seemed to be concentrating on the heavyset man, his sleeves rolled up, coming toward them. 'Listen, I told you now. No niggers allowed. Now move that car or I'm calling the police.'

'Why?' Belle questioned.

The man turned to her, and from behind the wheel Billie Rose could see the look in his eye. She'd grown up with it in Little Rock, where she had been raised by her aunt. Now as remnants of fear crept over her from her childhood, she renewed her grip on the steering wheel and ordered as sternly as she knew how, 'Belle, get inside the car this minute. You two as well.'

But if Belle heard, she gave no indication of it. Instead, with that disarming innocence, she approached the man.

'Sir, I'm afraid I don't understand. My friends and I just wanted to stop for a cherry Coke and – '

'You go to that fancy-ass school up north of town, don't you?' Immediately the dividing line grew deeper.

'I go to Hillcoat,' Belle replied politely. In the meantime Stacy and Fanny displayed the good sense they were born with and crawled onto the backseat, locking both their doors.

'Why?' Belle questioned, meeting the man in front of the car.

'No reason,' he said, 'except I think they forgot to teach

you pretty little things a major fact of life around this here place.'

'Which is?'

'That niggers like her' – and he pointed a finger at Billie Rose through the windshield – 'don't mix or mingle with decent white folks like us.'

'Why?'

The man blinked once. Belle held her ground, as Billie Rose knew she would.

From the backseat came an urgent whisper. 'We better get out of here.'

Billie Rose's plan exactly. But Belle took a step closer to the man and smiled up at him sweetly. 'I asked you why, sir?'

For a moment the man was taken off guard. He looked over his shoulder toward the glass booth where orders were picked up. Billie Rose saw three men looking out at him, two teenagers and one older man. All were scowling.

'You see, sir,' Belle went on with unfailing politeness, as though politeness might make a difference, 'all we want are four cherry Cokes. That's all, and we'd like very much to go inside and drink them. Now, is that all right?'

Not immediately receiving an answer, Belle plainly assumed that it was and had just taken a step toward the side of the car to reissue the invitation to Billie Rose when suddenly the man reached out and grabbed her by the arm.

'Now, you wait just a minute, little girl, you hear? You may set people hopping where you come from, but this here belongs to Scooter,' and he jabbed himself in the chest several times, still maintaining a grip on her arm.

His tone of voice changed. Only a moment before it had been menacing and surly. Now he stepped closer and peered down on Belle as though he were hungry and she was something to eat.

'Ain't you the tender piece of meat,' he sneered.

From the backseat came a fearful, 'Oh, dear . . .'

Belle tried to pull herself free. The man reached out with both hands and held her firm. He was being encouraged now by the teenagers, who were hanging out of their cars, as well as by all the help from inside the drive-in.

Then before Billie Rose's eyes, the man jerked Belle close and tried to kiss her.

'Stop it,' Billie Rose cried as she flung open the car door. 'Stop it this minute, do you hear?' And as she scrambled around the side of the car, she saw the man's dull-witted eyes and slack jaw.

Immediately he lost interest in Belle, as she knew he would. He turned in her direction. Two of the men from the drive-in became involved in this encounter and approached rapidly on her left.

'Get into the car, Belle, now,' she ordered, and then the man was upon her.

'Nigger, that's what you are, jest a dumb nigger drivin' around in that fancy car.'

As he talked he kept coming closer. Over the man's shoulder, she saw Belle's frightened face, and that was the last thing she saw clearly, for the other two men behind grabbed her arms while the man in front started striking her.

She heard Belle scream and saw her jump onto the back of the man named Scooter. Thus distracted, Billie Rose was given a few moments to absorb the pain. But then the two behind whirled her about, and to the background shouts of 'Nigger!' she took repeated blows to her face and head.

She never completely lost consciousness. She felt her knees buckling, was aware of the taste of blood in her mouth, and ultimately heard a siren in the distance.

'Billie Rose, are you – '

Somehow she ended up sitting on the curb, Belle hovering over her, blood streaming from her nose and several cuts over her eyes.

'Billie Rose . . .'

'I'm fine,' she lied as she looked up and saw two police officers.

She heard the man named Scooter protesting something,

heard several others chiming in to tell exactly what had happened.

'Here,' Belle said, and offered Billie Rose her handkerchief.

'Thanks,' Billie Rose muttered, and discovered that it hurt to talk.

'You all right?' the police officer asked.

'No, she isn't,' Belle said. 'Look at her. She is bleeding, and those men are the ones who – '

'What's your name?'

'Belle.'

'Belle what?'

Billie Rose tried to stand and failed. 'Leave the child alone. Just let us go home.'

'No,' Belle protested. 'Why did that man hit her? She had done nothing to him.'

The police officer smiled. 'Oh, but she had, little girl.'

'What?'

'She don't belong here.'

Belle lost patience. 'Why does everyone keep saying that? Why doesn't she belong here?'

''Cause she's colored.'

'Belle, please,' Billie Rose murmured as she tried again to stand and this time succeeded. 'I'm sorry, Officer,' she said, keeping her eyes down. White men didn't like for a colored person to look them square in the eye. 'Please, may we leave now?'

The police officer continued to write something in his book. 'Who do you work for?'

'Mr Malcolm Burgess.'

This seemed to make a difference with the police officer. 'Does Mr Burgess know what you're up to?'

Belle was there again, struggling for understanding. 'We weren't up to anything, Officer. Why do you keep implying that we were? All we wanted was a cherry Coke. Is that against the law?'

'For you, no. For her, yes.'

'I don't understand.'

'Look, little girl. We have laws here. I don't know where you've come from, but we got laws here, and those laws say that coloreds and whites don't mix.'

'Why?'

Billie Rose moved slowly toward the car. Surrounding them she saw a gallery of faces, some chewing hamburgers, others sipping drinks, still others just staring. All she wanted was to get out as fast as possible. 'Come on, Belle, please, let's go.'

She opened the car door, grateful for something to lean against. She looked back to see Belle still in conversation with the officer.

'But if she wants something to drink,' Belle persisted, 'where is she to go?'

'With her own kind.'

'And where would that be?'

'She knows. She also knows she was wrong to come here.'

Though Billie Rose ached to offer a rebuttal, she knew she dared not. The owner of the drive-in was leaning against the wall, grinning. Apparently no charges would be made.

'Get into the car, miss, I mean it. Now!' the police officer ordered.

'Well, if you ask me,' Belle said, still defiant, 'I think your rules stink. I think this place stinks, and I think you stink.'

'Belle, please,' Billie Rose advised, and gingerly eased behind the wheel of the car, catching sight of Fanny and Stacy in the backseat. 'I'm sorry,' she said to the rearview mirror, and hadn't the faintest idea what she was apologizing for.

Billie Rose saw the police officer lead Belle to the car door, open it, and all but push her inside. Then quickly he slammed the door as though feeling a need to contain her before she spilled out again with embarrassing questions.

Blessedly the keys were in the ignition. As Billie Rose turned the key, the officer's face appeared suspended beside her. 'I'll lead you home. I don't want Mr Burgess to hear any story but the truth. And I want to talk to him.'

Belle leaned over, undaunted. 'And he'll want to talk to you, too, and to him.' And she pointed at the man still leaning against the wall of his drive-in, surrounded now by admirers who obviously liked the way he'd handled things.

'Officer, I have to take these two girls home first.'

'Then give me their addresses. I'll lead the way.'

From the backseat came the information the officer wanted, first Fanny, then Stacy, in high, piping voices made thin by fear.

Belle shot them a withering glance.

'Thanks,' the officer said to the girls in back. 'And never mind. I know where the Burgesses live. Who doesn't?' He strode away from the car in a swaggering gait.

From the backseat came advice. 'You shouldn't have said what you said, Belle.'

'And just what did I say that was so wrong?'

Billie Rose concentrated on backing the car out of the drive-in, fully aware that there were offended parties all about. Two teenage boys in the car next to them shouted something and raised their hands, one finger pointing upward.

Stacy stared glumly out of the window. 'You really should have known better, Belle.'

'Why does everyone keep saying that?' Belle exploded.

'Haven't you ever been around coloreds before?' Fanny asked.

'No. Why?'

'Because if you had, you would have known that they don't go places that we go.'

'Why?' Belle begged.

'Because!' Fanny replied succinctly, and continued to look out of the window as though she'd explained everything.

Billie Rose backed out into the street and stopped until the police car pulled in front. She continued to dab at her face with Belle's bloodied handkerchief.

'Here, let me do that,' Belle offered. 'I'm so sorry,' she whispered. Up close Billie Rose saw tears in Belle's eyes and knew that the greatest pain was still ahead of her, the necessity to sit down with her and tell her about prejudice and make her understand that it was a very real part of this world, always had been, always would be, and as such it must be faced and accepted . . .

Malcolm Burgess stood on his driveway spraying the great banks of yellow-and-bronze chrysanthemums for late season pests. There was always something that seemed dedicated to destroying the beauty of the world.

He glanced at his watch. Belle should be home soon. They were later than usual.

He shivered in the late cool gray afternoon. Out of the corner of his eye he caught a flash of red coming toward the entranceway, a police car leading Billie Rose's car into the bottom of the drive, both moving slowly, as though –

Quickly he put down the spray can, wiped his hands on his work-shirt, and started a few steps toward the cars, alarm increasing. Accident? The car appeared to be all right.

He moved to the opposite side of the drive, ready to speak to Billie Rose. Belle? Had something happened to –

But there she was in the front seat beside Billie Rose.

Then he saw Billie Rose's face.

'Billie Rose? What happened?' he asked, bending low to the open window, walking alongside the car until Billie Rose brought it to a halt.

'I'm sorry, Mr Burgess,' she said, and he noticed fresh blood seeping down her chin.

'Is Belle – '

'She's fine.'

Belle leaned across the seat, and Malcolm had never seen her so angry. 'Mac, we have to talk. Don't listen to anything that idiot back there says. Promise?'

As the 'idiot' was approaching from his patrol car, Malcolm lifted a staying hand to Belle's anger and straightened up for the greeting.

'Good evening, Officer, I'm – '

'Mr Burgess, I know,' the man replied. 'And I'm Officer Cantrell. I'm afraid there's been – '

At that moment Malcolm heard Charlotte calling to him from the porch. Clearly she'd seen the police car. As she started down the steps Malcolm opened the car door for Billie Rose and was shocked at her appearance. Her clothes were torn and blood-streaked. She'd lost a shoe somewhere, and at first she appeared to be unsteady on her feet.

'Malcolm, what is – '

Charlotte reached the car seconds after her question. Seeing Billie Rose, she reached out. 'Lean against me, come on, we'll talk later. Let's get you to bed.'

'Belle, you run along with them.'

'No.'

This flat refusal came as a surprise. 'Belle, please, I think that – '

'No, Mac, I need to stay. I want to hear what Officer Cantrell has to say.'

Malcolm looked back at Officer Cantrell, who was standing feet apart, hands on hips.

'Officer Cantrell, would you – '

'Sure would, Mr Burgess. With pleasure. Seems like that young lady there needs some educating.'

'I don't understand.'

'They, that is to say your colored, drove into the Juke Box Drive-In just plain as day, like she belonged there. Naturally old Scooter took exception to it. Bad for business, you know. Well, the little miss there got out and started fighting with old Scooter – '

'I wasn't fighting with him, Mac,' Belle said. 'Why would I fight with him? He's as big as a truck. All I asked was why Billie Rose couldn't come into the drive-in for a cherry Coke with the rest of us.'

Officer Cantrell laughed, then continued with his explanation. 'Well, of course we weren't there when the ruckus started. We was sent for a few minutes later, but apparently old Scooter got mad at Miss Impudence here – '

'I wasn't being impudent, Mac. I just wanted to know.'

'– and so he just lays a hand on her shoulder, and your nigger got her dander up, come charging out of the car like a mad bull, leaps all over poor Scooter, and likes to claw his eyes out – and would have if it hadn't been for some friendly bystanders who drug her off and put her back in the car.'

Suddenly Belle exploded in anger. 'That's not true and you know it. You're lying. You're telling a lie.'

Malcolm grabbed her by the arm and turned her about. Forcibly he walked with her a few yards up toward the house.

'Belle, if you'll – '

'He's lying, Mac, and he knows it.'

'If you'll be patient – '

'No. They hurt Billie Rose and for no reason.'

'Belle, I'm begging you. Please stay right here. I know the man is lying, but for now all I want is to get rid of him. Then I promise you we will talk.'

As he bent over her, he could see the fury in her eyes. Obviously she did not take injustice lightly. Good for her. Still, one had to be careful.

He gave her a look, part plea, part command. She wasn't happy, but she turned away and started up to the house, took about five steps, then stopped, hands shoved into her sweater pockets.

Caught in the middle, Malcolm started back toward Officer Cantrell. 'Thank you, Officer, for seeing them safely home.'

'Oh, that wasn't what I was doing,' the policeman said, grinning. 'I think those two could get safely home from the moon. A pair of real hell raisers. I just didn't want you and your wife to think that your nigger had been roughed up for no reason. We don't have people like that in this town. Most folks around here like their niggers. Take real good care of them and make sure they don't go where they are liable to get hurt.'

'I know. I'm sorry. I had no idea.'

'Of course you didn't. And you might set that one down and tell her a thing or two. If you ask me, she's the one who got the nigger into trouble. If she'd been – '

'Yes, of course,' Malcolm said, and placed his hand on the man's shoulders, in order to turn him around and head him back toward his patrol car.

The officer extended his hand, Malcolm shook it, then watched as he backed his patrol car down the long curved driveway. Then he turned back to face Belle.

But she was gone. Good. That meant he had a few more minutes to conceive of a way to explain to her that in this world people with skin of one color go to certain places and people with skin of another color go to other places, and never, never can the two meet . . .

Belle stayed with Billie Rose in her apartment over the garage until the doctor had gone and Charlotte had brought up a tray fixed by Spoons. She would have stayed all night, except Billie Rose said that the Burgesses wanted to talk to her in the study at seven-thirty.

Belle slouched on Billie Rose's big maple rocker. 'I don't want to go.'

'But you're going,' Billie Rose said, sitting up on the edge of her bed, trying to eat and drink around the stitches in her lip.

'Why? They're just going to tell me – '

'You don't have one idea what they're going to tell you. Now you get on down there. Those two think the world of you, and you owe them at least the respect of listening.'

'Mac wouldn't even let me stay and talk to that policeman. You should have heard the lies he was telling, Billie Rose.'

'I've heard them all, child. I've heard them all and more besides.'

'It's not right.'

'No, but it is the way things are. Now come and tell me good night and get on down. Now!'

Reluctantly Belle dragged herself up out of the rocker and kissed Billie Rose on the forehead. 'I'm so sorry they hurt you.'

Billie Rose reached one hand up and touched Belle's face, then drew her close and hugged her.

'I'll take your tray down,' Belle offered.

'No. Don't you do it. I'll bring it down in the morning when I come.'

Surprised that her offer of help had been refused, Belle backed away from the bed. 'I don't understand,' she said quietly.

'I know you don't. That's why you must go down to the study now and talk to the Burgesses. Promise?'

'I promise.'

'Sleep tight.'

'You too.'

Belle closed the door behind her and started down the steps of the garage apartment. For a moment she seemed literally to be suspended between two worlds, the white world of privilege and ease down below and Billie Rose's world of uncertainty and pain up above . . .

Malcolm and Charlotte had been waiting in the study since dinner for Belle to appear. Malcolm had not insisted that she join them for dinner, well aware of her affection for Billie Rose and her reluctance to leave her.

'Shall I go and fetch her?' Charlotte asked, looking up from her knitting.

'No,' Malcolm said, relighting his pipe. 'She'll be along. Billie Rose will see to it.'

He broke off, having heard Belle's footstep.

'Hi . . .'

'How's Billie Rose?' Charlotte asked, putting her knitting aside.

'She says she hurts all over. But she ate a good dinner.'

'That's good,' Charlotte said. 'Come over by the fire. You must be chilled. Look – I have a sleeve and part of the back.' She held up the royal blue sweater she was making for Belle, who now went eagerly toward the fire.

Malcolm was tolerant of the small talk. It seemed a safe prelude to the larger, perhaps less harmless talk. He paced around the room, slowly making his way back toward the warmth of the fire. 'Did you know any colored people when you were living with the Shodas in California?'

'No.'

'Did you know any with the other family?'

'The Melvilles? No.'

'You'd seen them, of course.'

'Yes.'

'Where?'

'Some black people used to come to Harold's produce farm.'

Malcolm drew up a chair close to her and thought, What a macabre lesson to teach a child, the reasons for bigotry and prejudice.

'Belle, what I'm going to say, I'm not certain that even I understand. But bear with me, will you? For some reason, human beings, some human beings, need desperately to feel superior to other human beings.'

'Why?'

'Why? Because they feel insecure and in many cases unworthy. So if they can find a person less certain, less educated, less . . . fortunate or different in some way, then they pronounce themselves better than that person, and before you know it you have entire races being discriminated against.'

'All because someone needed to hate someone else to feel better?' Belle asked as though disbelieving that Malcolm could be that stupid.

Malcolm looked up for air, for guidance, for anything, and caught a glimpse of Charlotte's bemused expression. The knitting needles were flying fast, but he had the distinct impression that all her concentration was focused on his dilemma.

'What you must know,' Malcolm said, deciding to skip the flawed philosophies and move directly to specifics, 'is that here in this town feelings run high against coloreds.'

'Why?'

'Because as I said, we are a rural area, and people are by and large uneducated and they need – '

'Someone to hate, I know.' Belle sighed and turned about on the hassock.

Still he persisted. 'When Billie Rose drives you places, please make no stops at white establishments, or I'm afraid the same thing that happened today will happen again.'

'No, it won't,' Belle murmured with a peculiar fierceness. 'I should have fought harder.'

'Belle, no,' Malcolm said. 'Please listen, just go to your lessons, drop off your friends after school, and come home, I beg you. They won't hurt you if you make trouble. They'll hurt Billie Rose. Do you want that?'

'No, of course not.'

'Then promise. Don't ask Billie Rose to do anything that will cause her harm. Promise?'

'I still don't understand, Mac.'

'I know you don't, but please just obey the rules. For Billie Rose's sake. That's all I ask.'

'Will things ever be different?'

'We can hope and work toward that day.'

'How?'

'By trying to be a good influence on those who respect our opinions.'

'Like Fanny and Stacy?'

'Yes, and all your other friends as well, by letting them come to know and love Billie Rose as much as you do, and by abiding by the unwritten rules of the society in which you live.'

'But if everyone abides by them, how in the world will they ever change?'

Malcolm puffed on his pipe. It was dead, as were his theories on discrimination. He knew it and Belle knew it. No need to pretend, not with this one.

'It's your safety,' he said bluntly. 'Yours and Billie Rose's. That is my primary interest. We'll have to deal with justice later.'

He felt a little dishonest. Apparently Belle saw this in his face and gave him a smile of triumph.

'I'll be careful, Mac, for Billie Rose's sake. But I don't

have to like what I see, and I certainly don't have to accept it as law.'

Malcolm smiled down on her. 'No.'

'Anything else?'

'Subject closed.'

'May I spend the night with Billie Rose?'

Charlotte looked up. 'Do you think that's wise? Doesn't she need her sleep? Wouldn't you be tempted to talk and keep her awake?'

Belle thought on what Charlotte had said. 'I guess so. Then I'll take her her breakfast.'

'Good,' Charlotte said. 'Now stand up. Let's see if this is going to be big enough to suit you.'

As Belle stood, the phone rang. Malcolm picked up the receiver and recognized Carl's voice at the security gate.

'Sorry to bother you, Mr Burgess. There's an officer here, a Captain Stanford.'

'Captain? Army?'

'Yes, sir. He's come to see Belle.'

Malcolm glanced at the two by the fire, talking easily, laughing. 'Did he say what he wanted?' he asked, lowering his voice.

There was a moment's pause before Carl answered. 'No, sir. But I think – '

'Yes, of course. Send him up in about five minutes. Thanks, Carl.'

As he put down the receiver, Charlotte summoned his attention. 'Malcolm, Belle and I were wondering if we could drive into Tulsa. I was telling her about that very good fabric store. We have decided that this sweater will require a special royal blue wool skirt, and we just can't find really nice – '

'I'm afraid not, Charlotte,' Malcolm said as gently as possible. 'Rationing, remember? I'm afraid we can't get to Tulsa and back on three gallons of gas.'

'Could we save up? June Fletcher says they do that all the time.'

'We'll see.'

'Good. I'm sure we can.'

Charlotte gathered up her knitting. 'If you two will excuse me, I'm going to bed. It's been a long day. Coming, Belle?'

Malcolm answered for her. 'I'd like Belle to stay for a few minutes.' He ignored the puzzled look on Belle's face as he kissed Charlotte good night and watched her disappear up the stairs.

A few minutes later the front bell rang.

'I'll get it. You wait here,' Malcolm said. As he stepped into the hall, he drew open the door to find a very tall, gaunt officer with receding hair and sad-looking eyes. He was leaning heavily on one crutch. Malcolm could see beyond him the silhouette of a driver behind the wheel of an army staff car.

'Good evening, sir,' the officer said. 'I'm looking for Belle Shoda. I have this address.'

'She's here,' Malcolm said.

'Good. My name is Captain John Stanford. I have . . . news for her.'

Malcolm noticed that the officer clasped a small metal box under his left arm. He'd seen them before.

'I'm Malcolm Burgess,' he said now with sinking heart. 'Belle is staying with us.'

'I know. Harold told me all about it.' The officer smiled. 'In fact, I feel as if I know all of you.'

'Won't you come in?' Malcolm invited. 'And your driver, would he like to – '

'No, sir, thank you, sir. He prefers to wait outside. Always.'

'This way, then,' Malcolm said, and led the way back down the corridor toward the study, where even now he heard the silence of anticipation.

'Belle?' Malcolm called out in an attempt to get the next few minutes over with.

She was standing before the fire.

'This . . . officer, Captain John Stanford, has come to see you.'

'I would have known you any place – ' the captain began but could not finish. His voice broke, his one good leg seemed to buckle, and he would have fallen were it not for Malcolm, who grasped his shoulder and led him to a vacant chair.

Within the moment Belle was at his side. 'Are you ill?'

'No,' the captain said, 'no, it was just seeing you after everything Harold has told me.'

'How do you happen to know Harold?' Belle asked, her face reflecting the love she felt for him.

'I first met him at Camp Shelby,' Captain Stanford said. 'We were both attached to the Seventh Army and landed in Sicily.'

'How is he? Is he still in Sicily? Harold and I are going back to San Bernardino after all this is over, back to our farm. He said so. He promised. I have a dog there . . .'

'Lil.' Captain Stanford smiled.

'Yes.' Belle grinned. 'Harold has told you about Lil.'

All at once Captain Stanford looked up at Malcolm, a desperate unspoken plea for help, as though he knew better than anyone that to prolong the truth was to make it even more painful.

Malcolm could not ignore such a look, and though he hadn't the slightest idea what he was going to say, he spoke.

'Belle, I think that Captain Stanford has . . . news for you.'

'About Harold?' she asked, looking at him over her shoulder.

'Yes.'

'Belle,' Captain Stanford began, 'I want to tell you something about Harold Shoda that perhaps you don't know. He was the most courageous man I have ever known.'

Something about the past tense caught her ear.

'I told you,' Captain Stanford went on, 'that we went to Sicily together. We were later attached to the Thirty-sixth Infantry Division. When we invaded Italy we encountered fierce fighting at Salerno. Harold – '

He paused a moment, wiped his forehead, and renewed his grip on the small metal box.

'Harold distinguished himself at Salerno. Once, aware of

the imminent danger to the rest of the men, he jumped from his shelter with his bayonet in hand-to-hand combat, killing approximately four of the enemy. When he returned to his position he administered first aid to the wounded and directed their evacuation as another assault hit the line.'

Malcolm listened with a sense of increasing horror. He was torn between the captain's narration, which sounded stilted, almost memorized, and the expression on Belle's face. She looked vacant, as though she sensed what was coming.

'Then,' the captain went on, 'I was wounded' – he tapped his leg lightly – 'and in the chest as well. Command of the platoon depended on Harold. He led the men in a frontal attack through direct fire and knocked out three machine guns with grenades. Withdrawing under machine-gun fire and a mortar barrage, Harold reached a shell crater occupied by five of his men when an unexploded grenade struck his helmet and rolled toward his men. He dived for the grenade and smothered its blast with his body.'

Malcolm heard Belle make one sharp inhalation of air.

Slowly Captain Stanford resumed speaking, though now his voice was formal. 'By his swift, supremely heroic action, Sergeant Shoda saved five of his men at the cost of his own life and did much to clear the path for his company's victorious advance.'

He looked at Belle, who stared back at him with that awful vacancy and said nothing.

'I'm . . . so sorry to be the one who – '

All at once she stood and started toward the door. Captain Stanford glanced at Malcolm, another plea for help.

'Belle,' Malcolm called out softly, 'I don't believe that Captain Stanford is quite finished.'

At the door she looked back. 'What else?'

'These,' Captain Stanford said, and held up the small metal box like an offering or an apology. 'These have all been awarded to Harold Shoda. They are medals of valor.' Slowly he unlatched the lid of the box. 'To be precise,' he repeated, 'one National Defense Medal, Sicilian Campaign with Two

Stars, Italian Campaign with Three Stars, two Purple Hearts, a Bronze Star, a Silver Star, a Distinguished Service Cross, A Presidential Unit Citation, and the Congressional Medal of Honor.'

Malcolm bowed his head out of respect for the unimaginable heroism represented by such an array of honors. Harold Shoda scarcely seemed a candidate for military bravery: slight, thin, soft-spoken. Where on earth had he stored such an awesome display of courage? He looked up to see Belle's reaction. But still there was none.

'These are yours,' the captain said quietly, closed the box, and with a degree of effort reached inside his pocket to withdraw a letter. The envelope, once white, was stained with ominous smears.

'And this . . .' Captain Stanford smiled. 'Harold wrote you a long letter the evening before his last battle. He asked me specifically to hand deliver it, if I survived. Here it is.' Carefully he placed the letter atop the box of medals and now extended the whole package to Belle.

She stared at them for ever so long, and Malcolm suspected she was afraid to take them. But at last she made her way slowly back to where the captain sat. She stood before him for a few moments, then took the letter and the box. She leaned over and kissed him on the cheek. 'Please hurry and get well,' she whispered. Then she kissed Malcolm and left the room.

'I must be on my way,' Captain Stanford announced with sudden brusqueness. He struggled up out of the chair, and Malcolm resisted every effort to help him, knowing better.

'Where are you off to?' he asked cordially. 'I wish you'd stay for a while. Coffee, a drink – '

'No, thank you, sir. I'm on my way back to the base, then tomorrow I'm going home.'

'Good for you. Your family is there?'

'Yes. My parents and my wife. We have a son, three . . .'

They filled the air with the smallest of talk as they made their way back to the front door. There the captain stopped.

'Do you think – I mean – will she be all right? Harold told me all about her. It seems an incredible story.'

'She's an incredible young girl.'

Malcolm opened the door to find that a chilly rain had begun. Within the moment the driver was out of his car and standing on the porch, umbrella aloft.

'Good night,' Captain Stanford said politely.

Both soldiers started down the steps, the driver holding the umbrella as well as lending support to the captain.

Malcolm waited until the car had disappeared down the drive, then he shut the door but could not shut out what the captain had left in his house, a death message, Belle's 'other family' gone now, no more dreams of returning to California and the big white farmhouse where Harold and Kim Shoda had loved her.

He wished with all his heart that Billie Rose was up and functioning. She knew best how to handle Belle and could set her vision in a different direction.

At the top of the stairs he started toward Belle's room. What should he do? She should be given the chance to talk, to express anger or grief.

Outside her door, he heard the sound of weeping. He stood for a moment, head down. Dear God, what should he do? Had she read the letter? Were the tears a reaction to Harold's words? Or were they a reaction to the entire tragic day?

Overcome by the sound of grief, Malcolm shook his head slowly and walked away from the door.

Let her cry, he decided. There were certain days in the life of every human being when tears were necessary. For Belle this was one of those days . . .

November 29, 1943
Tulsa, Oklahoma

R. C. waited in the kitchen for the coffee to finish perking and looked out through the serving window.

'One piece of toast or two?' he called out the length of the dining room.

'One will do, thank you,' Martha called back, and never lifted her head from the newspaper.

R. C. knew she was worried about the war and when he would have to go, about how long they could stay in the abandoned mission before someone came to tear it down, and about how long they could live on what she managed to earn as day help to some of the ladies who used to drop off charity bundles. He bowed his head over the smoking toaster and felt useless. They had argued endlessly about his quitting school and going into the service. On his pay she could rent a small, comfortable apartment.

But she'd hear none of it, and it seemed to upset her every time he brought it up. Still, something was going to have to happen soon. The wrecking crew had stopped by last week and said their equipment was being repaired but they hoped to be back in business before Christmas, and then – what?

The toast was burning. Quickly he pulled it out and determined that he could scrape away the charcoal.

While trying to repair the burnt toast, he turned on the radio. Anything to cancel the confusion in his head.

'A kiss is still a kiss, a sigh is just a sigh . . .'

'Turn it up,' Martha called. 'That's a nice song.'

R. C. arranged the tray with two cups of coffee and three pieces of damaged toast. At the same time he tried his best to alter his black mood.

It was just – what was he supposed to do? Let her care for him for the rest of his life? He knew her motivation. Having lost Belle, she refused to let him venture too far away for fear she couldn't get him back.

Belle.

He froze over the tray. The torment and loss went with him everywhere.

'R. C.? What's the matter?'

'Nothing. Coming.'

He lifted the tray as the sad romantic song was coming to an end. Good. Now for something jazzy and upbeat.

'Ain't Misbehavin'.'

Perfect.

As he started across the large empty room, he kept his eye on Martha seated in that one patch of sun, bundled up in her heavy sweater.

'When is your first class?'

'Ten o'clock.'

'Don't miss the bus.'

'Have I ever?'

'And you're enjoying college?'

'No.'

She looked up from her coffee, surprised.

'I'm enjoying college,' he amended, 'but I'm not enjoying working a hardship on you. I can't tell you how much it hurts me to think of you on your knees scrubbing other people's houses, people who aren't good enough to – '

'Shhh.' Gently she reached up and touched his lips. He brought his diatribe to a halt, but it continued inside his head.

'Let's not go through it all again, R. C., please?' she asked. 'It serves no purpose.'

'Well, where will we go next month when this place is torn down?'

'God will provide.'

'Baloney.'

'Don't say that. You have no idea how often in my life one door has closed only for another one to open.'

'That's good luck, not God.'

She shook her head with conviction. 'No, but you'll understand one day. I promise you.'

He finished his coffee and changed the subject. 'Where are you working today?'

'Mrs Preston. Her car is coming at ten-thirty.'

'What do you do for Mrs Preston?'

She looked up and gave him a smile. 'You don't really want to know, now, do you?'

'Why not? You know everything I do.'

'Okay.' She laughed and held up her hands. 'Today I most likely will be polishing silver in the morning. The Prestons do a lot of holiday entertaining. Then in the afternoon I'll most likely clean the bathrooms.'

'I wish you wouldn't.'

'Why? Cleaning someone else's toilet is good for the soul.'

'That's nonsense.'

'Oh, my dearest, don't be so serious. Do you really think that getting down on one's hands and knees and sloshing cleanser around inside a porcelain bowl does permanent damage to anything that is truly important?'

He gazed back at her across the sun-dappled table and thought again, as he'd thought at least once every day of his life, how fortunate he was that fate had led him to her.

'Now what does that expression mean?' She laughed.

'It means how much I love you and how eager I am to repay you for all you have – '

'Any more coffee?'

'I'll get it.'

As he returned to the kitchen, he saw a shadow on the step outside the door and looked up to see Sam, the mailman.

Martha must have seen him as well, for she called to him even before he was in the kitchen. 'If those are Salvation Army bills, Sam, you know what to do with them. Just send them right on to Captain Meeks in Oklahoma City. They belong to him, not me.'

'You want coffee?' R. C. asked, and held up the pot.

'Sure. Why not?' Sam lowered his heavy pouch to the floor.

R. C. saw him rubbing the side of his neck and thought that Sam was too old for such a job. But then he probably was all the postal service could get, the younger men all gone off to fight in the war, all except himself.

'Here you go,' R. C. said, and handed him a mug.

Sam took his coffee to the table, sat next to Martha, and dropped several letters beside her cup.

'I told you, Sam,' Martha said. 'I don't want to see them if they are bills belonging to the army.'

'These ain't bills, Martha,' Sam said as he sank heavily onto the chair and placed his coffee mug on the table.

'Then what are they?' Martha asked suspiciously. 'I don't carry on a correspondence with a lot of people.'

'Well, let's see,' Sam said, taking a swig of coffee as he began to sort through Martha's mail. 'Here's a letter from somewheres in Texas.'

Martha sat up and tried to see the letter. 'Where in Texas?'

Sam laughed. 'Well for God's sake, why don't you open your own mail?'

He tossed the letter across the table, and R. C. caught a glimpse of a printed name in the upper left hand corner, a business letter from someone.

'It's from Hitchings,' she said, 'but I don't know the name.'

Sam looked around at the cavernous empty mission. 'Don't know how you two manage to stay here. This place gives me the creeps.'

R. C. laughed. 'It gives me the creeps sometimes, Sam. For the last several nights we've been hearing footsteps down here, and when we come down with a flashlight, there's no one here. Martha says it's the ghost of some poor man who passed through here.'

R. C. glanced back at Martha, who looked as if she'd just seen the ghost. 'Martha? What is – '

At last she put the letter down, looked directly at R. C., and announced with a curious tone that was part victory, part relief:

'My father died.'

Sam reacted normally. 'Gosh, I'm so sorry, Martha.'

'Don't be. He was a bastard, Sam. Now he's gone. It's over.' This last was spoken more to herself than anyone else, a private benediction on a very painful part of her life.

'And that's not all the good news,' she went on, lifting the letter. 'Remember what I said, R. C., about doors opening and closing? Well, seems I got that old farmhouse and some land in Hitchings, and according to this letter from the attorney of record, a Mr Denver, there's some good black Texas oil underneath the land. Oh, not much, mind you. But enough, I suspect, to get us what we want. Now what do you say to that, R. C.?'

His silence was based on many things. His navy scholarship was here at Tulsa University. He couldn't quit school. It was the only path that would lead him where he eventually wanted to go, a full professorship at a good university and a chance to share his passion for history.

'R. C.?' Martha prodded, clearly worried by his lack of response.

'I'm happy for you, Martha.' He smiled. 'You deserve it.'

'*We*. Shouldn't that be we?'

'What about school?'

'We got schools in Texas. Good ones. Ever heard of the University of Texas? SMU?'

'I don't have a scholarship there.'

'You don't need one now.'

'You don't know how much your oil royalties will be. What if they just barely put food on the table?'

'Then what about you?'

The obvious solution was there and waiting. 'I'll join up. With my salary – '

'No.'

'– I can send almost all my salary back to – '

'I said no.'

'Martha, I'm almost eighteen. I think I have a right to – '

'You have no right to go off and get yourself killed. No right at all.'

She was on her feet now, as angry as R. C. had ever seen her. Sam stood quickly, drained his coffee, and pushed away from the table. 'Congrats, Martha,' he said, walking away. 'Now maybe you two can get out of this creepy place.'

But if Martha even knew that Sam was present, she gave no indication of it. 'Now listen, R. C.,' she began, still holding the letter in her hand. 'This is what we've been waiting for. We didn't even know it, but this is it. Now I'll write to the navy and see if we can get your scholarship transferred to either University of Texas or SMU. You'll have to live on campus during the week. But you can come home on weekends.'

'Martha, you don't even know the condition of the house. What if – '

'We'll fix it up.'

'On what?'

'A loan if need be. Don't forget, people know me in Hitchings. It will be easier to manage almost everything.'

'Why don't you see how simple it would be for me to sign – '

'*No*! If you stay in school, you'll become a commissioned officer. The war might even be over by then – and I wouldn't lose you, too . . .'

This last was part plea, part cry of terror. The expenditure of emotion was too much, and she sat back down on her chair.

'I'm sorry, Martha.' He pulled a chair up beside her.

Belle was as present at their table as though she were literally seated opposite them. Martha would never let go of R. C. until they found Belle. He was her link, her witness to the fact that Belle existed, her faith that one day they would find her.

'Martha, it's going to be all right,' R. C. soothed, and offered her his handkerchief. 'I'll talk to the dean today and the naval commandant, see what I can find out. When do you want to leave?'

She took the handkerchief and mopped at her face. 'When is your semester over?'

'December eighteenth.'

'Then that's when we'll leave.'

She shook her head and blew her nose. 'Lord, I didn't expect this. Tell the truth, I'd forgotten about that old man.' She lowered her voice and studied the hem of the handkerchief. 'He *was* a bastard,' she said quietly, 'though I'm sure he had his reasons.'

R. C. sat beside her and let her talk. The sun was striking her directly in the face, highlighting wrinkles and lines he'd never noticed before. Still, to him she was beautiful, possibly the most beautiful woman he'd ever seen, and he would not cause her grief in any way if he could help it.

'Well then, I'd say we're headed for Texas.'

'Do you remember anything about it?'

At first he was taken off guard by her question, then he remembered. Texas had been his destination when he had lost Belle.

'Not much.'

'It's pretty, or it can be. I remember that Charlie and I used to – '

'Who's Charlie?'

She shook her head. 'A fella.'

'Yours?'

'I thought so once. Now . . .'

'What happened?'

'According to my pa, he went off to Amarillo and married another woman.'

'Did you like him?'

'We grew up together. We did everything together from about age four on. We used to ride out across Charlie's pa's spread until we could see the sunset from one end of the horizon to the other, point to point, that whole end of the world nothing but blazing red. Never seen anything like it before or since.'

R. C. watched as she stared at the table. Time was passing. He'd miss his bus. She should get ready for Mrs Preston's car when it came for her.

He bent over and kissed her on the forehead. She took his hands. 'We're going to be all right, R. C. I promise.'

'Of course we are. Besides, I want to see those sunsets.'

'And you will. Hurry home. We'll do something special tonight to celebrate.'

He thought she was watching him across the dining room, and as he reached the door he looked back and waved.

But she wasn't watching him. Instead her vision seemed fixed on the surface of the table, where clearly she was seeing the old house in Hitchings, seeing a sunset and a man named Charlie . . .

June 6, 1944
South Coast of England
Operation Overlord
D-Day

Though he had served with these men in North Africa, Sicily, and Italy, only now did First Sergeant Charlie Groveton realize that he scarcely knew any of them. Only their names. He'd made a point of knowing little else.

'Move it,' he shouted as his company filed past him onto the troop carrier. 'Rain's over, now the fun begins. Let's go! Let's go!'

As man after man in full battle gear clamored aboard the ship, Charlie tried to see if he could read in their eyes any apprehension of what was ahead for them.

'You think you're gonna have a chance to use that, soldier?' he joked with the kid from Kentucky, whose gold-tipped Jew's harp was still clenched between his lips where he had been entertaining the men on the dock before the midnight departure.

'Just never know, Sarge.'

I know, Charlie thought, and stepped back as the boarding continued three abreast now.

Good men, all of them, hundreds of thousands of good men, on their way to do – what? What was it Eisenhower had said – '. . . the free men of the world, marching together to victory, a struggle to preserve our civilization and to set free a suffering humanity.'

Charlie grimaced. Did they have to do all that?

'Keep that gun wrapped!' he shouted as he saw the plastic covering of a rifle flap free in the still damp early morning darkness.

Daylight in several hours. Behind he could see the outline of Torquay. In good times it probably was a sun-drenched seaside resort. But for the last several days it had been a gigantic and sodden makeshift army camp for over a hundred thousand American soldiers.

'Come on, soldier, step lively. Can't keep Hitler waiting. Let's move it!'

All along the dock Charlie watched his men scramble aboard the troop carriers, and he was suddenly overcome with the realization that this same scene was being carried out in every seaport in southern England. A quick glance at his watch told him that the airborne troops were already on their way, probably over the English Channel by now.

'All men aboard, Sergeant,' a soldier called out.

Charlie looked up and recognized Corporal Matt Horner. 'Okay, Horner, tell the ship's captain we're ready to get under way.'

Charlie saw an officer on the dock give orders to remove the gangway. Then other orders were being shouted, mooring lines were being cast off, whistles were sounding, and the troop carriers were slipping away from the docks.

Charlie knew that at long last it was going to happen. In just a few hours one-hundred-fifty-thousand men in five-thousand ships would assault the fortified beaches of Normandy. Briefly he entertained a pleasant thought. He imagined a sleepy German sergeant standing his watch in his pillbox on the coast of France, looking out across the Channel through the morning fog and seeing this armada coming steadily toward him.

Charlie grinned, looked around for someone to share his thoughts with, and saw Matt Horner. He was alone, always alone, come to think of it. All the other men had always paired off or joined in safe groups of three and four for card games and beer sessions.

But Charlie had never seen Horner with anybody. He kept strictly to himself. And he was a damn good soldier, though no green twig like most of the others.

'Horner?'

As he heard his name being called, the man looked about.

'Yes, Sarge,' he said.

'Did you ever think we'd pull it off?' Charlie asked, feeling a mysterious need to get to know at least one of his men before they landed on Omaha beach.

'Yes,' Horner replied. 'Just a matter of waiting.'

'We couldn't have waited forever.'

'Didn't have to.'

'No.'

Silence. The man rationed his words as though they were gold coins.

'Where are you from, Horner?'

'Texas.'

'Whereabouts?'

'El Paso.'

'Good country?'

'Yeah.'

'I'm from Texas, too.'

No reply, not that one was called for.

They were just beginning to make their way out into the Channel now. The wind whipped up the water, and in the early morning darkness he saw whitecaps dancing. Behind them the lights of Torquay glittered.

'You married?' he asked Horner.

'Yeah.'

Charlie looked out across the Channel toward France. 'What do you do in El Paso, Horner?'

'My dad owns a tire shop. I work for him.'

Another silence, thicker than the fog on the Channel. Somewhere near the front he heard the Kentucky boy's harp. Sounded like a jig, but no one was dancing. No room.

'Is it a good life?' Charlie asked.

'Depends.'

'On what?'

'Why are you asking me all these questions, Sarge?'

Embarrassed, Charlie laughed and shook his head. 'I guess I thought that talkin' was better than just staring out at the whitecaps. I didn't mean any offense.' His embarrassment increased, and he started to move away. Maybe getting to know at least one of his men was not such a good idea.

'Wait, Sarge,' Horner called after him. 'Come on back. Talking is a good idea, but if a talk is gonna go anyplace, both parties better know about it. Otherwise it sounds a lot like an interrogation. Hell, I thought I'd done somethin' wrong.'

Charlie looked back and found him grinning. 'All right,' he agreed, and made his way over to the railing despite the slight pitching of the craft as it began to encounter Channel currents.

For several moments both men stood railside. 'Shall I start,' Horner asked, 'or do you want to take it again?'

Charlie laughed. 'You take it,' he said. 'I've done about all the damage I can do.'

There was a pause. 'All right,' Horner began, clearly uncomfortable. 'What about you? You married? You got a girl?'

'No. I had one, but she got away.'

Charlie fished into his inside pocket and produced the photo of their high school graduation. It was the only picture he had of Martha.

'She's something,' Matt Horner said approvingly. 'What's her name?'

Charlie hesitated. 'Martha was her name,' he said to the black water rushing by. 'She was . . . special. We grew up together, and I thought . . . I don't know . . . something happened. One day she was gone.'

'Did you ever try to find her?'

'No. I figured she knew where she was. Now sometimes I wish I had.'

'It's not too late. After the war – '

'We'll see. Tell me about life in El Paso,' Charlie suggested, wanting to move away from the discomfort of the present subject.

'What do you want to know? It's hot and dusty, but I love it better than any place on earth.'

'You going back to it?'

'If we get out of this.'

'We will.'

Charlie listened and marveled as Matt Horner relaxed and began talking about his life in El Paso, about his close relationship with his dad and his wife, named Sally. Why in the name of God had he waited until now to get to know this man? To get to know any of them – all of them, for that matter? Then he remembered North Africa, his first combat experience, and the eight friends he had lost. He had vowed never again to know his men. Never until now. Matt Horner had always looked as though he could use a friend, and Charlie realized that he needed one as well.

Sometime during the night the two men moved away from the ship's railing and settled with their packs near a cargo hatch, where they continued to talk, humorously, intimately, and always compulsively.

They were still talking four hours later when dawn broke over the Channel, when the beaches of France became more than shadowy outlines. The artillery barrage had started now, harmless since they were still out of range. But Omaha beach was straight ahead, and the range was shrinking.

All at once a shell exploded about fifty feet out in the water. Charlie ducked, as did Horner.

'To be continued later.' Matt smiled. 'I guess this is when we start killin' Germans again.'

'Good luck,' Charlie said, and extended his hand. Matt

took it, and it was with a sense of accomplishment that Charlie realized he had done what he had set out to do. He knew one of his men now, knew most everything about him, his losses, his successes, his fears, his triumphs.

On either side now he saw men climbing down the cargo nets and into the landing crafts, saw the barrage of tracer bullets and artillery shells exploding on the beach.

'Last on, first off,' Matt said. 'Keep your head down, Sarge. After we finish here, you come to El Paso. I'll treat you to the best enchiladas you ever tasted.'

'It's a deal,' Charlie said, and gave Matt a thumbs-up. He looked back at his men, saw them return his gaze, their eyes wide, now fully aware of what was ahead of them. All at once in the moment before they started down the net webbing, and without any warning, he saw right through to an awful truth, that they weren't here for civilization, free men marching to victory.

They were scared men, who had interrupted their lives because their country had asked them, and who now were faced with one goal, to take that stretch of sand, and, if still alive, take the cliffs behind and, if still alive, take the Germans firing relentlessly down on them from those concrete bunkers.

'Over we go,' someone shouted, and in the last second Charlie realized he was holding up the parade. He looked down into the landing craft and saw Matt Horner grinning up at him. Then he too went over the side, scrambled down the cargo net, and dropped into the craft, which started forward immediately through the turbulent waters and toward the hostile shore.

He felt a bump, felt the rough scrape of sand beneath the landing craft. Then the bow fell open like a gigantic beast opening its mouth to disgorge something poisonous from its system. He stumbled into the water, seeing only tracer bullets and smoke, hearing only screams and shellfire.

Someone behind shouted, 'Keep down!'

Keep down, where? Charlie thought. Even the center

of the earth would not be safe from this unending, ever-increasing bombardment.

Then he was aware of water lapping at his leggings, and quickly he hoisted his gun over his head, realizing belatedly that he'd not removed the plastic wrap.

As his own men pushed past him, he struggled with the plastic covering. 'Damn,' he cursed, unable to slip the gun free, though he still was moving forward, over sand now, past casualties already fallen, some still moving, some not.

There, the gun was free at last, and as he lifted it for action a large artillery shell exploded not twenty feet in front of him. It knocked him down and set his ears to ringing, but a quick inspection assured him nothing more was wrong as he struggled up, weighted by battle gear and fear. He pushed forward again, trying not to stumble over the fallen soldiers.

He glanced in both directions and saw the beach swarming with men, tanks, and amphibious supply carriers. The beachhead was expanding.

Then he heard an ominous whistling, faint through the din at first, then growing louder, then –

'Get down, Sarge,' someone yelled.

The shell exploded directly in front of him and lifted him up into the air, then hurled him back onto a piece of beach already strewn with bodies.

For a moment he blessedly lost consciousness. But the world called him back as though to show him how really despicable it could be, and it was in the first few moments of consciousness that he discovered there was something wrong with his left side. And his left leg was –

He looked up at the sky, thinking there was a good direction for the last minute of life. But he discovered he also had time to look to his left, where he saw the familiar face of Matt Horner, eyes closed, skull opened, face covered with blood.

Charlie tried to speak but couldn't, and as the pain crept upward, he closed his eyes, sent his right hand crawling into the sand for something of substance to cling to, and felt a small metal object. He opened his eyes and in his last moment of consciousness saw a gold-tipped Jew's harp and wondered where the boy was who had played it.

'Matt?'

There was no answer, and Charlie lacked the strength to call again. All that preparation, all those plans, all the hope, for this? Why had they come?

He couldn't remember . . .

July 4, 1944
Hitchings, Texas

After four months of the most backbreaking work they had ever done, Martha and R. C. stood in the middle of the road and looked up at the farmhouse, shining white with dark green trim, and at the flower beds filled with zinnias and marigolds flanking the front steps.

'A miracle,' Martha murmured.

'I have blisters on my hands, knees, and feet,' R. C. muttered, 'and there's nothing miraculous about them.'

Martha took his arm. 'You know what I mean.'

For several moments they stood and admired their handiwork and let the heat dance in shimmering waves about them.

'Remember what it looked like when we first saw it?' Martha asked, wiping perspiration from her forehead.

R. C. chuckled. 'Remember? I'll never forget.'

Nor would she. The farmhouse she'd grown up in had been on the verge of falling down, and between them they'd had seventy-six dollars and twenty-four cents.

Then the miracles had started, those little right things that come in a chain when one is working in harmony with oneself and others.

Mr Denver, the lawyer who had written her the initial letter concerning her father's death, had informed her that he would have to collect fifteen hundred dollars for legal fees and burial expenses for Mr Drusso. While Martha and R. C. were reeling from that, the very nice Mr Denver told them not to worry because Mr Drusso had left a ten-thousand-dollar insurance policy. He would take the expenses out of that, then pass along to them eight thousand five hundred if that was all right.

'What are you smiling at?' R. C. asked.

'I was remembering the day old Denver told us we had eight thousand five hundred dollars coming.'

R. C. laughed. 'I wish you could have seen your face.'

'I wish you could have seen yours.'

They walked across the road and looked back at the house. 'I don't think it's ever looked better,' Martha mused. She spied the comfortable rocking chairs they had bought to go on the highly varnished front porch. 'Come on, those two chairs are just waiting for us.'

A few moments later they were rocking in the shade. 'I can't thank you enough for your help, R. C.'

'It's my home, too,' he said. 'You know what I hated most about leaving Tulsa?'

'What?'

'When I was a kid I used to think that one day Belle would come back to the mission and find us.'

The name, so unexpectedly mentioned, took Martha by surprise. It always saddened her to have her suspicions confirmed. R. C. would never know peace until Belle returned or was found or accounted for in some fashion. To the best of her knowledge, he had made no close friends in Tulsa, male or female. He kept to himself, attended classes, came home, studied, and helped her.

Yet he was a vital young man who –

'How are we going to celebrate, Martha?' he asked, interrupting her thoughts.

'Go out to the garden and dig me some new spuds and pick some peas, and I'll fry us up a chicken and make some cornbread.'

'And slice tomatoes.'

'And ice-cold lemonade.'

They both laughed. 'Who said we aren't having a celebration?'

Martha watched him the length of the porch until he disappeared around the side of the house toward the vegetable garden in the back. She lifted her face to the hot dry Texas wind.

Belle. How strange to be held captive by the memory of a three-year-old. Yet they both were. Neither she nor R. C. would ever be able to fully complete their lives as long as Belle was missing.

She would be fourteen now, almost fifteen. Was she alive? Was she happy? Was she loved? Was she lonely? Did she sense an emptiness as acute as theirs?

A blowing tumbleweed caught her eye as it skittered down the dirt road. Then it was gone. She looked at the flowers on either side of the front steps. They could use a watering. Later. For now she had a chicken to fry, cornbread to make, and a life to live. The first two were easy.

It was the third that sometimes stopped her dead in her tracks . . .

August 15, 1945
Fort Smith, Arkansas

Belle kept her eye on the soldier all afternoon. She'd never seen anyone quite so handsome. Now he sat on the side of her pool, dangling his legs, watching the Hillcoat sophomores and his fellow officers play water volleyball.

Did she dare to speak to him? Why not? She was the hostess.

She looked about at the pink-and-white umbrellas dotting the Burgesses' lawn, Billie Rose presiding over the barbecue where hot dogs and hamburgers were beginning to fill the air with a delicious aroma. Stacy had stacked the phonograph high with Johnny Desmond records. 'Long Ago and Far Away' was playing now.

Across the pool in the shade of the patio she saw Charlotte chatting with Miss Hepplewhite. Miss Hutsell was there, too, but saying very little. And walking out across the lawn toward the roses were Mac and Dr Priestly. They had been endlessly discussing FDR's death and 'that man from Missouri.'

Entertaining the young officers from the base was Hill-coat's belated contribution to the war effort. Now with the war almost over, Belle shuddered to think that these pleasant afternoons were coming to an end. This was the third swimming party they had held at her house this summer. But it was the first time she'd ever noticed that particular soldier.

At last she slipped quietly into the pool, took a deep breath, gave the volleyball players a wide berth, and swam underwater until she saw his legs by the side of the pool. She considered pulling on his toes but decided that would be too forward, so instead she surfaced, quickly wiped the water out of her eyes, and asked, 'Why don't you come on in? The water is great.'

'I'm sure it is' – he smiled – 'but I'm afraid I don't swim.'

Don't swim? Wasn't everybody born knowing how to swim? 'My name is Belle.'

'I know. My name is Brad. Brad Compton.'

'Where are you from?'

'California.'

She giggled, slipped underwater, and reappeared on his other side. 'A boy from California who doesn't know how to swim?'

'I know. It's a terrible lack.'

'It isn't at all. I could teach you.'

'I'm afraid not. Others have tried.'

'Not me.'

'All right. When do we start?'

'Where in California are you from?'

'Los Angeles. Beverly Hills.'

For a moment she could think of nothing further to say. On the far side of the pool Stacy laughed, and the three soldiers surrounding her laughed with her. It was so easy for some people.

'I like your parents very much.' Brad smiled down on her with the most dazzling smile she'd ever seen.

'They're not my parents,' she said matter-of-factly, and heard a slow, mournful rendition of 'I'll Be Seeing You' on the phonograph.

'I . . . beg your pardon?' Brad said, and braced himself on either side in an attempt to look more closely at her face.

'I said they were not my parents. I just live with them.' She looked out over the pink umbrellas, the high blue sky, the turquoise water, the enormous terra-cotta pots filled with pink geraniums. 'It's nice here,' she concluded, and really wished the subject of families and parents hadn't come up, at least not so soon.

'Who are you?'

'I don't know,' she said blithely. 'I used to live in California, too,' she said, and pulled herself up and down in the water, enjoying the sensation of shifting pressure.

'Where?'

'San Bernardino.'

'It's pretty there. Good farmland.'

'Oh, yes, and Harold had the best.'

'Your father?'

'No, Harold and Kim Shoda took care of me for a while, but – ' Again she broke off, amazed at how fresh and painful those memories still were in her heart. She ducked under the water for a respite from his questions. Suddenly he was in the pool beside her, holding on to the edge.

'Hey, be careful. I thought you didn't know how to – '

'I don't.'

'It's deep here.'

'I know.'

For a minute they bobbed side by side.

'Where are these people now?' he asked, holding on to the side while letting his body float out behind.

Belle did the same. 'You're in the right position for swimming. Now kick, like this – ' And she demonstrated the flutter kick and hoped he'd change the subject.

But he didn't. 'Why did you leave San – '

'Harold and Kim Shoda are Japanese,' she said, hoping she didn't sound too impatient. 'They were moved to the internment camp outside of town, and I came with them.'

It was clear to see by the puzzled expression on his face that very little she was saying made any sense to him. Yet somehow she knew he wouldn't give up until he understood.

'Kim died of pneumonia,' she said to the side of the pool. 'Harold joined the army and was killed in Italy. I have a box of his medals. Would you like to see them?'

'Yes. Very much.'

'I'll show them to you sometime. Now as for the rest of it, the army said I couldn't stay with them at the camp, so they took me to the Baptist Orphanage, and the Burgesses took me out of the orphanage and here I am.'

She gave a broad smile, struck a stupid pose, and really hoped that that would be the end of that.

But it wasn't. 'And you don't know – '

'Anything,' she said airily, 'about anything.'

He seemed to want to ask a million questions but couldn't think of the words for even one of them. Instead he gazed at her for several long moments with a combination of interest, which she loved, and pity, which she hated.

'You two hungry?'

It was Billie Rose, glaring down at them from pool's edge, her interest in Brad pointed and embarrassing.

'And your name is . . . ?'

'Brad Compton.'

'Well, you'd better mingle, Brad Compton,' Billie Rose said in a mild scolding. 'I've heard all these young ladies comment on how much you look like a movie star.'

Brad laughed and blushed and said nothing. Belle shot Billie Rose a withering look that plainly said, *'Leave us alone.'*

'Come on, hot dogs are ready,' she commanded, ignoring the look.

Then, thank God, Charlotte called. 'Billie Rose, I think we'll need more frankfurters.'

Belle grinned. 'See you around,' she said in a singsong voice.

They both watched as Billie Rose stamped off, promising first that she'd be right back.

'She seems nice,' Brad said.

'She's a dictator,' Belle said. 'Some of my friends call her Miss Hitler.'

Now it was his turn to look away. Concerned, she moved closer. Had she said something wrong? 'Brad?'

He looked back. 'My father called three days ago. He had received word that my aunt and uncle were killed in a concentration camp in Poland. My uncle was American, my aunt Polish. They were living in Warsaw when the war broke out and thought they would be safe.' He paused. 'My father was crying. I've never heard him cry before.' As he talked he brushed his hand lightly back and forth across the water as though deriving comfort from the sensation.

Belle felt sorry for him. Here she'd been rambling on about herself, which was nothing compared to what he had just told her.

'Does your father live in Los Angeles?' she asked.

'Yes, he works in the film industry.'

Her interest vaulted. 'Is he a movie actor?'

Brad laughed. 'No, he directs some, produces some.'

'Do you know any movie stars?'

He looked self-conscious.

'Who? Oh, please, tell me.'

'I thought you were going to teach me how to swim.'

'We've got time for that. We have all the time in the world.'

'We have to be back on base by eleven-thirty.'

'That's a long time. What do you do in the army?'

'I'm in the Signal Corps.'

'What does that mean?'

'I string lines for telephones, for all communications.'

'Can you come back to my house tomorrow?'

'I . . . don't know.'

'Can you find out?'

'I'll try.'

'Good. Now this is the way you swim. Hold on to the side, kick in steady, strong strokes, and move your arms like – this.'

As Belle demonstrated, she had the strangest feeling that he wasn't paying the slightest attention to what she was saying. 'Brad?'

'I'm doing it. Look!'

'All right, turn over and let's try floating. You have to know how to float if you're going to swim.'

'What do I do?'

'Turn on your back. I'll hold your head and just let the rest relax. Go ahead. Close your eyes and play like you're floating on white clouds.'

She loved touching his head. His hair felt like silk.

'How am I doing?' He grinned up at her.

'Just fine. Relax. I'm here. I won't let anything happen.'

On his chest were tiny black hairs, tightly curled. His hands, floating at his side, were white with graceful fingers. He was not too tall, not too short, not too heavy, not too thin. He was – perfect.

She looked up to see Charlotte smiling at her from beneath the umbrella. Standing close beside her was Billie Rose, scowling. As for what the rest of the party was doing, she really didn't care. She concentrated with all her might on Brad's face, studying it from all angles in the event he wouldn't be able to come back tomorrow . . .

Brad Compton had never seen anyone quite like her. Not that he wasn't accustomed to being around pretty girls. His father's pool in Beverly Hills was generally filled with ambitious starlets and scheming actresses who simply wanted to be near the great Cy Compton.

But this girl was different, with a natural beauty that alternately took your breath away, then strangely calmed you.

'You're doing fine,' she soothed, her voice low.

Suddenly a brightly colored beach ball landed in the middle of Brad's chest, and he struggled with the water, went under briefly, and came up blowing.

'Sorry, Compton,' one of the soldiers called from poolside. 'Didn't mean to –'

Belle tossed it back, then looked at Brad. 'Are you all right?'

'I'm really afraid of water.' He laughed and shook his head. 'When I was a kid, I almost drowned in my parents' pool, would have if my mother hadn't dragged me out.'

'How awful. Does she like you being in the army? Your mother, I mean?'

'She's dead.'

'I'm sorry.'

'When I was eight. Cancer.'

For a moment they stood in the center of the pool at the shallow end and let the water lap against them.

'You think you can come back tomorrow?'

'I don't know. I'll try.'

'I could teach you then, I'm sure. For now there are too many people around.'

'Belle. That's a pretty name.'

She laughed. 'I'm branded. Look – ' And she turned her head to one side, pushed back her hair, and pointed to the small birthmark in the shape of a bell.

He was fascinated by it. 'May I touch it?'

He lifted a finger and ran it gently over the smooth flesh of her throat. Then he cupped his hand about her neck and drew her close. She looked startled but did not pull away.

'Belle,' he whispered, and for an indefinite period of time, the rest of the world, and everyone in it, fell away. He was transfixed by her nearness, her beauty, and in the dream that this moment would never end.

'Hey, listen everybody, listen!' The excited voice came from poolside, from Bill Frazier, a guy Brad had gone through officer training with at UCLA. In his hand he held a portable radio that at the moment was giving off nothing but static. Still, the tone of his voice seemed to have gained everyone's attention.

The mood was broken, and Brad felt curiously shaken. Belle too seemed subdued as they made their way to the side of the pool and hoisted themselves up onto the edge.

'There it is, listen,' Bill commanded again, and as the static faded, Brad heard the voice of a news commentator.

'And so, after the devastation of Hiroshima and Nagasaki, the Japanese have surrendered unconditionally – '

There was more, but it was drowned out in the cheers and whistles of everyone at poolside.

'I guess we showed them. Dirty Japs – '

'With one bomb we blasted them right back where they belong – to the Stone Age.'

As his fellow officers exulted in the victory, Brad glanced across at Belle to see her reaction.

She was sitting poolside, dangling her feet in the water, a look of sadness on her face.

'Belle,' he murmured, and reached for her hand. 'You said you would show me Harold's medals. Would you do that now? Please?'

He stood and extended his hand to her, and she took it. Everyone was laughing, dancing, and cheering, but Brad saw one face of concern focused on Belle.

'I'm so sorry,' Mr Burgess said as he had hurried to her side. 'They mean nothing. They don't realize.'

'I know. May I take Brad upstairs? I would like to show him Harold's medals.'

'Of course.'

'Mac, this is Brad Compton.'

Brad extended his hand for the second time. They'd met

when the officers had arrived. Behind them now some of the soldiers and girls were doing a wild samba dance around the pool. The radio commentator was droning on, but no one was listening.

'Run along,' Mr Burgess said. 'I'll cover your backs from Billie Rose.'

Belle reached for Brad's hand, and he marveled at how small it felt inside his own. At the patio door they slipped on beach robes over their wet suits. Then there was her hand again, and he took it, fully aware that he would follow her anyplace . . .

She had shown him Harold's medals. She had shown him her room. She had shown him Mac's study. She had introduced him to Spoons in the kitchen and Spoons, in turn, had invited them to sit down at the kitchen table with her and share a turkey sandwich.

Then there had come an awful fifteen-minute separation while she had run back up to her room to put on a pale blue sundress, brush up her long blond hair into a ponytail, and secure it with a pale blue satin ribbon. The other girls were changing as well and were giggling all around her. But she paid no attention to them, not even when Stacy teased her about 'her new boyfriend.'

Belle didn't know anything about boyfriends and didn't really care. She just knew that when she was with Brad she felt better, happier, more excited, more – everything.

She hurried back down to the patio, where he'd already dressed.

Johnny Desmond was on the phonograph again. 'Long ago and far away . . .'

'Would you like to dance?' he asked.

She felt his arm go around her waist.

Other officers were drifting out now. Billie Rose had strung paper lanterns about the pool. The colors reflected off the water. The night was warm, but there was a pleasant breeze. It all was going too fast. It would be over. And then what would she do?

'Did you find out if you can come back tomorrow?'

'No, but I'll be back.'

'When?'

'As soon as I can get here.'

'I'll wait for you.'

He tightened his hold on her.

Every sensation was good, the feel of his body next to hers as they danced, everything was perfect, except that she knew he would be leaving soon to return to the base. Against such a loss she opened her eyes and looked up at him.

He was looking down on her with a curious sense of relief as though she were the answer to all the questions of his life . . .

Billie Rose kept grumbling, but Malcolm wasn't too worried. He'd had personnel checks made on all the young officers before he'd invited them to his home, wise enough to know that an attraction like this might occur, not just with Belle and young Compton, but with any of the young ladies as well, all of whom were daughters of his friends.

'She hasn't danced with anyone but him all night,' Billie Rose complained, hovering over Malcolm's shoulder where he sat at the table.

Charlotte was still occupied with Miss Hepplewhite and Miss Hutsell, though she seemed to be enjoying their non-stop conversation, which as far as he could tell consisted of everything from quilting techniques to the morality of using the new atomic bomb on the Japanese people.

Of course the latter was enough to give any sane person pause. He'd read the early statistics. Seventy-one thousand dead or missing, sixty-eight thousand injured.

For a moment the lovely setting blurred into one of unimaginable horror. He would have to address the issue in an editorial soon. Sides must be taken in something so devastating. The defenders of the bomb claimed an equal number of American lives saved by dropping the bomb and shortening the war. Perhaps these very young men had been spared by the sacrificial slaughter of seventy-one thousand others.

For several minutes he pondered the dilemma, and only a shift in tempo coming from the phonograph brought him back to the safe and secure setting of his lawn and terrace. Sinatra was crooning 'Night and Day,' a mellow and very danceable tune. He looked longingly toward Charlotte. How he would love to show these young bucks what a real lady looked like dancing. But now, at least, it was out of the question, and as a substitute for that pleasure he focused on Belle and young Brad Compton, keeping to themselves on the far side of the pool.

'See? There they go again, drifting away,' Billie Rose complained. 'Now if you want my opinion, you'd best take that young man aside and tell him that he better keep to this side of the pool in the light, or else.'

Malcolm finished his Scotch. 'We can see them plainly from here, Billie Rose,' he soothed.

'But we can't hear what they're saying.'

Malcolm laughed. 'She's growing up,' he reminded her, reminding himself as well, coming to face the awful truth of parenting, that one way or another, you ultimately lose them.

'Well, I think I'm just gonna march over there myself and – '

'I wouldn't if I were you,' Malcolm advised kindly. 'They're just talking. He's a nice young man. I assure you everything will be all right.'

At last, partially reassured that the young lieutenant was not going to kidnap Belle, Billie Rose headed back into the house.

Malcolm eyed his empty Scotch glass and contemplated going for a refill, but he changed his mind. Later he'd enjoy a nightcap with Charlotte. She always loved discussing the fine points of all her parties.

So for now he contented himself with sitting back, listening to Sinatra croon, and watching the pretty young girls with their handsome young officers. The night sky beyond the colored lanterns was ablaze with stars. A half-moon hung in precisely the right place. The honeysuckle and night-blooming jasmine were doing their parts in perfuming the air.

The war was over. Time to begin again . . .

Part Three

September 2, 1945
Hitchings, Texas

R. C. had always dreaded a separation of any length from Martha. Now with the war over, hopefully he could concentrate on his studies. The navy had transferred his full scholarship to SMU, and ultimately he would have to put in two years of service, but for now he would like to get his first degree.

To that end he placed his suitcases in the trunk of the Ford that Martha had given him. Once her father's, it had seen better days, but at least it would get to Dallas and back every weekend. That would leave Martha with the old pickup of ancient vintage and unknown origin, which started when it wanted to and got you there when it suited itself.

Now R. C. closed the trunk, looked through the back window at his boxes of books, his favorite desk lamp, and an assortment of his favorite knickknacks. On top he saw the gold-framed sketch of Belle. He had done a recent one for Martha, a projection of what Belle might look like at fifteen.

He stared at it through the window and fought off the persistent feeling of loss.

'Here we go.'

At the sound of Martha's voice, R. C. saw her just coming down the steps, a huge picnic basket in hand.

'I'm going to miss you.'

Curious how he just slipped that in. Briefly it took her off guard.

'Now, in here, you've got meat loaf sandwiches for the road. No need to stop and pay high restaurant prices.'

He took the hamper and placed it carefully on the front seat beside him. He had known the moment would be difficult but had no idea how difficult. 'I don't really want to go back, Martha. Isn't it funny? It's what I thought I wanted most in the world. Now I don't want to go.'

'Of course you do. It's what you've wanted all your life. You have a fine mind. How many people have told you that, and teaching is the most honorable profession in the world because you are in charge of tomorrow. I do love you, R. C.'

Perhaps it was the declaration of love coming fast on the heels of the lecture. He took her in his arms and held her and remembered the countless times she'd held and comforted him.

'There now,' she said. 'We've had our hugs and we've said our good-byes.'

He was behind the wheel now. 'You promise you'll call if you need me.'

'Of course.'

She threw him a kiss. He turned on the ignition. The old Ford started immediately.

'Treat her good,' Martha called out over the noisy engine. 'She survived my father. She's special.'

Slowly he stepped on the accelerator, and the separation was under way. She followed after the car for a few yards, then gave it up, and he increased his speed, the better to settle the tires into the rutted dirt road.

He was on his way then. His first degree would take three more years, then his master's for two years, then his PhD three more years, and at the end of all that time and all that study, he knew one thing for certain.

He would never be smarter or wiser than Martha Drusso . . .

As hard as she tried, she knew she'd never get used to things that disappeared, things and people, like Charlie Groveton, like Belle, now like R. C.

She stood in the middle of the road waving until the car disappeared and the dust settled.

He'd be all right, she knew that. She turned once in a slow, aimless circle. Surely something needed doing. Halfway up the steps she looked about to see if they needed sweeping. They didn't. On the second, shorter flight that led up to the porch, she was certain she would find a stray leaf. She didn't.

Now she sat on the rocker and slowly began to rock, back and forth, back and forth.

All dressed up and no place to go, she muttered to herself. Never before in her life had she sat idle with no one needing her.

Then what?

All at once she took the steps two at a time, hurrying toward the barn. She pulled open the doors and stared at the ancient pickup.

'Well, let's see,' she said, and inserted the key into the rusty ignition. She turned the key. The engine coughed and died. She turned it again, and the engine coughed and turned over. Carefully she backed the pickup out of the barn, gripping the steering wheel with both hands and guiding it down the gravel drive to the slight incline that led to the county road, where she turned right toward Hitchings.

About twenty minutes later she approached the outskirts of town. Her destination was the community center, a cinder-block building that sat at the edge of Blacker Park and was the place where anyone in need went for help. When she was a kid it had been run by a roly-poly man named Casper Decker. At Christmastime Casper had always played Santa Claus for the various churches. She wondered if Casper would still be there.

Ahead she spied the building. Good Lord, someone had painted the concrete blocks pink. As the pickup rattled to a halt by the curb, she jumped down from the running board.

She pulled open the front door and saw a large room containing a scattering of mismatched tables and chairs. Behind the desk to the left sat a woman with gray hair, plump and heavily corseted in a blue voile dress.

'May I help you?'

'Maybe.' Martha smiled and approached the desk. 'I was looking for Casper Decker. Could you – '

The woman's eyebrows went circumflex, and her mouth formed a lipsticked O. 'I'm so sorry, my dear, Mr Decker went home to be with God.'

Martha had thought as much. 'When?'

'Oh, five years ago, maybe six. My name is Leota Bynum.' The woman smiled and straightened a stack of invoices. 'I took Mr Decker's place, though hard shoes they were to fill.'

'Of course,' Martha said, and glanced back toward the bolted door at the rear of the big room.

'And you are . . . ?'

'I'm Martha Drusso. I live outside – '

'Oh, Miss Drusso, yes, of course. I knew your mother, God rest her soul. I'm afraid I didn't know your father. Can I help you with anything specifically? We're having a fall canning demonstration here shortly, conducted by Mrs Jasmine Overland of the Extension Division at Texas Tech. We would love to have you stay.'

'No. No, thank you,' Martha said politely, and wondered how she could phrase exactly what it was that she had come for. 'When I was growing up, Mrs Bynum, if there was anyone in Hitchings who . . . needed anything, you know, a meal, a bed, a place to – '

All at once she heard something, a faint noise. Hard to tell even where it had come from. She stepped closer to the desk, as though shortening the distance between them would enhance understanding. 'Mrs Bynum, I have a new house and plenty of food. Now surely you know of someone who could – '

She heard it a second time, a whimpering noise, like someone trying not to cry.

'Who's back there, Mrs Bynum?'

'Oh, that's none of your concern,' the woman said with a stern look.

'Please, Mrs Bynum,' she insisted. 'Who is back – '

Reluctantly the woman spoke. 'Scotty got a call out to the motel last night,' she said, holding her hand to the side of her mouth as though to prevent her words from sliding away. 'Mr Foreman called, said someone had set up a prostitute in his motel and he wanted her out of there. So Scotty went out and got her – them, really. She has a child, no doubt illegitimate, and Scotty's gone now to get the squad car to run her over to Amarillo where they are holding the man who left her out there.'

'How did Mr Foreman know she was a prostitute?'

Mrs Bynum spoke in hushed tones. 'Well, for the last several nights he's noticed a solid parade of men going and coming out of number thirteen. That's the end one, you know, and they've been parking their cars in the field across the highway so Mr Foreman wouldn't notice. But he noticed.'

This last was said with a pronounced sense of accomplishment, as though Mrs Bynum herself had had something to do with it. 'We certainly don't want her kind spoiling our town.'

'No, of course not,' Martha said, staring with renewed interest at the closed and bolted door. 'Where did you say Scotty would take them?' she asked.

'To Amarillo, and hopefully to a nice tight jail cell somewhere.'

'And when do you expect Scotty to be back?'

'Well, he had to see about getting a squad car. He didn't want to run his truck all that way on police business.'

'No, of course not.' Martha paced for a moment in front of the desk, still keeping her eye on the door. 'Mrs Bynum, let me take them.'

Mrs Bynum looked up, shocked. 'Take them where?'

'Out to my farm.'

'Forevermore why?'

'To get them off your hands.'

'Lord, they're not on my hands.'

'But she's going to jail. Now, does she deserve that?'

'You haven't even seen her.'

'Doesn't make any difference.'

'What would Scotty say?'

'He wouldn't have to drive them over to Amarillo then.'

'No, it's out of the question, out of the – '

'Why? You're a good Christian woman. Surely you believe in forgiveness?'

'But she is a . . . prostitute.'

'People change.'

'I'm afraid it's out of the – '

'Why?'

In desperation Mrs Bynum let her hands drop noisily onto the desk. She glanced at Martha, then at the closed door. 'Right now, Miss Drusso, I'm going to the little girl's room. I will probably be in there no more than five minutes. When I come back, perhaps there will no longer be a problem.'

Martha grinned and watched her until she had disappeared. Then she ran toward the locked room at the rear of the building. She wasted no time in throwing the latch and yanking open the door.

They were seated on the floor. The 'prostitute' was Mexican with dark hair and eyes. In her lap sat a little boy, no more than two, if that. Both looked scared, tired, dirty, and hungry.

'Come on,' Martha said with dispatch. 'Let's get out of here.'

But she reached the door alone and looked back, surprised to see the two unmoved.

Frustrated, she squatted in front of the girl and looked at her earnestly. Around her mouth was a telltale smear of lipstick. She looked no more than fifteen, Belle's age.

The thought was devastating, and without thinking she reached for the girl's hand and literally jerked her upward. The little boy spilled out one side, but Martha caught him up in her arms and commenced to drag them from the storeroom and across the community center.

At the front door, she peered out in search of a black-and-white squad car. Seeing none, she led them across the lawn to the pickup parked at the curb.

'Get in,' she said, opening the door. She helped the girl up, then handed up the little boy. He was dark, beautiful, and very frightened. She hurried around to the driver's side, pulled herself up, and inserted the key in the ignition.

Nothing.

She tried again. Two coughs, like an old man clearing his

throat. And then again nothing. She looked to her left and saw a squad car coming straight for the community center. For one brief moment she panicked, considered taking the children and running on foot.

But reason moved in, and as the police car came closer she said, 'Get on the floor, both of you, keep your heads down and keep quiet whatever you do.'

To her amazement the girl crouched down immediately and drew the child after her, covering him with her own body.

Quickly Martha reached for the old canvas cloth that R. C. had used to cover the torn upholstery. While the police officer was slowly getting out of his car, she dropped the cloth over the children and again warned, 'Not a word, don't even breathe.'

'Good morning, Officer,' she called out cheerily as he headed in her direction.

'Good morning to you. Car trouble?'

Martha laughed. 'Not really. It just goes when it wants to. It doesn't happen to want to right now.'

The officer was still approaching, nearing her window. 'You new here in Hitchings?' he asked, pushing his hat back on his head.

'New?' she exclaimed with a bit more energy than was necessary. 'I'm older than you are and been here longer.'

He looked puzzled. 'Ain't never seen you before.'

'Been away. My name's Drusso. Martha Drusso.'

'Oh, the old Drusso place out on the County Road.'

'Yes.'

'So you're the one been fixing it up.'

'Yes.'

'I ain't been out, but folks say it looks brand new. Sorry about your pa.'

'Thanks.'

'You out there alone?'

'I have family, but they come and go. I got a boy in school at SMU.'

He nodded soberly to all this, and she was fairly certain

that it would be repeated before lunch at the Sunup Cafe downtown, where all of the regulars brought a bit of gossip to have with their coffee.

'Well, I'd best be getting on out,' she said. 'Lots of things to do, you know.' Again she turned the key. Blessedly the old engine caught and turned over.

'See you around,' Scotty said, grinning.

'Yeah,' Martha said. Then she stepped on the accelerator and felt the old pickup shoot forward and did nothing for a few minutes but concentrate on getting through town and out of it.

About ten minutes later, when there was nothing on either side of the road but empty fields, she reached down, lifted the old canvas, and saw two very hot and very scared faces staring up at her.

'You did good' – she smiled – 'both of you. Now crawl back up here and take deep breaths of fresh air. Come on . . .'

She drove with one hand and extended her other to the young girl on the floor, who scrambled up beside her, the child still on her lap. Martha saw her lovingly brush the hair out of the boy's eyes and wipe a smudge from his cheek.

Did she speak English or didn't she?

No need to hurry and find out. For now they were safe. For now they didn't have to worry about jail or foster homes or separations. For now all Martha wished she could do was erase that scared lost look from both their faces. A song might help.

She grasped the wheel, took a deep breath, then lifted her head and sang out at the top of her lungs: 'Old McDonald had a farm, Eeee-I-Eeee-I-oh. And on that farm he had a duck . . .'

At first she seemed only to add to their fear, for they both looked at her with wide, apprehensive eyes. But Martha persisted, running through every chorus.

They were just approaching her farmhouse when she did the pigs. Whether it was the oink-oink or whether at last she'd convinced them that she meant them no harm, the little boy grinned, the young girl smiled, and repeated softly, 'Oink-oink,' and Martha laughed and announced, 'We're home . . .'

November 10, 1945
Dallas, Texas
Veterans Hospital

It was the hardest thing that Dr Swaddoes ever had to do, to tell these men that they were healed, at least as far as medical science could heal them, and that they were no longer required to remain in the hospital and were now on their own.

As he turned the corner into the large, sunny recreation room, his eyes searched for his target this morning and found him, over there by the window, alone and not wearing his prosthesis, though the entire staff had worked long and hard to help him use it with a degree of skill.

The man – Charlie Groveton was his name – had been here for over a year. Wounded at Omaha beach on D-Day, he had been more dead than alive the first time Chris Swaddoes had taken a look at him. The shell had blown off his left leg at the knee, had opened up his left side in its entirety.

Now six surgeries and seventeen months later, he was not as good as new. He would never be that. He would have to live with a degree of discomfort for the rest of his life. But he was alive and upright and all parts were capable of functioning, and when he wore his prosthesis he walked with only a slight limp. He would never run the fifty-yard dash, but he probably hadn't done that before the war. He could hold a desk job, could have a family, could enjoy quite possibly another thirty years of life, and that was a hell of a lot more than could be said about some of the men.

Swaddoes started across the crowded recreation room filled with men who had left various parts of themselves scattered all over Europe. Most spoke. A few joked. Some invited him into their poker games. The only pocket of nonmovement was the man in the wheelchair, sitting in a patch of sun by the French doors, saying nothing to anyone.

'Good morning, Charlie.'

After he spoke, he saw the man turn and look up as though Swaddoes had summoned him back from a more desirable place.

'Doc?' was his only word, and it served as greeting.

'How you feeling?'

'Lopsided.'

It was his standard reply.

'No need. Back in your room you have a perfectly good substitute. You know how to put it on, you know how to take care of it, you know – '

'I know everything, Doc.'

'Then why aren't you using it?'

'Don't like it.'

'Why?'

'It hurts.'

'It shouldn't.'

'But it does.'

'Use the padding.'

'Still hurts.'

'Then get used to it.'

Dr Swaddoes walked past the chair, sorry that he had snapped at the man. He stood by the doors, hands in his pockets, gazing out across the grounds of the hospital. Some paraplegics were playing basketball on the concrete court, manipulating their wheelchairs with skill, energy, and strength. Other patients were scattered about the lawn, enjoying the warm, healing rays of a late Indian summer.

All right, then, nothing to do but do it. 'Groveton, we're finished here. We've done all we can do. You're fit. And now you need to get on with your life. Do you understand?'

Swaddoes wasn't certain if he'd understood or not. His face was a blank, though his hands seemed to be gripping the arms of the wheelchair with renewed strength. A blanket covered his missing leg.

'Did you hear me, Charlie?'

'Yes, sir, I heard.'

'Most men are pleased to be given their release papers.'

'Yes, sir.'

'Where's your home?'

'Place called Hitchings. Up near Amarillo.'

'Good wheat country.'

'Yes, sir.'

'Do you have a family?'

'No, sir. None that are still alive.'

'Friends?'

'No, sir. They're all dead, too.'

'What was your line of work before?'

'Oilfield.'

That stopped Swaddoes cold. There was nothing a one-legged man could do on any oil rig. He looked about as though for help and saw none. 'We do have a facility in south Dallas, Oak Cliff, a place men can go while they're . . .'

'Trying to decide where to go.'

'Yes.'

'I'll figure something out.'

'I'm sure you will. And I promise you it will be easier with your prosthesis, easier to get around, to meet people on your feet, as it were.'

'I guess I'm just not a man for fake parts.'

'Do you want me to call the place in Oak Cliff?'

'Can I let you know?'

'Sure.'

'How much time . . . when do I have to – '

'Today is Tuesday. Say, Friday?'

'Friday.'

The man looked lost. 'Look, Groveton, take your time . . .'

'No, it's best.'

'I'd like to take another look at your leg, let the other people look at your prosthesis. Maybe it hasn't been fitted properly. It shouldn't hurt. I'll schedule an exam for you in the morning.'

Swaddoes waited a moment to see if there would be any further response. But he knew there would be no more questions. He'd worked too long at cleaning up the remains of war not to know that there was one kind of man who, regardless of the nature of his wounds, had taken a fatal blow to his pride.

Charlie Groveton was such a man . . .

Friday.

Dear God! Fear vaulted as Charlie rolled his chair through the doors onto the broad terrace, heading at top speed toward the steep flight of stairs that led to the lawn below. A nurse reached out and caught his chair only inches from the steps.

She gasped, 'Hey, soldier, try the ramp. It'll be a smoother ride.'

Charlie didn't even bother to look up. He turned his chair about and pushed toward the terrace.

Rolling effortlessly down the ramp, he headed toward the dark and inviting stand of trees about a hundred yards away. They reminded him of the big cottonwoods along the creek behind his farmhouse at home.

'Where is your home, Mr Groveton?'

He rolled faster as though trying to escape the voices inside his head.

'We do have a facility in south Dallas, Oak Cliff, a place men can go while – '

Charlie pushed on the wheels with all his strength. Somehow he felt if he could make it to that stand of trees, he'd be all right. He just needed time to think, to put a plan together, to –

The wheelchair wobbled dangerously across the bumpy lawn. One wheel lifted, tilted him to the right, and briefly all of his energy was channeled into maintaining his balance.

Closer, trees coming closer, and once there everything

would be all right. He could close his eyes, open them, be home again and see Martha –

He saw her face as clearly as though she were standing before him, and he rolled even faster, his hands burning from the wheels that spun across his flesh.

Thirty feet, twenty feet, shade ahead, ten feet, and all at once the left wheel struck a rock concealed in the high grasses and the chair spun crazily out of control and hurled him into the bushes. The chair fell on top of him as the stump of his leg struck something hard, and pain erupted beneath the wound.

Upended, the wheels of the chair whirled eerily for several seconds. Charlie lay perfectly still in the grasses, looked up at the blue sky, and wished with all his heart that the shell on Omaha beach had finished him as it had finished the kid from Kentucky, as it had finished Matt, as it had finished over eighty-five percent of his platoon.

Somehow he had survived, half a man now, not fit for life, not capable of death. He couldn't hold a job, he couldn't earn a wage, he couldn't pull his weight, he couldn't, wouldn't ever go home to Hitchings again. What if someone were to see him like this?

The thought could not be borne, and Charlie Groveton turned his face into the grasses, smelled sweet clover, and did something he hadn't done since he was a baby.

He wept . . .

June 4, 1948
Fort Smith, Arkansas

Belle held as still as she could, considering the special evening ahead, her senior prom.

'It looks fine, Billie Rose,' she said, 'it really does.'

And it did, her prom gown made of yards and yards of pale peach dotted Swiss.

As Billie Rose straightened up, Belle stood before the full-length mirror. 'It's beautiful,' she said, smiling, 'the prettiest dress I've ever seen.'

In the reflection of the mirror she saw Billie Rose looking not at the spectacular gown, but at her.

'Why did you go and grow up on us all of a sudden?'

'Brad said he has a surprise for me tonight. Do you know what it is?'

'If I did, I wouldn't tell you.'

'Do you, Billie Rose? Oh, please tell me.'

'I don't know,' Billie Rose said with emphasis, and began to scurry around, picking up from the dressing process.

Belle didn't know whether to believe her or not. Billie Rose and Brad Compton were great friends now, although in the beginning, way back at that first swimming party, Billie Rose had openly disliked Brad. But Brad had won her over as he'd won Belle from the beginning.

Thinking on him, she walked slowly to her gallery of Brad Compton pictures.

And there he was, his newest eight-by-ten photo at the center surrounded by smaller pictures of Brad and Belle on a hayride, Brad and Belle playing tennis, Brad and Belle in the pool, Brad and Belle in front of a Christmas tree, Brad and Belle making a snowman.

She did love him. It had taken her a while to realize that. She'd never had a boyfriend before, so she really didn't know how or what she was supposed to feel. But the first time they were separated, when Brad had been shipped back to California, Belle thought quite simply she would die. She'd missed the sound of his voice, his laugh, his jokes, the touch of his hand.

Then she heard the doorbell downstairs and whispered, 'Brad,' and took a final look in the mirror. She hoped he could stay longer this time. He'd visited her in May, but his father had called him back to Los Angeles, where he'd stayed for almost three weeks. Now she hoped he could stay for the rest of June, for the rest of the summer, for the rest of her life, because when Brad was around she felt less lost, more complete than she'd ever felt before . . .

Malcolm knew that if he lived to be a hundred, he would never see anything to equal the beauty of the moment when Belle appeared at the top of the staircase and looked down at Brad, as handsome in his white dinner jacket as she was lovely in her prom gown.

The dress made her appear older than her seventeen years, assuming that was her age. Briefly Malcolm felt the frustration of the last two years, when he'd hired skilled private detectives to search out every clue they could find from Belle's past.

They'd found nothing. Apparently the first family of record, the Melvilles, had disappeared from the face of the earth, and before the Melvilles there was no trace at all.

Now, as Malcolm and Charlotte looked back up, he noticed that Belle's eyes were fixed on only one, young Brad Compton. Since that first swimming party after the war, Brad had spent a portion of almost every week in Belle's company.

About a year ago, when he'd been honorably discharged from the army, he had taken a small apartment in town so he could be near her. Lately he seemed to be spending more and more time in Los Angeles, working for his father, but without fail every weekend he'd fly back to be with Belle.

Now the focus of these two was so private, so intimate, that Malcolm almost felt embarrassed to be a witness. Someone had to break the spell.

'How about a glass of sherry, Brad, to fortify you as it were against all of those pretty graduating seniors?'

'Yes, sir, thank you, yes, I'd like that very much.'

Belle looked baffled but said nothing and took Brad's hand, and together they made their way to the study. Malcolm could tell from Belle's face that this invitation for sherry was without precedent. Not once in two and a half years had Malcolm ever invited him to the study for a glass of sherry.

But tonight Brad was going to surprise Belle with a certain phone call, and in honor of the occasion and in an attempt to help Brad stall, Malcolm asked, 'Belle, would you like a thimbleful?'

'No, sir, I've tasted it. It tastes like cough medicine.'

Malcolm laughed and poured three glasses and handed one to Brad and one to Charlotte, along with a pointed expression designed to say, *'I don't know how much longer we can stall.'*

Then at last the phone rang. Brad grabbed it and lifted it to his ear. 'Yes? Of course, yes, she's right here.'

He extended the phone to Belle. 'It's for you.' He grinned, and at last Malcolm sat down, weary of making Brad's surprise work.

'Me?' Belle asked, puzzled, and took the phone. 'Hello?'

Malcolm was in a perfect position to see her face. 'Oh, yes . . .' She smiled. 'It's nice to meet you, too.' She covered the phone with her hand and gasped to the entire room, 'It's Mr Compton, Brad's father.' Then back the receiver went to her ear.

'Yes, sir.' For several minutes she was listening quietly. 'Really, sir, are you serious? Does Brad know?'

Malcolm found himself grinning. Everyone knew the secret surprise but Belle. Mr Compton was inviting her to come out to California with Brad for three weeks, to be a guest in Mr Compton's Beverly Hills estate.

'Thank you, sir. I'll look forward to it.'

She extended the phone to Brad. 'He wants to speak with you.'

Brad took it but first kissed Belle on the cheek. 'See? I told you I had a surprise for you.'

As he talked with his father, Belle started toward Malcolm and Charlotte, a look of surprised excitement on her face. 'Did you know about this?' she whispered, aware that Brad was still on the phone.

Malcolm smiled. 'For weeks,' he said wearily. 'Mr Compton and I have spoken often on the phone. I think they have some very special events in mind for you.'

'Did you know about it?' she asked Charlotte.

Charlotte laughed. 'Of course. You think Malcolm could

keep a secret like this from me? Besides, someone had to see to your new wardrobe.'

'Where?' Belle gasped, excitement still building. 'Oh, please, let me see, Charlotte!'

'Later. You go to the dance now.'

Brad put down the phone. 'My father asks a favor of you.'

'What?'

'That you will sing for him. I told him about your voice.'

'Oh, I couldn't.'

'He's expecting it. He will be disappointed.'

'Was all this your idea?'

'Partly. And partly my father's. I've told him so much about you, he insisted upon meeting you.'

'Why am I scared?' Belle said with a mock shiver.

'I have no idea,' Brad replied. 'You'll steal his heart as you manage to steal everyone's.'

Malcolm knew that neither Brad nor Belle had the slightest idea that there were others in the room. He kissed her very lightly, tenderly. 'I think you two had better get going or the dance will be over.'

Belle started toward the door, then stopped abruptly. She looked back at Malcolm and Charlotte, then slowly retraced her steps until she stood directly before them.

'I've never said this, but I should have. Thank you for letting me share your life. I . . . love you.'

Malcolm felt her kiss on the side of his face and saw her kiss Charlotte.

'See you soon,' she whispered. Then she was gone.

Malcolm could still feel her kiss and hear her words. He took Charlotte in his arms and felt her nestle close in familiar fashion.

'Do you know what I'm thinking?' she whispered.

'What?'

'I think Lenora would have liked her so very much.'

Shocked, Malcolm looked down on her. 'You've known?'

'Yes.'

'Since when?'

'Since the beginning. At first I needed for her to be Lenora. Now I want her to be Belle . . .'

June 5, 1948
Hitchings, Texas

R. C. rolled down the windows of his old car, glad to be out of the Dallas traffic but dreading to tell Martha his bad news.

Well, he had two weeks before the summer term started. Surely he could think of a way by then. He was eager to see her and to see the additional strays she'd picked up since Easter.

He switched on the radio and caught the end of a newscast; Truman had authorized airports in Anchorage and Fairbanks, Rita Hayworth and Orson Welles had filed for divorce, and the weather in the Dallas-Ft. Worth area would be hot and dry with highs in the eighties, a chance of rain late tonight.

Then a popular music program took over, with Frank Sinatra singing 'Bewitched,' and for the first time in several weeks R. C. relaxed, smelled alfalfa somewhere, and thought of –

Home.

It was a good word, a good feeling, marred only by an ancient loss. A performer named Belle Whiteside had been on campus last month, and R. C. had bought a ticket, only to find a heavyset blues singer, quite good, though clearly not the person he was looking for.

It was like an old wound. He could go for days, weeks sometimes, and never think of her. Then suddenly something, a blond-haired little girl in a restaurant, a tall slim pretty teenager, would catch his eye, and it was as if no time at all had passed.

Belle –

He sat up and grasped the wheel, angry that he could not cleanse his mind. It did no good to think on her, to wonder where she was and if she was well. A long time ago Martha had confessed that now and then she feared that Belle was dead.

No. R. C. had never once entertained such a notion. She was alive, she was well, and it was only a matter of time before R. C. found her.

He had no idea where the conviction had come from. But the thought brought him a degree of peace, and he accepted it gratefully.

Hitchings was about three hours away. Martha and her new brood would be waiting. Should he tell her the bad news when he arrived or save it until he was ready to leave?

He'd think about it and decide when he got there . . .

June 5, 1948
Hitchings, Texas

It never failed to amaze Martha, the number of lost people in this world. She lifted the baby in her arms, tilted the bottle to make it easier for him, and thought of Belle.

It was beyond comprehension the degree of pain the thought still caused. A south wind blew across her face and carried the voices of Juan, Rufus, and Molly. They were playing in the sandbox on the side yard, and their toys were some coffee cans and old wooden spoons.

Juan was four, Sara's son. Sara was seventeen, the young prostitute whom Martha had found at the community center. She had come from a village outside Mexico City, had gotten pregnant by her boyfriend, and her religious family had exiled her. A man had picked her up at the border, waited for the baby to be born, then had put her to work as a prostitute. Now she was a good friend.

Rufus was five. She had found him one morning about a year ago sitting on her front steps. No sign, no instructions, just a frightened little boy with lots of Indian blood in him who had spent most of the first day crying. Martha had held him all night, and by morning he was ready for scrambled eggs and two of Sara's tortillas.

Molly, the teller of the tallest tales Martha had ever heard, was seven and had been found in a tornado shelter of a burned-out farm about fifteen miles north of Hitchings. Everybody thought the farm had been abandoned; therefore when it burned no one thought much about it until they peered down the 'fraidy hole' and saw two eyes peering back. All she could tell them was that her name was Molly, her age was seven, and that her mother and daddy had said they would come back for her. They hadn't.

And last there was Ezra, the small, sleepy bundle in her arms. He was only three weeks old. His mama had died giving birth to him, and Mrs Bynum had told her she could have him if she'd come and get him.

Martha smiled. She couldn't remember ever having driven the old pickup that fast before.

Now she stood and put him over her shoulder and with the other hand lifted the playpen. Thus loaded, she was just starting carefully down the front steps when she looked up and saw a car coming.

She squinted into the distance and then hurried to the side of the house, put down the playpen, and gently placed Ezra in it. To Molly she said, 'Keep an eye on him. I'll be right back.'

The little girl nodded solemnly, and then she too caught sight of the car. 'It's R. C.!' she squealed, and was out of the sandbox along with Juan, both of them running for the car as fast as their legs could carry them.

Martha smiled. He was early. Good. The kids adored him. 'Come,' she said to Ezra. 'Can't leave you alone. Might as well go and join the welcoming committee.'

'R. C.?' she called out, waved, kissed Ezra's smooth cheek, and went to rescue R. C. before the kids buried him . . .

'All right,' R. C. shouted amidst a tangle of bare arms and legs that were crawling all over him, causing him to feel like Gulliver.

'Here, Molly, you get that hand. Juan, you get to sit on the shoulders. Ally-oops – up we go! And you, Rufus, come on, you get this hand.'

At last, with each child settled happily, he started toward the steps to see Martha at the top, a roly-poly baby on her hip.

'Ezra?' he marveled.

She nodded, clearly proud.

'My God, what have you been feeding him?' He laughed and delivered a kiss to Martha's cheek.

'It's good to see you.'

'And you.'

'How were finals?'

'Not too bad.'

'When are you due back?'

'Two weeks.'

She grinned. 'Two whole weeks. We'll have a picnic every day, and we'll go see if Charlie Groveton's creek still has water in it. It used to be the coldest water in Texas.'

The children were dancing around him now, Indian fashion.

'Listen, kids,' he said, 'why don't you let me talk to Martha for just a few minutes. Then I promise we'll go find us an adventure. Would you like that?'

Their response of high-pitched squeals indicated that they would.

Now R. C. was faced with Martha's wholehearted attention.

'All right, what is it?'

'I received a letter shortly before I left school,' he began.

'From who?'

'The NROTC commander.'

'And?'

'After graduation in December I am to report to officers indoctrination in San Diego for two years of mandatory military service.'

There. He'd said it. He watched Martha's face for the first sign of alarm, fear, anger, whatever.

But there was nothing. 'Well, we knew it was coming, didn't we?' She sighed and strolled back toward the porch, the baby still in her arms.

'I thought you'd be upset,' he said.

'Well, I am,' she confessed, 'but at least the shooting wars are all over. You'll make a good officer, and you'll get to see a part of the world you've never seen before, and – '

She broke off and looked back at him. Her face suddenly altered. 'And if anything happens to you, I swear to God I'll – '

Quickly he went to her and hugged her, baby and all. 'Nothing will happen,' he promised. 'And did you hear where I'd be stationed? California,' he added, still seeing the blank look on her face despite the fact that both had frequently been told that it would be easier to launch a search for Belle at the last place she possibly was seen.

Then it dawned on Martha. 'You won't have time.'

'I'll have leaves.'

'What will you do?'

'I'll start in Los Angeles and work backward to San Bernardino.'

For a moment he saw the light of new hope on her face. Then wisdom and prudence moved in and only slightly tempered the light.

'Good,' she said with a brisk nod. 'Though don't neglect your duties.'

'No, of course not.'

Ezra squirmed, wanting down. 'Come on,' Martha said, 'let's go and see if we can help Sara.'

She proceeded on up the step and had just pulled open the screen door when she looked back. 'What will they call you? In the navy, I mean.'

'Ensign R. C. Drusso.'

A smile lit her face. Then she was gone to corral her children.

Slowly R. C. sat on the very steps that he'd built only a few years earlier. He looked out over the vast land of west Texas.

The children, laughing inside the old white farmhouse, were like himself. For them, as for him, home would forever be where Martha was . . .

June 8, 1948

Belle had never dreamed that flying would be so noisy and nerve-racking.

'Will your father be there to meet us?' she asked, trying at least to appear relaxed.

Brad shook his head. 'No, he hates airports and crowds.'

The stewardess moved down the narrow aisle pushing a cart. Brad lifted his empty glass. She passed him a small bottle of whiskey. 'More ice, Mr Compton?'

'No, this is fine.'

She watched as Brad poured the bottle of whiskey into melting ice cubes, continued to watch as he downed it in one swallow, took one hard gulp, then settled back even more relaxed against the seat cushion.

'Are you scared?' he asked almost sleepily.

'No. Should I be?'

'Most people are upon meeting the great Cy Compton.'

Belle leaned back in her seat. 'I won't be afraid of him if he won't be afraid of me,' she said, and saw the stewardess coming back, two single bottles of whiskey in hand. How had she known?

Brad took the bottles, opened them both, filled his glass, drained it, and looked at Belle. 'You know what's going to happen, don't you?' he said on a laugh that sounded almost sad. 'My father will fall in love with you and you with him, and both of you will kick me out.'

'Oh, Brad,' she whispered, worried to see him drinking so much and not liking what he'd just said. 'Are you sorry you invited me out to California?'

'Are you crazy? For the first time in several years I may manage to arrive at Los Angeles Airport only moderately drunk.'

This baffled her, and she was on the verge of asking why when he volunteered. 'You might as well know now. My father and I . . . well, how to put it? I love him, at least I think I love him. But I'm afraid if he were here, he couldn't in all truth say the same thing about me.'

'Why?'

'I don't know. I've never been able to please him, though God knows I've tried. Cy Compton is a brilliant man, as everyone will tell you, including Cy Compton himself. I'm afraid I've turned out to be a very ordinary man.'

'You're not ordinary to me.'

For a moment her affection seemed to do more harm than good. He looked quickly out of the airplane window.

'Where will I be staying at your father's house?' she asked, attempting to break his pensive mood.

'I don't know. One of the guest houses, perhaps, or maybe he'll want you to stay in The Stables.'

'The stables?' she asked.

Brad laughed. 'That's what everyone calls my father's house.'

'Why?'

'His father, my grandfather, came out from New York City about 1917 and got in at the beginning. He directed silent movies. He bought up large portions of the valley and for himself forty acres in what is now Beverly Hills. He built stables on his land, that's all, just stables. He was crazy about horses, racehorses. At one time he had seventy-seven horses and a small cottage attached to the back of the stables where my father and his mother lived. Everyone called it The Stables, and when my father built the big house in the mid-thirties, the name stuck. It's still The Stables.'

He looked at her with an expression of sympathetic amusement. 'You really have no idea what's ahead, do you?'

'I suppose I don't.'

'It's not like the Burgesses, it's not sedate and graceful – '

He broke off and gazed out of the window. 'It's a circus, that's what it is, a damned circus.'

'Your mother,' Belle asked quietly, always a magic word where she was concerned. 'Did you know – '

'I loved her very much, as did my father. Everything you will see at The Stables that is beautiful, tasteful, elegant, creative, and original is the result of my mother's hand. She died the year the house was finished. My father was devastated. He ordered a shrine of Carrara marble and brought over artisans from Italy to finish it. Inside the mausoleum is an altar of pink marble, and her ashes are contained in a gold chalice. Fresh pink roses are placed there everyday by my father, who talks to her as though she can hear.'

His eyes glazed as he spoke of this difficult part of his life. 'I talk to her, too,' he confessed. Old grief surfaced unexpectedly. 'They'll be serving lunch in a few minutes. Are you hungry?' he asked.

'Not particularly.'

'Then we'll wait. Hannah will have something ready when we get there.'

'Who's Hannah?'

'My father's cook.'

'Is there anyone else I should – '

Brad laughed. 'Just a small army. Gerald will meet us at the airport. He's my father's driver, has been for almost eighteen years. Then there's Inez Cooper. Everyone simply calls her 'the Person in Charge.' There's Jules Schaeffer, my father's personal attorney. Then there's Paul, head gardener and groundsman, and he has a staff of twelve. Then there's – '

She lifted her hands in mock surrender. 'Never mind. I'll take them as I come to them.'

June 8, 1949
Los Angeles, California

As the plane touched down, Brad regretted having told Belle so much about what lay ahead for her. As with any ordeal, perhaps it was best to discover the details a step at a time.

'Are you all right?' he asked.

'I'm fine . . .' She smiled. 'Just a bit nervous.'

After the plane came to a stop, he led the way down the narrow aisle, one hand reaching backward for Belle. Several times during the long walk through the crowded terminal, he looked back to see if she was all right. An incredible transformation was taking place. She seemed to be getting younger. At home around the Burgesses' pool or in the library she looked mature, almost sophisticated. Here she was beginning to resemble a very young girl.

'Come on,' Brad called back. 'We're almost home.' Renewing his grasp on her hand, he fairly dragged her through the doors and saw Gerald, his father's driver, adjust his cap and snap to attention.

'Gerald,' Brad called out warmly. 'Good to see you.'

'And you, too, Mr Compton. Your father sends his regrets. A meeting, you know.'

Brad knew. 'Gerald, I want you to meet Belle Burgess. Belle, this is Gerald. He's driven for my father – forever.'

'Miss Burgess, my pleasure, I assure you.'

'It's good to meet you, Mr Gerald. Thank you for coming to pick us up.'

Brad saw the confusion on Gerald's face. 'No, Miss Burgess, it's not *Mr* Gerald. It's just Gerald.'

'You have a last name?'

'Yes.'

'What is it?'

'Gerald Townley.'

'Then it's nice to meet you, Mr Townley, and again thanks for coming to meet us.'

For the moment Gerald didn't quite know what to do. He took the small gloved hand that was being extended to him because to ignore it would have been rude.

'Sir, if you'll give me your claim checks . . . We brought two cars, one for the luggage.' He pointed to the second car behind the limo, the wood panel station wagon.

As Brad handed over the luggage checks, Gerald suggested, 'Why don't you two get in and make yourselves comfortable. There is refreshment.'

'Good for you, Gerald.' Brad winked and took Belle by the arm.

Once inside, the noise of the airport muted, Brad saw on the drop table two filled champagne saucers and an open champagne bottle resting in the ice cooler. In a small dish nestled on a bed of ice was black caviar surrounded by cream cheese and toast squares.

But the greatest pleasure inside the car was Belle herself.

'You are amazing,' he whispered, wanting in the worst way to take her in his arms and kiss her.

'I don't understand.'

'I've known Gerald forever, and I've never known his last name.'

She looked surprised. 'Did you ever ask?'

As the limousine pulled away from the curb, Brad watched Belle take a swallow of champagne, make a face at it, and hand the glass back to him.

'It's an acquired taste,' he said, and drained her glass, then concentrated on his own.

A short while later Gerald turned into the palm-lined boulevard that led to Beverly Hills.

'Just ahead.' Brad motioned to Belle and only belatedly realized how much it sounded like a warning.

Then there it was, the enormous Italian Renaissance villa, one hundred and fifteen rooms that sat on the crest of a hill behind a black wrought-iron fence.

Gerald paused at the gatehouse and waved to the man inside. A moment later the gate opened automatically, revealing a complete vista of the vast, meticulously landscaped grounds that featured a waterfall and a small golf course, a well-stocked trout pond, a bowling green, an aviary, two greenhouses, one garden house, four guest houses, servants' quarters, three swimming pools, two tennis courts, and an eight-car garage.

'Would you like to drive around before we go up to the house?' Brad asked.

'Yes, please,' Belle said.

About halfway around the grand tour, Belle pointed to the left. 'What's that?'

'My mother's shrine.'

'May we stop?'

At once the limousine came to a halt, and Belle was already opening her door as Gerald arrived. Brad stood beside her, and both stared down at a lovely marble building that sat in a grove of willow and mimosa. A brick walk led to the door. On either side of the door were pink roses, flowering luxuriously and filling the air with a lovely scent.

'It's beautiful,' Belle said. 'Could we – '

'Of course.'

Brad took her hand, led her down to the shrine, pushed open the door, and closed it behind them. There was the hand-carved altar and on the altar the urn filled with his mother's ashes and above the urn an oil portrait of Sylvia Compton.

Belle moved a step closer.

Then all at once the door to the mausoleum was pushed open and a sudden rush of sunlight flooded the dark corners. They both turned with a start and were momentarily blinded by the unexpected illumination.

Brad shielded his eyes and saw Belle do the same. Adjusting to the light, he saw a figure silhouetted in the door, a tall, well-built figure, instantly recognizable.

He was wearing white slacks, a white silk shirt, and a white silk ascot. Over his shoulders was a pale cream sports jacket, draped with careless abandon. He stood, legs apart, with his hands behind his back.

Brad started to speak, a simple and affectionate greeting. But then he saw him approach Belle and bow in a courtly manner and in so doing revealed what he held behind his back, one dozen long-stemmed pink roses.

'My dearest Belle, please accept these as a token of my hospitality and allow me to personally welcome you to The

Stables. Brad has spoken endlessly of you, so I feel as if I know you.'

Belle took the flowers. Brad was certain of one thing. She had never, even in her varied and mysterious background, known anyone remotely resembling the man whom he was about to introduce to her.

'Belle, I would like you to meet my father, Cy Compton . . .'

Watching him was like watching a piece of mercury as it darted first this way, then that. Belle was fascinated.

'Brad,' he said now with a warm smile, and moved toward his son, who at this moment appeared uncertain as to whether he should advance or retreat.

But at last Belle saw the two men embrace, and though it seemed warm it also was short-lived.

'And how was the flight?' Mr Compton asked, his head cocked in interest. He seemed fairer compared with Brad, who clearly had inherited Sylvia's dark beauty. But Mr Compton had curly sandy hair and tanned skin. In his white slacks and white silk shirt, he looked like a movie star himself.

As the two men discussed the basic discomfort of air travel, Belle glanced toward the oil portrait of Brad's mother. If Brad had his mother's coloring, whose coloring did Belle have?

As the oil portrait of the dead mother reminded her of her own uncertain origins, she felt a deprivation of air and hurried out of the mausoleum in search of a breeze.

Within moments they had joined her, both concerned.

'Brad, what on earth possessed you to bring her here?'

'I wanted to come, Mr Compton.'

Cy studied her intently for a moment. 'Of course you did. And now that you've seen this place, I'm certain that you'll want to return. Sylvia was a remarkable woman. The power of her soul extends beyond the grave. That's why this place is such a magnet. But you've just had a long and exhausting journey. You should rest. I have had a special guest suite designed just for you, so may I suggest . . .'

He didn't complete the sentence but gestured toward the

brick walk that led to a strange-looking vehicle, part golf cart, part child's toy, with a fringed awning in candy stripe pastels. Behind this whimsical-looking vehicle, Belle saw the black limousine, Gerald Townley still waiting by the door.

'Gerald,' Cy called out as they started up the walk. 'I'll take the children up to the house with me. Many thanks.'

Belle glanced at Brad and saw his eyes slide heavenward. He took her arm and drew her close. 'Are you all right?'

'I'm fine.'

She saw Mr Compton at the top of the walk holding open the small half door next to the driver's seat.

'You don't mind the jump seat, do you, Brad? When you were a little boy you refused to ride anyplace else.'

As Brad hopped wordlessly into the small half seat in the back, Belle eased onto the passenger seat and readjusted the large bouquet of pink roses.

She watched as Mr Compton moved rapidly around to the driver's seat and swung into place, as excited as a child. 'These are called putt-putts,' he said to Belle as he started up the motor. 'If you ever want to go anyplace at The Stables and don't feel like a hike, just call for one of these, though I doubt seriously if you will be alone for so much as a minute during your stay here.'

As Cy pulled out onto the driveway, Belle glanced over her shoulder at Brad. He looked uncomfortable wedged into the small seat.

'Tell me, Cy,' Brad called out from the back with a massive wink at Belle.

'Anything.'

'Do you know Gerald's last name?'

'Who?'

'Gerald. Your driver.'

'His last name?'

'Yes, that's what I said.'

Belle saw a premature look of triumph on Brad's face. Clearly he wished to catch his father in a lapse of memory.

But unfortunately the triumph was short-lived. 'What a ridiculous question.' Mr Compton laughed. 'Gerald's last name is Townley. He's been married to a lovely woman named Marsha for over twenty-five years. They have two children, a girl fifteen, Esther, and a boy nineteen, Ronald. Compton Productions pays his tuition at Stanford. Why do you ask?'

Belle turned about on her seat, not wanting to see Brad's embarrassment.

'I can't tell you,' Mr Compton was now saying to Belle, 'how truly happy we are to have you here. My son has been distraught, responsibility here, heart elsewhere. Now for a few blessed days we have unity. Don't you admire unity? Most of our lives are so shattered that we scarcely know where to go to find ourselves. Look! There it is, The Stables. Here's the best view. Look up, Belle.'

As his voice and authority washed over her, she followed his command, looked up, and saw the imposing façade of The Stables.

Then he accelerated the putt-putt and took the rounding driveway at top speed as Belle held on to the side of the vehicle, closed her eyes, and hoped that Brad had recovered from his minor disappointment. Then she realized belatedly that where Cy Compton was concerned, it probably was every man for himself . . .

As his father pulled up beneath the overhang in front of the house, Brad saw Inez Cooper, 'the Person in Charge' at The Stables for as long as he could remember.

Now, as he caught sight of her slim figure and fine gray hair, he jumped out of the vehicle even before his father could bring it to a stop, took the flight of steps in one bound, and greeted her with surprising affection, surprising in that he'd seen her less than two weeks ago.

Nonetheless she played her part, which undoubtedly was one of the main reasons for her longevity at The Stables. 'I say, Brad!' She grinned and kissed him on one cheek, then the other. Then she whispered, 'Is that her? Oh, she *is* smashing. And look at old Cy about to turn himself inside out.'

Brad glanced over his shoulder to see his father assisting Belle out of the putt-putt.

'Let me show you one more item of interest,' he said with tour guide formality, and took her arm, led her about fifty feet back down the driveway, and pointed toward the west.

'His arboretum . . .' Inez sighed. 'You'd think it was his greatest accomplishment.'

Now Brad turned back to Inez with an urgent question. 'What has he done, Inez? He said something about a redecorated suite?'

She tried to be reassuring. 'He brought in a decorator friend of C. B. DeMille's. Your father gave him free rein.'

'And the result?'

'You wait. You just wait.'

'Inez – '

'Shhh – here they come.'

And here they came, his father with his arm about Belle, pointing first in one direction, then the other. 'Ah, there she is.' Cy gestured toward Inez, who straightened her dress and smoothed back a stray curl of gray hair.

'All of this that you see around you' – his voice lifted as he gestured broadly on all sides – 'requires the greatest organization and leadership, a small village, that's what we are, really, isn't that right, Inez? And Belle, can you even imagine who stokes the furnace, drives the horses, and rings the bell that keeps The Stables operating at clocklike precision?'

Though it was a rhetorical and silly question, Brad heard Belle produce an answer.

'This lady, I imagine,' she said, and stepped forward with perfect aplomb, perfect innocence, and introduced herself. 'My name is Belle Burgess. And you are . . .'

'Inez Cooper,' came a warm response.

As the two women chatted, Brad moved to the end of the portico, saw his father approaching, and felt somehow threatened. It was a natural response.

'She is perfection,' Cy murmured. 'Merely perfection. I've only seen it once before, you know. Your mother . . .'

'Yes.'

'How long will she be among us?'

Oh, Lord, this was his theatrical mood, when every word, every nuance, was staged and phrased as though for a performance. 'She will be among us,' Brad said, walking a few steps away, 'about three weeks. At least that was the agreement I struck with Mr and Mrs Burgess.'

'Mr Compton?' It was Inez. 'I believe your guest is ready to be shown her quarters. Shall I, or would – '

'No, no, I'll escort her,' Cy said. 'Come along, Brad,' he repeated enthusiastically. 'You too, Inez. This should be fun. Did I tell you, Brad? In honor of our beautiful guest, I've had the guest suite completely redecorated. You won't believe it. Come – '

Cy took Belle by the arm and led her up the gray stone steps to the carved double doors, which an agent had purchased for The Stables in Milan. It wasn't until Brad felt Inez at his side that he recognized it had happened again, that peculiar and awful paralysis that always came over him when he was in the presence of his father.

'Coming, Brad?'

He took Inez's arm and led her up the steps, through the door, and into the vestibule-rotunda, an immense stone circular hall, colorful Italian mosaic on the floor and the great stone walls expanding two floors up and serving as a gallery for Cy's collection of Italian Renaissance paintings.

'And this is a Signorelli. He did the frescoes, you know, in the Chapel of St Brizio, and is best known for his manipulation of the human body. And this column, Belle, look at this beautiful Salviati, the figures are so delicate, don't you agree? And one of my very favorites, Pontormo. Look, look carefully, see the chain of human elements is matched by the chain of human reaction which binds the figures to each other by glance and gesture and also includes the spectator.'

Brad recited the last few lines under his breath, having heard this particular speech countless times.

But Belle appeared interested and impressed as she turned

her head first one way and then the other, always carefully following the direction of Cy's hand.

Then all at once he heard his father's bellowing voice. 'But enough of dead Italians. Later I'll give you the complete tour of the artwork at The Stables. For now I know that both of you are tired from your flight and you must be rested and beautiful, for tonight we are giving a formal dinner in your honor. Come, Inez, give the children a hint at who will be joining us tonight in the dining hall.'

Inez looked uncomfortable, thrust unexpectedly into the spotlight. 'It – will be a comfortable and relaxed gathering,' she said, smiling. 'Some of Cy's oldest and closest friends.'

'Orson Welles,' Cy said, not at all reluctant to drop the names of his friends. 'And let's see, Gary Cooper, of course, and Mr Howard Hughes, all accompanied by three of the most beautiful women in Hollywood.'

There followed an awkward moment during which time the dynamo named Cy Compton shut down. He seemed to focus on Belle as though seeing her for the first time.

Then without warning he was scolding them all. 'Well, for heaven's sake. What are we standing about for? Come along,' he commanded, and again led the way around the twin staircases that led to the second and third floors.

Inez caught up with Brad and lightly squeezed his arm. 'Be prepared,' she whispered.

Brad was on the verge of questioning her further when he saw Cy standing before the double doors that led to the guest suite. 'Ready?' he said, grinning.

Then all at once Cy turned about and pushed open the double doors to reveal –

'What in the – ' Brad passed by Belle, who apparently was unable to determine whether or not it was safe to move.

'Well, come, all of you,' Cy called out, and Brad reached back for Belle's hand, leading her forward into what resembled a jungle.

'It's a lanai,' Cy explained, obviously seeing the confusion on their faces. 'A tropical paradise. That's what I wanted and that's what I got.'

Brad was prepared to argue the point but decided against it and settled instead for a close inspection.

There were banana trees everywhere, great clusters of them in all corners, and between the banana trees and the other foliage were enormous arrangements of orchids mixed in with Spanish moss. The furniture was bamboo. On the floor was a woven mat, and ahead, in the place where a fireplace had once been, was a waterfall, real water cascading down to a reflecting pond filled with huge goldfish and water lilies.

Considerately, Cy gave everyone time to look to their heart's content. Brad did not have the nerve to turn and investigate Belle's reaction. First he would have to deal with his own.

'And look,' Cy said, pointing upward. All followed his direction and saw a parrot perched in the tallest banana tree.

'Is it – alive?' Belle asked.

'Of course it's alive, and trained to speak, though I've not been able to coax a word from it. Her name is Baby. I'm sure she'll speak volumes for you.'

For several minutes all gazed up at the multicolored parrot, who stared down on them condescendingly.

Then Brad had seen enough. Belle couldn't stay in this – this greenhouse. It was out of the question. She –

'How do you like it, Belle?' he heard Cy ask.

'I like it very much. It looks like fun.'

'Exactly! Precisely! The purpose of a lanai is to make everyone feel carefree and chatty, like monkeys at a cocktail party.'

Belle laughed at this, and Brad pushed open the double doors with more force than was necessary and proceeded to the terrace, trying to rein in his resentment.

'Oh, yes, the terrace,' Cy said, apparently unaware of Brad's mood. 'Come and look, Belle,' he called back, and within the moment Brad was joined by the others.

'How lovely,' Belle exclaimed softly, gazing down on the pool.

'I'm glad you like it,' Cy said. 'We brought the tile over from Greece. And there at the end you see a real Greek temple. It rivals old Bill Hearst's at the ranch.'

The water in the pool was crystal clear, revealing the intricate mosaic design of flowers, birds, and creatures of mythology.

'So you think you'll be comfortable here?' Cy now asked.

'Yes. Very much so. Thank you for all your efforts on my behalf.'

Cy drew near and kissed her hand, his eyes lingering for an appreciative moment on her face. 'You're being selfish, you know, Brad,' he added. 'This beauty should be shared. You know where she belongs. On the screen, of course.'

Brad was horrified and started to protest. But as always he wasn't given a chance. Cy backed away until he reached the terrace steps. He turned about just before another step would have sent him tumbling down. The drama of almost falling was good stuff. Both Belle and Inez had taken a step of assistance toward his father when he turned at the last minute. 'I must go to my office now, children. I'm sure you understand.'

Then he was gone, moving nimbly down the steps with the gait and energy of a man of twenty-eight instead of forty-eight. He disappeared below the terrace, heading toward his office, and Brad quickly moved away from the terrace and back into the ridiculous room.

'Inez, this is out of the question. Is there another suite prepared that Belle could – '

'Brad?' It was Belle, a look of alarm on her face. 'This is fine. It is. In fact, I think it will be fun.'

'It's absurd.'

'Perhaps. But still, we don't want to hurt your father. He's gone to a great deal of trouble. This will be fine, Inez.'

Brad saw Inez nod. Clearly she understood. He wished to hell he did.

Now Inez took her leave, welcoming Belle again, promising to have her luggage brought up as soon as possible and send along a maid to help her unpack. She reminded Brad and pointed out for Belle's benefit the small though complete kitchen, which mercifully had escaped the lanai influence and was hidden by a small grove of banana trees.

'The fridge is stocked' – Inez smiled – 'and if there is anything you want that you can't find, just give the kitchen a call.'

As the door closed behind her, Brad struggled to put the pieces of his personality back together. 'I'm sorry,' he said.

'For what?'

'For everything. For this room, for my father – '

'There is nothing to be sorry for,' she said. 'I think the room is delightful, even Baby.' She looked back over her shoulder at the vibrantly colored parrot, who seemed to be listening critically from her perch.

'And your father,' she went on, 'is equally delightful. I've never known anyone like him.'

'That's because there is no one like him.'

'You do love him very much, don't you?'

'On occasion, I suppose, and other occasions I could cheerfully murder him.'

Then he tried to lighten his mood. 'Unless I miss my guess,' he said, standing back, 'you'll find swimming suits in the bathroom in a variety of sizes and styles along with robes. You change, and I'll be back in about twenty minutes.'

'Brad, are you – '

'Fine.' He smiled and started back toward the door. 'God, whatever possessed him?' he muttered, glancing to the right and left at the garish tropical environment . . .

Cy Compton hurried down the wisteria-covered arcade that led to his office, maintaining aplomb and energy until he pushed open his door, then closed it behind him.

At last he let the pose drop, leaned against the closed door, and drew several deep breaths, cursing this new fatigue. Slowly he unknotted and drew off the ascot, wiped his brow with it, and looked about at his office.

He loved it. It was white on white and always seemed

to regenerate him. This bright, airy room was like the Mediterranean sun on a Greek village.

God, but she was beautiful, Brad's little girl –

He walked slowly past walls of white leather to his immense white desk. Next to the desk was a white tile bar and by the window a white Steinway concert grand. Behind his desk on the wall was a gallery of photographs of good friends. One special of FDR, one of Mr Truman, one of Louis B. and David O., one large one of his father, and an even larger one of his beloved Sylvia.

Also behind his desk on a white standard stood an American flag, a gift from the Veterans of Foreign Wars for his film *Above the Stars*. On a special shelf next to the photographs were his three Oscars, two for directing, one for producing *Above the Stars, Summer of the Swan,* and *River to the Hills.*

He stood for a moment beside his desk and saw his office as a stranger might see it. Luxury was here, all the signs and signatures of success, the proof of stature. Then why did he continue to feel driven, frequently hollow, always the charlatan?

The questions were rhetorical, and the lack of an answer led him to the bar, where he poured himself a Scotch, drained it, poured himself another, and returned to his desk to sit on the large white leather chair and eye the clutter.

Had Dory already contacted Uris?

If so, then he must move more rapidly and go after a far greater talent in his opinion, in the person of Louis Rosen, the brilliant young writer whose novel *Resurrection* had been at the top of every bestseller list for the past year.

A haunting story of the Holocaust culminating in the rebirth of Israel, the book was full of bitter ironies, accusations, and recriminations aimed not only at the Nazis, but at the Allies as well. It begged to be filmed, and Cy knew he was the one, the only one, to do it.

There was only one major question. Did he want to do it?

He leaned back in his chair, rocked gently back and forth,

and tried again as he had tried every day for the past two weeks to wring an honest answer out of himself.

This was 1948. The world was still recovering from the war. Hollywood was still putting itself through the unnecessary agonies of repression and punishment. Why, he had no idea. Perhaps it was because generally speaking the industry had flourished during the years of great sacrifice for everyone else. Now a toll had to be extracted for all that good fortune.

He stared forward at the white carpet and saw a solitary roly-poly bug moving steadily but slowly toward the light at the door. Poor bug, so vulnerable in that vast field of white.

Cy watched him for several minutes, charting his tortuous yet determined progress.

Now to work. What to do about Louis Rosen and his brilliant *Resurrection*. 'First, examine your motives,' he muttered to himself.

Before he could find an answer, his mind wandered back upstairs to the new lanai room. Had Brad taken her to bed yet? There was a remote possibility he hadn't. Sylvia had done a good job with him, creating a wholly civilized young gentleman, sometimes too civilized for his own good.

If not *Resurrection*, then what?

The world was a difficult and painful place of disappointment and broken dreams. A worker with a few dimes to spare enters into a kind darkness, where he will find people meeting all sorts of odds and dealing with them. He'll find love, hope, and dreams worth pursuing. That same worker will leave the theater two hours later, renewed by the spirit of imagination.

Cy blinked rapidly through his thoughts. He leaned forward and reached for the script in the green folder, the book for the smash Broadway hit of last season, a musical entitled *Harvest of the Heart*, set in Iowa, an American *Romeo and Juliet* with a more promising ending, a simple story filled with the old values of trust, honor, and decency.

He lifted the script as though weighing it. This was what he wanted to do.

Strange, this new feeling of rightness. The fatigue, if not gone, was at least eased. He wanted to find new faces for this property that all America loved, he wanted a new ingenue, a new leading man, everything new, his signal that it was time to move forward into tomorrow and leave behind the diseased ideologies and brutal prejudices that had poisoned the century.

He heard laughter on the terrace steps leading down to the pool and started out from behind his desk, drawn to the sound. As he reached the door he looked down and saw the roly-poly bug nearing the threshold.

Cy smiled. He'd made it. The gritty and gutsy little creature had made it. Carefully he bent over, tapped him into a safe ball, cradled him in the palm of his hand, and deposited him outside his door beneath a hibiscus. He looked up from his rescue mission to see Brad and Belle approaching the pool.

Cy was entranced. What fun to stand, hidden by wisteria and hibiscus, and watch. Not a voyeur, dear God, he hoped not, more like that worker sitting in the darkened theater, tired, frustrated, and disappointed. He wanted to gaze forward at bright sun on blue water, on a beautiful young woman and a handsome young man laughing, their hands touching, then parting.

Which was the real world, the one of accusation, recrimination, anti-Semitism, communism, and fascism – or that one of beauty, grace, and love?

While Cy wasn't certain which one was the real world, he knew beyond a shadow of a doubt which one should be . . .

There were times, quite unexpected, when Belle thought of Harold and Kim Shoda with an ache that took her breath away.

Poised on the edge of the pool at the very instant of diving, her eye caught on a profusion of roses and she remembered Kim's pride in her rosebushes.

Then she split the surface of the clear water and took her longing with her to the bottom of the pool, where she ran her fingers across the tiles from ancient Greece. And caught between the longing she'd felt on the surface of the water and the lostness she experienced at the bottom, she foundered momentarily and let the pressure of the pool rock her first one way, then the other, before she began the slow ascent back to the surface.

She broke through at the center of the pool and saw Brad in his bathing suit dangling his feet in the water and watching her. She drew even with his legs, his beautiful legs, muscular and well formed.

'I love you.' His declaration caught her by surprise.

He pushed off from the edge, stood in the shallow end, reached out for her hand, and drew her near. She closed her eyes and with the tip of her tongue tasted the flesh of his shoulder.

'You've just arrived and I already dread your leaving. I'll have to stay here. My father is determined to make me earn my keep.'

'What is it you do for him?'

'Everything, anything. I check books, make phone calls, take care of correspondence. A poorly trained secretary could do it all better, but I think he likes to see me doing it.'

His voice had changed. He locked his hands about her waist now in a playful stance, and she felt his legs against hers.

'Why don't you stay?'

'Here? I can't stay here forever.'

'Why not?'

'Because my home is – '

'You don't know where your home is. It might as well be here.'

All the time he spoke, she shook her head. 'The Burgesses, they would never – '

'Well, we don't have to decide now. And you're right to practice caution. You've probably had enough of this place already.'

'No, I didn't mean – '

'Then please, just let me hold you.'

He drew her close, and she went willingly.

Then all at once something caught her eye at the top of the terrace. 'I believe we have an audience,' she whispered close to Brad's ear.

'I know.'

'Your father?'

He nodded.

'Why doesn't he join us?'

'He'd rather spy on us.'

'I'm not sure he's spying, Brad.'

'Then what?'

She started to answer, then saw Cy Compton start down the terraces heading toward the pool.

Brad saw his father approaching at the same time. 'Damn,' he muttered. 'Goddammit,' he repeated in escalating anger. And even before she had a chance to soothe him, she heard Cy calling to her from the second terrace. For a moment she foundered between this son and that father, sensing incredible need on both sides.

'You dive beautifully,' Mr Compton called out, still striding toward her with an impressive aura of power and authority. So different from Brad, who sometimes seemed to be uncertainty itself.

'Thanks,' she called back, and again glanced toward Brad, who had pulled himself up out of the pool on the opposite side and was now drying off, apparently ready to sunbathe. She wished he would glance her way for just a moment so she could reassure him with a smile. But he didn't.

'Who taught you?'

This voice came from directly above her where she stood at the edge of the pool in the shallow end. She looked up and stared straight into the sun, his face darkened in silhouette. 'Who – ' she stammered, momentarily losing her train of thought.

'Who taught you to dive and swim? You are grace itself.'

'I took swimming lessons at Hillcoat. My instructor was an Olympic diver. She was very good.'

'Obviously. And what and where is this Hillcoat?' As he talked he slipped off his shoes and rolled up the cuffs of his white slacks and lowered himself to the side of the pool, his feet dangling in the water.

'It's where I went to school,' she faltered, still a bit intimidated by this man who seemed so confident of himself and his place in the world.

'In Arkansas?' he asked. He was so close that she could catch the scent of his cologne.

'Yes.'

'Did you enjoy it?'

'School?'

'Yes.' He lifted his bare feet pleasurably in and out of the water.

Before she answered, she again glanced across the pool and saw Brad stretched out on a chaise, his eyes closed, though for some reason she knew very well that he was aware of everything that was going on.

'Well?' Mr Compton demanded playfully. 'This school, this Hillcoat, did you enjoy it?'

'Not at first, but later, yes, very much.'

'Why not at first?'

She ran her hand across the surface of the water, embarrassed by his question. 'At first, I was – new, and they didn't know where I had come from.'

'And?'

'The girls made fun of me.'

'Stupid girls.'

'But not for long.'

'I should hope not. There's enough cruelty in the world. Coming from all corners sometimes, or so it seems. Do you agree?'

She did so wordlessly, not quite knowing what response to make.

For a moment the world was silent, although there were birds somewhere persisting with their song. She dared not look up because she was absolutely certain that he was looking down at her.

'You are so beautiful,' he said, his voice low. 'If unknown origins are responsible for such perfection, then we all should be cast out like Moses in his basket.'

His words flattered her, and the image amused her as she smiled up at him, impressed anew with his tanned good looks. He appeared more like Brad's brother than his father.

'Do you swim?' she asked.

'Me?' he repeated with mock incredulity. 'Beneath this shirt are fins. If there is any problem, professional or otherwise, that I can't resolve on dry land, I strip to my swim trunks and dive down and run my fingers across the face of Zeus from ancient Greece and feel instant relief.'

'I did the same thing only a few moments ago.'

'There, you see,' he exclaimed with a proper sense of awe, though she wasn't absolutely certain what it was she should see.

'You know what,' he said with a new sense of melodrama. 'I think I am coming in for a swim. Would you mind very much?'

'No, of – '

'Very well.' And without a word of warning he fell forward into the shallow end, fully clothed.

She burst out laughing and moved back as he surfaced, spluttering. 'As I thought,' he said, still wiping water from his face, 'the water is perfect.'

'Your clothes,' she gasped, still laughing.

'Are soaked, yes, but never mind. Now we can talk as equals, though I think I will shed this.' Gingerly he unbuttoned his white silk shirt and dragged it to the side of the pool, then cupped his hands and threw water on his face and smoothed back his fair curly hair.

And throughout all of this, Belle watched, fascinated by everything, his movements, the mass of tightly coiled hair on his chest, his muscular and tanned forearms, his wonderful unpredictability. She was fast learning that when you were with Cy Compton, you didn't have time to watch anything else.

'Now, this is better' – he smiled – 'though I think we'd both be more at home in the deep end, don't you?'

At first she thought the question was rhetorical and concentrated on controlling the massive waves of self-consciousness that were washing against her along with the crystal-clear water. But when he posed the question again, she looked up to see him watching her with a new intensity.

'The deep end,' he said quietly, his voice and eyes reflective. 'There are those people who hunger for the deep end in all areas of their lives, finding nothing challenging or regenerative or imaginative in the shallow and safe end of anything. Which are you?'

'I've never really thought about it.'

'Of course not. Your entire past has been a deep end with mysteries and currents that push you one way and then the other. And still you have survived, more than survived. You've flourished, blossomed into perfection.'

All the time he spoke he seemed to be looking at her with growing respect, his voice and manner becoming more reverent, until at last he eased a step backward in the water.

'I can't begin to tell you how very much I admire you, making your way through your difficult life as you have done. Brad has told me a great deal about you and some of the ordeals you've faced. I can't even conceive of the amount of courage you must have, how much fortitude, to emerge from such a harrowing journey not only unscathed but intact, beautifully intact.'

At some point his voice had fallen to a whisper, and she found herself mesmerized not only by his gentle tone, but by his remarkable words. She sincerely hoped that he was not waiting for a reply because at the moment she was incapable of giving him one. Everything else had fallen away except his gentle eyes and a most peculiar and contradictory sense of excitement and security.

'I'm afraid I've embarrassed you, and I'm sorry,' he apologized. 'I propose that we meet down at ancient Greece for a touch of hands, then I must be off to the office. Work, I'm afraid. All right, you wait here. I'll flog my way to the other end, and on the count of three, we surface dive to the bottom and meet on the face of Zeus.'

At first she didn't understand, but then she did and was instantly caught up in his sense of play. She dog-paddled until he was in position at the end of the pool, then saw him raise his arm, hand extended.

'Ready?'

'Ready!'

'At the count of three – one, two, three!'

Effortlessly she jackknifed and cut the surface of the water and propelled herself downward toward the large tile medallion. Eyes open, she saw him coming at her from the opposite direction, tiny bubbles escaping from his nostrils, his hair wavy and extended, his white trousers billowing out, causing him to resemble some ancient winged figure from mythology.

She reached the bottom first, though he was only seconds behind her and took her by the hand and placed it on Zeus' face and covered it with his own.

Then all at once he let go and shot his way to the top, and she followed after him to the sun and surface. By the time she shook her face and eyes free of water, he was pulling himself out of the pool without a backward look, without a word. He grabbed a towel from the stack on the table and dried his face, then wrapped the towel about his bare shoulders and started up the terrace walk as though he'd just realized he was late for an appointment.

She clung to the side of the pool and watched him until he disappeared from view into his office. Perplexed by his hasty retreat, she wondered if she had angered him in any way. She hoped not. Well, enough. She shook her head and face free of water and decided to join Brad for a bit of sun. Poor Brad, to have spent his life with such a mercurial and unpredictable man. Poor, lucky Brad.

'Brad?' she called out as she turned and started swimming back across the pool.

But to her surprise she found the chaise empty. At the center of the pool she dog-paddled and searched in all directions, thinking perhaps he was at the bar for a drink or a sandwich, thinking he'd changed positions in search of the best sun, thinking he would reappear at any moment.

But he didn't, and she continued to dog-paddle until her legs and arms were tired. Then slowly she swam to the edge of the pool, uncertain and confused, still looking in all directions, not knowing whom she was looking for, whom she was missing.

Brad?

Or Cy Compton . . .

June 12, 1948
Hitchings, Texas

It was hot and still. Not a sign of a breeze. R. C. had taken the old pickup into town to see if someone could make it more reliable. He'd be leaving tomorrow. How Martha hated to see him go.

The kitchen at four o'clock in the afternoon was easily over one hundred degrees. Martha had set up a small fan on the table, but it only pushed the hot air about. Perhaps this was the wrong day for R. C.'s favorite dinner of fried chicken, mashed potatoes, okra, tomatoes, and big slices of sweet white onion.

'Keep drinking lots of water, Sara,' Martha advised.

'It's not a good hot,' Sara said, peeling potatoes, then dropping them into the pot of salted boiling water.

Not a good hot. She was right there. A blast furnace wind had blown most of the morning, then it had stopped dead.

'Let's get finished here,' Martha said, and felt sweat rolling down the small of her back. 'Then we'll join the kids outside in the shade.' She tested the grease, dropped the floured chicken in piece by piece, and stepped back to avoid the splattering.

'All done,' Sara said from her side of the stove, and clamped the lid on the potatoes.

Martha watched her and took comfort from her company. In all the time Sara had been living with her, almost two years now, she'd never heard her complain once, had never seen any sort of behavior except that of a sweet-natured young girl.

Her thoughts brought her pleasure, and she reached for a clean towel, dabbed lightly at the sweat on Sara's forehead, and saw a surprised look in her eyes.

Without warning Sara put her arms around Martha and hugged her and kissed her on the cheek, the first affection she'd ever shown. 'Your chicken,' Sara gasped, and pointed to the smoking pan.

As Martha lifted out the crispy pieces of chicken, she placed them on a clean towel and suddenly felt a breeze. Behind her the window curtains over the sink were beginning to stir. She leaned toward the window and saw churning black clouds.

As she started toward the back door, she heard the children coming around the side of the house. She pushed open the door for them. 'Hurry on in. Play in the house until the wind decides what it's going to do.'

As she rushed them into the front room, she heard Sara at the back door calling above the wind, 'Juan – '

Martha took the baby from Molly and heard the front screen door slamming open and shut. 'Where's Juan, Molly?'

Suddenly the wind began to buffet the house with a fury that caused the children to scream. Martha looked up out of the front door with sickening recognition, seeing the dark, threatening wall cloud like a massive shade being lowered over the earth. Directly beneath the black wall was a crystal-clear band of blue that hugged the ground. It was from this combination that tornadoes whirled to life.

She'd seen several as a child, had seen more than once the destruction they were capable of causing.

'Come along, kids,' she ordered, backing away from the door but leaving it open. 'Hurry, down to the root cellar. Here, Molly, take the baby. There's a candle down there. Keep them as quiet as possible. Sing to them.'

She threw open the small door behind the kitchen cabinet and herded them down the narrow steps into the safe darkness. 'Where did you say Juan was, Molly?'

'The wind blew the pictures away. He went after them.'

Martha waited until Molly was all the way down, then lowered the door and looked about for Sara. She had last seen her at the back door, calling for Juan. Now she was gone.

'Sara? Where – '

Martha made it as far as the door but not beyond. The wind had turned into a dynamo. She felt her face flattened by the force, and even though she was clinging to the door frame with both hands, she felt at any moment that the sheer force of the wind would dislodge her.

'Sara . . . Sara! . . .'

She heard a sound resembling an express train, heading toward her farmhouse. The high-pitched scream was already deafening. She had two choices, go after Sara or take refuge in the root cellar with the others and hope that Sara and Juan could survive on their own.

Then nature made the decision for her as the wind, doubling up like a fist, broke the window glass in the back door and at the same time tore loose the ceiling. As Martha heard the sounds of destruction above the sounds of the wind, she looked up and saw a large ceiling beam falling. She tried to protect her head by lifting her arm, but the heavy piece of timber collided painfully with the side of her head. She fell, losing consciousness on the descent, thinking it was to be expected. She'd been content of late, and generally speaking in her life contentment did not last.

It had always been the case, and apparently it would always be so . . .

* * *

It had started raining just as the old mechanic had dropped the hood on Martha's pickup. Carburetor, he had said without elaboration.

R. C. had paid him, glanced up at the churning sky, and decided he'd better head for home.

'Don't worry none, son,' the old man had said with a grin. 'Twisters don't like rain. You're safe in a rain.'

To tell the truth, R. C. hadn't thought about twisters. He'd seen pictures of them, and he'd seen *The Wizard of Oz*, and that was about as close as he wanted to come. Now, as he guided the truck down Hitchings's main street, he saw people running for shelter, saw a group of men standing in front of the bank pointing up at a solid black cloud slipping closer and closer to earth.

A few miles out of town the rain stopped, but the cloud continued to grow and spread until ultimately there was only a single band of blue hugging the horizon.

Then came the wind. He'd scarcely felt any wind back in Hitchings, but out here on the flat land the wind had increased to such an extent that he could feel it pushing against the old truck.

Up ahead he saw a portion of the black cloud drop down, just finger-size from a distance, as though part of the cloud's fury had broken off and decided to go it alone. He watched the moving finger with fascination as it whirled, churned, and danced, always connected with the mother cloud from which, without a doubt, it was drawing its energy and taking its direction.

Now he was having a hard time keeping the pickup on the road. The wind was still increasing, and the air was full of loose debris, a rainstorm of tumbleweed, dirt, and blowing papers. It pushed the truck to one side until it was balancing precariously on two wheels and falling to earth again.

Then no more than five minutes later, the storm passed him by, the funnel disappeared back into the atmosphere from where it had come, and all that remained was a layer of dust.

Slowly he sat up, tasting grit between his teeth. He peered out of the window like a cautious child and now smelled the sweet scent of rain. Then he saw it, great half-dollar-size drops of rain, making imprints on his dust-covered windshield.

Good. Rain would cool things off. Martha's picnic might have to be moved inside, but –

Martha.

Quickly he sat up, brushed the dirt off his shirt, and stepped on the accelerator. The rain was steady now and cooling. He had no idea where the twister had gone. All he could think of was, Good riddance.

A few minutes later he saw the farmhouse on the left side of the road, saw the mailbox uprooted and lying in the mud. Then he saw more.

'God,' he whispered and eased the old truck over. He looked up and saw half a house, as though a knife had cut cleanly down between the front door and the back and had left one side standing, the other side destroyed.

'Martha – '

He called her name even before he had left the truck. 'Martha,' he called again as he started in a run up the steps.

He saw no one. He heard no movement. Then he cried out, 'Martha, where are you? . . .'

June 24, 1948
Hollywood, California
Beverly Hills

Belle loved to dance to 'Sentimental Journey.' It was her favorite, and apparently someone had told the orchestra. They had played it at least half a dozen times. Brad was handsome in his white dinner jacket, and the terrace had been strung with lights. She was wearing the pale yellow organdy gown that Billie Rose claimed was her prettiest.

Already that evening she had met Mr Kelly and she'd met Mr Warner and she'd met Mr Power and Mr and Mrs Cooper, and she'd met so many more that she couldn't keep track.

'I'm afraid I have a request from my father,' Brad whispered as they danced.

'What?' she asked, curious. She'd not seen Cy Compton alone since the day they had swum together.

'He wants you to sing tonight.'

'Oh, Brad, why?'

'Why what? Remember I warned you. He said he had a favor, and you agreed. Sing something from your senior recital at Hillcoat. The orchestra will know anything you select.'

She lifted her eyes heavenward and wished she could claim laryngitis. 'Couldn't I sing just for him later tonight or perhaps tomorrow after breakfast?'

Brad laughed and they resumed dancing, though the good mood was gone, replaced by rising terror at the thought of having to face all these people.

'What should I sing?' she whispered, peering over Brad's shoulder at faces that suddenly had turned threatening.

'I have a request.'

'What?'

'"People Will Say We're in Love."'

She knew it very well. 'When do I have to do this?'

'Don't worry. Cy will find the right moment and let you know. For now, let's – '

But he never finished his sentence, and she heard a new somberness in his voice. 'Sentimental Journey' was followed by 'I'll Be Seeing You,' and as one romantic ballad followed another, Belle relaxed in Brad's arms and began to dread the day when her visit here would be over and she would have to return to Arkansas.

All at once Brad held her at arm's length. 'Look, if you really don't want to sing, I'll just tell him so. He has no right to force you into a command performance.'

Suddenly there was a burst of applause and she looked up,

frightened to see the entire party focused in their direction. The next voice she heard was unmistakable.

'Ladies and gentlemen . . .'

As Cy Compton came down the terrace steps, Belle saw the crowd part to make way for his passage.

'I am pleased to announce a special treat. I want Belle to sing for us. Would you do that?'

'I'd be happy to sing, Mr Compton, if it pleases you.'

'No, no "Mr Compton." Please call me Cy.'

She agreed and took Brad's hand and let him lead her to the orchestra. He introduced her to the orchestra leader, Percy Kincaid, who asked her for the name of her selection and a key.

'"People Will Say We're in Love,"' she said, then gave him the key, kissed Brad lightly on the cheek, and urged, 'Please don't go too far. I want to be able to see you.'

'I'm here,' he said, and sat on the edge of the terrace ledge.

Behind her she heard the orchestra play the refrain. She'd never sung with an orchestra before. It was good to know that it was there in the event she faltered.

But she really didn't plan to falter. Even in her dreams she could never imagine a setting more lovely. The guests, easily a hundred, were all gazing up at her, and to the left, having taken himself away from the crowd, as he frequently did, stood Cy.

She sang the song as she had never sung it before, and a few minutes later the applause startled her. She looked up to see Cy approaching until he was standing directly in front of her.

'Now I want you to sing another song. And not just me, we all do, don't we?' And he raised his voice to the company with a rallying cry that stretched all the way back up the terraces to the house itself, where she saw a line of servants looking down on the party.

In all, Belle sang eight songs, practically her entire senior recital at Hillcoat, though she was certain that the songs sounded better here with all those violins and cellos behind her. The crowd seemed to like her and moved closer until they were less than four feet away. Cy moved to a position at the end of the orchestra, where a waiter brought him a chair and a glass of champagne. He sat unmoving for the entire evening, smiling at her, joining in the applause, calling out, 'Bravo!' always encouraging her to do 'just one more.'

After almost an hour, she'd had enough. She was tired of being the center of attention. Besides, she'd seen Brad at one of the bars and knew he was drinking too much. So at the conclusion of the last song she thanked everyone, waved toward Cy, and walked out of the spotlight.

But she'd only managed a couple of steps before Cy caught up with her.

'Please, Belle, I beg you, only a moment or so more of your time. I know I've monopolized you terribly this evening, and I ask your forgiveness and Brad's. But there are so many people who want to meet you and thank you for sharing your remarkable voice. Please, only a few moments. Is it asking too much?'

His manner was so sincere, almost naive. He resembled a small boy asking one more favor of an adoring adult. Torn, Belle glanced over her shoulder in the direction of the bar and saw Brad watching closely as though he'd overheard everything and, like Cy, was waiting for her decision.

'Belle? Please. Just a moment or two, I swear. Then I'll return you to Brad safe and sound.'

How could she say no to him? After all, he was her host. And he'd promised her that he needed her for only a few minutes. She glanced back at the bar to see that Brad was no longer watching her, as though he'd known her decision at the instant she had made it. She saw the bartender refresh his drink. He'd be content as long as the drinks were flowing.

'Very well . . . Cy.'

'Oh, good, thank you, my dearest. Come, let's see. Where shall we start?'

And as Cy took her arm with gentle authority, she took a final look back at the bar to see Brad engaged in a close conversation with a young woman. Belle watched for as long as she could until Cy summoned her attention with an irresistible invitation.

'Belle, I would like you to meet Mr Clark Gable . . .'

June 24, 1948
Hitchings, Texas

Martha awakened in a white room that smelled suspiciously like a hospital. At first her vision was blurred, but she blinked her eyes several times and brought into focus a very worried looking R. C.

Now, as she smiled up at him, the worry was eased. 'Thank God,' he breathed, and sat on the edge of the bed. 'Martha, can you hear me?'

'Of course I can hear you. I'm not deaf.'

'Are you all right?'

'How would I know? I just got here.'

She tried to lift her head and instantly regretted it.

'Easy,' R. C. urged.

She closed her eyes to wait out the discomfort and gradually let small bits of consciousness back into her memory. There had been a storm –

'Sara,' she gasped. 'And Juan – '

Quickly R. C. went to the door and pushed it open. There they were, a very shy looking Sara and, clasping her hand, the dark-eyed Juan.

'They're all right,' R. C. soothed. To Sara and Juan he said, 'Come on in. She wants to see you.'

Martha reached out for Sara's hand. 'I was so worried . . . And the others?' she asked, looking around the room for the rest of her brood.

'Outside in the hall.' R. C. smiled. 'We didn't know if you would – '

'Bring them in,' she said, and felt a thick bandage that encircled her head. 'What in – '

'You've heard of the ceiling falling on people,' R. C. said. 'Well, it happened to you. You had a cut on your scalp. The doctor took twelve stitches.'

She listened to the explanation, amazed that all this had happened without her knowledge. 'Have I been here overnight?'

'You've been here for ten days.'

She was certain that he was joking. But the laughter never came. 'We've been worried sick,' he went on. 'I found you that day, half-buried by the kitchen ceiling. I couldn't find the children, I couldn't find anything – alive.'

'Poor R. C.'

'Then at last Sara came back with Juan – '

'Where were you?' Martha interrupted. 'I called and – '

'I found Juan in graveyard,' Sara explained. 'We held on to a gravestone till the wind stopped. We're sorry we worried you.'

Then R. C. led the others in, Molly carrying the baby and Rufus trailing behind. It was a good reunion, the kids crawling all over the hospital bed, playing with the controls on the side while R. C. helped Martha to a chair.

'How much of the house is left?' she asked, feeling the need to hear all the bad news at once.

'It's fine except for the kitchen and a couple of windows in front. I found two men who have been helping me. We've almost finished it. And Sara here has been a godsend, looking after the kids, cooking and washing and – '

As the list went on, Martha reached for Sara's hand and thanked God for the day she had rescued her from the back room of the community center. 'So where are we now?' she asked with a sigh.

'You are to stay right here,' R. C. instructed, 'until the doctor says you can leave. The house should be finished in a couple of days. We'll be back to see you tomorrow.'

The children were getting restless. A nurse poked her head in, a disapproving expression on her face, and then quickly disappeared.

'Come on, kids,' R. C. said, lifting Rufus off the bed and

into his arms. 'The rest of you as well. Martha needs her – '

Then the door swung all the way open and a stout man in a white coat glared at all of them. 'We need to examine her now, you'll have to get them out of here. They look filthy. This is a hospital.'

The arrogance of the man infuriated Martha. 'Sara?' she called out to the chastised little group just leaving the room. 'What are you having for dinner?'

Sara looked back, surprised. 'Meat loaf.'

'My favorite. That's it. I'm going home.'

She stood with a degree of success and looked about the room for a closet where clothes might be hidden, all the while enduring the heated protestations of both the doctor and R. C.

At last, clad in her old rose-colored chenille housecoat and her floppy slippers, she took R. C.'s arm, Sara's hand, and with the children giggling all around her, she led the parade down the corridor of Hitchings Medical Clinic and out into the sun of the late June day.

R. C. helped her up onto the high seat of the old pickup. The children and Sara piled in the back.

'You all right?' R. C. asked. 'I really think you should have stayed at least until they examined you, at least to see what you need.'

'No, thank you. I want to go home. That's all I need . . .'

June 29, 1948
Hollywood, California
Beverly Hills

It was midnight. Belle stood on her balcony and looked out over The Stables, everyone sleeping, a pearllike patina of moonlight casting all the buildings and grounds in an unreal glow.

She should be tired, but she wasn't. How could anyone

sleep in a place as beautiful as this? She shivered though she wasn't cold and drew her robe more closely about her.

She would be going home soon, back to Arkansas, and though she had missed Mac and Charlotte and Billie Rose, she would miss this paradise as well. But perhaps it was for the best. She seemed to be seeing more and more of Cy and less and less of Brad, and she was sorry for that. But Brad seemed never to be around anymore.

Someone was always making excuses for him, either Inez Cooper or Cy himself. He'd appeared at breakfast and promised to be with her at the last party that Cy was giving in her honor. He had kissed her softly and a little sadly on the cheek, and despite her entreaties for him to stay and spend the day with her, he had claimed to have work to do at the studio for his father. And as Cy had been absent as well, Belle had spent the day by the pool, talking with Inez Cooper, the feisty little Englishwoman whom she had grown to like very much.

Still, she felt out of kilter somehow, despite the beauty around her. Brad seemed to be growing more and more distant, though at one time when she'd first arrived, she had sensed that he had been on the verge of proposing. Not that she was ready for such a step. But she did love him. Didn't she? She had certainly loved him back in Arkansas. Of course she loved him. There was no doubt about it. Was there?

Abruptly she pulled on her slippers, tightened her robe about her, hurried down the terrace steps, and headed across the long driveway, which in turn led to Sylvia's mausoleum.

Breathless from her run, she stopped in the moonlight, curious as to why this had been her destination. Carefully she pushed open the door and was surprised to see a soft light filling the chamber, illumination that apparently burned night and day.

She stepped inside, planning to stay for only a moment. She looked up at the beautiful Sylvia, Brad's mother, who seemed to be smiling down on her.

Mother . . .

Why was she alone?

Where was the family that everyone else seemed to take for granted – the aunts, uncles, and cousins, some proof that everyone was part of a continuing chain?

She walked to the altar, where the urn rested between two bouquets of pink roses. She lifted a hand to touch it when all at once she heard a step behind her and turned, expecting to see the concerned face of a security guard. Instead she saw –

'Cy!'

She was embarrassed that he had found her here and was on the verge of making a quick apology and returning to her rooms. But Cy came all the way in and to her surprise sat on the small step just inside the door.

'Sit down, Belle,' he invited, and patted the step beside him. 'Please – just for a moment.'

She sat and tried to explain her presence in his wife's shrine. 'I'm sorry that I came here.'

'Why?'

She studied the mosaic of tile on the floor. 'It's your place, yours and Brad's.'

'Nonsense. It's anybody's place who wants a quiet harbor from all the hurly-burly, and I'd say that of late we have had our share of hurly-burly.'

She smiled in quick agreement and felt his leg press ever so lightly against hers.

'Dear Belle,' he whispered, and put his arm around her. 'I can't tell you how happy you have made me. What fun it is to be young again with you, to see everything through fresh and innocent eyes.'

She looked up at him, ever and endlessly fascinated by this unique man.

'Come,' he said, stood, and extended his hand to her. 'You need to be in bed. No red and sleepy eyes for the party tomorrow.' He lifted her to her feet, put his arm around her, and walked with her until they were standing in front of Sylvia's oil painting.

'Sylvia.' He addressed the woman in the painting, his arm

still about Belle's shoulder. 'Sylvia, this is Belle. I think you would like her. She is very beautiful, very gifted, and very lost, just like you. And I'd like to ask you to look after her if you could. She needs you. Come to her, comfort her, soothe her, and most important of all, love her as only a mother can do. Will you do that for me, Sylvia?'

Belle found herself mesmerized by his words and the kindness of his thoughts, and when at last he said, 'She has agreed, as I knew she would,' Belle felt a new security, a new ease, as though all her wishes had been granted.

'Now, that accomplished,' Cy said in his customary manner of moving from one finished task to another, 'you must return to your rooms. I want dawn to find you dreaming the sweetest dreams. But first, one last favor. May I hold you, just hold you? For tomorrow it will be out of the question.'

In answer to his request she said nothing, for no words were needed. She stepped into his arms and felt them tighten around her waist, felt his hand guide her head downward until it was resting on his chest, and for a lost number of minutes they stood there before the smiling Sylvia.

She could feel his heart beating and could hear him breathing. Then it was over.

His voice sounded husky when he said, 'Thank you.'

He walked with her to the door and summoned a passing security guard to escort her back to her room.

Clearly he was going to stay for a while. The last thing she saw as the guard started down the road was Cy, still standing before the portrait of his wife, as though still speaking with her . . .

At nine o'clock on 30 June 1948, a most beautiful midsummer night, two hundred and fifty highly favored and carefully selected guests gathered on Cy Compton's upper terrace to honor Belle Burgess of Arkansas.

At first Inez Cooper had had doubts about the beautiful young girl with the dazzling smile, though she'd certainly kept her opinions to herself. But then Inez had fallen in love with Belle, as had everyone, and hoped that this evening would culminate with the announcement of Brad and Belle's engagement.

But now she was fairly certain that no such announcement would take place. For one thing Brad Compton was not to be found anywhere. First Belle had searched for him, then Belle and Inez had searched for him, and at last they had enlisted Cy, who had pressed dozens of security guards into service both at The Stables as well as at the studio. To no avail. Now, while saddened, Inez was forced to admit to herself that she wasn't too surprised. Time and again she'd seen Cy take over Belle's attention and leave poor Brad to watch and wonder.

What precisely would happen, she had no idea. Now she stationed herself in her customary lookout post, the extreme west corner of the top terrace, where she scanned the scene below, not surprised to see perfection in every aspect of the evening from the flowers, to the orchestra, to the expectant company turning now and then to see if the guest of honor had yet appeared at the top terrace. No, she had not and wouldn't for another twelve and one-half minutes, the exact amount of time to build suspense and yet not court boredom.

In the interim Inez felt one of her few reflective moments coming on, for she was not by nature a woman who tended to look back. There was so little to see looking back. Still, in quiet moments she remembered the Knightsbridge section of London where she had been born and raised proper and prim in an upper-middle-class English household. Her father had been killed in the Great War in 1916, and for the next nine years she had served a virtual sentence of prisoner/companion to her demanding and critical mother. The only way that Inez had retained her sanity was to escape every afternoon to the American cinema. There, with the help of those beautiful actors and actresses who had reminded Inez of precocious children, she would for two hours be free of her mother's incessant demands and cruel criticism.

Then when she turned thirty, Inez had taken the small inheritance left to her by the terms of her father's will and emigrated to America. She had known exactly where she was going and what she was going to do.

All those beautiful Hollywood children would always need someone British and sensible to look after them and their affairs. So she went directly to Los Angeles, enrolled in the best business college she could find, and in 1929 when Sylvia Compton called wanting a private secretary, Inez Cooper and destiny were waiting.

After Sylvia's death, a death that almost proved Inez's undoing, she became generally recognized at The Stables as 'the Person in Charge.' She signed checks, dealt with all members of the staff and service people, and ran The Stables as she would a four-star hotel.

Enough woolgathering. Hopefully Brad had been found. She glanced at her watch. She moved a step to the left to check the seating, there the Dore Scharys, there the L. B. Mayers. There the Powers, Flynn and friend, and Colbert. She adored Claudette. And there dearest Jules, Julian Schaeffer, quite possibly Cy's best and closest friend, and most trusted ally, his personal attorney. Cy and Jules had known each other in New York as young men. Julian Schaeffer was the most gentle, considerate, and kind man Inez had ever known. If it weren't for that stunningly beautiful woman now standing at his side, Lorna, his wife of over thirty years, Inez would set her cap for him.

Now Percy brought the Strauss waltz to a close. There was a moment's silence.

She glanced back toward the top of the terrace, where still no one had appeared, though she'd lost count of the number of times she had gone through the staging with everyone – first Belle, followed a step behind by Brad, and then about five steps behind after them Cy, where all would come together on the central terrace and address the party with whatever news of the evening needed announcing. If it was an engagement, well and good, all the more cause for celebration. If it was simply an announcement honoring the grace and charm of their house guest from Arkansas, still well and good and certainly less complicated.

But now apparently there was to be no announcement of any kind, for as yet no one had appeared. Inez could feel a degree of nervous tension building in the company, and understandably so. She caught Percy's eye with only a glance but successfully conveyed an urgent message: *'Play!'*

Then, as the tentative sweetness of another Strauss waltz began to fill the night air, she slipped up the terrace steps and took quick refuge in the wisteria arcade, heading first for Cy's office. But the office was empty. Cy was missing as well.

Alarm increasing, she hurried down the wisteria arcade and up to the side terrace steps that led to the family wing and the new lanai suite where the gracious little guest of honor had settled in among the palms and waterfalls like a regular trouper.

As she turned the last corner that led to the lanai suite, she saw an ominous gathering of servants at the end of the corridor. And more ominous than anything else was Cy leaning against a closed door, calling out, 'Belle, please, you must let us help, please, I beg – '

At Inez's approach, the other servants parted as though to make way for an ultimate authority. 'What?' she asked briskly of a maid named Dot standing on the edge of the gathering.

'Beats me,' Dot replied with admirable bluntness. 'Someone delivered her a special letter brought by courier, and I was told she read it once, started to cry, closed and locked the door. And that's about the long and short of it.'

Though Inez might have wanted more in the way of explanation, she had the feeling that the salient points of the melodrama had been contained in Dot's succinct explanation.

It wasn't too difficult to figure out what had happened. Good old Brad had taken another powder. She'd lost count of the number of females he had loved and left. The only trouble was this one was different, clearly more sensitive to such abandonment.

'Ah, Inez!' The voice of relief was Cy's. 'Come,' he now urged, and cleared a path for her through the small audience of household staff.

As she passed through them, she very gently but firmly suggested that they all get on with their various duties. With only slight grumbling that they had been shut out of what possibly was the best show of the evening, they all turned about and muttered their way back down the corridor.

'I came to fetch them,' Cy began, 'remembering that you had told us to take our places exactly at nine.'

'Yes . . .'

'But when I got here, the door was locked and – ' He paused, a stricken expression on his face. 'I think she's crying, Inez. I think – '

'I know,' she soothed. 'Why don't you go on out to the party and try to stir some life into it.'

'What about Belle?'

'Let me tend to her.'

'And Brad? Where in the hell is Brad?'

'Cy, I could be wrong, but I think that Brad has taken off for parts unknown.'

A massive look of incredulity covered his face, followed by anger. 'The son of a bitch!'

Then he was gone and the corridor was hers, as was the painful silence coming from behind the door.

'Belle?' She knocked once, softly.

'Belle? Please let me in. I think I can help. I'd like to try . . .'

Belle sat on the edge of the bed and watched two goldfish fight the currents at the bottom of the waterfall. She felt dead. The letter was still in her hand. Twice she tried to put it down and twice she rejected the command, feeling somehow if she held it long enough, the words and declarations of the letter would either change or disappear.

She'd stopped crying, at least for the moment, and for that she was grateful. Earlier she had been aware of a commotion outside her door, had been aware of Cy knocking and calling to her. Dear God, he was the last person she wanted to see now. How embarrassed she was, how embarrassing for him, trapped with his son's house guest while his son –

There were the tears again. She bowed her head, closed her eyes, and tried to digest the pain caused by the letter in her hand.

So brief. No more than six lines, so terse and cold, as though a stranger had written it. No greeting of affection, not even of friendship, just –

Belle,

Sorry I won't be there tonight. Or tomorrow. Met up with an old girlfriend. Passion rekindled. She needs a traveling companion for Europe. I'm very good at that.

I wish you the best, as I know you wish the same for me –

Brad

The words on the page blurred. She didn't have to read them. She knew them by heart: old girlfriend . . . passion rekindled . . . traveling companion –

Why?

As fresh pain cut down she stood abruptly and tried to move away from it. But it merely followed after her, past the waterfall and goldfish, past the bougainvillea. Through her grief she saw the lavender organdy gown in which she was to have made her entrance on Brad's arm. Crushed now, the material appeared as defeated, as wilted, as she felt. She could not, would not, put in an appearance on this night or any other. She was finished here and had only one real desire, to go home.

Home.

The word alone was capable of conjuring up security, contentment, Charlotte doing her endless needlepoint beside the fire, Billie Rose bullying everyone, and Spoons calling out for a taste tester.

For just a moment the pain was eased in the onslaught

of good memories. It hadn't worked out here, it was that simple.

'Belle, it's me, Inez. May I come in?'

She looked toward the door and the soft voice beyond. Inez. She would understand. Still, how embarrassing.

For now she needed to try to put Brad Compton out of her life, out of her mind, and most difficult of all out of her heart.

Could she do that?

Only time would tell. Now she faced a more difficult task. Make the hurt stop. Make the embarrassment stop. Make the truth go away, that Brad didn't want her, as the Melvilles hadn't wanted her, as her own mother hadn't wanted her . . .

July 1, 1948
The Stables
Beverly Hills

Inez Cooper sat on the terrace steps and looked out over the pristine early morning beauty of Cy's personal kingdom. She listened for sounds coming from the suite behind. She'd left the door open, in order to hear Belle in the event she called.

Of course it was fully expected by everyone that Belle would go back to Arkansas today. In fact, last night her luggage had been brought over from storage.

Now she looked up and thought she saw movement at the end of the curved brick terrace. She blinked her eyes in an attempt to clear them, then looked again and saw nothing. Only a morning shadow. Her watch said ten minutes until eight.

There – she did see someone at the end of the walk. She adjusted her bifocals the better to see the figure just emerging from behind the hedge. It was –

Cy.

Good heavens, what was wrong with him? He was walking as hesitantly and as shy as a schoolboy. And what was that in his hand? A small bouquet of violets? There were no violets in any greenhouse at The Stables, certainly none growing in any garden. Those had been especially ordered and delivered for . . . some purpose.

'Good morning, Inez,' he called out when he was about fifteen yards away. 'Inez, would you – do you happen to know – is . . . Could I – is Belle able to – '

'I don't know,' Inez interrupted, anything to bring a halt to his painful stammering. 'She's in her room. Why don't you go on in?'

He looked grateful, as though he'd been afraid Inez would not let him pass. He stepped around her and lightly touched her shoulder. She found the gesture particularly moving and listened to the tread of his step on the stairs.

What would he find? She had no idea . . .

The hardest thing for Belle were her good memories of Brad. If she could just manage not to think for five blessed minutes. But she couldn't, and the remembrance of what had happened would strike her with a force that left her reeling.

A soft knock.

'Belle?'

It was Cy. He looked terrible. She felt sorry for him and at the same time felt a degree of resentment. If only she had spent less time with –

'May I come in?'

She said yes and sat straighter on the side of the bed, uncertain if she was in the presence of a friend or an enemy.

'Belle, I'm sorry to bother you. I probably shouldn't have come at all, but I had to see you.'

He appeared so self-conscious, so ill at ease.

'What I'm trying to say, Belle, and saying it very badly, is that although you have only been here for a short time, I wish with all my heart that you would stay at least for the rest of the summer. The Stables is a wonderful playground. Inez would love to have the pleasure of your company, as would I. I would hate to have you leave here thinking so ill of us. Please, I beg you, stay for a while.'

She focused on the intricate Oriental design at her feet and saw it blur.

'I'm sorry. I didn't mean to upset you further.' He placed the violets in her lap. 'All I ask is that you remember what I've said, how much we all would love to have you stay here. Please, I beg you, consider it.'

She wished he'd leave now. And as though he had heard her wish, he turned immediately and closed the door behind him, and she was alone.

Slowly she reached for the violets and thought on everything he'd said to her. And thought, No, her place wasn't here. It wasn't really back with the Burgesses. Where was her 'place'? Would she ever know?

'Please,' she whispered as though asking for mercy . . .

July 14, 1948
Oak Cliff Rehabilitation Center
Dallas, Texas

Charlie had no idea what the note meant, a summons for him to come immediately to the front office, signed by Captain Wayne Tarkington.

For a moment he felt like a misbehaving schoolboy called to the principal's office. But how had he misbehaved? And why after two years in the rehab center was he now being summoned to see Captain Wayne Whateverhisnamewas?

Charlie wheeled his chair closer to the window of his cell-like room. One good push in any direction was about all he could manage.

Still, it suited him. He didn't need much.

He glanced again at the summons. He'd better go find out what it was all about.

A few minutes later he rolled himself out into the hall and past the rec room, a large hot room that always smelled of body odor and tobacco. Then he maneuvered his chair to the right and toward a long corridor, illuminated by the amber rays of a late afternoon sun. He could hear someone's radio in a distant room. Bob Wills was playing 'San Antonio Rose.' Slowly he began to turn his wheels. The chair was old, made an awful squeak. The last thing Charlie wanted to do was call attention to himself.

A few moments later he rolled into the reception area and saw the captain's office to the right. The door was open. He saw a WAC working on a typewriter behind the desk.

'Yes?'

'I'm here to see Captain Tarkington.'

'Do you have an appointment?'

'I have a note,' Charlie said, and held up the message he'd found beneath his door.

'Go on in,' she said, and turned back to the typewriter.

Charlie wheeled toward the door. 'Sir?' he said to the officer behind the desk.

'Charlie Groveton?'

'Yes, sir.'

'Thanks for coming so promptly.'

'What is – '

'I have received notification,' the captain began, and commenced to riffle through the cluttered surface of his desk, 'that . . . wait a minute, it's here someplace. Yes. The army feels,' he went on, looking at the letter, 'that we need to have an assets conference.'

Charlie frowned. 'I am afraid I don't – '

'Since you were wounded in . . . let's see, June of forty-four, you have elected to roll over all of your pay as well as your medical benefits.'

'Yes, that's – '

'So now, according to this report, your accumulated funds amount to . . .' The man's eyes scanned the page and stopped at the bottom.

'Good heavens' – he smiled – 'did you know about this?'

'About what, sir?'

'About your accumulated earnings?'

'No, I – '

'You've sent nothing to your family?'

'I have no family, sir.'

'Nothing for your own needs?'

'My needs are simple.'

'Apparently.' The captain laughed and lifted the letter, as though wanting to be accurate. 'Your earnings on the books at present are . . .' He paused again. 'Nineteen thousand seven hundred sixty-seven dollars and thirty-two cents.'

He looked up at Charlie with an expectant expression. 'Well?'

Charlie blinked. He thought he'd been paying attention, but the numbers had simply gone right past him. 'I'm sorry, sir, I didn't quite – '

'Nineteen thousand seven hundred sixty-seven dollars and thirty-two cents, Groveton. How much clearer can I make it? Here, see for yourself.'

With that he handed the paper across the desk.

'Nineteen thous – ' Charlie began, his hands trembling as his eyes struggled to find such a number on the page.

Then he found it, at the bottom of a long column opposite which were designations such as back pay, combat pay, medical disability benefits. There it was, neatly tabulated.

He looked up at Captain Tarkington, who was grinning back at him. 'Yeah, it's something. I've only known a couple of other guys to accumulate more, and one of them was in a prison camp for four years.'

Charlie looked down again as though fearful that perhaps the number had disappeared. But there it was, a fortune. Perhaps there was a catch.

'How is, under what terms is this amount – to be paid?' Charlie asked, not looking up, half afraid to.

'How about this?'

Captain Tarkington reached into his top drawer and withdrew an army issue check. He read, '"Pay to the Order of First Sergeant Charles Groveton, nineteen thousand seven hundred sixty-seven dollars and thirty-two cents." How's that?'

Charlie shook his head, still certain that there was a catch.

'It's yours, soldier.' Captain Tarkington smiled and leaned across the desk, pushing the check toward Charlie. 'Now take it and go home. You don't belong here. And if you haven't got a home, buy one, and if you don't like the bus, we can get you a car redesigned for an amputee. You got your stake now. So just clear out, you hear? Whether you like it or not, you've got a lot of good years left, so go on and start living them.'

Charlie heard.

'If you haven't got a home, buy one –'

'Where are you from, soldier?'

'West Texas, sir, the Panhandle.'

'Then go on back to west Texas, where you got roots if nothing else. They'll serve a man even if they once were severed. The heart remembers, and that's all that counts.'

Charlie listened closely to everything the man was saying.

Home.

It was safe now, he was certain of it, nobody there who would bother him or hurt him.

'Hey, you all right?'

'Sorry, sir. I'll go now,' Charlie said hurriedly. 'Would you keep this for me, while I make some plans?'

'It'll be in the safe.'

'And that car you mentioned?'

'Yes, let me give you the guy's name. He's right here in Oak Cliff. What he does is he takes a good used car and rigs it to suit your needs.'

'I'd like that.'

'Then I take it you'll be leaving us?'

Charlie looked up at the direct and very difficult question. He felt safe here. The thought of someone from Hitchings seeing him like this was more than he could bear. Yet he ached for the sight and sound and smell of the earth again.

'What do you say? Are you going home?'
'Yes, sir, I'm going home . . .'

December 25, 1948
Oak Cliff, Texas

Christmas morning and Charlie felt exactly as he'd felt on that Christmas morning years ago when he'd discovered, next to the Christmas tree, his first bicycle. Dark blue with black leather seat cover, chrome fenders, and the promise of freedom.

Now he stood at the curb beside his car, again dark blue, a Ford, 1946, with black seat covers and a clever mechanism on the steering wheel that enabled him to operate the brakes and the gearshift. The accelerator had been relocated into the center of the floor so he could reach it easily with his one good leg.

A marvel of a car, the design belonged to a genius of a mechanic in Oak Cliff named Marley, an amputee himself who kept busy turning out his special cars for veterans like Charlie. Once Charlie had asked him why he didn't submit his design to Detroit. Marley had burst out laughing. 'Now Charlie Groveton, who's gonna pay serious attention to an ignorant, one-legged nigger?'

Charlie had placed the order four months before, but there were others ahead of him. Then Marley had called two weeks ago to say the car was ready. Charlie had paid twelve hundred dollars and taken three test drives. Marley had gone with him to get his license and finally had pronounced him 'ready to fly.'

And ready he was. In the backseat were his crutches, his collapsible wheelchair, the black case with the hated prosthesis, and one small cardboard suitcase, everything he had in this world.

He'd always dreaded Christmas Day in the rehab center, so he'd planned purposely to leave on this day and thus avoid the visiting families with their sad faces.

Now he eased himself behind the wheel. He'd said his good-byes to his checker-playing buddies and had thought that one or two might come to the front door and wave him off. Yet when he looked back he saw nothing but the lopsided paper Christmas wreath.

Then so be it. He was free, the day was mild, a warm sunny Christmas Day, and for the first time since Omaha beach he was beginning to feel almost like a man. A man could drive his own car, a man had some money in the bank, a man could pick and choose where he wanted to go.

Charlie's destination was the farmhouse outside Hitchings in the west Texas Panhandle, the place of his birth, of his growing-up.

He had wings beneath him now in the shape of wheels, and all he wanted was to go to that old farmhouse, sit on the porch, watch the wind blow through the wheat, and somewhere in the distance listen to the lullaby of a pumping well, hear an owl hoot or a coyote howl.

'Son of a gun . . .' He grinned and tapped the horn lightly with the palm of his hand. Then he struck it a bit harder, honked the horn, laughed out loud, and turned on the ignition, shifted into gear, looked both ways, and pulled away from the curb.

Charlie Groveton was back among the living . . .

December 25, 1948
Hitchings, Texas

It had been a strange Christmas Day, one of the happiest Martha could remember and one of the saddest. She looked around at the cluttered living room, still strewn with wrapping paper at six-thirty in the evening, Christmas carols being sung on the radio, the remains of the turkey dinner still on the kitchen table, and amidst all the clutter not one human being in sight.

She sat comfortably on the old rocker and mentally called the roll: Rufus and Molly, of course, were riding their new bicycles hell bent for leather up and down the road in front of the house. Juan was riding his tricycle on the front walk under the watchful eye of Sara, and Ezra was taking a late afternoon nap.

Now she should be up and about doing dishes, straightening, seeing if she could help R. C. with his packing. There was the sad part of the day, the inevitable good-bye, but not merely back to school this time. This time he was driving all the way to San Diego to fulfill his military obligations, and the only good thing that Martha could find in all of it was that there was no war going on. Thank God for small favors. Two years. Then he'd be out and free to pursue his education, a master's degree, then his Ph.D. Imagine!

She shook her head, thinking how sad for the real parents of all her children not to be able to watch them grow and develop. But then someone somewhere might be saying that about Belle.

Abruptly she stood, not that it was the first time she'd thought the name all day. It wasn't. Then get busy doing something, go to R. C.'s room, sit with him while he packs, talk with him, store up memories against the long months that he would be far away.

She snagged an olive as she passed the kitchen table and went to R. C.'s room at the back of the house. His door was open, but she heard no sound. She started to knock, then peered in and saw him seated on the opposite side of the bed, his head bowed. She heard him sniffle as though he had a cold.

'May I come in?' she called out, and saw him hurry to repair himself. 'I'm sorry if I – '

'No, no, of course not. Come on in. I was hoping . . .'

'What?'

He looked self-conscious. 'I was . . . packing. I'm almost finished. I was getting ready to give you your Christmas present.'

'I told you I wanted nothing. I have everything.'

'Oh, I think you're wrong. I think you'll want this.'

He stepped back to the side of the bed. 'In one of my

classes last spring, there was an interesting man. He has a degree in anthropology and he was getting a degree in psychology. He worked part-time for the Dallas police. He had an extraordinary talent of being able to sketch how a person might look years later from an early photograph. He was used primarily to help locate missing persons and now and then to try to identify skeletal remains.'

Martha listened closely.

'We were having coffee one day and I showed him the sketch of Belle that I had done when we last saw her at three. I asked him if he could – '

He broke off. 'He could and did. I was going to give it to you this morning when everyone was opening presents but decided to wait until tonight before I left.'

Slowly he bent over and pulled something out from beneath the bed. He brought it to her, and she saw in his eyes a warning of some sort.

Then she turned it about and gasped as she surveyed a beautiful young girl, about eighteen, with shiny blond hair, quite long, with wide-set blue eyes and a smile that seemed to encompass the whole world.

'I almost didn't give it to you,' he said.

She still was unable to speak and sat down on the edge of the bed, R. C. beside her. 'She's beautiful,' she said.

'I – don't know quite why it always tears me apart . . .'

She put her arm around him. 'R. C., will we ever find her?'

'Yes,' he replied without a moment's hesitation. 'Yes, we will. For some reason I'm more certain than ever. When I get through these next two years, come to California with me. I'd like to study at UCLA anyway, and I have the strongest feeling that she is in California, that she rode that train to the very end, to LA, and someone found her. And now – with this – ' He held the portrait higher, and again they studied the lovely young face that they'd last seen fifteen years ago.

Martha heard one of the children calling out front. 'Martha, is R. C. ready to go?'

'Not yet. We'll be there in a minute.'

R. C. closed his suitcase. 'I'm leaving a bunch of stuff here. Is that all right?'

'Of course.'

'Books, primarily. I doubt if there will be very many opportunities for research.'

'I wish you didn't have to go.'

'So do I. But you taught me that an obligation is an obligation.'

'Me and my big mouth.'

'I'll miss you, Martha, and I'll worry about you. Out here on this deserted road alone.'

'I grew up on this deserted road, as you put it. And who would bother an old woman and a mixed bag of kids?'

'You're not old.'

'Sometimes I feel it.'

'We will find Belle, for the simple reason I won't let either of us die until we do.'

This heartfelt pledge weakened her dangerously.

'You take care.'

'And you, too.'

'Call me when you get there.'

'Of course.'

'Then I guess that's it.'

R. C. handed Martha the portrait of Belle. 'Keep her safe for both of us.'

'I will.'

They walked arm in arm back through the house to the front porch, where Sara had managed to corral Juan, Molly, and Rufus. Their faces glistened with perspiration in the unseasonable warmth of the evening.

Behind her, coming from the radio in the living room, Perry Como was singing 'Jingle Bells.'

'No dashing through the snow tonight,' Martha said, laughing, and together they all walked down to the road where R. C.'s car was parked. As R. C. was putting his luggage into the trunk, Martha saw Molly and Rufus tie a red yarn Santa Claus to the front of his car.

'Looks like you won't be traveling alone after all,' Martha said, and pointed out the new decoration and the two grinning 'decorators.'

'Now gather around, all of you,' R. C. commanded in his best teacher's voice. 'I want you to promise me to look after Martha as well as yourselves. Is that clear?'

'Yes, R. C.,' came a solemn choral reading.

'Well, then, come on, I want a kiss from everybody.' As the parade lined up to dispense kisses, Martha looked down the road, amazed at how much lonelier it already seemed.

Then he climbed behind the steering wheel, closed his door, waved a final time, and started slowly away. The wind picked up the red yarn Santa Claus and made it look as if *he* were waving as well.

The distortion delighted the children, who ran after the car as far as they could, though all that was left was the dust raised by the car's passage and Bing Crosby on the radio in the living room singing 'Silent Night.'

'Shall I round them up for their baths?' Sara asked.

Martha shook her head. 'No, let them ride their bikes and trikes a while longer. Come on, let's you and me sit on the porch and have a cup of coffee. Ezra will be wanting his dinner. We'll sit a spell, then we'll clean up.'

They sat in perfect silence until the western sky was ablaze with red, orange, and gold. 'No place in the world for sunsets like west Texas,' Martha said.

And that was all that was said for the next hour. Then: 'You bathe the kids. I'll wash the dishes.'

As each went to her own tasks, Martha thanked God for the routine of living. There were times when it was the only thing that kept a human heart from breaking . . .

It had taken Charlie Groveton all day to go three hundred and fifty miles. But that was perfectly all right with him, and with apologies to no one he'd stopped three times for barbecue at the very best places, those smelly, dusty little shacks alongside the road with the big cookers fired up behind. He'd forgotten how good barbecue, baked beans, and crusty golden rounds of cornbread could be.

Then on the outskirts of Amarillo he'd stopped at a big market to lay in a supply of groceries and to get out of the traffic for a while.

Amarillo had grown and changed. He'd come in on a big highway past all sorts of shopping buildings and salvage yards, past a shiny new place called the Sun River Motel, past places where they sold just about anything a mind could think of. He'd used his crutches in the store, and everyone had stared at him like they used to back in Oak Cliff, but he'd pushed one of those big carts around and chocked it full of canned goods and coffee, dried beans, rice, and bottled water in case his well had gone dry. Then with his backseat and trunk filled, he had headed out on Highway 54 toward Hitchings.

He'd passed the outskirts about dusk and immediately noticed a change or two in Hitchings as well. Bigger, more spread out, with one of those motel places, only this one wasn't as fancy as the one in Amarillo. And where Thompson's Market used to be was now a sprawling supermarket like the one outside Amarillo. And on the main street the tire shop had expanded, and where Mullins Diner used to be was now a place called the Chicken Shack. Changes, everywhere he looked.

In fact, if Charlie had just dropped down out of a plane, he wouldn't even be absolutely certain he was in Hitchings. Of course some things were the same. There was the big water tower, though someone had painted it blue, and the bank was still there, and there was the billiard parlor and Starling's Feed Store. And there on the corner of the intersection with the county road was Hoskins Filling Station, though according to the sign it wasn't old man Hoskins anymore, which was just as well.

Now he pulled into the small station, so familiar from his past, and watched a young boy, broken out in pimples, heading for his car.

'Fill 'er up,' Charlie said with a smile, and received no

reply from the kid, who obviously was mad because he had to work on Christmas.

For the first time since he'd left Dallas, Charlie began to relax. He was tired as hell, and all that barbecue wasn't riding so well. But he was grateful for one thing. The weather was mild, which meant he would be comfortable in his bedroll in the event the old house had not aged any too good. Of course his overriding fear was that someone had moved into the house. Then what would he do?

As the kid came around to get the windshield, Charlie asked, 'What's up the county road these days?'

The kid looked at him through the bug-splattered windshield as though he hadn't heard or understood.

'This road here,' Charlie repeated, 'anyone live up this way now?'

The kid shook his head. 'Just some old lady and a bunch of kids.'

'Do you know the old Groveton place?'

'Empty.'

Thank God, Charlie breathed, fished through his pocket, and paid the kid for the gas. 'Merry Christmas,' he called back, and was just about to pull out when a car passed in front of him coming from the direction in which he was headed. A man was driving, fairly young, and on the front of the hood was tied a small red Santa Claus.

Slowly Charlie pulled forward and to the right, heading down the road he knew better than the back of his hand. About two miles down the road he saw the Drusso place, saw a boy and girl with their bikes at the side of the road, and saw the house newly painted with fresh shutters and lights blazing throughout.

Charlie passed by the house and the kids in a blur. Ahead by three miles was his place.

Home.

He really didn't care what condition it was in. He'd clean it and take care of it for the rest of his life. This was all he wanted. He realized that now. He'd done enough wandering and roaming.

It was almost dark, so he couldn't see much, but he found the dirt road of a drive, turned on his headlights, and saw the fallen gate and the front of the house.

He stopped the car and clung to the steering wheel.

'Charlie, you're home,' he whispered in the darkness . . .

January 5, 1949
Hitchings, Texas

As Martha set the table for dinner, she heard the rain beating against the window and drew the shade.

All the tinsel of the sunny, warm Christmas had been put away. Early this afternoon a cold rain had come up, and she had brought in two loads of firewood, though she knew the fire would do little to warm the chill deep inside her.

She missed R. C., though he'd already called twice, praising the beauties of San Diego and promising to send photos as soon as possible.

The two older children, Molly and Rufus, were going back to school tomorrow, which would leave only Martha, Sara, Juan, and Ezra. She planned to make tonight special for the kids, and she wanted very much to have a private talk with Molly, whose propensity for exaggeration and just plain wild stories was getting out of hand.

R. C. had encouraged her shamelessly when he'd been home, claiming that her red hair and freckles spoke clearly of a few loose Irish genes, and to an Irishman a good story was perhaps the most important ingredient in life, having absolutely nothing to do with morality or lying.

So egged on by R. C., Molly had treated them nightly to the most bizarre stories Martha had ever heard, white horses that flew through the sky, two mice in the barn that spoke to her of distant places, and now this latest, the one-legged man she'd seen standing on the roof of the old farmhouse down the road.

'Dinner!' Martha called out. 'And wash first,' she added,

surveying the table set with the new red oilcloth, a special purchase for Christmas and one she couldn't bear to pack away with the other decorations. It made the kitchen look cheery.

Sara and Juan arrived first, Molly and Rufus came into the kitchen next. The pair had become like Siamese twins since they'd both received new bikes for Christmas. Up until today when the rain had started, they would disappear after breakfast in the morning and reappear throughout the day only when hunger and thirst drove them home.

'You two look as if someone had died,' Martha said, and tied a bib around Ezra's neck.

'School tomorrow,' Rufus muttered.

'I know. I should think you'd be ready to go back.'

'I'm not,' Molly pronounced with conviction. 'And it's raining.'

This last was added as though it were the ultimate offense.

Martha lifted the bubbly casserole of macaroni and cheese out of the oven, smiled at the hungry reaction around the table, and quickly served generous portions to everyone. There was little talk on any subject for several minutes as everyone ate heartily.

Then, 'Saw him again today,' Molly said between bites.

'Saw who?' Sara asked.

'That man with one leg, down at that old farmhouse. Rufus and me rode down there before the rain started, and there he was, that one-legged man trying to chop firewood. But he couldn't do it, 'cause he needed both hands for his crutches, and he fell a couple of times. Then Rufus and me, we helped him.'

Martha listened, astounded. Apparently the child was capable of creating a whole world in her head. 'And how did you help him?' she asked with strained patience, curious to see just how far Molly would go.

'Well, Rufus stood on the end of the wood and I chopped it. Then we picked it up and carried it into his house. He's very nice, the one-legged man, he doesn't have much, just a chair and a cot and a few dishes. But he thanked us and said he'd appreciate it if – '

She looked at Rufus, who returned her stare with a hard glare of condemnation.

'Well, I forgot,' Molly whispered.

'You promised.'

'I said I forgot.'

'Hey, you two, what's going on?' Martha interrupted, alarmed. 'Rufus? Did you see this one-legged man as well?'

'Yes, ma'am.' Rufus nodded, and at last the kids had Martha's attention. If there was a drifter, one-legged or not, squatting in the old Groveton house, she wanted to know about it.

'Did he say anything to you?' she asked Rufus.

'Yes, ma'am.'

'What?'

'He asked about you, asked your name, asked if you had a – '

'A husband.' Molly giggled, claiming center stage again, as though it were her story and she'd answer the questions.

Alarm rising, Martha put down her fork. Someone wanted to know if there was a man here? Why? Easier to rob –

'Tell me more,' she invited both children.

Molly spoke first. 'He's real old,' she said, wrinkling her nose, 'and he walks on crutches like he hurts. He doesn't say much. He carried in the wood, and that's when he asked all those questions about us and this house and you, mostly you.'

Martha and Sara exchanged a glance. If only Rufus hadn't confirmed Molly's crazy story. But the prospect of a strange man less than three miles away making inquiries about her and this house was not a matter to be taken lightly.

'Finish your dinner,' she said, and as they ate she thought on what they had told her. If R. C. were here, she'd ask him to go down and see what, if anything, was going on. But R. C. wasn't here.

So it was up to her . . .

* * *

After the children had been put to bed and against Sara's wishes, Martha slipped into her dark jacket, loaded her father's hunting rifle, and flipped on the safety.

'Martha, please don't. Tomorrow we call the sheriff, let him go. Remember what R. C. say to you.'

'I'm not going to do anything,' Martha said, zipping up the hood of her jacket. 'I just want to take a look for myself. You know as well as I do that it probably is just Molly's imagination again.' She gave Sara a kiss on the cheek, told her to lock the back door and leave on the porch light.

Alone on the back steps, she fished through her pockets for the keys to the old pickup. Sidestepping the big puddles, she jumped into the truck, turned on the ignition, and backed out.

There was a small lake at the bottom of the drive, but she plowed through and fell easily into the main rut of the old road, always keeping her eye on skittering shadows. Molly's silliness had made her jumpy.

When she was about fifty yards from the old Groveton place, she turned off her headlights and pulled the truck over as far as she dared on the muddy road. Then quietly, without slamming the door, she started walking the last few yards, always keeping a close eye on the farmhouse.

She smelled wood burning. She looked toward the chimney and saw a pale wisp of smoke and felt her heart accelerate. Someone *was* there. Molly had told the truth.

As she drew nearer to the road that led to the house, she kept close to the lilac hedge. She saw a pale yellow light coming from inside, as well as a shadow that passed back and forth in front of the light.

Martha stopped. She was shivering, partly from cold, partly from fear. Perhaps Sara had been right. Maybe she should go back to the house and call the sheriff. It could just be a squatter, a drifter, or it could be someone far worse.

She stood for several seconds, trying to decide on the best course of action.

She'd come this far. Maybe she should try to get close enough for one quick look. She didn't like the thought of a stranger in Charlie's house. And it *was* still Charlie's house to her, and he'd want her to see who was trespassing on his property.

So she crept forward, her heart beating in her throat, and got close enough to the living room window to peer in . . .

Charlie stared glumly into the fire and tried to decide what he should do.

Every instinct commanded, 'Leave. Leave now – spare yourself.' The little red-haired girl had said the woman who looked after her was named Martha.

It was no mere coincidence. Martha had come home. No wonder the Drusso place looked so spit-and-polished. Martha always was one for pretty and neat.

But then both children had said there was no man, and if that was true, then where was her husband, the one she'd ran off with years ago according to old Max Drusso?

He leaned back in the rocker and closed his eyes, amazed and angry at how much it still hurt.

Well, if it was Martha – and who else would it be – then it would be best for him to keep moving. He had wheels now and some money. He could go anyplace, do anything he wanted.

He opened his eyes and stared down into the fire. The truth was he didn't want to go anyplace else, didn't want to do anything else but stay here, wait for spring, and plant a garden.

Martha –

The last time he'd seen her was what, eighteen, almost twenty years ago. Yet he'd know her anyplace, even now. Some things about Martha he was certain would never change, like her capacity for love.

Abruptly he leaned forward and rested his forehead in his hands. If he were certain that he would recognize her, he was less certain she would recognize him. Look at him, a damn cripple, his whole body thrown out of kilter by the missing leg, and there was gray in his hair and he couldn't begin to do the work he'd once done and sometimes his back hurt from where they'd had to leave some shrapnel in, and –

He wanted to get up and move away from the fire and the rocking chair but realized he'd left his crutches on the other side of the room. His wheelchair was close by, but he was sick of that chair, and the only way he could get to his crutches was to hop like a damn rabbit, hop-hop-hop. And suddenly without warning he stood on his one leg, lifted the rocker, and hurled it with murderous ferocity halfway across the room. In the fever of anger he lost his balance, fell onto the floor, and lay there studying the fire from a different perspective. After several moments of cursing he pushed himself up into a sitting position and faced the hard truth.

There were options. Self-pity was not necessary, productive or fun.

If he decided to stay here, he knew one thing for certain. He did not *ever* want Martha to see him with one leg. If he stayed, he would have to wear the prosthesis. He sat on the floor, propped up by one hand, and knew that what he needed was over there, beneath his cot.

He stared at it over his shoulder for several minutes, then half dragged, half pushed himself across the floor, reached under the cot for the black case, and righted the chair he'd recently hurled in anger. He placed the case on the seat of the chair and pushed the whole thing back in front of the fire, the only place in the room where his teeth didn't chatter.

Slowly he opened the case and lifted out the heavy pad that he was to place between his bare stump and the prosthesis itself. He examined it, saw dried bloodstains where he'd tried to work with the therapist at the VA Hospital. It had hurt like hell then. Maybe the skin of the stump was tougher now.

At last he lifted out the thing itself, complete with harness and fake black shoe. Now he wasn't even certain that he remembered how to put it on. Slowly he stood, using the chair for support, and balanced on his good leg. He unbelted and unzipped his khaki trousers, slipped them down, and sat back down in the rocker. Clad only in his wool plaid shirt and undershorts, he stared down at himself and felt sick at his stomach, wondering how long it would take before he got used to the sight. He'd been told that some men never got used to it, never accepted it.

Well, he wasn't sure what else he could do with it but accept it. There it was for all the world to see, one good leg and one reddish purple stump with sinews and scar tissues running crisscross where the flap of skin had been brought down over jagged bone. He had scar tissue all the way up his hip and side where the shell had ripped him open. But he'd recovered in all aspects except for – that.

And now more to cover it and get it out of his sight than anything else, he reached down for the pad, held it in place, and at the same time fitted the joint of the prosthesis to his leg. Then he stood and brought the harness up about his waist, then down the side of his leg, pulling all of the straps tight as he remembered the therapist telling him to do, at last securing them in appropriate buckles. Now he dared to test just a portion of his weight on the piece of dead material attached to his knee.

It didn't hurt so much, and he tested it again and yet again until at last he was standing on both feet.

The feeling of balance was good. Standing upright, without crutches or support of any kind, he gave a quick smile and whispered, 'Damn,' and grew brave and tried to manipulate the fake leg forward into a step. Thinking it had moved when it hadn't, he tried to bring his real leg forward and fell hard on his knees. His teeth grated together, and he bit his tongue.

He stayed on his knees to wait out the pain, then remembered the therapist crying, 'Operate it from the hip. The power has to come from the hip. Try again . . .'

And he did, reaching back for support, angling the fake leg out, then up, and dragging his good one after it. Using both hands, he grabbed his upper leg and swung his hip out, seeing the fake leg and foot move all of about an inch. He tried again, harder, and this time the leg moved too far too fast. Again he went down, in the manner of a split this time. Waiting out the discomfort of a cramp in the calf of his good leg, he tried again and again, moving the leg forward, always falling, always rising and trying again.

After about an hour, he could go three steps without falling, though by now his knee was bloodied and his hands bruised. Still he tried, falling, rising, falling, rising, always encouraged enough to keep on, knowing if he ever wanted to look upon Martha Drusso again, he'd have to do it standing on two good legs.

Martha moved as close to the window as she dared and saw a man standing awkwardly. Then he lifted the chair in which he had been sitting and hurled it angrily across the room.

The sudden violence startled her, and she was on the verge of withdrawing when she saw the man fall and noticed the missing leg for the first time.

'And I saw an old, one-legged man.'

Molly had not lied this time, though the man didn't seem so old, just tired and weak. She watched him as he raised up and half dragged, half pulled himself toward the cot, watched as he pulled out a black case of some sort and straightened the chair he'd recently hurled, watched him place the case on the seat of the chair and then push the whole thing back toward the fire.

Not until he turned and started back toward the fire did she see his face.

She made a sound, just a brief outcry, and quickly covered her mouth with her hands. 'Charlie?' she breathed, the name a question because she wasn't certain. He was older, gray in his hair, and he'd been ill, for he was thin. But worse than that, his leg –

The hand that covered her mouth trembled, but she kept it firmly in place to keep from making a sound and watched as he slipped off his trousers and frowned at what he saw.

'Oh, Charlie.' She spoke his name again, just an inhalation of air, and wondered what had happened to him.

She pulled her jacket more closely about her as he withdrew an artificial leg from the black case, struggled into the harness, tightened the straps, and at last stood on uncertain feet. He tried to walk and fell, and she started forward, ready to run around to the front door to help. But abruptly she stopped. She couldn't do that. She knew Charlie too well and still loved him far too much. She suspected that this was the first time he'd tried the artificial leg, and when he was ready . . .

Again he fell and again he stood, and she hid by the window for almost forty-five minutes, feeling his pain through the side of the house, aching to go to him, watching him wipe the blood from his knee and wishing she could absorb some of the pain for him.

Every time he fell she spoke his name and wiped at her tears, knowing that she would have to wait for him to come to her. At last she hurried back to her truck and sat for a long time in the cold dark, though she was aware of neither the cold nor the dark. All she could think of was, 'Charlie is home . . .'

January 16, 1949
Hitchings, Texas

For the next ten days Martha got up each morning, put on a clean dress, brushed her hair, put a dab of lavender behind each ear, and went about her chores, always keeping an eye on the road out front.

But so far he hadn't come.

She'd told Sara and the kids all about him, how he'd been her beau, and she'd had to explain to all of them what a beau was and that somehow they'd gone different ways and she hadn't any idea what had happened to him, but that she was fairly certain he'd come calling soon and when he did, they were all to behave themselves, please –

Then, on the eleventh day, a bright sunny Friday afternoon, Sara came running into the kitchen, her face flushed with excitement. 'He's here, Martha, your beau is here. He just drove up out front.'

Martha was making cornbread and had just taken the heavy black skillet out of the oven, almost dropping it on her foot.

'Here,' Sara offered. 'You go on.'

'How do I look?'

'Beautiful.'

Martha's hands were shaking. Her heart felt as though it had ceased to beat altogether, and as she started through the living room, she saw children grinning at her from all sides.

'Don't be monkeys,' she whispered, and kept her eye trained on the man just starting slowly up the front steps, walking unaided on what appeared to be two good legs.

She pushed open the door and let it slam behind her, and this summoned his attention. Slowly he released his hold on the railing and stood erect. He was wearing clean khaki trousers and a clean white shirt opened at the neck. His hair was gray at the temple, freshly combed, and he'd shaved too close. One cheek was scraped pink.

She proceeded on a few feet and felt suddenly so weak at the sight of him, she too was forced to stop.

'I declare, it's Charlie Groveton,' she said, her voice scarcely audible.

'Martha,' he said, shy as always. 'I didn't mean to surprise you. I wanted to bring you some flowers, but I couldn't find any growing.'

'It's January.'

'Yes.'

'You look grand.'

'You too – '

'I've . . . missed you.'

'I've missed you.'

Then she knew she didn't stand a chance of keeping back the tears.

He didn't look as though he were doing any better, so she moved a few steps closer, slowly put her arms around him as she felt his tighten around her.

He felt thin to her, yet so familiar, and she hated the thing that had hurt him and knew she'd hear all about it in time because there wasn't anything or anyone on earth that was going to take this rare man from her again.

She had twenty years of love stored up to give him, and that was just the way it was going to be . . .

February 20, 1949
The Stables
Beverly Hills

Somehow summer had stretched into fall and Belle had tried several times to leave, but Cy had always made some irresistible proposition. 'Stay until Thanksgiving, just stay until after I complete this film, then we will . . .'

She had managed to escape back to Arkansas for Christmas with every intention of staying there. But Cy had phoned her on the second of January, claiming that Inez was very lonely, that there was a special project he wanted to share with her, and please, please, if it was all right with the Burgesses, could she fly back out for just a short visit?

Of course it had been all right with the Burgesses. They had grown very fond of Cy Compton, his courtesy and thoughtfulness, though both were still puzzled and hurt by Brad's behavior. Both Cy and Belle had received brief friendly letters from Brad, apologizing, claiming that he had never been happier, living with his girlfriend on a houseboat in Chelsea on the Thames. She was an artist, and he was learning to paint as well. So. Matter closed, and the twinges of hurt that Belle still felt occasionally were receding, healed by Cy's sweet consideration.

Belle had heard music coming from Cy's studio all morning and had been intrigued by it. A piano expertly played. She recognized the songs, all hits from the Broadway musical *Harvest of the Heart*.

Slowly she sat up, the music still forming a beautiful backdrop, wiggled her toes beneath the sheets, and thought on last night. Cy had invited her for dinner at the Brown Derby. So many people had stopped by their table that Cy scarcely had a chance to eat. When she'd commented on this, he'd patted her hand and said, 'The last thing people come to the Derby to do is eat.'

Now she heard Inez padding about out in the corridor, no doubt wanting a decision on the day's activities. Unfortunately Belle didn't have one, though at last she managed to get out of bed and slip on a pink cotton robe. She drew her hair back and secured it with a clip, then walked out onto the balcony, the better to hear the music.

There was a knock at the door. Inez. 'Come in,' she called, looked over her shoulder, and waved the cheery little Englishwoman out onto the balcony.

'Good morning,' Inez said.

'And good morning to you.' Belle smiled and moved some magazines off the glass table so that Inez might set down the tray of coffee and orange juice.

'Did you have a good time last night?' Inez asked.

'I guess.'

'You don't sound very enthusiastic.'

'Cy talked business most of the evening.'

'Typical. If you really want his attention, get him to take you to a place where movie folk don't go. And what will it be today? The style show at the Coconut Grove?'

'Inez, could it, I mean would it be all right if it was nothing today? I'd like very much to take a long swim and write to Charlotte and Mac.'

Inez seemed relieved. 'Whatever you wish. I have plenty to do here.'

'Why don't you come for a swim with me?'

'Later, perhaps. Cy has business guests. One I'm told has dietary restrictions. I have no idea what, but I must go and find out. So you're on your own. All right?'

'Fine.' Belle smiled and lightly brushed Inez's hand as she passed, a gesture of affection that was not lost on Inez, who passed her by a step or two, then came back and lightly kissed the top of her head.

A few moments later Belle left the chaise and waved to Inez on the flagstone below, then went back into her room, showered, and slipped on a black bathing suit, white terrycloth robe, grabbed a towel, and hummed along with 'Man in the Shadow' all the way down the steps.

Once or twice she looked up toward Cy's studio and saw all the doors and windows open. Peculiar. Usually he worked with all doors closed. When she reached the center steps leading down to the pool, she sat for a few minutes on the stone ledge, head down, still listening to the score. It was very beautiful, though why the songs were being played over and over again, she had no idea . . .

March 10, 1949
Hitchings, Texas

Martha stood over the steamy sink doing dinner dishes and tried to sort out exactly what she would tell R. C. Of course she really didn't have a lot to tell him yet, only that her old friend named Charlie Groveton had reappeared and now was having dinner almost every night with them.

She rinsed a glass and frowned at it. Not much news in that. She heard Sara in the bathroom cooing to Ezra as she gave him his bath. And in the front room by the fire, Charlie had been lassoed by the Three Musketeers, Juan, Molly, and Rufus, and they had insisted upon 'Telastory Time.'

Now she turned off the water so she could hear Charlie's voice. She never tired of listening to him, and apparently neither did the children, for they all had heard in dizzying repetition about his life in Venezuela, they had heard about his experiences in the oil rigs, they'd heard about the characters who were the roustabouts. The children had *not* heard, though he'd told Martha, about the man he'd attacked in Oklahoma City for accidentally killing his best friend, nor had he told the children about the state penitentiary.

He wore his prosthesis almost all the time now and was getting very good at manipulating quite normal movements. She'd never seen such a mutual attraction, Charlie, Molly, Rufus, and Juan – Four Musketeers, really, for Charlie was waiting by the side of the road every day when the school bus arrived, and from midafternoon until bedtime these four were constant companions.

Now Martha rinsed the last dish, put it in the basket to drain, dried her hands on her apron, and caught herself hurrying to get in to the storyteller herself.

She had told Charlie all about R. C. and had tried once to tell him about Belle but couldn't quite bring herself to do it. Maybe later.

In fact, the two of them had talked endlessly, piecing together the puzzle of the past, discovering her father's cruelty in driving them apart with stories that each had gone off with someone else.

The bitterness of this last recollection was canceled when from the living room she heard Molly and the others begging for just one more story. She approached the door quietly and marveled at the tableau, Charlie on the big overstuffed chair, with children nestled all about.

'Bedtime,' she announced to a chorus of groans. But after a moment's argument everyone lined up to give and receive a kiss, and then they were gone.

Alone.

Charlie stretched. Martha yawned. Good grief, it was only eight-thirty. Charlie leaned forward, took the poker, and nudged the fire. An explosion of sparks caught their attention and died a quick, lovely death.

'Where did you learn so many stories, Charlie?'

'I didn't learn 'em. I just make 'em up as I go.'

'The kids love them. And they love you.'

'They're great kids,' he said with sudden conviction as though someone had challenged him on the point.

'I know.'

'I'm glad you took 'em in.'

'It's amazing how many people get lost in this world, Charlie.'

He looked at her with a strange intensity. He pushed laboriously up out of his chair, stood for a moment, then walked to the sofa and sat down beside her.

She liked the feel of him next to her, liked it when he took her hand and separated her fingers as though he were looking for something.

'Martha . . .'

'Yes.'

'I've been thinking . . .'

'What about?'

'Us.'

She held her breath.

'What would you say,' he went on, 'to . . .'

'To – what?'

'To marrying me.'

For what seemed minutes neither moved, neither spoke.

'Martha, ah . . . don't cry.'

But she was, and there wasn't a thing she could do about it. He took her in his arms and kissed her, shyly at first, but gathering courage along with passion. The tears dried rapidly and were replaced by a longing she had given up hope of ever feeling again. At the end of the kiss they rested their foreheads together, each touching the other in shy and yet intimate ways.

She felt his hand move down her back to her hip, to her leg, and as their mutual need and longing grew, she thought, *Now I have news for R. C. . . .*

March 20, 1949
San Diego, California
On the Destroyer Collett

R. C. waited in line to use the dockside telephone and re-read Martha's worrisome note –

Dear R. C.,

Call me immediately when you can. I've tried to write a dozen letters to you and can't say it in a letter –

Say what?

We're all fine here. The children send their love.

Please call!!!

Love,
Martha

And that's just the way it was written, followed by three exclamation points.

He studied the note. It had been waiting for him when his ship had returned to San Diego following maneuvers.

There were four destroyers in his division, and all had docked. Now the dockside phones were jammed. He was next. Hopefully the man ahead would have a brief message.

As though he had read his mind, the officer turned about. 'You go ahead, Drusso. I can't get my number. I'll try later.'

R. C. smiled his thanks, refolded Martha's note, and slipped it into his pocket. After three rings he looked up, remembering the time difference. Five in the afternoon here, early evening there. She should be home.

He heard her voice, faint on the other end. 'Martha? Is that you?'

'R. C.?'

'Yes, I'm here. It's good to hear your voice. I just got back. We've been on maneuvers. Your letter was here. What – '

'Are you all right?'

'Of course.'

'What are maneuvers?'

He laughed. 'I'll tell you all about it later. Now what's the news? In your letter you said you'd tried to write. What's going on?'

At first there was no response. He thought he heard her talking to someone in the background. Sara, most likely.

'Martha? You there?'

'I'm here, R. C. I . . . uh I have something to – I want to tell you something.'

Something was wrong. He knew it. He'd never heard her so nervous, so uncertain of what she was going to say.

'Martha, is everyone well?'

'Of course.'

'Are you well?'

'Yes, R. C. That's not what – what I'm trying to say is . . . well, do you remember me telling you about Charlie Groveton?'

'Of course I remember,' he said, cupping his hand about the receiver as the line behind him grew longer.

'Well, he came back.'

He blinked forward at the plain statement. 'What do you mean, he came – '

'He's home. The kids, Molly and Rufus, kept riding their bikes down by his place and telling me about this one-legged man. You know Molly and her stories, well, it turned out not to be a story. The man was Charlie, and he was in the war, R. C., and he lost his leg, but you sure couldn't tell it none now, and he came up a few weeks ago and we just got to talking and the kids love him and he tells stories, you know this bunch, anyone who can tell a story . . . R. C., you there?'

'Yes, I'm here, go on.'

'Well, Charlie's back, and well . . . a few days ago, seeing as how he's up here for almost every meal and he's been helping out around the place and his house is a mess, a real mess, worse than ours if you can believe it, well, a few days ago – '

Her voice broke.

'What, Martha?' he prompted.

'Charlie Groveton asked me to marry him.'

R. C. smiled. There was one problem. 'What about the woman he went off with?'

'There wasn't any woman, R. C.' she said, a note of triumph in her voice. 'It was my father who told Charlie I'd gone off with another man, just like he told me Charlie had gone off with another woman. He lied to both of us.'

R. C. shook his head.

'R. C.? You still there?'

'I'm here, Martha, and believe me when I say I couldn't be happier for you.'

'Do you mean it, R. C.?'

'Of course I mean it.'

'Charlie's here. Right beside me. Would you . . . I mean, would you like to – '

R. C. made a quick face. Not that he didn't want to speak with Charlie. What the hell was he going to say?

'Here he is, R. C.,' Martha said. And R. C. was certain he'd never heard her so excited.

'R. C.?'

The voice was deep and possessed a slight Texas drawl.

'Yes, here, and you're Charlie.'

'I am that. Martha has talked about little else but you. I feel as if I know you.'

'Same here.'

'I need to ask you something, R. C.'

'What's that?'

'If you'd have any objection if I put a gold ring on this lady's finger. I should have done it years ago, but we both got lost somewhere along the way.'

R. C. liked him, liked the strength in his voice, the gentle manner in which he spoke.

'Listen, Charlie,' R. C. said. 'My only objection would be if you do it before I can get home. You better plan it so I can be there.'

'And when would that be?'

R. C. looked over his shoulder at his ship. Rumor had it that they would be out of here by June on fleet maneuvers at Pearl Harbor. 'How about a May wedding?'

'I'll let you talk to Martha about that. Sounds good. I look forward to meeting you.'

'And I you, Charlie. Congratulations.'

R. C. heard a quick conversation on the end of the line, then Martha was there. 'How about May? May third. Lilacs will be out then as well as my pink peonies. And R. C.? Will you give me away?'

He thought a moment, head down. 'No,' he said softly, his hand cupped about the receiver, 'but I'll be more than happy to share you with Charlie.'

Martha laughed. 'You're a scoundrel, always have been, always will be.'

'Then May third,' he repeated. 'I'll put in for leave right now. Anything else I can do?'

'Just get yourself here safe and sound. Are they treating you okay? Are you eating well?'

'Very well. It's not as good as your cooking. But I won't starve.'

'We miss you so much,' she said. 'I miss you.'

'And you're happy, Martha?'

'Yes, very. Not quite complete, but it will be one day.'

He closed his eyes, knowing that she meant Belle. 'Yes.'

'Then May third it is. Hurry home.'

'I will, Martha. I love you, and congratulations.'

'I love you.'

Then the connection was broken.

'About time,' the sailor behind him grumbled.

'Sorry,' R. C. muttered, and walked away from the phone.

Home. May third. For Martha's wedding. In a strange way, her happiness made him feel even lonelier, and he started off down the dock, his head whirling. Submit a leave request, get dress whites cleaned, find a suitable gift, make travel arrangements, get something for the kids, and on and on the list grew. Briefly his mind went blank, and then out of all the recent voices and memories, his mind predictably selected one.

Belle.

He increased his pace in a futile attempt to outwalk the memory . . .

May 3, 1949
Hitchings, Texas

Charlie stood on the front porch in his new dark blue suit. He and R. C. had talked too late last night, had drunk too much beer, and had shared a portion of their lives with each other. He liked R. C., liked the fact that he loved Martha.

Now he examined the flower that only a few moments earlier Sara had pinned to his lapel. A white rosebud from the trellis out back. R. C. had gone into town to pick up Reverend Parkhurst, the new young preacher from the Sunrise Methodist Church. Charlie had the license in his right pocket and the ring in his left. He'd begged Martha to take a honeymoon trip to Galveston, but she'd declined, saying she'd rather save the money and put it toward the new bedroom that Charlie was building onto the west side of the house. Construction was already under way.

Charlie was doing all the work himself, though he was a bit rusty. It had been a long time since he'd worked with boards, saws, and hammers. But the frame was up and Martha had said it was all the wedding present and honeymoon she wanted, an airy bedroom with big west windows, white organdy curtains, and her mama's wedding ring quilt on the old four-poster.

Just thinking on Martha was enough to make Charlie go weak. He had loved her all his life, and they'd always known somehow that they would be there for each other.

And they had been until old man Drusso had stuck his nose in where it didn't belong. Martha had not known that it was her father who'd paid the back taxes years ago and had bought Charlie's farm out from under him, nor had she been aware that she'd been paying taxes on both spreads until a few weeks ago when a trip to the courthouse had revealed all.

Now it was Charlie's hope that next spring he could work the land again, a good wheat crop, some new farm equipment, their combined spreads making for one impressive farm.

Why not? The prosthesis was second nature to him now. He could easily pull himself up onto a tractor or a combine. And they had most of his mustering-out pay in the bank, along with his monthly disability check and her oil royalty. Things looked pretty good.

A dust cloud coming out from Hitchings caught his eye. It was R. C. with the preacher. Charlie lifted his face toward the flawless blue sky and tried to the best of his ability to accommodate this new sense of happiness.

The woman he loved more than life itself had agreed to become his wife. There would never be another moment in his life exactly as perfect as this one, and he intended to enjoy it to the fullest.

R. C. felt stiff and out of place in his dress whites and would have been perfectly at home in a sports jacket. But Martha had wanted him to wear his uniform, and that had been motivation enough, particularly when she'd promised him he could change right after the ceremony.

Now he stood in the kitchen, waiting for Martha to make her appearance. He admired the table filled with the best-looking food he'd seen in a long time: huge platters of chicken, a whole sugarcured ham, potato salad, fruit salad, Martha's best deviled eggs, and at the exact center of the kitchen table the wedding cake, a two-tiered angel food creation that Sara and Martha had both worked on, pale yellow frosting and a small nosegay of yellow roses on top.

As for the rest of the house, it was flower-filled, lilacs everywhere filling the house with their spicy scent and on the dining room table a big glass bowl filled with pink peonies.

Then the door opened and there she was, looking extraordinarily pretty in a white silk dress. She wore a white garden hat and white shoes and carried a small bouquet of white lilacs, and she looked as lovely as R. C. had ever seen her. And as scared.

'You're beautiful,' he whispered, kissed her on the cheek, took her arm, and felt her trembling.

R. C. smiled. 'Are you – '

'I'm fine, it's just that I've never gotten married before.'

'I hear it's painless. The trouble starts later.'

'Don't joke.'

'Who's joking? Are you ready?'

R. C. gave Sara the sign to go to the upright, and in the sweetest, most tortured one-fingered rendition of the 'Wedding March' ever heard, he and Martha started through the dining room and into the living room, where Charlie was waiting along with the preacher and the children.

Sara made it to the end of the basic melody, all that Martha had been able to teach her in the last month, and then the service began.

Starting with 'Dearly beloved,' R. C. watched closely as these two people spoke their vows. They were both almost forty, both bearing the marks of a difficult life, both speaking now only to each other with an intimacy that caused R. C. to blush.

At the end, Charlie placed the ring on her finger, then kissed her with such force that her hat fell backward and was caught by Molly, who promptly slapped it on her head in comic fashion, thus providing everyone with a much needed laugh.

Of course Reverend Parkhurst and his wife stayed for food. R. C. shed his stiff dress whites for more comfortable blue jeans and a sports shirt. Charlie did the same, then everyone loaded their plates and took them out to the front porch, where an early evening spring breeze perfumed the air. The music was provided by a gifted mockingbird and his equally vocal mate.

R. C. and Charlie drove the reverend and his wife back into Hitchings at dusk and returned in time to see nature's wedding gift, a spectacular mauve, rose, and gold sunset that stretched the limit of the horizon.

The children sprawled on any lap they could find that would still accommodate them, and with both Charlie and R. C. on hand, they had a storytelling marathon, first Charlie, then R. C., then Charlie, and again R. C. At last Sara ushered them off to bed.

After Martha had tucked the children in, she came up behind the rocker on which R. C. was sitting, hugged him, and kissed the top of his head. 'I'm so glad you're here.'

'Wouldn't have missed it.'

'We both want you to know this has always been your home and will always be your home. Do you understand what we're saying?'

'You can't get along without me. That's what you're saying.'

'Exactly.'

The expression of love moved him. 'I tell you what,' he said, changing the subject, 'I'm going to take a stroll down the road here to try to walk off dinner.'

Charlie stood, put his arm around R. C., and started to say something but settled for the pressure of his touch, which spoke volumes.

R. C. walked down the steps to the road. The moonlight was as bright as the sun. He strolled about twenty yards down the road, hands in pockets, and looked back to see what the newlyweds were up to.

They were gone. No place in sight . . .

May 4, 1949
Hitchings, Texas

They awakened simultaneously to the five A.M. crowing of the rooster. Martha stretched, found the side of his leg with her toe, and enjoyed a brief tingling resurrection of all the glorious sensations from the night before.

'One day I'm going to kill that bird,' Charlie muttered sleepily.

'Without him and his harem you wouldn't have breakfast eggs.'

'Right now I don't want breakfast eggs.'

As he raised up on one elbow and looked down on her, she brushed back the mussed hair from his forehead.

'I was right.' She grinned.

'How's that?'

'There is nothing a one-legged man can't do except run the fifty-yard dash.'

Beneath the cover his hand found her breast. 'You know, for two people who both claimed they weren't very good at it, I think we did all right.'

'I agree, but I'm wondering . . .'

'What?'

'If we don't need a little more practice, just to make sure we're getting it right.'

She drew him down, kissed him, and heard footsteps outside of the room. 'Shhh,' she whispered, slipped from the bed, put her shoulder to her mother's mahogany dresser, and pushed it forward about three inches, just enough to cover the door and keep anyone from coming in.

When she looked back at the bed, she saw Charlie lift the covers. And without a moment's hesitation, she hurried back across the room and slid right into paradise . . .

June 16, 1949
The Stables
Beverly Hills, California

As Inez watched Belle at the dressing table, brushing her hair, she settled on the chintz rocker, enjoying both her beauty as well as her bewilderment.

Inez knew exactly what Cy was up to. He was playing one of his games, but for one of the few times in her long association with him, she didn't altogether disapprove.

'What time are we to be there?' Belle asked Inez's reflection in the mirror.

'I believe he said four.'

'Who else will be there?'

'I haven't the slightest.' Inez shrugged. 'We've arranged cocktails and hors d'oeuvres for thirty.'

'Thirty?' echoed a very surprised Belle.

'With Cy you never know. What dress are you wearing?'

Belle shook her head, indicating indecision as well as lack of interest.

'May I?' Inez smiled, gesturing toward the wardrobe.

'Sure.'

Inez stood a moment, lost in the rows of clothes, all gifts from Cy. 'All right, how about this?' She withdrew a pale lavender linen, cut low off the shoulders.

Belle agreed, drawn now to the balcony, where the overture for *Harvest of the Heart* could be heard coming from the studio. Played by a small orchestra this time.

'Come on, let's not be late,' Inez suggested.

Belle took off her dressing gown and stepped into the dress. Oh, yes, Inez thought as the material tightened and clung to Belle's figure. She slipped on a pair of lavender pumps and a single strand of pearls.

'Ready?' Belle asked.

Inez smiled. 'Ready.'

They made their way downstairs and up the flagstone path, across the drive and onto the middle terrace, following the sounds of the overture.

Belle quickened her pace, calling back, 'I'm afraid we're late.'

And Inez followed after, not wanting to miss a thing . . .

Cy saw them come in right on the button. He'd started fifteen minutes early to make them think they were late. Inez and Belle came in the side door from the terrace, a vulnerable entrance that brought them into the crowded room at midpoint and caused all heads to swivel.

Quickly, with a slight bend of her neck, Belle hurried

down the side of the room past the rows of white folding chairs that had been set up for this 'performance.' And it *was* a performance, perhaps one of the most important productions Cy had ever staged.

He caught her eye as she neared the back of the room and stepped forward with two folding chairs.

'Sorry we're late,' she whispered. 'Our clocks must be off.'

Cy noticed that the audience had settled down after Belle and Inez's entrance. It was a group made up of old friends as well as trusted professionals, men and women who had in some way been involved with past Compton productions: technicians, film editors, art directors, voice coaches, cinematographers, script writers, good people all, loyal to a fault and necessary both to Cy and to Compton Productions.

Now he felt the kind of excitement he always felt at the beginning of a big project, that peculiar combination of imagination, talent, and technology that would produce flickering shadows in a darkened theater and bring people to tears and laughter, perhaps change their lives forever.

'May I have your attention?' he called out over the chattering crowd. 'I think you know why I called you here, to bring the greatest love story since *Romeo and Juliet* to the screen. I want you to hear the music, the words, perhaps, more clearly than you've ever heard them before, I want all of you to have a script, take it home, study it, scene by scene, sequence by sequence, line by line. I don't want us merely to make this movie. I want us to become one with it, with its purity, its innocence, its sorrow, its joy. Only then will we succeed in making that young girl in, say, Carthage, Missouri, or Dublin, New Hampshire, know exactly what it is to find a true love, to lose it, and to find it again.'

He looked toward Belle, saw her head bowed. Good. Something he'd said had caught on a raw nerve.

'Now I have a surprise for you. I have invited Danner Rush to be with us here today – no small feat, as he just finished filming in Mexico yesterday. And to perform with him, Emily Mark.'

He gestured toward the back of the room. Now Danner Rush was making his entrance. He was tall, with dark good looks, a very good voice, and three recent hit movies.

Danner acknowledged the applause of the company, though instead of going straight to the stage, he veered toward Cy, a worried look marring his handsome features. 'Mr Compton,' he said, 'one of your assistants asked me to tell you that Emily Mark's agent called. She's ill.'

'Oh, no,' Cy groaned, and clapped his hand to his forehead.

'I can't sing the songs by myself. They were meant for harmony.'

'Indeed they were, and I assure you they shall be sung in harmony. Come . . .

'Ladies and gentlemen,' Cy said, 'we've just received sad news. Emily Mark is ill, according to her agent. And here we have one of the best voices in America, and he lacks only a musical partner.'

Cy glanced toward the back of the room to see what the initial reaction would be. At first, nothing. Belle appeared to be totally caught up in the drama of others, still unaware that the spotlight was now on her.

Cy walked through the company to the back of the room where she sat. He bent over and took her hand. 'In view of the fact that I have invited forty-five very busy professionals here to listen to the music from *Harvest of the Heart*, will . . . ?'

He raised up with a massive smile of pure helplessness.

'What – do I have to do?' she whispered, her eyes darting nervously from Cy to the musicians to Danner Rush to the waiting company.

'What you do – effortlessly, like breathing. Sing,' Cy said simply, and made an outstretched gesture with both hands as though to suggest he'd asked nothing at all of her.

He studied her face as the war raged. Then at last the magic words: 'All right, if you wish.'

Cy winked at Inez, nothing more than an affectionate acknowledgment of 'We know how to handle them, don't we?' He took Belle by the arm and led her back through the silent company, who now appeared grateful for a legitimate excuse to stare at the vision in the lavender dress.

'Allow me to introduce Belle Burgess. Belle, this is Danner Rush.'

Belle extended her hand. Reluctantly the young man took it and seemed not at all impressed with her beauty but concerned with whether or not he was going to make a fool of himself.

'All right, Belle, here's the score,' Cy said, handing her a stack of music. 'Start with "A Long Way Wandering," and Danner, you come in on the chorus. Let's just see how it goes, shall we?'

As Cy moved to one side out of the range of vision of his audience, he heard Percy strike the chord, saw Belle study the sheet music in a nervous manner, then lift her head and hit the first note. Her eyes closed as she began slowly to submerge herself in the emotion of the song, the lost child searching for love, for roots, for a place to belong.

After about a minute into the song, she carefully refolded the score and placed it on top of the piano, singing now by heart as well as from the heart, a stroke of genius, gathering the attention of the room to her and holding it fast.

Each time he heard her, Cy was impressed anew with her incredible range and the hypnotic quality of her voice. The audience appeared to be in a trance, not even breathing, or so it seemed.

And Cy was pleased to note a grin on Danner Rush's face. Clearly the 'little unknown' would not embarrass him. In fact, he had his work cut out simply to keep up.

As far as Cy was concerned, the two leads were cast. But he hadn't yet decided whether he'd produce and direct or just produce. There was a gifted young director named Stanley Bracer available who had expressed an interest in the film.

Then it was over. The audience stood. Percy's little group tapped their music stands with their bows.

Then Cy came up between them, like a referee at a boxing match, lifted their hands into the air, and claimed them both winners. As the applause fell silent, he turned toward Danner. With his voice low in order to quiet the room, he said, 'Ladies and gentlemen, may I present Joseph Anderson, the young man who wanders straight into everyone's heart.'

More applause. Young Rush appeared duly modest and very pleased.

'And . . .' Cy announced, topping the noise in the room with one word. 'May I present Cassie McQuinn, who teaches everyone about the true harvest of the heart, and who – '

Even as he spoke he felt Belle tug free from his grasp. 'No,' she murmured, and he saw a degree of fear that astonished him.

'Belle, listen, we – '

'No, please, Cy, I must go now.'

'But – '

'No, thank you – ' And with that she was out the side door. Inez was after her, having first shot Cy a look of pure condemnation.

'All right, ladies and gentlemen,' he said, as though trying to bring control to an unruly class. 'There's a buffet and a well-stocked bar waiting for you in the dining room. Please help yourselves. I'll join you in a moment.'

He started toward the side door in pursuit of Belle. 'I'll see if I can't bring back our Cassie for you.'

That promise sparked another round of applause, and Cy gave a mock salute and ran out of the door in search of the only girl in Hollywood, in the United States, in the whole world, capable of playing Cassie precisely as she must be played . . .

All Belle could think of as she ran out of the door was, He's lost his mind.

She took the second terrace at a run. How in the name of God did Cy think she could play Cassie? The only acting she had ever done had been in the Hillcoat Thespian Club, the only singing in the Baptist Orphanage Choir and in the Hillcoat Glee Club. Now she was going to leap from that to starring in Cy Compton's production of the Broadway hit *Harvest of the Heart?*

By the time she reached her bedroom, her hands were shaking and she felt mildly sick to her stomach. She reached behind and unzipped the lavender dress, kicked off the heels, let down her hair, and slipped into her favorite uniform, a pair of shorts, a cotton blouse, and no shoes.

She felt suddenly drained and stretched out across her bed.

A knock at the door. Probably Inez.

'Come in – '

It wasn't Inez.

Quickly Belle scrambled to a seated position on the side of the bed, bare feet dangling. Her discarded clothes still lay in a heap on a chair. Cy looked first at the clothes, then at her, an expression of apology on his face.

'I'm so sorry.'

'No need, I just – '

'You sang so beautifully. That's why I thought – '

'I couldn't, Cy. Please . . .'

As she held up both hands in a heartfelt plea, he quickly dragged a chair forward and sat, confronting her on the side of the bed. 'All right,' he began, businesslike, 'let's take this apart and examine it carefully.'

'There's no – '

'You are by the general and sincere consensus of everyone present this afternoon *the* one to play Cassie.'

'No – '

'Now these are not amateurs, Belle. You must understand that. These are seasoned professionals who are trained to make the best objective judgment they can make. So leave me out of it. I'll be the first one to concede that I may be prejudiced. But they aren't. They simply want to make the best film possible. Their reputations are at stake, their standings in the film community . . .'

Even as he spoke, Belle could hear Brad's voice. *'He can*

persuade you to do anything. I've watched him. His approach is like Chinese water torture – drop, drop. Ultimately he'll wear anyone down.'

'All right, and then we come to what must surely be your basic sense of insecurity.'

'Yes,' Belle said with conviction. She had no desire to become the laughingstock of the town.

'All right, first of all, God in His infinite generosity has provided you with more than most people possess after a lifetime of vigorous training. But I realize I'm not going to convince you of that, so let's consider something as simple as lessons.'

'There's no time,' Belle said, her alarm increasing as she saw how serious he was.

'No time? What do you mean? This is June. Filming wouldn't even start until possibly October. That's five months.'

Belle bowed her head and closed her eyes. 'Cy, I'm not an actress.'

'Oh, but you are, the best kind, a natural actress.'

'I've had no experience.'

'For what I'm asking you to do, experience would not serve you at all. Now if I was asking you to play Desdemona or even Juliet, that would be another matter.'

At least they were in agreement on one point. But still he wouldn't go away.

'What you lack, Belle, I can provide you with in a matter of weeks. A good voice coach to take what you already have and simply polish it a bit, a good dance instructor to show you how to open up and use what God has given you, some fencing lessons, perhaps, for balance, for grace, for fun, what the hell.' He laughed and inched his chair closer.

'Cy, I've never done anything like this.'

'That's the point,' he said quickly, possessing an answer for every argument. 'Neither has Cassie. Cassie is a young, innocent, untried girl from an Iowa farm. There is a natural kinship. Don't you see? And more important, you are young and gifted and at the moment wasting both these rare gifts.'

He inched the chair yet closer and took her hand. 'It will mean a chance for us to get better acquainted,' he said, his manner changed. 'I'd like nothing better, but my greatest pleasure would be in presenting to the world one of the most beautiful voices I have ever heard in combination with one of the sweetest souls I've ever met.'

Belle found herself almost mesmerized by his voice.

'Please, Belle, let's share this adventure, just the two of us. I'll take all my cues from you. More work, less work, time out to go back to Arkansas, time out for general principles, just say you'll do it, please, I beg you, please – '

She felt as if she were drowning, in desperate need of a lifeline and not one in sight. By way of surviving she stood and brushed past him, thinking she couldn't, thinking she had no desire to make such a monumental commitment, thinking she didn't want to be involved in such a grand project, and thinking she'd fail for certain.

'Will you, Belle?'

Still thinking no, she turned about and said, 'Yes.'

December 23, 1949
Compton Studios
Soundstage B

Cy stood at the window of his office and stared out at the chill rainy day, wondering whether or not he should go and check on the rumor.

He'd heard it swirling about for several days, that his young director, Stanley Bracer, was in fact a bully, causing at least one unpleasant scene every day on the set.

Cy drained his coffee, set the cup noisily on the tray, and realized with a wave of relief that he'd heard those rumors about every director in Hollywood. In fact, the better the director, the more potent the rumors.

Still, it might be advisable to visit Soundstage B. He reached for his raincoat and at the same time signaled his secretary. 'I'm out for a while, Betty. Take all messages and I'll return calls when I get back.' He buttoned up his raincoat, snagged an umbrella from the stand, and pushed open the door.

A few minutes later he entered the soundstage and heard the general buzz of voices that always accompanied a break. The shadows by the door provided him with sufficient cover, so he decided to stay in them. Carefully he shook off his raincoat, placed it along with the umbrella on a pile of canvas, then slowly eased around until he had a view of the stage and set.

It was the interior of the McQuinn living room. According to the shooting schedule for the day, they were to be filming the sequence of Brock McQuinn's discovery that his daughter, Cassie, was seeing Joseph Anderson. The scene was one of parental rage, culminating with Brock dragging Cassie down the steps and locking her in her room. The sequence consisted of dialogue, no singing.

'All right,' he heard someone shout toward the general confusion.

'We're wasting time here. Mr Bracer's ready, and he hopes you are.'

Cy craned his neck forward in an attempt to see precisely what it was that Mr Bracer was doing. He saw him bent over the production book, apparently planning camera angles.

'Now!'

He heard the single word shouted like a command and saw Bracer on his feet, a tall young man, well over six feet, with a great shock of blond unruly hair that always looked as though it had never known comb or brush.

Cy looked closer. Dear God, Bracer was wearing jodhpurs, a white shirt with a paisley scarf hung loosely about his neck. In his hand he seemed to be carrying a pointer or swagger stick of some sort. Cy was appalled and amused simultaneously. Mr Bracer seemed to be more 'in costume' than the actors, who were beginning to gather on the set now. Well, maybe it was just his method. Cy really didn't care what he wore. He simply wanted him to bring his best talents to this project, for Belle's sake.

'Now where is our little Miss Star?' he heard Bracer call out. Bracer turned affectedly in all directions, apparently looking for Belle, who had already appeared and was standing center stage.

'I'm here, sir. I thought you'd seen me.'

Bracer turned toward the voice. 'Now why would I have called you if I had already seen you?'

Belle smiled nervously, shook her head, and looked uncomfortable. She also happened to look very beautiful. Her costume was a simple white cotton nightgown. In the scene before, she had been dreaming of Joseph, then her father learns from the foreman of his crew that he has seen Cassie kissing the man named Joseph from Summerfield Farm.

Outraged, Brock drags Cassie out of her sleep and down the stairs, confronts her with the story, and waits for her to confirm or deny it. She confirms it, and the sequence culminates with Brock striking her and carrying her back up the stairs, where he locks her in her room. The scene ends with Cassie pounding on the door and screaming to be set free.

'All right,' Bracer shouted, 'let's walk through it. You, Brock, stand there where you've come in from outside. What you have just heard enrages you. Think beyond the words of what you are saying, think of the betrayal of trust from this daughter you worship. Think with your soul, do you understand?'

Lawrence Craig, one of the finest character actors in the film industry, nodded yes. Of course he understands, you idiot, Cy thought. Lawrence Craig's little finger probably knows more about acting than your whole costumed body.

Cy drew a deep breath, amazed at the hostility he'd just loosed on the young director of his choice.

'And you,' Bracer said, pointing toward Belle with his swagger stick. 'Wait, what in the hell is that?' He hurried to Belle's side, placed the palm of his left hand on her forehead, and pushed her head awkwardly to one side.

Cy saw Belle struggle once, then submit to a close personal examination of some sort.

'Is it dirt?' Bracer said, staring closely at something on the side of Belle's neck.

'No, sir, it's a birthmark.'

'I've never seen it before,' Bracer replied, something accusing in his voice.

Belle laughed. 'I assure you, sir, I was born with it.'

Bracer took a closer look, as did several of the actors and crew members. And all the while Bracer's hand held Belle's head at a stiff bowed angle.

'A little bell, isn't that sweet? Your mother must have been totally bereft of imagination to name you after a birthmark.'

Cy shook his head, feeling that the small humiliation was totally unnecessary.

'Makeup!' Bracer bellowed. 'Get in here and cover this thing.'

Cy started out of the shadows, angrier than he'd been in a long time. But at the last minute he caught himself. What he'd seen had been the antics of a bully. But Belle was strong enough to survive.

The makeup girl began applying cosmetics to the tiny bell-shaped birthmark. Cy still couldn't believe the man had made such a fuss over it.

A few minutes later, repaired and still intact, Belle followed Bracer's shouted instructions to get to the top of the stairs and through the door and 'think all of the appropriate things that will at least give you the illusion of being a real actress.'

Cy looked puzzled at the verbal assault. What was the point? What in the hell was going on?

'Now stay behind the door until your father comes for you, then protest, resist. Do you understand?'

'I understand, sir,' came the voice from behind the door.

'All right, now you,' Bracer said to Lawrence Craig,

summoning him forward. 'I'm afraid you're going to have to act for two. I want you to drag her from the room and down these steps, the irate and betrayed father. Do you understand? Good, let's take it that far.'

Cy stepped forward to watch the rehearsal. He saw Lawrence Craig burst into the room, fists clenched, his face distorted by anger. He called for Cassie once and, receiving no answer, thundered up the stairs, losing his footing once in his anger and at last jerking open her bedroom door. A moment later he reappeared, clasping Cassie's arm in a death grip.

'Wait, wait, wait!' Bracer shouted, both hands raised in the air, approaching the scene at a melodramatic pace, all the time shaking his head rapidly.

'Wrong,' he said, at last looking primarily at Belle. Then he placed his arm about Lawrence's shoulder. 'What I want to happen here is that on the top step, the girl loses her balance, and Brock, refusing to let go of her arm, drags her down the stairs.'

For a moment Cy thought he had heard wrong. But then he saw old Lawrence step back from the director. 'I can't do that, Bracer,' he said, his beautifully trained voice bristling in anger.

'What do you mean you can't do it?' Bracer challenged. 'Here, let me show you.' Quickly he grabbed Belle by the arm, ran back up the stairs, and turned her sharply about for the descent. Then he jerked her forward off the top step, and Cy watched, horrified, along with everyone else, as Belle fell forward, striking the banister first, then the steps, as Bracer proceeded to drag her the length of the staircase, impervious to the shocked expressions around him. Lawrence Craig was the first to reach Belle as she lay on the floor at the bottom of the steps.

Cy had seen and heard enough. He stormed out of the shadows, shouting with each step, 'Out, Bracer. That's it. Out! You're fired. Get off of this soundstage and out of this studio. You will never work here again. Do you understand?'

As Cy repeated Bracer's favorite question, he was amused and not too surprised to hear applause on all sides as he passed through the technicians.

But his primary concern was Belle, whom Lawrence Craig had now helped up to a seated position. Holding her arm, she was obviously in pain.

'You bastard,' Cy muttered to Bracer. 'You goddamned bastard. There was no point to that.'

'She is not a trained actress.'

'She doesn't have to be, for God's sake! She's playing herself.'

'She's . . . undisciplined.'

'How would you know? All you've asked her to do is fall down the stairs. This is not the theater. We have stuntpeople to fall down stairs.'

'If she were trained, she'd know how to fall.'

'You pompous idiot, you're fired. Do you know how to get out of here?'

'We have a contract.'

'Not any more we don't.'

'Then I'll sue – '

'You do that,' Cy said, leading the man toward the door. 'Oh, please do that, and I'll produce an endless line of witnesses, all willing to testify to what they saw here today.'

Bracer attempted a stammering reply, but Cy topped him. 'Get out! I said, get out!'

On the third command, Bracer muttered something beneath his breath, gathered up his minions, two young women and one young man armed with clipboards and subservient smiles, and out they went, the lot of them.

For a moment Cy felt sick. He should have checked sooner, should have listened to the rumors sooner. Now God alone knew how much damage had been done to these people, this production.

Belle –

At the thought of her, he turned immediately, hurried back onto the set, and knelt before her where she sat, still cradling her arm. Old Lawrence was in faithful attendance, as well as several extras.

'Are you – '

'I'm all right.' She smiled, though there was a stiffness to her smile that suggested otherwise.

'I think a doctor should see her,' Lawrence advised.

'Of course, of course.' Without another word Cy lifted her effortlessly into his arms.

He was aware of the feel of her body, the softness of her hair beneath his chin, and the manner in which she relaxed in his arms as though in absolute trust . . .

December 24, 1949
The Stables
Beverly Hills

Inez had heard her up at six-twenty in the morning. Cy had left strict instructions that he was to be called the moment she awakened, so Inez had telephoned his suite, then had sent for a tray of hot tea and toast.

Twenty minutes later she stood, tray in hand, just outside Belle's door. To her surprise Cy was already there in his bathrobe, seated on the edge of the bed next to Belle. Belle's arm was wrapped tightly in a support bandage. Though only a sprain, work would be out of the question for at least two weeks.

It was just as well. Cy had called a week-long holiday recess anyway, and as he now was directing he could reschedule other shots for the second week of Belle's absence. Though Inez was terribly sorry that Belle had been hurt, it would insure a pleasant and relaxing Christmas for all of them.

And Cy had such plans. As a surprise for Belle, an enormous Christmas tree had been set up in the dining hall. There were dozens of packages beneath the tree, and hidden safely in one of the garages was a white Cadillac limousine complete with a red satin bow and her own driver. Inez had never seen Cy so excited.

'Tea for anyone?' Inez called out, interrupting their quiet conversation.

'Just what the doctor ordered,' Cy said. He took the tray from Inez and placed it on the coffee table. A few moments later Belle drifted toward the fire.

'Cy,' she said after one sip of tea, 'may I ask a favor of you?'

'Anything. You know that. Anything.'

'I'd like very much to go back to Arkansas for Christmas. Just for a few days.'

Inez looked down into her tea and thought, Oh, dear, what now?

'Of course. Do you feel up to traveling?'

'Yes, though I haven't even told Mac and Charlotte that I'm coming.'

'They'll welcome you, I'm sure.'

'You had nothing planned here, did you?'

Cy missed only one beat before replying, 'Here? No, nothing at all, nothing but work.'

Belle smiled, her first that morning. 'Good. And thank you, Cy. If you'll excuse me, I'd better call Malcolm. When can I leave?'

Cy put down his tea cup and swung into action. 'I'll call the airport immediately. It'll take a bit to get the plane ready. How about one o'clock? That will put you in Fort Smith at early evening. Christmas Eve homecoming. How lucky for the Burgesses.'

Only Inez heard the sadness and longing in his voice. Poor Cy. People in his life were always dying or walking away. Who now would enjoy the enormous Christmas tree and all the gifts?

'Then one o'clock it is,' Belle said. She stopped by Cy at the end of the sofa and lightly kissed his cheek. 'Thank you so much,' she said, 'for everything.' Then she disappeared into her dressing room.

Slowly Cy placed his cup back onto the tray. 'She needs

to go home,' he said. 'Help her, Inez, in whatever she needs. I'll be at the studio.'

And he was gone, walking like a man of eighty. Inez felt sorry for him. He had so looked forward to this Christmas with Belle.

'Inez, can you give me a hand? I seem to be missing one.'

Did that cheery voice coming from the wardrobe belong to the same young girl who recently had sat moping on the edge of her bed?

'Coming,' Inez replied. She drained her tea cup and felt a few extra years herself, wondering how much longer she'd be able to look after the children . . .

December 24, 1949
Fort Smith, Arkansas

Malcolm Burgess stood at the end of the tarmac and saw Belle's plane touch down. He turned up the collar of his raincoat and hoisted the umbrella in some protection against the rain that had just started.

It was already dark at six o'clock, a chill and wet Christmas Eve. Charlotte had insisted upon putting on makeup and a new bed jacket so she 'wouldn't look too awful for Belle.' Billie Rose had been a virtual whirlwind about the house, unpacking Belle's favorite Christmas decorations, cleaning and airing her rooms. And Spoons had found a last minute fresh turkey and had made her chestnut dressing and a pecan pie. So it was going to be Christmas after all. Malcolm was very pleased.

Then there she was, waving at him. He hurried across the tarmac and noticed her coat slung over a bandaged arm. 'You're hurt,' he said at the end of their embrace.

'I fell on the set,' she said simply, and looked back as the stewardess brought her luggage down the steps.

'Thanks, Anna.'

'Have a good Christmas, Miss Burgess.'

'Thanks, you too.'

As they started toward the car, Malcolm thought she was changed. Something was wrong. But he decided not to pry. In time they would talk. He was certain of it . . .

Belle reached for the umbrella with her good hand as Malcolm picked up her luggage, and together they started toward the car.

Inside, Malcolm turned up the heater and promised 'snow by morning, at least according to the weatherman.'

How perfect, Belle thought, and as he drove through the quiet streets she was impressed anew with the beauty of a landscape minus neon and horns.

'Are you all right?' Malcolm asked after they both had caught their breath.

She started to tell him everything, including her decision that she was not going back. Then she decided to wait. The moment was too good, too perfect, too filled with everything she'd come home for.

'How is Charlotte?' she asked.

Malcolm took a moment too long to answer. 'Not well,' he said. 'The doctor says her heart is growing weaker.'

'And nothing can be done?'

'Nothing.'

'I'm sorry, Mac.'

'I have not yet been able to conceive of life without her. But I imagine I'll have to start soon.'

Outside the window a fine snow had started to fall. 'I'm glad you're here,' Malcolm said.

About twenty minutes later, he pulled into the long driveway that led up to the house. The front door opened and there was Billie Rose.

Belle was out of the car and moving toward the steps, her coat slipping from her shoulders as she ran toward the woman she loved most in this world, the woman who had seen her through every hurt, every scrape, every mystery, every puzzle of her adolescence.

'You're home,' Billie Rose said in her ear, and tightened her arms around her.

Belle closed her eyes inside the fortress of love. Billie Rose whispered, 'You look awful. Don't they feed you out there?'

All at once Belle started to laugh. When was the last time anyone had been honest enough with her to tell her she looked awful?

At some point the laughter mysteriously turned into tears, and Billie Rose held her throughout.

'It's all right. Billie Rose is here . . .'

It was well after midnight on Christmas morning when Belle and Billie Rose finally told Malcolm good night.

They had stayed in Charlotte's room until ten, opening their presents until Charlotte had grown tired. Belle had marveled at the transparency of her skin, so white, so deathlike.

She'd held Belle's hand ever so long, worried over the sprained arm, and begged them not to go, even though she'd dropped off to sleep only moments after she'd said it.

Belle, Billie Rose, and Malcolm had sat in his study and watched the lights on the Christmas tree as Belle had told them about her life in California and about the film that Cy was making. Now, as they watched Malcolm slowly climb the stairs to bed, Belle suggested softly to Billie Rose, 'A cup of hot chocolate?'

Billie Rose grinned. 'In the kitchen. Like we used to.'

A few minutes later they were settled across the big wooden table on which Belle had consumed countless bowls of chicken noodle soup and equal numbers of peanut-butter-and-jelly sandwiches. As the hot fragrance of chocolate wafted up, she closed her eyes and smiled at her new happiness.

'You look just like the cat that swallowed the canary,' Billie Rose said.

'I feel like it,' Belle replied. Then she asked a curious question that had just popped into her mind before she could censor it. 'What did you think, Billie Rose, when Malcolm brought me home as a substitute for Lenora?'

The question clearly caught Billie Rose off guard. 'My Lord, you *are* going back a ways, aren't you? Why do you ask?'

'Just curious.'

'No big mystery. You were a little girl in need of a family, and we were a family in need of a little girl. Somehow everything fit. Are you sorry?'

'Oh, no, no, of course not,' Belle hurried to reassure her. 'It's just that we're not the real McCoy.'

'No . . .'

'Do you think you'll ever find them?'

'Once I did.'

'Now?'

'I . . . don't know.'

'Poor Belle.'

'Not poor Belle,' she said on a burst of energy. 'I have a surprise for you.'

'Another one?'

'I'm not going back.'

Billie Rose was lifting her cup of hot chocolate to her mouth but slowly put it down. 'You're not?'

'No. Oh, no, Billie Rose, it's so – it's hard to explain. No one really means anything they say. Everyone out there is only interested in one thing. Themselves. Everyone thinks that all that matters in this world is their project of the moment. And for that, life stops, courtesy stops, decency stops.'

Billie Rose shook her head and said nothing. Belle knew her too well. Something was on her mind. 'What's the matter?'

'Nothing,' Billie Rose said in that tone that indicated something was very much the matter.

'Billie Rose, come on, what is it? I thought you would be glad that I – '

'Me? Glad?' Billie Rose parroted, and sat up straight on her chair, a look of disappointment on her face. 'I wanted nothing more than for you to come back here. I knew you didn't belong out there. If you'll recall, I didn't want you to go in the first place.'

'So what's the problem?'

'You are,' Billie Rose said bluntly. 'You have obligations now, responsibilities, you have entered into an agreement that involves a large number of people, and you have no right just to walk away and leave them high and dry.'

Belle laughed and shook her head. 'Do you really think I'm important to this film?'

'I doubt if Mr Compton would have asked you to be in it if he didn't feel – '

'There are hundreds of actresses who could do this part as well as if not better than I'm doing it. Do you know how this happened?' She held up her injured arm, still wrapped in support bandages. 'I'll tell you. The director, admittedly an ass, was angry because in his words I was untrained, an amateur, who, as he put it, failed to understand the direction he was giving me.'

Abruptly she stood up from the table, the memory of the ugly scene still fresh in her mind. 'He was demonstrating how I was to come down a flight of steps. He demonstrated too hard. I lost my footing and fell.'

Billie Rose murmured, 'I'm sorry.'

Belle shook her head. 'So I'm not going back,' she concluded, and wished that Billie Rose might have been happier with her decision.

'What about this Mr Compton?' Billie Rose asked.

'I'll call him, all right?' Belle said, really angry now, and terribly hurt. 'I don't understand you,' she said. 'I thought – '

'You thought I'd be happy to watch you walk away from a responsibility and an obligation? You don't know me very well. And I could have sworn I taught you better than that. How many times in high school you would come to me and say, "It's hard, Billie Rose," or, "I don't like the people," or, "I can't do it," and we'd take those flimsy excuses one at a time, turn them over, and remember what we always found?'

Billie Rose didn't wait for a response. She never did when she was making a point. 'What we always found was Belle, poor little Belle, poor lazy Belle, or poor scared Belle, or poor disinterested Belle. No matter. It was always Belle who was the problem.'

'This is different.'

'How different? Just bigger as far as I can see. More people dependent on you, bigger obligations, higher stakes.'

All at once Belle felt very tired. 'I'm going to bed now,' she announced.

'You do that,' Billie Rose called after her. 'Go to bed, put your pillow over your head, and try to convince yourself that this world and all of its problems and your part in it will just go away. But don't be too surprised come morning if nothing has gone away. Your feelings are important, Belle, but the cost is too high when you fail to consider others as well.'

From the door Belle looked back at Billie Rose as though she were the enemy. 'I thought you'd be happy.'

Then she left the kitchen, but not without first seeing the stricken look on Billie Rose's face.

Duty, responsibility, obligations. What did Billie Rose know? She wasn't the one who had to endure their criticism, their endless and brutal criticism.

Belle wasn't one of them. They had made that clear. So she wasn't going back, and nothing and no one could alter her decision . . .

For the next ten days a bitter cold rain set in, and Belle spent most of every day in Charlotte's bedroom reading to her from all her favorites. Charlotte seemed deeply appreciative, and the two women had long chats until Charlotte would tire and fall asleep.

She spent the evenings with Malcolm, listening to the latest crises that had developed at the newspaper office or talking politics. She hadn't told Malcolm of her decision not to return. She was still smarting from Billie Rose's reaction.

As for Billie Rose, the worst thing that could possibly

happen to them had happened. They had grown polite. There had been one or two occasions when Belle had ached to take Billie Rose in her arms, apologize, and explain that some people belonged in Hollywood, others didn't.

But the moments for reconciliation had come and gone, and no one had made a move.

Then on January 4 the rains had stopped, the sun came out, and the air felt as though it had gone overnight from winter to spring. Belle tested her arm, found it strong, and removed the heavy white bandage.

In her closet she found an old pair of blue jeans rolled up at the cuffs and one of Mac's oversize white shirts. Slipping quickly into the clothes, she drew her hair back into a ponytail and appeared in the sunny breakfast room.

'Good Lord,' Mac said, grinning. 'You look just like you did – '

'Five years ago,' Billie Rose said, completing his sentence as she filled his coffee cup.

'Mac, may I borrow a car and Billie Rose this morning? There's someplace I want to go.'

'Sure,' Mac said without hesitation. Then he noticed her unbandaged arm. 'Are you – is it – '

'Strong. The doctor said two weeks should do it.'

'If you're sure.'

'Billie Rose? Could you spare me a couple of hours?'

'I can spare you the rest of my life. I thought you knew that.'

'Then let's go,' Belle said.

Surprised, but not objecting, Billie Rose untied her apron, shrugged at Mac, and followed after Belle.

They took Billie Rose's car. She handed Belle the keys and said simply, 'You drive.'

Belle drove out into the country about five miles until she spotted the barbed-wire fence first, running alongside the road, leading finally to the big wooden gate, fallen now and beginning to rot. Billie Rose sat up, aware at last of where they were.

'Want to come?' Belle invited. She opened her door and started off toward the fallen gate.

The wooden frame barracks used as the clearing center was still standing. Belle was aware of Billie Rose behind her and was aware of little else except the clamor from the past.

'Men, form a line there, women and children here – '

'Stay close, Belle – '

'Kim, don't let them take me – '

Belle stood perfectly still and let the past swirl about her. She heard herself breathing as though she'd run a great distance.

Then she started down the central avenue. In the intervening years nature had reclaimed most of it, and now the once broad street was a mere path. Still, she knew where she was going and increased her speed until she arrived at the graveyard.

The tombstones were simple gray markers. And there were hundreds of them. With remarkable ease, as though some force had been guiding her footsteps, Belle found the one marked

KIM SHODA

FAITHFUL WIFE OF HAROLD SHODA

1907–42

She bent over to pull away a Virginia creeper that had wrapped itself around the marker. She pulled up the dead weeds and grasses until this one area was clear. Then she looked back over her shoulder to see Billie Rose standing about ten feet away. 'This is Kim,' she said, and realized how foolish it sounded, like an introduction.

'I know,' Billie Rose said.

'Kim,' Belle repeated softly, and searched the grave marker as though searching for the woman herself.

She got on her knees and ran her hands back and forth across the marker and saw in loving memory the white farmhouse in San Bernardino, Kim's kitchen, Kim's roses, Harold teaching her to jitterbug –

'You're a shiner!'

She had been afraid she would cry, but she didn't. The longer she knelt, the more she felt Kim's strength coming from the grave. There was an unholy alliance between these two women who had never met, the dead one beneath Belle and the live one standing behind her. They both knew what a lost child needed and gave it generously, without question. They both loved her and in return asked for a certain caliber of performance. They both had told her to 'leave footprints.'

'We can bring some plantings out in the spring if you like,' Billie Rose suggested.

'I'd like that.'

A few minutes later Belle stood. She wavered, searching for a center of balance, and Billie Rose's hand was there to help her find it.

Belle took it, and the two walked slowly back to the car. Though Belle had regained her balance, she never once let go of Billie Rose's hand . . .

January 5, 1950
The Stables
Beverly Hills, California

Looking back on the last two weeks, Inez was prepared to swear that she'd never passed a drearier time in her entire life. The holidays might as well not have happened.

Cy had sat in the lanai suite for the last two weeks. Occasionally he had read production notes, occasionally he had taken an important phone call, occasionally he had had something to eat and drink, but he had turned down all social invitations and had gone back to his own suite late at night only to sleep, then to return before six the following morning to take up his vigil again by the telephone.

Inez sighed noisily and took the breakfast tray from one of the maids.

'Cy? You must eat something. Look – French toast. Your favorite.'

'You're always telling me it's too rich.'

'Occasionally it won't hurt.'

'Inez, tell me the truth. Do you think she's coming back?'

The direct and painful question caught her off guard. 'I don't know, Cy. She was very unhappy.'

'I know, I know.'

'Though it was nothing you had done,' she hastened to add. 'She just never felt at ease.'

'Why?' Cy asked, his manner almost pleading, as though his disappointment might be relieved with just a bit of understanding.

All Inez could think of was, 'She's a lot like Brad. He never took to the business either.'

'But Brad has no gifts, not like she has. Inez, she is talent-laden. Everyone who sees her says that. Everyone. Oh God, I just wish . . .'

He shook his head. 'We need to get on with production. Costs are soaring. Most of the actors have other commitments, as do the technicians.' Carefully he leaned back in the chair, and she saw the ravages of doubt on his face. 'She is so . . . perfect.'

Inez stood by helplessly and could think of nothing to say that would lessen his frustration.

The ringing of the phone shattered the silence and caused Inez to jump. She reached for the receiver, but Cy had already scooped it up.

'Yes?' he demanded.

Inez poured his coffee and was just straightening up when she caught sight of his face. It resembled a pitch black room being slowly warmed with brilliant sunlight.

'Yes, of course, of course, fine, and you? Are you – ' He held the receiver with both hands as though caressing it. Inez found herself grinning.

'Yes, they'll be there. I promise. Yes, yes, yes, of course. See you then.'

He stood perfectly quiet for a moment, the receiver still at his ear. Then he lowered it and clasped it with both hands and let out a yell of pure jubilation.

'She's coming home!' he announced. 'Belle is coming back. She wanted to know if I could have the plane pick her up. Could I have the plane – '

He laughed at the question and started moving about the living room like a man possessed.

'She sounded so good, Inez, so damn good, her voice strong. She's coming back, she's coming back today. Oh, Lord, so much to do. Help me on this now, Inez. This place. I guess we don't have time to redo it. No, of course not. Then get people in, have it cleaned from top to bottom, and fill every room, every room, with flowers. Order more if we don't have enough in the greenhouse. And have her car brought around and waiting outside. You might take that damn ribbon off. I'll take care of the plane. I need to call the airport and Harry. Oh, God, so much to do, so very much to do, but the important thing, Inez, the really important thing is she's coming home, she's coming home, she's coming home – '

And with that he took the front door running and opened it with such force that it crashed back against its hinges. Inez continued to watch as he ran down the terrace and across the lawn and disappeared at last into his office suite.

Inez blinked once, then twice. Her mouth fell open. The sudden silence exploded around her. Cy Compton had acted for all the world like a man who had fallen in love.

No.

Oh, no.

He couldn't, he wouldn't, he hadn't, he mustn't . . .

It was almost midnight when Belle and Cy crawled into the limousine and left the airport for The Stables.

'Tired?' Cy asked.

'A little.'

'It's so good to have you home.'

She looked out at the passing neon lights and their glittering reflection on the wet pavement.

'Are you enjoying it, Belle? The making of the film?'

She thought for a moment before she responded, sensing it might be important to him. But just as she was on the verge of speaking, he answered for her. 'You don't, do you? You're not really one of "the children," as Inez calls us. Sylvia wasn't either. Oh, she tried. She did one film for me. She was very beautiful and had a nice Garbo quality on screen. But she didn't like it, said she didn't care for the fussing and the phonies and the boredom of waiting.'

Belle thought, What a peculiar feeling to have a dead woman express your exact thoughts.

'It's sad, though,' Cy went on in a reflective mood, 'to find two great talents in one lifetime, neither one of whom was interested in participating in what is basically my lifeblood.'

She could only see his face in partial shadows, and even those flickered and shifted as the car moved through the midnight streets. Abruptly he said, 'I'm canceling the film.'

She looked at him, not quite believing. 'You can't.'

'Of course I can. And will. I don't want to be a participant in anything that causes you pain.'

Her sense of relief was powerful and sweet. 'Cy, I – '

He settled back close to her, his shoulder slightly overlapping hers. 'Nothing more to be said, except – May I make a request?' he rested his head on the cushioned seat.

'Of course,' she said, amused at his sudden outbreak of formality and still not quite able to believe that he had sacrificed his film for her.

'May I just, for a moment or two, with your permission, of course, hold your hand?'

She started to laugh at the simple request so elaborately spoken. But shifting shadows allowed her to glimpse his face, and she saw not a trace of humor or amusement on it. He was a remarkable man, and she was so glad she was here sitting beside him. She'd missed him, and she loved him.

'You may hold my hand,' she said with matching formality, and felt like a seventh-grader.

He took it in a memorable way, by first studying his own as though for defects. Then slowly he placed his hand palm down over hers and gathered it up in a strong gesture that left her wondering what there was about holding hands that could create such a turmoil inside . . .

June 25, 1950
Sasebo, Japan
The Officers Club

The jukebox in the Officers Club was playing Nat King Cole's 'Red Sails in the Sunset.' R. C. shifted uncomfortably on the rattan chair. He put down his pen, stretched the stiffness out of his neck, and gazed through the open shutters toward the twin green mounded hills that the enlisted men lovingly called 'Jane Russell.'

The configuration did resemble a woman's breasts, though he'd better not share that piece of local color with Martha. She still worried about him, about his apparent inability to find a 'nice girl.'

Well, the point and purpose of the letter he was writing to her now was to share the good news, that he was coming home, and while the search for a 'nice girl' certainly wouldn't be at the top of his list of priorities, he had no intention of erasing it from the bottom, either.

Behind him he heard a friendly game of poker, friendly because they too were going home, all going home after this brief stint in the Orient. As for R. C., he'd seen all he cared to see, thank you. He had seen poverty beyond description, a rudimentary sanitation system, not enough food, not enough medicines, a world of sorrow, sickness, and deprivation he could never imagine. He'd tried to convey some of it in his letters to Martha and Charlie, but no one could fully understand unless they had seen it for themselves.

He withdrew his handkerchief, mopped at his brow, and loosened the top button of his uniform. And then there was the heat, heat such as he had never felt before, wet heat, tropical heat, debilitating heat.

Still, enough bellyaching. He was going home. Going home. Surely the two most beautiful words in the English language – or any language, for that matter.

Now he lifted his multipaged letter to Martha and Charlie and reread the last page, replete with his plans for the future. First, discharge. Hallelujah! Then a trip to Hitchings to see what the 'newlyweds' were up to and to check on any new faces that might have appeared in Martha's home during his absence – and there were sure to be some.

Next an orderly transfer of all his academic credits to UCLA, where it was his intention to pursue his Ph.D. and after that to settle comfortably into a life of teaching in some pleasant grove of academe and to continue his search for that part of his heart that had been missing for almost twenty years.

Slowly R. C. lowered the letter and wondered if he should put in that line about Belle. It seemed so farfetched now, so utterly impossible. She would be a grown woman if she were still alive, with no memory or knowledge of her past.

R. C. leaned forward on the desk and shaded his face with his hands. Incredible the extent to which he still felt grief and guilt. Slowly he lowered his hands and heard raucous laughter at the poker table behind him. Leave it in, he decided, the part about Belle. Every reference to her served as a kind of a memorial, a reminder that there was yet in this life a massive piece of unfinished business.

Well then, seal it, stamp it, and send it on its way to Hitchings, Texas, at least give her fair warning that a grand homecoming soon would take place.

'Hey, Drusso, you're wanted.'

At the sound of the voice, R. C. looked over his shoulder and saw Lieutenant Greg Hogan framed in the doorway.

'Where?' R. C. asked.

'Out here,' Hogan replied.

He took Martha's letter, left the desk, and pushed past the poker game, focusing on Hogan, who was still out in the corridor.

'What is it?' R. C. asked while he was still several feet away.

'We're at war.'

'We're what?'

'We're at war. The damn North Korean forces crossed the Thirty-eighth Parallel today and invaded South Korea. A declaration of war was broadcast on Northern Pyongyang Radio. All officers are to report back to the ship immediately.'

R. C. frowned at both the message as well as the messenger. 'Surely there's some mistake.'

'No mistake,' Hogan said. 'MacArthur is on his way to Korea. Truman hasn't declared war, but the scuttlebutt is that he is going to extend everyone's tour of duty. Now come on, we've got to get back to the ship. Well, don't just stand there, Drusso. At last we've got ourselves a real war.'

R. C. became aware of a flurry of activity throughout the club: poker games were breaking up, men were trying to pay their bar bills or finish a last drink before scrambling back to the fleet landing. Now, as Hogan sprinted toward the bar, R. C. hesitated a moment longer, trying to digest everything he'd just heard. He wasn't going home. There would be no reunion, no homecoming feast, perhaps not even a future.

He lifted the letter that he had written to Martha and Charlie, studied it for a moment, then with deliberation tore it neatly in half and tossed it into the wastebasket.

'At last we've got ourselves a real war.'

Well, what if we don't want ourselves a real war?

No answer, just the ache of disappointment and the apprehension of what was ahead . . .

July 31, 1950
Hitchings, Texas

Martha had taken a vow not to read the Amarillo papers or listen to the radio newscasts until after the children were in bed each night. The news from Korea was grim, and all she had received from R. C. was a hastily scribbled note from a place called Sasebo in Japan telling her that his ship was headed to – Korea.

Now with Rufus and Molly at last settled, she took off her apron and hung it on the hook behind the kitchen door and headed toward the front porch.

There was not a hint of a breeze. Halfway across the living room she stopped to pick up Juan's catcher's mitt. The boys had played a heated game of baseball on the side yard with Charlie playing any position as needed. As she bent over she heard the radio perched on the open window between the living room and the front porch.

'Any news?' she asked as she stepped out onto the porch and saw Charlie in the swing.

'Sit you down,' Charlie invited, and took her hand as she passed in front of him.

She sat and listened to the annoying jingle of a Brylcreem commercial.

'Ball game going on in Amarillo,' Charlie said.

'Who's playing?'

'Not sure.'

'Any news?'

'Some coming up, I believe, 'least the man said so.'

Then they heard the familiar voice of Edward R. Murrow:

'Today General Douglas MacArthur arrived for talks with Chian. America's involvement in Korea will by and large depend upon the outcome of these talks. If General

MacArthur recommends it, President Truman will send thirty-three thousand troops to South Korea.'

Martha closed her eyes and wished that she could close her ears as well. Charlie saw her distress. 'Hey, look, R. C. isn't a foot soldier, remember? I don't know how many times I wished I was a sailor, safe and sound on some destroyer. This doesn't mean nothing, Martha, nothing at all. You hear?'

She heard, but of course it did mean something. It meant that R. C. was somewhere in the middle of what was fast taking on all the appearances of a major war. And she was at great risk of losing someone else.

Suddenly the confinement of the porch swing was too great, so she got up, left the porch, and walked into the front yard until the road stopped her.

She knew Charlie was coming behind her.

'I can't bear the thought of losing him, Charlie. I can't even think about it.'

'Then don't,' he comforted. 'Think about the day R. C. comes barreling down that road, driving too fast like he always does. Did you know that? R. C. always drives too fast. In fact, I plan to speak to him about it when he gets home. And another thing. He promised he'd help me fix the roof on the barn. And I'm gonna hold him to it. If we're gonna run a few head of cattle, I've got to have a dry place to store feed. You hear me, Martha?'

'I hear you, Charlie. If R. C. is going to get lectured on driving fast and held to a promise of fixing the barn roof, then he'd pretty near have to come home in one piece, now, wouldn't he?'

'Yes, he would.' Charlie and Martha stood for a time in silence.

'You know what I did this afternoon?' Charlie asked.

'What?'

'I fixed that big oscillating fan we found in the attic, fixed it so it's running smooth as glass. And you know where it is now?'

'Where?'

'It's aimed right down on our bed, blowing cool breezes every which way.'

'Is it now?'

'It is.'

'Well, what do you think of that?'

'I'm thinking that big bed of ours might be a pretty cool place right now.'

'Think so?'

'I do, I do, yes, sir.'

'Well, I'm plenty hot. I could use some cool.'

'Do you want me to show you where you can find some?'

'If you please . . .'

'Oh, I please.'

She laughed, kissed him, took his hand, and walked with him back into the house, where his closeness would at least dull the ache of apprehension she felt for R. C.

Keep him safe, she prayed as she undressed. Then Charlie was there and the oscillating fan blew cool breezes over their bed and Martha drew him to her and wondered why it was that she always seemed to be losing someone she loved just as she was finding someone she loved . . .

August 6, 1950
The Stables
Beverly Hills, California

Inez was the first to realize that love had returned to The Stables. She had no idea how serious it was or how reliable, but there it was for anyone with eyes to see. And there were times, amazingly enough, when she even wondered if the two major players, Belle and Cy, knew precisely what had afflicted them.

But the truth was that Cy practically lived in the lanai suite now except, of course, for his exits each night before midnight. Then he wouldn't return until breakfast the following morning. And curiously enough he insisted that Inez be in their company at all times. He seemed to be aware of the delicate nature of his relationship with this young woman.

Now, as Inez watched them playing in the pool, she felt for all the world like a Peeping Tom. Why was it that a person could watch two people who were not in love and not feel guilty of trespassing? But now she felt sly and scheming and intrusive.

She tried to get comfortable under the umbrella, despite the August heat, and watched them playing ball in the pool. Cy was trim, fit, and full of energy as though a man twenty years younger had reached forty and walked right through it as though it were a non-existent barrier. And Belle at twenty, when she was around Cy, seemed older, more mature. The result was a curious shedding of years on Cy's part and an equally curious gaining of years on Belle's part so that they seemed to meet in some mutually agreeable age.

'Catch it,' Cy shouted at Belle, who in return caught the big yellow ball and hurled it back at him, then promptly disappeared underwater in one sleek surface dive.

Inez watched as Cy turned this way and that in the pool, searching for telltale air bubbles or a flash of red from Belle's bathing suit.

But nothing. Apparently she'd gone straight to the bottom of the deep end. Either that or –

All at once she surfaced directly behind him with an explosion of water. In mock fright he grabbed her and drew her toward him, while she, laughing, struggled free and swam to the edge of the pool, pulling herself out effortlessly.

Cy was less than three feet behind her, the approximate distance he'd maintained for the last several months. He grabbed a towel and dried her off, then held her terrycloth robe for her. As she knotted the cord, he slipped on his robe, dried his face, and eyed the champagne and the melon salad that had just been brought out from the kitchen.

'Come on, Inez,' Belle called out. 'Cantaloupe, your favorite.'

'I've eaten, my dear. You two go ahead.'

Inez saw Cy next to the phonograph making record selections, and a few minutes later she heard the sound of a mellow clarinet hit the opening note of 'It Had to Be You.' Cy slowly returned to the table where Belle was seated and extended his hand to her in an invitation to dance.

Inez took note of how their bodies fit together, the manner in which he held her hand and clasped her waist, the way Belle rested her head on his shoulder. Their bare feet were scarcely moving to the music.

She felt a searing blush on her cheeks and realized she could watch no longer. Quickly she gathered up her newspaper and empty coffee cup, hoping that neither Cy nor Belle would notice her departure and call her back.

They didn't . . .

September 30, 1950
Hitchings, Texas

Charlie read the official US Navy commendation twice in order to avoid the concern in Martha's eyes.

'What does it mean, Charlie?'

'Not sure. Let me – '

Again he lifted the piece of paper and read the dread words:

> To the Commander of the USS *Collett*: The ship under your command distinguished itself by extraordinary heroism in action with the enemy and exhibited gallantry and determination in overcoming difficult and hazardous conditions beyond the call of duty . . .

The commendation went on, more about gallantry and courage and self-sacrifice. But not one word about Ensign R. C. Drusso.

Charlie shook his head. 'I'm not sure, Martha, so don't hold me to nothing, but I'd say offhand that if R. C. were . . . well you know – if he were – that message would have come before this one.'

'But why haven't we heard from him, Charlie?'

'Can't answer that one.'

'Is there anyone we can call?'

'I don't know who. Let's be patient a while longer.'

'Charlie, watch Ezra for me, will you?'

'Where are you going?'

'I need to go up the hill.'

'Martha, no need to expect the worst.'

'Until I hear, Charlie, I don't know what to expect. Just watch Ezra for me, please.'

'Of course.'

Slowly she stood and pushed away from the table. The commendation had come in the noon mail amidst a scattering of bills. Charlie had known what it was the moment he saw it, all reeking with official gobbledy-gook, which, plainly spoken, meant bad news.

He looked up out of his thoughts and saw her climbing the hill where her family was buried. He glanced back at the commendation. Sitting ducks. A hell of a way for a man to die, sitting dead in the water just to draw enemy fire.

He pushed back from the table, gathered up their coffee cups, and put them in the sink. He heard Ezra in the playpen in the living room.

'Coming, skipper,' he called, then looked out of the kitchen window and saw Martha almost to the top of the hill. He'd give anything to be able to put her mind at ease, to reassure her that R. C. was well and would soon be safely home with his nose in a book.

But he couldn't do that, and he personally could testify as to how fast death came in war, how a man could be alive, dreaming and planning one minute, and half-alive, half-unconscious, then dead the next.

'Damn,' he muttered to the kitchen sink, and wondered how long it would take mankind to figure it all out and get it right so ordinary folks could just get on with their living . . .

October 4, 1950
Hitchings, Texas

Martha was sitting on the front steps, helping Molly and Rufus with their multiplication tables, when she saw Mr Hawkins's old Ford churning up the dry October dust of the road.

'Seven times two is fourteen, seven times three is twenty-one, seven times four is twenty-nine – ' Molly said.

'Twenty-eight,' Martha corrected, never taking her eyes off the old Ford as it pulled off the road.

'Afternoon, Martha,' Mr Hawkins called out, and held up a red-, white-, and blue-striped envelope for her to see. 'Come special delivery for you. Thought I'd run it right out.'

Death comes in telegrams, she thought. That wasn't a telegram, though maybe the newfangled navy had a newfangled way of doing things.

'Thanks,' Martha said, and pushed up off the steps. Behind her she heard the screen door slam. Charlie coming out to see what was going on.

She took the letter. Skinny-looking thing it was on that thin paper that was hard to write on. She was aware then of four sets of eyes on her, Mr Hawkins, Molly, and Rufus, who were old enough and wise enough to sense precisely what was going on, and Charlie at the top of the porch steps, his walking stick raised as if he weren't certain whether he should advance or retreat.

Well, then . . . And with trembling fingers she split the seal. The first line read:

Dear Martha,
Just a note to let you know I'm all right . . .

'Martha? What is it?'

The shout was from Charlie, who clearly was tired of all the silent waiting.

'Says he's all right,' Martha called back, lifting the letter in the air.

All at once Molly and Rufus jumped up and started a crazy squealing Indian dance around in a circle. Martha looked at the letter and was so relieved. 'Thanks, Mr Hawkins,' she said, her hands still shaking. 'Please excuse my manners. Can I offer you something? Charlie's making his special cider – '

'No, Martha, I best be getting back. Glad it's good news. I was hoping it would be.'

As the old Ford did a U-turn, raising more dust, Martha eased past the shrieking 'Indians' and approached Charlie.

He reached for her and missed, and she backed away quickly, laughing, the first time in many days when she'd felt like laughing. 'If you got so much energy,' she said coyly, 'put those two through their multiplication tables. Molly's hopeless after the sevens. I think she just guesses and gets half of them right.'

'Where are you going?'

'To fry us up some chicken for dinner.'

At the door she looked back, met his eyes, and saw love there and understanding.

Fried chicken was for Sundays and celebrations.

And it wasn't Sunday . . .

December 1, 1950
The Stables
Beverly Hills, California

In all his life there had been only four people whose opinion had really mattered to Cy and whose advice he might under certain conditions follow.

Two were dead. His father and his wife. The third, Inez Cooper, had already given him her opinion, and the fourth person whose opinion he respected was seated across his desk from him, a big black Cuban cigar held firmly in the side of his mouth, his eyes calm, knowing, mildly amused by this ongoing circus called life.

Julian Schaeffer – Jules, as Cy called him – his personal attorney, had seen him through more legal scrapes than either of them cared to admit. They'd known each other as boys back in New York.

'So what am I here for, Cy, or can I guess?'

'You want brandy?'

'If I'd wanted brandy, I would have got brandy.'

'Of course.'

Jules smiled. 'You look like a goddamned schoolboy, Cy.'

'Funny, I feel like one.'

'Talk to me,' Jules urged. 'I can read the gossip. I know what they're saying. But tell me about your friends. What do they say?'

Still with his head back, Cy talked to the ceiling. 'They say sleep with her.'

'Have you?'

'No.'

'What else?'

'They say play with her, get her on a slow boat to China, send her back to Arkansas for ten years to grow up – '

Jules laughed. 'Only thing wrong with that is that while she's growing up, so are you.'

'They say take her on a cruise, live with her for a year on an island, basically do anything, anything but marry her.'

'Where is the young lady now?'

'She's in her suite.'

'How do the two of you pass the time?'

Cy frowned at the peculiar question. 'We meet for breakfast about eight . . .'

'Where?'

'In the lanai suite. Then I drive in to the studio. Sometimes she joins me for lunch. We go for a swim late afternoon, sometimes we will walk around the grounds afterward. She loves the aviary. Dinner at seven and I'm back in my office here by nine.'

'Truth now, Cy. You've never slept with her.'

'I swear to God.'

'What do you get from her company?'

Cy was pleased that this was a question he could answer with pleasure. 'Renewal,' he said flatly. 'When I'm with her, I see the world through her eyes. She has extraordinary vision, Jules. She reminds me so much of Sylvia. There's an innocence there and yet a wisdom, something that needs protecting, and yet a strength beyond anything I can imagine. At her center is a pure fire that burns with compassion, a grace that mesmerizes, a beauty that transforms, and an energy that revitalizes. I was not aware of my half-life until she completed it for me. I do love her, Jules, more than I could possibly convey to you or to anyone else.'

'There will be talk amounting to the "Anvil Chorus."'

'I know.'

'I've already heard . . .'

'What?'

'You don't want to know. Don't pollute your ears. It could affect your career, the studio . . .'

'How?'

'Child bride, child molester.'

'My God, she's twenty.'

'I know that and your critics know that. But they will conveniently forget it when it comes time to start slinging mud. Remember Chaplin.'

Abruptly Cy left his desk and walked rapidly to the door as though he were going to leave the room. Two things stopped him, his respect for Jules and the sight of Belle down by the pool, slipping out of her robe and testing the heated water with her toe.

Jules's cigar smoke preceded him, and Cy knew he was standing behind him without looking.

'What do you see down there?' Jules asked with detachment.

'My life,' Cy replied.

'Then I'd say the opinions of others, including my own, matter little.'

Cy looked astonished over his shoulder. He grinned. 'You're a real bastard, Jules, you know that, don't you?'

Jules shrugged. 'You'd better go tell that little girl to fasten her safety belt. The ride ahead may be very rough.'

Cy pushed open the door and started across the upper terrace, aware of Jules watching him. But for some reason nothing mattered except the young woman waiting beside the pool who just now had looked up and smiled at him with a warmth that he felt across the terraces. Taking the steps down two at a time, he focused on her face, until at last he stood a scant three feet before her.

'Will you marry me?' he asked, his voice breathless from his sprint down.

'Yes,' she replied, and stepped into his arms and fit as smoothly as though they were merely two pieces of the same puzzle cut apart and now rejoined . . .

December 24, 1950
The Stables
Beverly Hills, California

With the exception of Belle's disappointment that Malcolm and Charlotte Burgess could not come – Charlotte had been hospitalized only the week before – Inez was certain that she'd never seen a happier bride.

On this balmy Christmas Eve afternoon, as Inez buttoned the back buttons of Belle's pale blue silk suit blouse, she asked casually, 'Who is Billie Rose?'

Belle's laugh was immediate and warm. 'Why do you ask?'

'Because I couldn't help noticing your two-hour phone conversation with her the other day. She seemed to have a lot to say.'

'She did. She always does. You'd like Billie Rose, Inez. You two are a lot alike.'

'How so?'

'You both are convinced the world would stop spinning without your capable and efficient hands.'

'Well, I can't speak for Billie Rose, but I know very well the world would stop without me.'

With the blouse buttoned, their eyes met in the reflection of the mirror. 'Inez, I want you to know that I do love him.' Abruptly Belle turned about and faced her with new urgency. 'I hadn't planned on this. In fact, when I first met him . . .'

Inez let her talk, certain that it would do her good, less certain that Belle understood fully what was ahead for her. The gossip columnists had already started, and so far they knew nothing about the wedding this afternoon. Cy had gone to great pains to keep it an absolute secret. Jules Schaeffer had managed most of it, obtaining the license, purchasing the rings, arranging for Nick Costain, a Unitarian minister and Cy's good friend, to perform the ceremony. It would all take place at The Stables about five in the afternoon of December twenty-fourth.

Belle had selected a pale blue silk shantung suit. Cy had given her a magnificent strand of matched pearls for a wedding gift, and she was going to carry a pink rose. Inez would stand up with Belle, Jules with Cy. There would be champagne afterward, and the newlyweds would honeymoon in the lanai suite.

Those were the complete arrangements, and though at first Inez had very serious doubts about the wisdom of the decision, she now was convinced that the two major participants really had had little choice in the matter. It was as though both had come down with the same illness at the same time and the only cure was marriage.

'How do I look?' Belle asked, worried. It was an ongoing part of her charm that she never really seemed convinced of her beauty.

Inez shook her head. 'There is no possible way that you could look any more beautiful, I swear.'

She lifted the one perfect long-stemmed pink rose from the vase and handed it to Belle. 'You know, I knew Sylvia Compton very well.'

'Yes . . .'

'I think she would like you enormously and be very happy to share Cy with you.'

All at once Belle embraced her, a spontaneous affection that moved Inez. 'Shall we?' she invited, and held out her hand to Belle.

'I'm ready if you are.'

'Then forward march – '

Together, hand in hand, like schoolgirls leaving on an outing, they left the lanai suite.

Inez's last prayer was that Cy and Belle be allowed the happiness they both so richly deserved . . .

'They're coming,' Cy exclaimed, and stepped back from the door of his studio.

Jules thought that he resembled a kid who'd caught his first glimpse of Santa Claus.

'Jules?'

'Here, Cy,' he said, and took a final puff on his beloved Cuban cigar, then sadly snuffed it out.

'Are you ready?'

'I'm not the one going anywhere.'

The terrace door opened and there she stood, by any man's account a vision of youth, innocence, and unlimited possibility. For just a moment Jules felt a pang of envy when he considered the paradise that awaited Cy later this evening and every evening, morn, and noon for the rest of his life.

Scoutmaster Inez eased past the two lovebirds who were conferring at the door and greeted Jules with the weary look of a parent who has just dressed, brushed, and groomed a child in her party garb.

'Is this Inez Cooper I see before me?' Jules grinned and kissed her on the cheek.

'All right, ladies and gentlemen, if we may . . .' Reverend Costain called out, warming up his ministerial voice.

Less than fifteen minutes later it was over. Jules had this to say for it if nothing else: It had been brief. With those few words, this man and this child had been bound together for life.

At Reverend Costain's invitation to do so, Cy kissed his bride. And blushed! Jules couldn't believe his eyes.

'Congratulations,' he said, and gave Cy a monstrous bear hug, adding, 'You know that Lorna and I wish you both every happiness.' And they did, for Jules could not imagine life without Cy's companionship and richness of spirit.

Then he faced the new Mrs Cy Compton. 'Belle . . .' He smiled and lightened his hug, though to his surprise she didn't and put her arms around his neck.

'Thanks, Jules, for being Cy's best friend,' she murmured.

There were torrents of kisses all around, the popping of cork, the obligatory slicing of a single-layered lemon cake. Then Reverend Costain took his leave.

Just as Jules was warming up to his fourth piece of cake, he heard Cy call to him from the door.

'If you'll excuse us,' he said with a lame smile, and Jules noticed that he'd already passed his bride through the door, where she was waiting for him on the other side.

'Oh, of course,' Jules said.

'Certainly, most certainly,' Inez said.

'Well?' Jules said at last.

'Well what?'

'Has he just blown his life and career out of the water?'

'No, I don't think so.'

For several minutes both Inez and Jules stared glumly down at the remains on the cake table. Then all at once Jules heard music and listened, frowning at Inez, trying to place the familiar tune.

'"Casey would waltz with the strawberry blonde and the band played on . . ."'

Inez heard it, too, looked at Jules, and then glanced toward the studio door.

'"He'd glide 'cross the floor with the girl he adored and the band played on . . ."'

'What in the – '

Jules reached the door first, glanced down toward the pool, and saw Cy and Belle waltzing to the music, which was coming from the hi-fi system.

They waltzed around the pool with a grace, a charm, and a simplicity that was irresistible.

Then Cy stopped and Belle stopped, and they appeared to look at each other for a long moment without speaking. All at once Cy bent down and lifted her into his arms as the music played on. He carried her across the terrace into the darkness heading toward the lanai suite.

For several moments there was silence. With nothing more to stare at down by the pool, Jules walked back to the cake table, finished off his cake, and wiped his hands on a napkin.

'Inez, I have an idea,' he said to the woman who was still staring out into the dusk where the two had just disappeared. 'Lorna has been fussing over a goddamn prime rib all afternoon. I think she hoped I could coax the newlyweds over for a wedding supper. Since that clearly is out of the question, why don't you – '

'Oh, I couldn't.'

'And what in the hell are you going to do here?'

'There are . . . things.'

'Come on, Inez. Sorry to say, I doubt very seriously if you'll be needed here tonight in any capacity. Lorna and I need you to help with that prime rib. What do you say? Come on.'

'Thanks, Jules. I really hadn't thought about what I'd be doing tonight.'

And with that he took her by the arm, steered her through the door, down the corridor, and out into the pleasant night air, where a large portion of Los Angeles was celebrating the birth of Christ and another was observing Hanukkah while the two in the lanai suite were having the best celebration of all, reveling in the pleasure and miracle of each other . . .

At the height of orgasm, Belle lifted her head off the pillow and with her hands pressed against his buttocks held him securely inside of her. She wrapped her legs around his and wondered if she'd ever draw enough breath into her lungs to accommodate the explosions inside her. They came in never-ending waves, each leaving her gasping, still holding him even more tightly while he covered her arched throat and breasts with kisses. At last both of them relaxed into each other, still locked in the closest of unions.

Against her breast she could feel his heart beating. Still enjoying his body, she thought with amusement how rapidly they had arrived at this point. Cy had moved on lovemaking as he moved on everything else, with purpose, with resolve. One minute they had been waltzing around the pool and the next he had lifted her in his arms and carried her into the suite, where they had taken off their clothes without speaking a word. Then he was lying beside her, still no words, and not until he was inside her did he speak, and then it was to whisper, 'I love you so very much.'

Beyond that point, no words had been needed. And now no words were possible. His body felt right and good, all aspects of it. 'Am I too heavy?' he murmured.

'No.'

'Are you sleepy?'

'No.'

And in that remarkably short time, she felt new energy being generated, felt him push up and look down on her, and thought how fine his face was, his eyes particularly. And even as she was concentrating on his eyes, she felt him start the slow rhythm inside her. With each new angle, each new pressure, the sensations started again, deeper this time, more explosive, both reaching orgasm in a simultaneous outcry of joy, pleasure, pain, and mutual recognition that no matter what they encountered in the world, no matter what they lost or gained, forfeited or sacrificed, each night they could return here to their private temple and renew themselves in the passion of their bodies and in the reality of their love.

It was an astonishing awareness and tended to make both of them feel indestructible . . .

December 24, 1950
Hitchings, Texas

Martha tucked the last excited child into bed. Rufus, born a bit too wise, giggled. 'Who is going to play Santa this year, Charlie or R. C.?'

'I don't know,' Martha said with dwindling patience. 'Go to sleep and when you wake up you can find out.'

She bent over and kissed him, checked on the others, already fast asleep, then tiptoed out into the hall and heard the special sound of the two men talking in the living room.

R. C. and Charlie.

She stood in the darkened hall for a moment and gave thanks to God for returning R. C., even though he could only stay three weeks before he had to report back to San Diego for duty.

She cut short the prayer as she realized that both men had been sipping the good bourbon that R. C. had brought Charlie. Unless she wanted a plastered Santa Claus come morning, she'd better get in there and at least help them kill the bottle.

But first . . .

As she came to the end of the hall, she glanced into the living room. Both men were seated on rockers before the fire, in stockinged feet, talking low of war and battles.

She would join them in a few minutes. Now there was one other ritual she always observed every Christmas Eve.

Through the kitchen she proceeded to the bedroom. She reached into the bottom drawer for her walnut box, lifted it out, took it to the edge of the bed, where she raised the lid and looked down on the small portrait of the young girl with blond hair and blue eyes.

For several minutes she sat there and thought of the little girl who had graced her life so long ago for such a short period of time. So lost was she in her thought that she didn't even hear him come in. Not until he sat on the bed beside her did she look up and see him.

'R. C.,' she whispered, relieved.

'Have you told Charlie about her?'

'No. Where is Charlie?'

'He's trying on the Santa Claus suit. We'll find her, Martha.'

'I used to think so.'

'Think so again.'

Martha kissed him on the cheek. 'Come on,' she said, tucking the picture into her walnut box and slipping it into the bottom drawer of her dresser. 'How do you feel about putting together a rocking horse?'

'For Ezra?'

'Yes.'

'Lead me to it.'

Together they walked out of the room arm in arm, renewed by hope, blessed by love, and made strong by faith, which was more or less what Christmas was all about . . .

April 10, 1951
The Stables
Beverly Hills, California

Cy tried his dead-level best to concentrate, but my God it was hard.

Belle was sitting on the window seat in the splash of warm April sun. She was barefoot and busily arranging several pots of butter yellow daffodils.

The wise man knew when he was defeated, and slowly Cy put down the script he was trying to read and watched her. Without qualification, he was fully aware that these last four months had been the happiest of his life. He hadn't even tried to get back to work until last week. There was absolutely no point. Every morning they would awaken to each other, then like irresponsible children they would plot the day. They had driven north to the redwoods. They had driven south to San Diego and Balboa. They had spent several weeks on Catalina. They had flown back to Arkansas for a splendid visit with Malcolm and Charlotte Burgess in their gracious home. Cy had met and fallen in love with Billie Rose. And for the rest of the time they had walked, ridden horses, played tennis, swam, talked, and made love.

Then last week someone had reminded him that he had a studio and people waiting for him to make certain decisions, so he had retreated to his office but had discovered that he simply could not work without at least seeing or hearing Belle. So he had his large desk moved to the lanai suite, and for the last several days he had been trying to get through a script. But the distraction of Belle in the same room proved to be too much, and now quietly he left his chair, walked around the desk, came up behind her, put his arms around her, and pulled her to him.

She said not a word, as though she had known all along that eventually she would drag him away from the script. She pressed back against him as though she knew what he wanted because it was precisely what she wanted. Then she turned about, ready to receive his kiss. Cy gathered her to him, resigned to another day of nonwork, for it was impossible to touch her any place without wanting all of her. Then he had an idea. Perhaps they should just have an appropriate honeymoon of indeterminate length, Europe maybe. Oh, what fun it would be showing off Belle to Europe.

'I have an idea,' he whispered, wondering how long he would be content merely to hold her.

'What?' she said, rubbing the back of his neck in a manner that discouraged concentration.

'Let's do this right.'

'What?'

'A proper honeymoon. In Europe. Let me show you everything. Athens, Florence, Venice, Paris. Would you like that?'

The smile on her face indicated that she would. 'But what about your work?'

'It can wait,' he replied with confidence. It would have to wait. There were those times in every life that offered such a richness of joy that to pass them up would be criminal.

'I'll make the arrangements,' he whispered.

'Yes, but in a minute. For now, could we . . .'

'Yes.' He gathered her to him and realized anew how much he loved her, how vital she was to his well-being, and how he could not bear to lose her. He would have to go first, for he could not endure life without her.

LETTERS TO BILLIE ROSE

Athens, Greece
Grande Bretagne
May 28, 1951

Dear Billie Rose,

Look at the front of the postcard I'm enclosing with this letter and observe the balcony with the X marked on it. I'm sitting on that balcony right now writing this letter to you.

I can't tell you how beautiful it is here. I've never seen Cy so relaxed. He had a bit of a stomach upset yesterday, but I think it was because we arrived here two days ago and our luggage is still lost somewhere.

I can't tell you, Billie Rose, how much I admire and respect and love my husband. He is truly a unique man. We are still wearing the clothes we wore on the plane. But yesterday Cy asked the hotel to pack a picnic for us, and we arose at six this morning, fetched our lunch, caught a taxi, and climbed to the top of the Acropolis and watched the sun come up through the columns. I've never seen anything so beautiful in my life. And Cy spoke to me of freedom and democracy and explained that we were sitting right where it was born.

By lunchtime we had lots of company in the form of other tourists, so Cy led us to a small Greek theater not too far away and we sat on earthen seats, ate big fat black olives, munched on feta cheese and hard rolls, and drank from great mugs of tart lemonade. We stayed until midafternoon and walked back to the hotel.

Cy is downstairs now trying to reach the airport to see when our luggage will arrive. On the way back from the Acropolis we stopped in a small clothiers, and I bought a peasant dress and Cy bought a Greek fisherman's shirt. I'm afraid that despite the native dress we will never pass for Greek.

Tonight we are going to the Plaka. Cy tells me it's the oldest part of Athens and he wants to show me all of it.

We are having so much fun, Billie Rose. We are the perfect couple. Cy has seen and knows everything. I have seen and know nothing.

I do love him.

Hope Mac and Charlotte are well.

Love to all,
Belle

Rome, Italy
Hotel Eden
August 10, 1951

Dear Billie Rose,

Sorry I haven't written in so long. During our last week on Capri we both caught some sort of virus, and if it hadn't been for the kind ministrations of the hotel doctor and nurse, I really think that we both might have perished then and there.

Poor Cy was hit the hardest. I've never seen him so sick. The doctor ordered him flat on his back in bed for three weeks, and he had to take something that would cause him to vomit.

Billie Rose, I got so frightened when he was so ill. I don't know what I would do without him. He is better now, thank

God, but so weak. The doctor says it will take time to regain his strength.

Well, I don't want to turn this letter into a list of nothing but complaints. From what I can see, Rome looks fascinating. I'm sure that one day we shall put on our walking shoes and take off for parts unknown. I miss you. How I long for one of our 'old-fashioned conversations.'

How is Charlotte? And Mac?

I do miss you so much and soon we'll be home –

All my love,
Belle

Florence, Italy
The Villa Medici
September 8, 1951

Dear Billie Rose,

Rain. Torrents of it, for the last three weeks. Cy seemed excited about coming to Florence, but since we arrived it has done nothing but rain.

One good thing. Cy seems to be regaining his strength. The color of his face has improved, his appetite has improved, and in a way even his sense of humor has improved.

Tell Mac he would love it here. There is a museum on every street corner and the world's greatest pasta.

Cy is calling to me from the other room, so I'll bring this to a close. I do hope we will be home soon –

All my love,
Belle

Venice, Italy
The Gritti Palace
November 1, 1951

Dear Billie Rose,

Great news! We'll be home for Christmas. Cy says it is time to know precisely where we can find a fingernail file.

Cy has fully recovered from his ailment. He is making copious notes on two projects he left behind. He is eager to get home.

I have news. A secret. I may be pregnant. I'm not sure

yet. I haven't told Cy. No need until I'm absolutely certain. A baby, Billie Rose. Can you imagine? Me a mother? Remember now, not a word to anyone until I have proof positive. Oh, I hope I'm pregnant. How pleased Cy would be. I want so desperately to make him as happy as he has made me. Despite his illness and how worried I was, we have had a wonderful time. Still, like Dorothy, I agree, there is no place like home. Especially if Cy is there. And now – a baby –

Keep your fingers crossed. I promise you will be the first to know. Well, certainly the second –

I love you so much,
Belle

December 20, 1951
The Stables
Beverly Hills, California

Inez had been working with her best cleaning crew night and day for the past week to get everything ready for the honeymooners' return. She had even managed Christmas decorations, a tree, several holly wreaths, and poinsettias everywhere.

She had received cards from Belle early on. Then they had stopped, and it was Jules who had informed her of Cy's illness on Capri that had persisted for a dangerous length of time.

She had almost flown over at that point, convinced they needed her. But Jules in his wisdom had talked her out of it, and so here she was, waiting with a sense of excitement that she hadn't enjoyed for years.

'Miss Cooper, telephone.'

'Thanks.'

She waited until the maid was on her way upstairs, then lifted the receiver. 'Hello.'

'Inez – '

'Yes, Jules.'

'Trouble, I'm afraid.'

'What?'

'Cy's plane has radioed ahead for an ambulance.'

'Uh . . . Jules, what – '

'It's Belle. She's suffered a miscarriage.'

'Oh, dear God – '

'They will be bringing her home first. The doctors will see her there. And determine if she needs to be hospitalized.'

'Yes . . .'

'Are you all right?'

'Yes, I'll be waiting.'

'Bad luck.'

'The worst.'

For several moments Inez held on to the receiver, though her eyes were fixed on the overstuffed Santa she had propped up against the back of the desk.

Poor Belle –

Still, women recovered from miscarriages. A baby. It would have meant so much to both of them.

She put down the receiver and turned the smiling Santa Claus toward the wall. He seemed out of place . . .

February 5, 1952
Fort Smith, Arkansas

On February 3 at nine forty-five in the morning after a valiant struggle with a failing heart, Charlotte Burgess passed away at Doctors Hospital.

Malcolm was with her, held her hand on her last breath, wept for her passing and for the fact that she had died long before the actual moment that her heart had stopped beating.

A large portion of Charlotte's heart had truly died the day their daughter, Lenora, had passed away, years ago. Her body had continued to function in a flawed way, but the soul was dead. All that had remained was for the heart to follow. Two days ago it had.

Now Malcolm sat behind his desk, staring out of his window at the dead lawn, awaiting the return of Billie Rose from the airport where she had gone to meet Cy and Belle. Malcolm had been opposed to Belle's coming, aware of her recent miscarriage.

But Belle would hear none of it. She had insisted on coming, and in private Inez had confided to him that it might do her good, implying that her problem was not an ill body, but rather an ill spirit.

Now Malcolm glanced at his watch. They were cutting it close. Exhausted, he leaned his head back and stared dully at the mountains of cards, telegrams, and letters.

On his desk were three eight-by-ten photographs. One was of Charlotte on the day of their wedding thirty years ago, one was of Lenora at her eighth birthday party, and one of Belle when she had graduated from Hillcoat.

Two dead, one gone. He glanced down the drive and saw the limousine just turning into the gate. They were here. He wiped at his face, then hurried out of his study and down the corridor, arriving at the vestibule in time to see Belle.

No words were spoken. He opened his arms and held her and heard her whisper, 'I'm so sorry, Mac.'

Despite everything her voice sounded strong. He found it hard to believe that she was only twenty-two. She handled herself like a woman twice her age.

'Mac, Cy couldn't come.'

'Not ill, I hope.'

'No. Still, not strong, but eager to get back to work. He wanted to stay in Hollywood to see if he could get someone to talk to him.' She shook her head. 'It's really remarkable. It's as though while we were in Europe, we became invisible.'

'And you?' Malcolm asked.

'I have been better,' she said honestly. 'The doctors tell us to wait a while before we try again. They are pretty sure there is nothing wrong. It was just . . .'

'I know.'

'I do want a child so badly, Mac. Lots of them, if possible. Can you think of a more perfect place to raise kids than at The Stables?'

'No, I can't.'

Malcolm took his raincoat from Billie Rose and helped Belle into a spare from the vestibule closet. He held the door for both women, grateful for their strength. Belle had surprised him. He'd anticipated justifiable weakness and weeping.

Now he discovered that her ease gave him courage and allowed him to hope that he might make it through this day . . .

July 10, 1952
Hitchings, Texas

As R. C. turned off the main street of Hitchings and onto the county road, he lifted his head and grinned at the heat-filled air and shouted at the top of his lungs:

'I'm a-comin' ho-o-ome!'

He laughed aloud, amazed at how really good he felt, though he had not slept for more than a few hours in the last thirty-six.

He had been discharged the day before yesterday. He'd put on a pair of blue jeans and white shirt. He'd picked up his car from a friend who had been keeping it for him. He'd stopped at a little cafe on the outskirts of San Bernardino for a bag of sandwiches, a thermos of coffee, and three Baby Ruth bars. Then he had started driving due east, aching for home, Martha, Charlie, and the kids. His family. That's what they were, and on more than one occasion during these last four years, the memory of them had seen him through many a difficult time.

He looked back over his shoulder to check on the enormous cardboard box on the backseat, a special surprise he was bringing to all of them, a new twelve-inch television set, RCA's best with four controls and a set of rabbit-ear antennas.

He couldn't be certain, but he doubted if any of them had ever seen a television set. How much they would enjoy it, Charlie watching the ball games, Martha watching the music shows, the kids watching anything.

Then he saw it, the steeply pitched roof of the farmhouse. Briefly forgetting the fragile TV set in the back, he stepped on the gas and at the same time covered the horn with his hand in a continuous honk, thus announcing his arrival.

He pulled up directly in front of the steps that led to the house, waited for the swirling of his own dust to settle, then waved his way through the dying clouds and came to a halt at the bottom of the steps, confident that at any moment a shrieking, laughing parade would come tumbling out and be all over him.

'Martha?'

He called out once, waited, and saw the breeze push against the porch swing as if a ghost were swinging. Baffled, he looked up and down the road.

'What in the – '

As he muttered to himself, he started slowly up the steps and called out again, 'Charlie? Anybody home?'

He proceeded onto the front porch, into the house, through the house to the kitchen, where he smelled a pot of black-eyed peas and ham hocks slowly cooking. But he found no one.

Still digesting his disappointment, R. C. went back to the car, lugged the boxed TV set up to the porch first, then went back for his sea bag. Just as he was slamming down the trunk of the car, he saw the telltale dust rising from the county road in the distance.

Quickly he sprinted back up to the porch and sat down beside the TV set on the steps, resting his chin in his hands with the attitude of a man who had been waiting forever. A few minutes later he saw them in Charlie's car, Charlie driving, Martha on the front seat, holding something, and Molly, Rufus, and Ezra on the backseat. Where was Juan?

Only then did he remember that Martha had written and told him that Sara and Juan had returned to her parents' home outside Mexico City. She was no longer ashamed of what she'd had to do, and her parents were growing old and needed her. With her self-respect intact, she had taken her son and returned home.

Then he heard it, the first outcry, as they drew close enough to recognize his car.

'It's R. C.!' he heard Ezra screech. 'Stop the car, Charlie, stop the car!' And even before Charlie could bring his car to a halt, he saw the kids in the back spilling out, Rufus leading the way and followed by pigtailed Molly and Ezra.

While they were scrambling up the stairs, he saw Martha ease out of the car, turn back, and place something very carefully on the front seat. Then she too was grinning, shaking her head, and wiping her hands on her apron.

Now the kids were upon him, two hugging him on either side, someone trying to scale his back, their squeals deafening in his ear as he stood in a pathetic attempt to defend himself. Martha stopped to give the kids all the time they needed for their greeting, but then apparently she could wait no longer and pushed through her brood for a private greeting.

'R. C., you're home,' was all she said, and took him in her arms just as she had done all his life.

'Are you out?' she asked, still holding him.

'Completely. My discharge is in my bag.'

'Thank God. Have you been waiting long? Why didn't you call?'

'Not long, and I wanted to surprise you.'

'What are your plans?'

'Later.' He smiled. 'I have a surprise for all of you.'

'And we have one for you.'

'What's keeping Charlie? Come on, you old reprobate,' he shouted down at the car. But the man was still seated behind the wheel.

'I asked him to wait there,' Martha said, something of a sly smile on her face.

'Why?'

Then Molly spilled the beans. 'We have a new baby brother.'

R. C. blinked, then smiled at the announcement, not terribly surprised. Two had left, Sara and Juan. Nature and Martha abhorred a vacuum.

'A baby?' he echoed. 'Well, I think your surprise certainly takes precedence over mine. Come on, let's go take a look.'

As the caravan started down the steps, he saw Charlie push himself out from behind the wheel. He extended his hand first, then a moment later pulled R. C. forward into an embrace.

'So good to see you,' Charlie said. 'We were expecting you sometime this month.'

'What have you been up to, Charlie?' R. C. joked, pointing toward the small bundle on the front seat.

'Not mine.' Charlie grinned as Martha hurried around to the passenger's side and carefully scooped up the infant.

'You know how it always starts, don't you, R. C.?' Charlie asked now.

'No, how does it start, Charlie?'

'With a simple phone call. Mrs Calvert at the community center or sometimes Sheriff Daley or some bureaucrat from Austin or Amarillo. And you know what they always say, R. C.?'

'No, what do they always say, Charlie?'

'"We got a kid down here with no place to go." And I tell you, those are magic words as far as Martha is concerned.'

With a look of pride Martha drew back the blanket to reveal an infant. 'Charlie named him Danny,' she said, 'because "Danny Boy" was playing on the radio while we were driving into town.'

'And how long will you keep this one?' R. C. asked.

Martha shook her head. 'Forever, I hope. Mrs Calvert said the mother was a transient, passing through, claimed she didn't want the child, didn't know who the daddy was, and after a day's rest she up and took off without her baby.'

Danny. R. C. took him as Martha handed him over. He nuzzled the infant and whispered, 'Do you have any idea how lucky you are to be here, with this woman to raise you? You will one day, I promise you.'

Martha touched his shoulder and hugged him lightly. Then in customary fashion she started all her brood moving again.

'Charlie, you take the car around back to the barn and bring in some of your cider. Molly, you go put clean sheets on the crib. Rufus, you take the groceries in from the trunk and put as many of them away as you can, then you and Ezra go round up a couple of chickens for dinner.'

This last command brought squeals from the kids and a grin from Charlie. 'The prodigal returns,' he said. 'No fatted calf, but something better.'

As everyone disappeared on their appointed chores, Martha took R. C. by the arm as he carried Danny. 'It's so good you're home. Lord, I was worried.'

'I know. But it's over now.'

At the porch she sat on the top step and looked out over the west Texas plains. 'You know, R. C., I doubt seriously if I'm really entitled to this much happiness. I've done nothing to earn it.'

'Nonsense.'

'No, I mean it. I love Charlie as I have loved him since we were kids. Molly, Rufus, and Ezra provide me with a hundred joys a day. You're home. Now Danny. There's only . . .'

'Belle.'

'Yes.' She laughed to hide her emotions. 'You know, if she's still alive . . .'

'She's still alive.'

'She obviously has a life now, people who love her. Why do we persist?'

'Because we loved her first,' R. C. said with a conviction that defied rebuttal.

Martha wiped the sweat from her forehead. Danny yawned and squealed, and R. C. drew back the blanket, amazed at his beauty, doubly amazed that no one wanted him.

'Martha,' he began, pleased that they had this brief time alone, 'before I left California, I was accepted at UCLA. I need my doctorate.'

'Of course you do.'

'Why don't you and Charlie and the kids move out with me?'

She looked up at him as though he had gone temporarily mad. 'Move out with you?' she parroted, the frown on her face supplying him with her response. Still he persisted.

'Why not? We'd all be together. You would love California.'

'I've been to California.'

'A long time ago.'

'No, R. C.,' she said with finality. 'My place is here. My home is here – '

As she broke off, he picked up the refrain. 'I have the name of a private investigator.'

She laughed. 'Not again. Remember the other one. Oh, what was his name, a real con man, the one back in Tulsa – '

'This one is not a con man. I plan to call him when I get out there.'

'When will you have to leave?'

'Not until September.'

'Good, we'll have you then for the rest of the summer.' She leaned over and kissed his forehead. 'You know, you look right at home holding that baby. There's no law that says you can't fall in love and have a family of your own.'

He felt a slight blush and hid it by nuzzling Danny again. 'No law, perhaps, but something as insistent.'

'And what would that be?'

'I haven't found her. If indeed she's even out there.'

'She's out there.' Martha grinned. 'You'll see. Mark my words.'

Then all at once she spotted the large cardboard box on one side of the porch. 'What in the – what is that, R. C.?'

R. C. stood and handed Danny down to her. 'Your surprise,' he announced. 'For all of you. A brand-new television set.'

'A – what?'

'A television set.'

Martha frowned up at him. 'What are we going to do with that?'

'Watch it.' R. C. laughed. 'Come on, Martha, welcome to the twentieth century. You just wait. I promise, you've never seen anything like it . . .'

After dinner, with the good smell of fried chicken filling every corner of the house, Charlie and R. C. lifted the television out of the big box and placed it on the table by the window.

Standing about in a transfixed semicircle were Charlie, Martha holding Danny, Molly, Rufus, and Ezra, all mouths opened.

'Now just keep your eyes on the screen,' R. C. instructed as he adjusted the rabbit ears at appropriate angles. Then in a rather dramatic flourish, he turned the knob and heard the first crackling of electricity, stood back next to Ezra, and watched.

'It's snowing,' Ezra said.

'Looks like snow,' Charlie agreed.

'Is it snow, R. C.?' Martha asked.

'No, let me try another channel.' Quickly he rotated the dial. More snow.

'It looks cold for July, doesn't it, children?' Martha asked, obviously trying to make the most of their disappointment.

'It's not supposed to look like that,' R. C. said, and rapidly rotated the dial to another number.

Still snow, great flurries of it dancing across the screen.

'That's really nice, R. C.,' Molly said with characteristic kindness, never wanting anyone to feel bad about anything.

Her kindness only heightened R. C.'s frustration. He reached forward and turned the knob all the way around, stopping briefly at each number, the snow increasing.

'It's fine, R. C.,' Martha urged kindly. 'Leave it. I rather fancy it. It cools you off.'

R. C. muttered a heartfelt, 'Damn,' and Charlie suggested that maybe the snow would quit after a while and 'some other season would come on.'

In despair R. C. turned off the grand surprise and saw the children grin, relieved that they didn't have to stand about and watch the snowstorm all evening. 'Can we have the box?' Rufus asked. And he saw the three kids dragging the big box off the porch down the steps to the side yard.

'It's probably in the reception,' R. C. muttered to Charlie and Martha. 'We're picking up the picture from Amarillo, and I should have known that rabbit ears would not do the trick. We'll have to install a long-range antenna on the roof.'

When he finished speaking he looked at Charlie and Martha and saw identical expressions on their faces, a look of pure bewilderment, as though for a short period of time he had lapsed into a foreign language.

Ultimately he put his arms around them and led them to the front porch, where Charlie took up with his rocking chair, Martha sank onto hers, and R. C. sat in the middle of the big swing and began to push against the floor with his feet.

Behind them he heard the children playing with the box, their imaginations transforming it into first a car, then a fort, and as well as he could make out from their animated conversation, now a cave.

The sun was down. The breeze was warm. The front lawn was alive with a million fireflies. An owl in one of the tall cottonwoods was hooting at the night. The cicadas were trying to outdo each other. The peace was deep and palpable.

Good Lord, what in the name of God did anyone need with a television set in this paradise? . . .

May 15, 1955
The Stables
Beverly Hills, California

Cy bowed his head, pretended to be reading, and waited for the discomfort to pass. Generally it was mild, a slight ache along the rim of his jaw that sometimes went down his shoulder. It never lasted long, but it was getting to be a real pain in the neck. Literally. He probably needed to see a dentist. God, he hated dentists.

Exactly as he had predicted, the discomfort was over in about two minutes and he continued what he was doing, which in this case was watching Belle, his all-time favorite indoor-outdoor activity.

She was seated at the Queen Anne desk in front of the leaded-glass window writing a letter to Billie Rose. He loved the way she turned her head. Was she happy? He would give all he possessed to insure her happiness.

Cy propped his feet up on the near ottoman and considered reaching for another cup of coffee, but he was afraid he would disturb her. Or maybe he wanted to disturb her. In a minute. Study her now. Commit her to memory. Thank God for her and pray that you are making her happy.

He shifted the manuscript in his lap and read a few lines of dialogue.

'Cy?'

'Yes, my darling.'

'How do you spell "quiescent"?'

'Quiescent? Q-u-i-e-s-c-e-n-t. Why do you ask?'

'I'm writing to Billie Rose.'

'Why quiescent?'

'I read the word somewhere and what it meant – becoming quiet, at rest, at peace.'

'Are we leading a quiescent life?'

She smiled. 'In a way. It's good, I think, do you?'

'In a way . . .'

'I'm sorry I bothered you.'

'You always bother me. Have you finished your letter?'

'Almost.'

'Would you come and sit beside me?'

Without hesitation she put down her pen, pushed the desk chair back, and walked toward him. She knelt beside him on the sofa, put her arms around him, and drew him toward her until his head was resting against her breast.

'Yes, quiescent,' he murmured, eyes closed. 'Most definitely.'

The discomfort along the side of his jaw was starting again. All he had to do was hold still and wait it out.

It would go away . . .

June 17, 1957
The Stables

Belle had never been so happy in her life, despite the five-month confinement in her bed, both Cy and Inez indulging her every whim. First it had been the classic dill pickle syndrome. Then she had grown more creative, pancakes with barbecue sauce and lately marsh-mallow cream and salami.

Drs Levinson and Routhe were in daily attendance, charting every millimeter of growth.

Then last night the most miraculous moment of all, the first movement, Cy beside her, his hand pressed against her belly while inside something very small and very persistent stretched and kicked and informed them that now they were three.

Belle stretched beneath the sheets and grinned at the ceiling. She had never seen Cy so excited. They'd hugged, kissed, and held each other until Inez had said it was bedtime – for two of them, at any rate.

Now dawn, rosy light just creeping up over the windowsills. She stretched again and felt a sharp pain on her right side, then it was gone. She had had them before. Uterus expanding, according to the doctors.

She'd slept well enough except for her dreams, persistent dreams where –

There it was again, sharper this time. Belle closed her eyes and waited it out, taking deep breaths as they had instructed her to do.

Please God –

Of course. She had to go to the bathroom. Relieve her bladder and the pain would –

But as her bare feet touched carpet, she doubled over and clung to the side of the bed, felt the pain cut across her abdomen and down into her groin.

No – *No*!

'Inez?'

As she called for help, she looked down and saw a trickle of blood running down her left leg.

'Inez?'

She called again and tried to straighten up, but now the pain was intensifying, like an enormous wringer inside her stomach, something trying to twist free.

'Inez – '

As she called a third time, she took one step toward the door, then the floor rose up to meet her, and she pressed her forehead into the carpet.

She heard the sound of running footsteps, heard Inez's shocked, 'Oh, no,' heard more footsteps, heard Cy's voice strained, breaking:

'Call the doctor. Ambulance – quick, hurry!'

She felt his hands on her back, felt them gently turning her over, and then she saw his face.

'Belle, I'm here,' he said. 'Try to lie still.' He lifted her into his arms, rocked with her, and held her close.

She must have lost consciousness because the next thing she heard was a siren, distant at first, now coming closer, and she was back in her bed, someone adjusting a blanket.

The pain in her abdomen settled into a steady assault, no waves, no contractions. Something wanted out.

'This way,' someone shouted.

She tried to raise her head but could not. A moment later she felt the prick of a needle on her arm, and all at once she was floating in the midst of white clouds. There were voices all around her, but none of them concerned her.

She had only one thought. She was sorry that she had so displeased God. He had taken away her past. Now He seemed determined to deny her a future as well . . .

Inez stood beside the door of Belle's hospital room, trying to stay out of the way of the endless parade of doctors and nurses filing in and out. They had just brought her back from surgery. The baby had been a little boy, not quite six months, perfectly formed but ill-equipped to survive outside the womb.

Cy stood by the broad window looking out over Los Angeles, his hands laced behind his back. Inez was almost as worried about him. He had become ill as they'd taken Belle to surgery. A resident doctor had attended him, diagnosed nerves, given him a mild tranquilizer, and suggested that he lie down for a while.

'A while' had been about five minutes, then he had started pacing outside the surgery door, not speaking, rejecting all nourishment, though he did stop a couple of times to sit down.

Jules had arrived about nine to lend support in any way he could. Inez had called Malcolm Burgess, who was going to try to catch an evening flight. The sight of Belle on the gurney, so pale and lifeless, tubes leading into and out of her body, had caused Inez to go weak. But Cy had rallied, had held Belle's hand all the way back to her room.

Dr Levinson had told Cy that he saw no reason why they couldn't have another child. All things considered, Belle should make a good solid recovery, though she would be weak for some time. Then they should wait about a year and try again.

To all this dispassionate and objective advice, Cy had simply nodded repeatedly, then he'd gone back to the window and taken up a vigil on the city of Los Angeles.

There would be no child, then, at least for a year. The new nursery would have to be dismantled before Belle came home. The toys and all the stuffed animals would have to be put away as well. Inez made a series of mental notes.

'Cy?'

She wanted to ask if she could get him anything, coffee, juice. But either he hadn't heard or was too deeply engrossed in private matters to respond.

Belle's first stirrings came about thirty minutes later, a soft groan, and Cy was at her side.

Inez started to leave, but Cy asked, 'No, stay. I may need – '

He never finished, and she took a chair to a far corner of the room, sensing an interlude between husband and wife to which there should be no witnesses.

'Cy . . . I'm so – ' Belle faltered.

'No,' he whispered. 'You're going to be fine. The doctor said so. They even said we could – '

'What was it?'

Cy bowed his head and sat on the edge of the bed. 'A – boy, not quite six months.'

Then Inez heard weeping as Cy lifted Belle into his arms.

She turned her chair toward the corner of the room, withdrew a handkerchief from her purse, pressed it against her mouth, and held it there . . .

July 16, 1957
The Stables
Beverly Hills, California

With the resiliency of youth, Belle made a spectacular recovery, and less than a month later she was swimming laps in the pool and chiding Cy for slowing down. Now she stared up at him from the edge of the pool.

'A swim would do you good,' she teased.

'In a minute,' he said, studying the script in his lap. He'd brought his work down to the pool and spread it out on the table beneath the umbrella.

Still, she looked at him, deriving energy from him as she'd always done. They had named their son Edward, after Cy's father, and had placed his ashes in the mausoleum along with Sylvia. In a macabre moment Cy had shown her where he would go and where she would go if she so desired.

She shivered in the warm water and let it lap against her. Then she pushed off the side and floated on her back, staring up at the high blue sky filled with fluffy July clouds.

Most of the time she tried not to think about what had happened. Instead she chose to consider it an illness from which she had recovered. That was far easier than 'they had lost a child.'

She closed her eyes and felt water rushing into her ears, causing a pleasant deafness. Abruptly she commenced to tread water, then she paddled back to the side of the pool.

'Cy?'

He sat with his head down, the script still in his lap, his pen poised in his hand. His concentration was deep. He had not moved in several minutes.

She flipped over into a surface dive and pushed to the bottom of the pool where the water was cold, shot back to the surface, cleared it with a splash, wiped the water from her face, and saw him, still bent over the script.

'Cy?'

Still no answer. She frowned at him yet knew if he was busy she mustn't disturb him.

All right, then, ten more laps. And off she went, loving the feel of water running across her body. At five laps she slowed as she passed him where he sat at the table. Still he had not moved, the pen at the same angle, his head bowed so that she couldn't see his face.

He was asleep, of course. Well she'd let him nap. He needed it. He had looked so tired lately, so discouraged.

The wall clock said twelve forty-five. Lunch soon.

She pulled herself up out of the water, reached for her towel, and dried her face. She slipped on her terrycloth robe and started around the pool, never taking her eyes off of him, confident that he would sense her coming, look up, smile, and say something remarkable.

But he didn't, and she stood less than three feet from him and considered kissing him awake. She'd done it in the past, and he always came up smiling. Then why not?

'Cy?' She stepped forward and kissed his forehead.

It was cold.

'Cy?'

She called again and reached for his hand, limp in his lap. It was cold.

'Cy? Wake up – Cy . . .'

She called again and again, touching his face, his shoulder, trying to find warmth, trying to stimulate movement, begging for a response. In her fear she brushed against him, and as she did so he fell forward, a slow, almost graceful descent, first to his knees, then over onto his side, where for the first time she saw his eyes fixed and staring.

Then she was screaming in a continuous siren of grief and despair and anger . . .

July 18, 1957
The Stables
Beverly Hills, California

For Inez it was simply a matter of doing everything for everyone, being everything for everyone, and when she could no longer serve in those two capacities, she'd quietly retreat to a linen closet, a pantry, a bathroom, or some private cubicle in which she could repair to the best of her ability and move out again into an arena where she was most needed.

Cy's sudden death by heart attack two days before had taken all of Hollywood by surprise. Yesterday a large memorial service had taken place on Soundstage B with Reverend Nick Costain presiding. The limousines had stretched around the studio grounds and out the gate, blocking traffic for almost a mile. The guest books read like a *Who's Who* of the American film industry.

So the death ritual had been carried out by all players except one – Belle.

She had refused to go and in that one act of defiance had clearly demonstrated what Inez had always expected, that she was not one of the children, not a bona fide member of this playground called Hollywood.

Now, forty-eight hours later, waiting for Cy's ashes to be delivered to the family mausoleum, Inez paced the dining hall in the big house, listening to Jules as he made phone call after phone call, setting into motion all the necessary wheels, which curiously must start to turn only when a man dies.

'Where's Belle?' Jules asked with a suddenness that startled her.

'Dr Levinson gave her sedatives. She's in the lanai suite. A nurse is with her.'

'You're a rich woman, Inez, but Belle is richer.'

Inez moved quickly to the far side of the big room. 'Excuse me, Jules.' She slipped out of the dining hall and into the pantry, where in the past she had overseen the serving of elegant dinners. Now all that remained in the pantry was a mild scent of disinfectant.

Cy. Dead. She leaned against the cupboard and tried to accommodate the pain. She was worried about Belle. The doctors couldn't keep her drugged forever. They would have to let her fight her way up to full consciousness and deal with the truth. Still, coming so close on the heels of the miscarriage . . .

She heard the phone ringing and at the same time heard a car on the driveway outside. The funeral home. Reverend Costain. Cy's ashes.

Quickly she bowed her head, recalling her days in chapel

as a schoolgirl. Then she had had a perfectly lucid image of God as a kindly, white-haired old man who always looked after her and walked with her, kept her strong, safe, and whole.

At some point in her life, she'd lost that friend of her adolescence. Now desperately she needed him back. She bowed her head and begged softly, 'Go with me, be with me, give me strength. Please . . .'

It was about the goddamnedest thing that Jules Schaeffer had ever had to do, to go down into that cold mausoleum where they had put Sylvia and the dead baby. And now Cy.

He had tried all day to reach Brad. There was no answer at his last London address. He had managed to reach a friend who had told him that the last he had heard, Brad was in India – somewhere.

Now, as he stood in the mausoleum next to Inez, he saw the preacher lift the urn and ask God to go with Cy's soul. And Jules had a hard time swallowing that, too. There should be a rabbi here. There should be a burial, *shiva* and *shloshim*, someone to say the right words for Cy. Who in the hell was this schlemiel? Jules had no idea, and all he wanted was to get it over with and get back to his office, where there was a bottle of good brandy waiting. It was his intention to get loop-legged drunk tonight. Then tomorrow he would arise and face the complexities of what old Cy had left behind.

He closed his eyes to the bleak existence without Cy. God, but he missed him already.

He heard a noise at the door of the mausoleum and looked over his shoulder. It was Cy's child bride, Belle, or what once had been Belle. A nurse had her arm about her, which was good because otherwise she would have collapsed. She looked god-awful. Her hair hung down about her face uncombed. There was not a sign of makeup. She wore a wrinkled white shirt, oversize, partially buttoned, one of Cy's, was Jules's guess, and blue jeans.

As they stopped in the door, Jules saw her try to focus her eyes and at the same time try to shake off the nurse who supported her.

'Let me,' she muttered and then she saw Inez. 'Inez . . .' She collapsed to her knees, and Inez hurried to her side.

The nurse apologized. 'I'm sorry. She insisted on coming. I couldn't – '

'It's all right,' Inez soothed.

Jules looked back toward the preacher, who appeared to be shaken by her appearance. Then he resumed his religious drivel about the soul reaching heaven and being reunited with those they loved and Jesus Christ.

In order not to hear the religious nonsense, Jules stole a glance backward at the young girl on the step between Inez and the nurse, looking now more like an escapee from a mental institution than one of the richest women in the country. Then he looked back at the urn filled with Cy's ashes and tried to remember the prayer for mourners he had learned years ago at Hebrew school.

Hamakom y'nahaim Etkhem . . .

But he couldn't do it. He had wandered too far from his roots, like Cy . . .

July 28, 1957
The Stables
Beverly Hills, California

At first everyone had said it was all right. Let Belle stay in the mausoleum as long as she chose. It was simply her way of working through her grief.

Now, ten days later, Inez wasn't so certain. Every morning Belle left the lanai at dawn and went directly to the mausoleum. She stayed there all day, frequently into the night, sometimes eating the food Inez brought to her on a tray, but most of the time leaving it. She was taking only two tranquilizers a day now, but still she refused to speak.

Malcolm Burgess had flown out twice since the memorial service and both times had tried to coax her out, but to no avail. Ultimately business at the newspaper had called him back.

Jules had tried. Certainly Inez had tried. Inez had even called in a psychiatrist, who had spent two full days seated on the cold marble step with Belle. All to no avail.

'She needs a purpose for leaving the dead and returning to the living,' the expert had said.

Don't we all? Inez had thought.

Then there was the incident this morning. One of the maids had called Inez at ten of six claiming that Belle was going crazy, that she was pulling everything out of her closets, saying something about finding metal.

Still half-asleep, Inez put on her robe, slipped into her sandals, and hurried down the stairs. When she reached the lanai, she found the front door open, two of the maids waiting for her, and a third ready to escort her to the master bedroom, which now appeared as though a tornado had struck. Yet there was a curiously ordered island directly at the center of the chaos, one of Belle's bed pillows, fluffed and straightened. Resting atop this shrine, she saw the box of medals given to Belle by the army and belonging to the Japanese man named Harold Shoda.

With understanding came greater pain, and Inez sat wearily on the edge of the bed. 'Where is she now?' she asked, unable to take her eyes off the medals and their position of order on top of the pillow.

'You know where she is, Miss Cooper,' one of the maids muttered. 'She scares me sometimes. When is she going to – '

'I don't know,' Inez said with dispatch, waving away questions she couldn't answer.

As she started down the path to the mausoleum, she tried to think of something, anything, that she could do or say that might make a difference. She couldn't and gently pushed open the heavy door, momentarily blinded by the contrast of bright sun and dark shadow.

But at last she found her, seated on the bottom step, still in her pajamas, her long hair mussed and tangled about her face. She was hugging her knees and rocking ever so faintly back and forth, back and forth.

Briefly Inez closed her eyes to rest them from the sight of such devastation.

'Belle? It's me, Inez. I was wondering . . .'

But it really didn't make a damn bit of difference what she was wondering. There was something about the gently rocking figure, the tuneless humming interrupted only by deep sighs, that suggested Belle was perhaps incapable of hearing Inez or anyone else. And if this was the case, then the problem had rapidly escalated into yet another tragedy.

Suddenly she had an idea, so simple, yet so apparent. Quickly she turned about, ran up the walk until, out of breath, she sank onto the chair behind the phone desk off the rotunda in the big house. She dialed the number, which she knew by heart, and was delighted to hear Malcolm Burgess's voice on the other end.

'Malcolm, this is Inez.'

'Inez, tell me, what – is she – I was going to call today.'

'No, no, she's the same. In fact, if anything, she's worse. Malcolm, I need a big favor.'

'Anything.'

'Could you send out Billie Rose? . . .'

Two days later Inez paced the driveway beneath the porch, waiting for the car to return from the airport.

She had no idea what to expect. In the past Belle had talked endlessly of Billie Rose. Now it was her most fervent prayer that Billie Rose could work her magic, whatever the nature of that magic might be, and resurrect the young woman who for the past three nights had not even bothered to leave the mausoleum.

Then Inez saw it, Cy's limousine coming slowly up the long driveway. Inez stepped back to make way for it beneath the portico. A few moments later a Negro woman stepped out. She was tall, slim, and stylishly dressed in a tailored navy blue suit with a white lace blouse, high heels, and a pert pillbox hat that she wore at a charming angle low on her forehead.

'Are you Inez Cooper?' she asked with efficient dispatch, and Inez did well to nod.

'My name is Billie Rose,' she said.

'Yes, of course.'

'Where's my girl? I'm surprised that she's behaving like this. She knows better. She's been taught better. Now where is she?'

Inez had thought to offer her luncheon, a chance to rest and wash up. But clearly she was interested in only one thing.

'This way,' Inez murmured, and led the way down the drive, hearing the efficient tap-tap-tap of Billie Rose's heels on the pavement behind her. She tried to think of something appropriate to say.

'Did you have a nice flight?'

'No. I don't care for airplanes. But I just kept my eyes closed the whole time and thought of Belle.'

'Over here.' Inez gestured and started down the walk that led to the mausoleum. As they approached the door she thought she ought to say something to prepare Billie Rose. Two weeks of personal neglect and emotional turmoil had taken a toll. 'Billie Rose,' she said before she opened the door, 'It's been hard – '

'I know.'

As the two women stood facing each other, Inez was astonished at the eyes staring back at her, calm eyes, wise eyes.

Inez smiled weakly. 'Do your best.'

'I always do.'

Then Inez pushed open the door and saw Belle seated on the bottom step, hugging her knees, her head resting sideways, rocking back and forth.

As far as Inez could see, there was no change of expression on Billie Rose's face. She watched Belle for several minutes without speaking, and then at last spoke full voice.

'Well, are we about finished in here?' she asked, and Inez saw the rocking stop. 'I think it's gone on long enough, don't you?' Billie Rose went on, not waiting for an answer.

'Do you have any idea how many lives you've upset?' she continued, speaking to Belle's unresponding back. 'Too many, let me tell you, including mine. Why, I had to get myself all dressed up to fly out to this place because no one else knew what to do with you. I was tempted, yes, I was, to tell them just to throw you on the junk heap. But Mr Burgess said I couldn't do that.'

She took a step closer. 'You know what Spoons said? She said you needed a dose of castor oil, said that would get you out of here quick enough.' And incredibly Billie Rose laughed, a foreign sound to the marble walls.

Still no response from Belle.

'Well, I haven't traveled all this way to give you a dose of castor oil, but I have traveled all this way to say something to you. I want you to listen carefully. It's time to get up now and move on with your life. You've lost a lot, I'm not denying that, but you've been given a lot, too. I've never seen such a place as this. Even the dead people in here want you to get up and get out. I thought I told you all about death, Belle. Did you forget? It's there for all of us, and it's not bad, it's just part of the same process of life. No big surprises. We all live for a while, do the very best we can, and we die. That's the plan, Belle, always has been, always will be. Nothing will change it, and all you're doing in here now is cheating yourself out of some of your life days. And that's really dumb, you know? You've been given a beautiful world, filled with people who love you, and you go ahead and bury yourself with the dead. Boy . . .'

Inez saw Billie Rose shake her head vigorously as though astonished by such stupidity. Then her manner changed again.

'All right now, this is what we're going to do. I can't hang around this place all day. Back home, I got two pecks of peaches waiting to be preserved. You remember how busy August is. I got a bushel of cucumbers waiting to be made into Mr Burgess's bread and butters. My old aunt in Little Rock is ailing, and Mr Burgess is worried sick over you. So this is what we're going to do. I'm going to give you five minutes to say your final good-byes to the people in here. This nice lady and I are going to wait out in the sun because I'm freezing in here. And I'm going to check my watch. And if you're not out of here in five minutes, I'm coming in to get you, because we got a plane to catch back to Arkansas, where for the next few days I'm gonna need all the help I can get and since you don't have anything better to do, you're going to be my helper.'

She paused a moment and lifted her head. 'Did you understand me, Belle? Five minutes. Say your good-byes. Now!'

Without another word, Billie Rose turned and walked out into the sun, followed by Inez, who shielded her eyes against the sudden brilliance.

'Four minutes,' Billie Rose called back through the door, which was opened a crack.

Inez walked a few steps away and raised her eyes heavenward. Did the woman really think that Belle would respond to what she had said? Jules had said approximately the same thing, and so had she.

'Three minutes,' Billie Rose called back through the door, and kept her eyes on her watch.

Inez looked back toward the door. Nothing. Nor would there be. Well, it would be interesting to see what Billie Rose tried next.

'Two minutes,' she called out as though it mattered, and Inez was already searching through her head for the next plan. The psychiatrist had suggested a clinic where she could be evaluated by a panel of medical experts. Inez didn't like the sound of that, but if it became necessary . . .

'One minute,' Billie Rose called out, and again Inez looked back toward the door. Nothing.

Then – something. Faint movement, one small hand pushing against the weight of the door itself.

Billie Rose took one step forward. Inez held her position. Then there she was, looking like hell, pale, weak, disheveled, in soiled pajamas, one trembling hand reaching out toward Billie Rose, who was there to take it, to take all of her into her arms and hold her through the worst tears Inez had ever heard.

After several minutes Inez saw Billie Rose withdraw a large handkerchief from the pocket of her suit and wipe Belle's face as though she were a child.

'There,' she said with dispatch. 'Now show me where your clothes are. We'll pick out something suitable, and maybe that nice man in the big car will drive us back to the airport. We'll get home in time for a midnight snack with Mr Burgess. Then tomorrow morning, you got a bushel of cucumbers to cut and trim and two pecks of peaches to peel. So what do you say? Should we be about it?'

As the two of them started arm in arm up the walk, Inez wondered with a wave of humor and relief if it would be all right if she went with them . . .

August 7, 1957
Westwood, California

There were no words in the world to describe Martha's sense of pride when R. C. walked across the platform, took his degree, switched the short thick gold tassel to the other side of his mortarboard, and graduated magna cum laude, now Dr Drusso.

As Martha waited for him outside the stadium at the appointed spot, she tried to move back out of all the foot traffic, happy graduates running to greet parents, girlfriends, and boyfriends. She found herself grinning at each reunion.

What a grand visit she'd had. R. C. had wanted them all to come out, but there simply hadn't been enough money, and two of Martha's new kids, Peter and Maggie, were just getting over measles. So Charlie had offered to stay with the kids, and Martha had accepted R. C.'s plane ticket on the condition that it be both her Christmas present as well as her birthday present.

She had arrived yesterday and was going back tomorrow, much to R. C.'s consternation.

'Come all this way for three days?'

'I have kids at home and a husband . . .'

As always, she had managed to jolly him into better spirits, and although he had wanted to take her out for dinner last night, she had cooked chicken-fried steaks, mashed potatoes, and cream gravy for R. C. and a colleague of his, a nice young man named Keith Wilmington who also was an instructor in history at UCLA.

She looked toward the door and saw more graduates coming out minus their robes, all grasping their tassels and degrees, all eager to march straight into tomorrow.

'There you are.' She turned at the sound of the familiar voice and saw R. C., looking even more handsome than usual in a blue sport coat, white shirt, and tie.

She put her arms around him. 'I'm so proud,' she said. 'So very proud.'

'I couldn't have done it without you,' he said, and for a long moment they simply stood in a quiet embrace and let the crowd swirl around them.

'All right,' R. C. said at last, 'you took over last evening. For the rest of this day, we're going to follow *my* game plan. And no argument, you hear?'

'I hear,' she said with meek obedience. She took his arm and allowed him to lead her through the crowds to the immense parking lot, where somehow they managed to find his car.

First he showed her his office, a neat cubicle where on the wall she saw his first two degrees. 'Now they have got the granddaddy of all to keep them company,' she said. 'What will you be teaching?'

'Twentieth-century American history at first, primarily World War One to the years leading up to the Depression.'

'You'll be a good teacher.'

'I love it. I always have.'

After the office, they made a brief stop at his apartment, a comfortable ground-floor suite with two bedrooms, one bath, and living room. It was located just two blocks from campus and was perfect for his needs. While he changed into more comfortable clothes, Martha made a few mental notes. He could use a clothes hamper and a new can opener and, in the area of his desk, a pencil sharpener and a holder for letters and –

She saw something that abruptly brought her inspection to a halt. There on his desk in a small gold oval frame was his early sketch of Belle when she was three. Slowly Martha lifted it, sorry in a way to see it here. Part of R. C.'s life had stopped on that day so many years ago when he had placed Belle on the wrong train.

Now she heard him returning and quickly put it down. But he saw her.

'You know, I have an appointment next week with Derrick Woodall, the private investigator I told you about. I had hoped that you would stay long enough to meet and talk with him.'

'I have to get back.'

'You don't mind if I – '

'No, no . . .'

'Then what?'

Martha walked away from the desk, trying to sort through all the elements of her despair. 'It's been so long . . .'

'This man, Mr Woodall, has just located the brother of a woman who has been missing for forty-six years.'

'How wonderful.'

'I didn't think it would hurt to – '

'No, no, of course not. I'll send whatever money I can.'

'No, I don't want that.'

'How are you going to – '

'I have some saved. Don't worry. Come on, I have exactly one night to show you all of Los Angeles. We'd better get started.'

During the next three hours R. C. showed her the Hollywood Bowl, Knotts Berry Farm, and Grauman's Chinese Theatre. He drove her past Paramount and MGM. He showed her the famous corner of Hollywood and Vine and drove through Beverly Hills to show her a few of the big Hollywood estates.

'What's that?' she asked, pointing to a large gate with a high wall that seemed to stretch forever in both directions.

R. C. slowed the car. He'd never been this way before. 'Some movie star's home, I imagine,' he said.

Martha looked backward at the words over the gate and laughed. 'It sure doesn't look like any stables I've ever seen.'

'Hungry?' R. C. asked as they continued to drive past the high wall.

'Yes, I am,' Martha said.

'Stick with me. I know all the best places.'

'I'd stick with you even if you didn't.'

'Martha, I can't thank you enough for loving me.'

'What choice did I have? I couldn't leave you tied to that lamppost for the rest of your life.'

'What will it be, steak or seafood?'

'Seafood, Mr Drusso.'

And they turned away from the great walled estate and headed toward the ocean where the best seafood places were . . .

Part Four

September 2, 1957
Fort Smith, Arkansas

Belle perched on the stool at the end of the long counter in the big kitchen peeling peaches, and for the first time in several months she felt safe.

Of course she'd always felt safe in this kitchen so long as Billie Rose was either at the ironing board or bending over the counter and Spoons was at the stove. Now here they were again, exactly in their right places, Spoons stirring peach preserves at the stove, Billie Rose ironing Mac's shirts while Mac himself was in his study working on his editorial for the next day's paper.

Everyone in their place, no one leaving or dying, everyone just where they belonged.

'How are those peaches coming?' Spoons asked, and grunted her way over to check on them herself.

'Almost finished,' Belle replied. 'You can take these if you wish.'

She saw Billie Rose glance her way, the hot iron suspended over the white shirt. 'You know, there isn't a reason in the world why you can't do this, then I could help Spoons more.'

'Iron a shirt? I've never – '

'Time you learned. Finish those peaches and get yourself over here.'

Belle grinned. Good. Something else to do, Billie Rose making certain that there was always something else to do. Quickly she finished the peaches and looked up to see Billie Rose expertly guiding a beautifully ironed shirt onto a clothes hanger.

'Ready? I got an old shirt here at the bottom of the basket for you to learn on. Come on, let's go.'

Belle slipped from the stool and took her place at the ironing board, Billie Rose opposite her. 'First, you have to dampen – '

The kitchen phone rang. Billie Rose hurried to get it.

'Hello? . . . Hello?'

Belle studied the hot iron, wet her finger as she had seen Billie Rose do a thousand times, touched the surface with a short sizzle.

'Hello, who is this? This is Billie Rose. What number are you – Caroline, is that you? Where are you calling from?'

Belle studied the iron and wondered if she dared touch it to the shirt.

'I'm so sorry,' Billie Rose said.

Belle looked up, alert to the tone of voice.

'Of course, I'll come immediately.'

Belle put down the iron.

'I'll be there,' Billie Rose repeated ominously. 'Just hold on tight. I'll drive over as soon as I can. I promise you. You take care now. You know what to do. Is Reverend Burton still there? Good. He'll help. See you soon, Caroline.' Quickly she hung up the phone but continued to stand by the table.

'Billie Rose, who was – '

'My niece, Caroline. My old aunt died. The one who raised me. In Little Rock. I have to go to – '

'Let me come with you,' Belle asked. 'Please, Billie Rose. Let me come. I – '

Billie Rose started to shake her head. 'It's nothing like you're used to.'

'I'm not used to anything. Please, Billie Rose, I can drive you. I won't be in the way, I promise.'

Then Billie Rose softened. 'Well, come on, let's clear it with the boss. Might do you some good after all.'

'What shall I pack, Billie Rose? How many clothes?'

Billie Rose snorted and shook her head. 'What you got on and one clean shirt for the funeral. Even then you'll probably be overdressed . . .'

Billie Rose backed her Ford out of the garage and handed the keys to Belle with a warning that she could drive only as long as there was light in the sky.

Belle took the keys. 'There might have been light longer

if we had left sooner,' she said, and guided the car down the drive.

Once she reached the highway and settled into a good solid fifty miles an hour, Belle glanced at Billie Rose, still mildly annoyed with her for postponing their departure just so that she could give Mac his dinner.

'We didn't have to stay, you know,' Belle said. 'Even Mac was suggesting that we take off sooner. I don't know why – '

'Are you finished?' Billie Rose cut in.

'All I meant was – I don't – '

'You don't understand much of anything, do you?' Billie Rose began, and Belle sensed a verbal barrage.

'I want you to listen,' Billie Rose went on, 'and try your level best to understand. What I did today back there in Fort Smith? That has little or nothing to do with Mr Burgess direct, you hear? What I did back there has everything to do with a commitment I made to Mrs Burgess on the morning before she died. She asked me to promise faithfully that I would look after Mr Burgess until the day I died. I told her yes, I would. I made a firm commitment, and she believed me and I think as a result came closer to dying in peace. So what I was doing back there is honoring a commitment. Do you know the word, Belle?'

'Yes – '

'It doesn't mean doing something just because it suits you to do it, or doing it because it's easy or convenient. It means being truthful with oneself and loyal to others.'

At last she turned back around on her seat and stared out of the window. 'You might want to think long and hard on the word, Belle. From what I hear from Mr Burgess, you got a commitment or two waiting for you back in California.'

Belle took her eyes off the road.

'Keep looking where you're going or you'll put us both in the ditch.'

'What are you talking about?' Belle demanded, still smarting from the lecture.

'You know what I'm talking about. Your husband left you

in charge of a great deal. Now he must have thought you had the sense to know what to do with it.'

'I'm not interested in any of that. I don't understand business affairs.'

'You're not an idiot, at least you didn't used to be. You could learn.'

'Jules handles all that.'

'Then why didn't Mr Compton leave it all to Jules?'

'Do we have to talk about this now?'

'You're all grown up now, Belle. Time you start acting like it.'

Then she settled back onto the seat, rested her head on the cushion, and warned Belle, 'Fifteen minutes more and the wheel is mine, you hear?'

'I hear,' snapped Belle, her spirit suddenly dampened by the woman sitting next to her.

Exactly fifteen minutes later to the second, Billie Rose ordered Belle to pull over to the side of the road. Then she stepped out of the passenger's side and marched to the driver's side. The only revenge Belle had was to slam her door with such violence that the car shook.

'Like I said,' Billie Rose commented airily as she pulled carefully away from the side of the highway, 'it's past time some of us did some growing up.'

It was after nine o'clock when they reached the outskirts of Little Rock. Belle had dozed the last few minutes.

Now she sat up, rubbed sleep from her eyes, and saw that the streets were lined with army vehicles. The car headlights caught furtive movement, soldiers crossing rapidly from one side of the road to the other, all carrying rifles with fixed bayonets. For a moment she thought she was still asleep and lost in a nightmare. Alarmed, she glanced toward Billie Rose and saw apprehension in her eyes.

'Billie Rose, what is – '

'I don't know, but let's just get out of here.'

As she pulled wide in an attempt to make a U-turn, she saw a group of soldiers approaching the car, two on either side, all carrying guns with bayonets.

'Just stay quiet,' Billie Rose warned. 'Don't – '

At that moment one soldier knocked on her window and indicated that she was to roll it down.

'Good evening, sir,' Billie Rose said.

Then a soldier on Belle's side knocked on her window and told her to roll it down.

Both soldiers bent low and peered into the car. 'What's going on here? Are you all right, miss?' the soldier nearest to Belle inquired.

'Of course, I – '

'Ah was jes' takin' my mistress home,' Billie Rose said suddenly with the funniest accent. 'I done work for her people an' she wanted a whiff of fresh night air is all. Ain't that right, honey?'

Belle started to laugh at the ridiculous voice, but something about the tense situation suggested she better not.

'Ah am real sorry, Officer,' Billie Rose went on. 'Ah didn't know nuthin' about all this goings-on.'

Over the top of the car one soldier asked the other, 'What do you think?'

'Makes sense to me. She looks like a working nigger.'

Then all at once the soldier's face reappeared in Belle's window. 'You sure you're all right, miss?'

'Yes. What's going on here?'

'Big trouble tomorrow. Niggers trying to get into Central High. Governor Faubus called us out to keep the peace. That's all. Don't you worry your pretty head none. Just let your maid take you on home, then you sit real tight tomorrow.'

Belle listened with a kind of horrified fascination. She glanced at Billie Rose and saw her gripping the wheel with both hands, eyes front, staring straight ahead.

'Take off now, miss. You'd best get on home.'

Belle rolled up the window as Billie Rose eased the car forward. They drove past Central High School and saw it surrounded by soldiers.

Then Billie Rose stepped on the gas, and they moved rapidly through the downtown, past deserted streets, past warehouses and freight docks, past used-car lots and dumps, and on down to Baconne Street, number twelve, a small cabin on a street of similar cabins.

'Nigger Town,' Billie Rose said. She brought the car to a halt, turned off the ignition, and continued to hold on to the wheel as though despite the absence of movement, there still was a need for direction.

'Billie Rose, I'm so sorry,' Belle said, and reached for her hand.

'Best not do that here, child,' Billie Rose said, shaking off Belle's hand and looking up toward the cabin.

Belle followed the direction of her gaze and noticed that they were directly beneath a streetlight, which illuminated a ghostly scene. The front yard was filled with men, all dressed in faded work clothes. There were at least thirty of them. Belle saw a few children playing in the dirt. A marble glinted now and then, but no one called out a score. No one laughed. It was as if they had lost their voices but not their need to play.

'Come on,' Billie Rose said, and with that she left the car and started across the yard. A few of the men nodded politely and moved back as she passed. Once she stopped to speak to a young man all dressed in black.

'Belle,' she called, summoning Belle to her. 'This is Reverend Burton.'

Belle took his hand. 'It's good to meet you.'

'And you,' he replied. 'All of us here on Baconne feel as if we know you. Billie Rose has kept us informed over the years.'

While Billie Rose and Reverend Burton talked, Belle looked about and saw the group of wide-eyed children staring at her. She tried to return a smile, but they darted away.

On the porch were several women. They looked down on Billie Rose, and all were there to embrace her as she stepped up onto the concrete block that served as a step to the porch.

Belle waited a few steps behind, glanced in through the

front door, and saw more women hovering over a coffin, most weeping, a few singing a hymn, 'Lord into Your Bosom.'

Then she saw Billie Rose with her arm about a tall young woman who was crying openly. 'Belle, this is my niece, Caroline.'

Belle took her hand. 'I'm so sorry to hear about – '

The woman shrugged and blew her nose. 'She was old and in pain and ready to go. But we will miss her so.'

Then Billie Rose took Belle's hand and led the way through the low door of the room as the women moved back, revealing a plain pine coffin, three white candles burning at each end, and lying in it a very old and very frail looking woman, snow white curly hair, her chin pointed upward, her gnarled hands folded over a black worn Bible. A piece of white shiny satin had been draped about her and seemed now to highlight her dark dignity.

Belle stood just inside the door and watched as Billie Rose smiled a greeting to the women, then slowly approached the coffin. Though her back was to Belle, nonetheless Belle could feel her grief. In an attempt to distract herself, she looked about at the shadowy interior and saw a small room with pieces of cardboard nailed over the windows, saw one chair, one table, one kerosene lamp. Through the doorway she could see into a kitchen, a lean-to room with a wood stove and another lamp and table.

On the wall nearby she saw a large calendar with a picture of the Eiffel Tower and next to it a picture of Jesus in his crown of thorns. All around was the strong smell of urine and unwashed linen. Belle looked up as the singing started in earnest, all the women with closed eyes and raised hands and faces begging, 'Lord for the Salvation of Our Souls.'

Belle looked in all directions and saw nothing but poverty and neglect, sorrow and pain. Billie Rose kissed the woman in the coffin and remained bent over as though she were whispering something to her. When she raised up, she looked directly at Belle and motioned her to come forward.

Slowly Belle approached and felt Billie Rose's hand tighten on hers. 'I want you to see her. She took me in when I had no place else to go. She fed me when there wasn't enough food to feed her own family. She taught me compassion and honesty, integrity, dignity, and most important, she taught me that you can't love somebody else until you love yourself.'

Belle put her arms around Billie Rose and held her close.

'I'm fine,' Billie Rose insisted. She looked about at the small room filling with more and more people. 'I can't keep an eye on you all night,' she warned, 'and all this is gonna be going on for quite awhile. If you get tired, there's a blanket in the backseat of the car. You can probably sleep there as good as . . . anyplace.'

'Don't worry about me,' Belle soothed. 'And I'm not tired. I want to stay if it's all right.'

''Course.' Billie Rose smiled. Then she was gone, joining the women singing around the coffin, shaking hands with everyone as they filed by to pay their last respects.

Belle made her way through the crowd to the wall and stood between the pictures of the Eiffel Tower and Christ, watching the open, honest emotion. She wondered if any of these people, besides Billie Rose, knew what was going on up at Central High School, where soldiers had gathered with fixed bayonets to make certain that black children did not sit down with white children.

Belle closed her eyes before the mystery of it all. She didn't understand. She would never understand.

The tempo of the gospel hymn increased, and keeping time was Belle's bewilderment, until at last she slid down the wall and sat on the floor and watched the feet of those who passed in front of her . . .

September 3, 1957
Little Rock, Arkansas

'Come on, come on, wake up. Let's go see what's going to happen.'

Belle opened her eyes in a sideward glance and saw the same room she'd seen last night, though now the room was empty except for the coffin.

'What – I – '

'You're okay,' said Billie Rose. 'I covered you up and left you where you were. Come on, I want to go into town.'

'What about – '

'Funeral's not till noon. Everybody's still asleep.'

Belle said nothing more and hurried behind Billie Rose toward their car.

A few minutes later they parked about a block from Central High School. The streets converging in front of the school were already clogged with people, trucks, and newspaper reporters.

'You walk on ahead,' Billie Rose suggested when they were only about half a block away from the school.

'No, I won't. Come on . . .'

She waited until Billie Rose had begrudgingly moved forward, then together they started up the street, heading toward the confusion of people and cars.

White boys lined the walk leading up to the door of the school. On the top step was a committee of official-looking men. Directly behind them stood half a dozen soldiers, rifles in hand, bayonets fixed.

Milling about in the street in front of the school were about fifty Negroes, some dressed in suits and ties, others in work clothes, and it was in this direction that the white boys were hurling small rocks and dirty words.

Then a few minutes later, they saw a yellow school bus approach slowly through the crowd. The bus stopped directly in front of the walk. The doors opened and nine Negro boys and girls stepped off into the bright sunshine. Even from that distance, Belle could see the fear on their faces.

The white boys were shouting continuous threats, joined by their classmates, male and female alike, pretty young girls in poodle skirts and penny loafers shouting the most unimaginable obscenities.

Belle pushed forward, the better to see. Now the nine

students started slowly up the walk, heading toward the steps of the school. At the bottom step they came to a halt, and at the exact same time all the shouting stopped, all the curses and obscenities fell silent.

Just as one boy started up the steps, the soldiers stepped forward, rifles lifted, and blocked his path. One soldier shouted so that all could hear, 'Governor Faubus has placed this school off limits to Negroes.'

All at once a deafening cheer went up all around. The spectators on either side applauded, shouted, and clapped each other on the back. Belle looked around for Billie Rose and saw her standing well behind the crowd.

She heard a collective intake of breath. A young Negro girl had dared to walk around the soldiers, and now one had stepped up to her and was holding a rifle directly against her head.

The sight was terrifying, no one moving, fear as palpable as the hot sun. Slowly emerging from the spectators, Belle saw a white-haired lady walk primly up the walk, take the young girl by the shoulders, whisper something to her, then lead all of the children back to the bus stop, where they boarded their bus and shortly disappeared.

There was a deafening ovation all about, men throwing their hats into the air, women hugging each other, white children laughing and whistling.

Belle turned back to Billie Rose. She saw an expression on her face that she had never seen before, part fury, part grief. Belle put her arm about her and led her back to the car. Then she eased onto the driver's seat and put the key in the ignition but did not drive.

For the moment, forward movement of any kind was out of the question . . .

Aunt Cornelia's funeral was held at noon on the same day the Negro children were turned away from the school door. The small Baptist church at the end of Baconne Street was filled.

Reverend Burton let the choir sing its heart out for almost

an hour before he took the pulpit and held up two books, one the Bible, the other the writings of W. E. B. Du Bois.

'Here we have a black man,' he shouted out over the hushed congregation, 'who feels as we feel, but God has given him a golden tongue so that he might express it and write it down.'

Belle sat between Billie Rose and Caroline and listened to Reverend Burton, transfixed by his voice and by the words of Du Bois.

'The nineteenth was the first century of human sympathy – the age when half-wonderingly we began to descry in others that transformed spark of divinity which we call Myself . . .'

For over an hour Reverend Burton spoke of the man Du Bois. 'He did his work nobly and well. His name today means little, and herein lies the tragedy of the age: not that men are poor – all men know something of poverty; not that men are wicked – who is good? Not that men are ignorant – what is truth? But that men know so little of – men.'

There was more singing, more testifying, more praise, but for Belle the service had come to a halt with Du Bois. She must find his work and read every word. She must learn precisely what he was saying and how it might affect her and everyone living today.

'Are you all right?' Billie Rose muttered. Belle said yes, though in truth she wasn't. In fact, she would never be quite the same as before. Somehow sitting in this plain church with these plain people she'd found the most extraordinary human voice she'd ever heard.

They stayed in Little Rock until the morning of September fourth. No Negro child tried again to enter Central High School, though everyone said it was far from over. Belle watched and listened. Like a ghost she sat on the edge of prayer meetings, on the edge of family dinners, on the edge of Aunt Cornelia's funeral, on the edge of late night porch conversations. She had never seen Billie Rose so relaxed or laugh so much.

When it came time to say good-bye, there were kisses

enough for everyone. Belle accepted them, returned them, and envied the children who were a natural part of this family.

Reverend Burton shook her hand and gave her a list of writers 'she might find interesting, Booker T. Washington, William Edward Burghardt Du Bois, James Weldon Johnson, Ralph Ellison.'

Billie Rose offered to drive home, and Belle accepted, welcoming the peace and quiet of the car to reflect on all that she had seen, heard, and felt.

'Thank you for letting me come with you,' she said after they had been driving for about an hour.

'My pleasure,' Billie Rose said.

'I liked everyone I met.'

'They liked you.'

'I'm sorry about what happened at the school.'

'They'll try again.'

Belle agreed and started to say something else, but a new quiet had settled over Billie Rose. No longer relaxed and laughing, she stared straight ahead.

All the way home, Belle watched her. The closer they drew to Belle's home in Fort Smith, the greater the change, not that Billie Rose was becoming more white, just that she was becoming less black . . .

December 16, 1958
The Stables
Beverly Hills, California

'So what is the excuse this time?' Jules grumbled, and stood behind Cy's desk as Inez put down the receiver, her third call to Fort Smith in as many days.

She shrugged. 'Christmas, what else? Though Mr Burgess has promised faithfully that he would send her back the first week in January.'

'Is he part of our problem?'

'No,' Inez replied quickly. 'Quite the opposite. He is fully aware that she has responsibilities here. It's just that . . .'

'What?'

'Well, she's going through difficult times.'

'Hell, we're all going through difficult times. Is she still in her missionary mood?'

'Come on, Jules, be patient. She's – '

'I know goddamn well what she is,' he exploded. Inez sat down on the sofa to wait out the tirade she knew by heart.

'She's just inherited over thirty-three-million dollars and is now in charge of a very complicated estate.'

'You've handled things very well for Cy for many years.'

'Goddamn it, Inez, use your head. I'm over sixty-five, and the clock's running real fast. I'm not going to be here forever to hold her hand and make decisions for her. Only God knows why Cy did this. Hell, he could have put it in trust, he could have named an executor, he could have done a dozen things more sensible than sign over the fruits of his lifetime and his father's lifetime to a young woman who's not yet thirty, who has a high school diploma and has exhibited absolutely no head for business.'

Inez waited, head bowed, for the barrage to end. Inez was the one who had said give Belle until Christmas. But all reports coming out of Fort Smith were not good.

'What else did Mr Burgess say?' Jules asked, sitting wearily on Cy's chair.

'Well, Mr Burgess said she was reading.'

'That's good.'

'Negro literature for the most part.'

Jules groaned.

'And she's doing volunteer work in a Negro school.'

The volume of the groan increased.

'And every other weekend she drives to Little Rock, where she is directing a choir of Negro children.'

'Just what we need,' Jules exploded again. 'A millionaire missionary!' He laughed. 'Too bad old Cy isn't around. It has the smell of a good movie to me. In the meantime – ' Abruptly he sat up and looked Inez straight in the eye.

'In the meantime,' Inez repeated weakly, 'we'll be patient and wait. If Malcolm Burgess promised to have her here the first week in January, I think she'll be here.'

'Too vague, too vague,' Jules proclaimed, fighting his way up out of the chair. 'Let's set a date, a time, and a place.'

'All right.'

'January seventh. At three P.M. In the grand dining room of the big house.'

'She'd feel more comfortable somewhere else.'

'I don't give a damn how comfortable she feels,' he said. 'I have got to make her aware of her new responsibilities because if someone doesn't, I'm gonna kick the bucket and you're gonna kick the bucket and the vultures are going to descend and everything Cy worked for is going right down the old toilet.'

He shook his head as though completely rejecting his own scenario. 'I won't let it happen, Inez. I loved Cy too much. If I have to, I'll sit on her until she is aware of what her husband left her.'

Inez agreed with everything. There was no cause for dispute.

'Remember, Inez, call Burgess back. Tell him that Mrs Cy Compton had better be seated in the grand dining hall of the big house at three P.M. on January seventh or else.'

She was tempted to ask, 'Or else what?' but didn't. She watched as Jules snapped his briefcase closed and adjusted his jacket. 'Lorna said come stay with us for the holidays.'

'Thanks.' Inez smiled. 'I may take you up on it.'

'You got other plans?'

'No, I just sit up there in my apartment and wait for the telephone to ring and think of the good old days. We had some times here, didn't we, Jules?'

'The best, the best.'

As she walked with him to the door, a question occurred. 'Why the grand dining hall, Jules? Why not Cy's office?'

'Because I need the big table.'

'What for?'

At the door he turned and kissed her on the cheek. 'For the goddamnedest show-and-tell you have ever seen.'

Puzzled, Inez started to call after him as he hurried out to his car. While his driver held the door, he called back, 'Be careful up there in your apartment, Inez. Just take care you don't start whispering "Rosebud."'

Inez smiled, waved, closed the heavy door behind her, and leaned against it.

Rosebud . . .

She remembered the time that Cy had given the formal dinner party for Orson Welles and Rita Hayworth. The center of the long dining hall table had been lined with orchids, all colors, over two hundred orchids. Cy had ordered fans of peacock feathers placed behind each chair, and five chefs had worked in the kitchen. Hedda Hopper had called it the party of the century.

Inez started walking slowly back through the cavernous corridors of The Stables. How she missed those days, those glorious days . . .

January 7, 1959
Los Angeles, California

As the plane started its descent, Belle stared at herself in the reflection of the window. She was not returning willingly or happily to The Stables. In fact, she had argued endlessly with Mac and Billie Rose over why she had to go back at all.

But she had been no match for their big guns, using words like 'commitment,' 'obligation,' and 'responsibility.' She could still hear their voices inside her head even as the plane touched down at L. A. Airport.

About an hour later the limousine pulled up in front of the big house and she saw Inez step out of the door. It was good to see her.

Belle hugged her warmly and started to lead her back to

the car. 'Come on around to the lanai with me,' she invited. 'I have so much to tell you. You'll never believe what I've been doing. Oh, Inez, so much has happened. Let's have a pot of tea and talk for the rest of the afternoon.'

Despite her eagerness, Belle saw a mild scowl forming on Inez's face. 'Let me take a rain check on that,' she suggested softly. 'Jules is waiting. He's most anxious to speak with you.'

Belle started to protest, then changed her mind. This was what she'd come back for. Might as well get it over with.

'Would you like to wash up?' Inez asked, and Belle heard her voice echo about the walls of the vast rotunda. She remembered the first day she had arrived here with Brad. Cy had taken her by the arm and given her a tour of the Italian masters.

Cy. Brad. A confusion of love and hurt. Brad had sent a wire of condolence a few months after Cy's death. It was from someplace in Tibet. He had married an English girlfriend, and between their two trust funds they were very happy and living well.

'Belle?' It was Inez, dragging her back to the present.

'I'm fine, lead me to Jules. I hope he isn't angry. I'm not up to an angry Jules.'

Inez laughed. 'He isn't angry at all. He simply wants . . . well, I'll let him tell you what he simply wants.'

As they walked down the corridor toward the grand dining hall, Belle wondered why the meeting was taking place there instead of in Cy's office. She started to ask and changed her mind.

'Inez, did you know that I'm directing a choir now? I am. About thirty children, give or take. Ages about ten to fifteen. Oh, I wish you could hear them. They – '

'Here we are,' Inez interrupted, and came to a halt before the doors that led into the dining hall. 'Belle, all I ask of you is that you be patient with Jules, as I'm sure Jules will be patient with you. Promise?'

Belle thought it a strange request and was a little hurt that

Inez had not shown greater excitement over the choir. But no matter.

Abruptly she leaned over and kissed Inez on the cheek. 'Don't worry,' she whispered. 'I'll be on my very best behavior.'

Then she pushed open the door and went in . . .

Inez held back for a minute as her mind snagged on a bit of memory, the time years ago that she had helped Ingrid Bergman pin up the hem of her dress in this very spot.

Then she heard their voices inside the dining hall and realized that if she didn't stay alert, something else this day might need repair. Quickly now she followed Belle into the vast room, closed the door behind her, and saw Jules on the opposite side of the long table, which was stacked high with boxes and files. A paneled truck and two guards had arrived that morning, and for the last several hours the men had been loading the boxes into this room and onto that table, with Jules giving them instructions every step of the way.

'Did you have a pleasant flight?' she heard Jules inquire of Belle, who glanced at the boxes but with no particular curiosity.

'Very pleasant, thank you.'

'We could have sent Cy's plane.'

'No, thank you, that wasn't necessary.'

'You're having good weather back there?'

'Yes, a mild winter.'

The stiff conversation died for lack of interest on both sides. Inez held her position by the door and wondered if she should intervene. She decided not to, and just as well, for Jules had decided he'd had enough small talk.

'Would you care to sit down, Belle?' he asked thoughtfully.

'No, I'm fine.'

'Now, Belle,' he began, not looking at her. 'I know you are familiar with the terms of Cy's will.' When there was no response, he peered out over the mountain of boxes. 'Well, you are, aren't you?'

'I think so. You told me some things.'

A brief look of exasperation crossed Jules's face. 'Brad's well taken care of. Cy left sizable gifts to certain individuals, but the bulk of the estate now belongs to you.'

'I understand,' she said, 'but I wish he hadn't.'

'But he did, and now you and I must decide what precise course of action we are going to take.'

'I – don't understand.'

'The estate,' Jules began, 'Cy's estate, breaks down very roughly into four main categories. Here we have stock investment – ' And he touched the first grouping of file boxes, all neatly aligned on the table.

'And here we have real estate, many holdings going back to Cy's father, who purchased land when there was still a lot of it to go around. And here we have energy investments, some oil, some gas, some minerals. All these were Cy's personal investments, and, I might add, he has done very well.'

Belle said nothing.

'And last,' Jules concluded, 'we have his film revenues and personal possessions, this house, this land, his studio, his equipment, his options on certain scripts, his artwork, the whole shebang. I've leased the studio, so that's no problem for the time being. Now,' he went on, mopping his brow with his handkerchief, though the room was cool, 'this is not a stagnant pool. Every investment must be guarded, checked, protected, maintained until it produces the maximum benefit for the estate. Is that clear?'

'Yes.'

'Since all of this is now in your name, what I need to know is, are you prepared to take over the reins?'

Belle glanced first at the boxes, then at Jules. 'Who has been looking after it since Cy died?'

'I have, along with a small army of accountants and stockbrokers.'

'Then why can't we continue like that? Why can't – '

'Because you may not have noticed, but I'm not getting

any younger. I don't want to check out, I don't plan to check out, but nature has a leg up on me. Nature says everyone must check out, including Jules Schaeffer.'

'What about the accountants and the – '

'They take orders. They don't give orders. They don't make decisions.'

'Inez could help.'

'Inez? Does she have the key to life everlasting?'

Now Belle stepped toward the table, her voice as snappish as Jules's. 'All I can promise,' she said, 'is that I'll do the best I can.'

'And what do you mean by that?' he demanded, coming around from behind the table for the first time and confronting her.

'Well, I mean . . .'

'What? That you'll fly in when it suits you, that you will trust Joe Blow and John Doe with a fortune in excess of thirty-three-point-five-million dollars that it took two men two lifetimes to accumulate, that you will sign your name to any piece of paper that is thrust beneath your nose? Is that what you mean by doing your best?'

'Then why did Cy leave it to me? I didn't ask for it.'

'I assume because he thought he knew you, thought you'd know what to do.'

'Then why don't we trust Cy's judgment?'

'Because for the first time in a fifty-year relationship, I think he made the worst decision of his life.'

'That's not fair.'

Their voices were rising. Inez saw two red spots on Jules's cheeks as he hurried down to the end of the table. 'Not fair?' he echoed in what appeared to be genuine anger. 'All right, here we have stocks. What is the difference between common and preferred? What is a debenture? What is meant by "selling short"? What is a bull market? What is a bear market? This is an easy one. What's a blue chip?'

With each question Belle blinked and did not answer. She

watched as he moved to the next category. 'Okay, here's real estate, something everyone knows at least a little about. So tell me, Belle, what is a casualty loss? What is meant by depreciation? What is a – '

Inez broke in. 'For heaven's sake, Jules, give her a chance to respond.'

'I'm so sorry. Please take the floor. What is depreciation?'

Belle looked back at Inez with a helpless expression. 'Depreciation is,' she began, 'when something isn't as good as it once was.'

Jules gaped at her for a long time without speaking. He tried to repeat her answer and apparently ran out of steam. 'Let's try another,' he said, his voice gentler. 'What is meant by capital gain?'

She shook her head.

'What is a variable mortgage?'

She shook her head.

'What is a wraparound clause?'

She shook her head.

Jules looked at Inez and said nothing.

'All right. Here we have energy. What is an overriding royalty, then?'

She shook her head.

'What is a lease bonus?'

She shook her head.

'What is a depletion allowance?'

She shook her head.

'Jules,' Inez said. 'Enough.'

'Oh, I agree,' Jules said, and paced the length of the table and back again until he stood before Belle.

Gently he placed a hand on her shoulder and with his other hand lifted her face. 'Look, I'm not the enemy. I want to help. Old Cy must have seen something in you to put this bundle in your lap. But you've got to know what to do with it. You have to know how to work it, how to make it work for you. Do you understand?'

'What do you suggest?' she asked in a faint voice.

He shrugged. 'School. Go back to school.'

'Where?'

'We've got one of the best in the country in our own backyard. UCLA in Westwood. That way you'd be near me if I needed you and I would be near just in case you needed me and old Inez.'

Inez saw Belle walk past the table filled with Cy's assets, studying the boxes. Then she saw a familiar black notebook resting on the far end of the table. 'Jules,' she called out, 'you forgot to show her that.' She pointed toward the notebook.

'Oh, yes,' he said, and moved to the end of the table and picked up the thick loose-leaf notebook. 'These were Cy's charities, a listing of every charity he has supported over the years. He was, as I'm sure you know, a very generous man.'

Belle looked up with new interest. 'Two favors,' she said.

'Name them.'

'That I don't have to start until September, that I can have the summer in Arkansas.'

'No problem. What next?'

'Do I have enough money to buy a car?'

Jules looked at Inez, then back at Belle and smiled. 'You have cars, about a dozen of them, complete with drivers.'

'I don't mean those kind.'

'Then what kind?'

Belle thought a moment. 'A Ford? Billie Rose has a Ford. I've been driving it. People don't stare at you when you drive a Ford.'

Jules smiled. 'I think we can manage a Ford.'

'Thank you.'

'I'll take care of your enrollment. You just be ready to go in September. And what they fail to teach you, old Jules will. How's that?'

'I'm grateful,' she said, and sadly Inez saw none of the

enthusiasm she had seen only a scant half hour earlier. She'd grown up even more in her discussion with Jules. Would she ever be granted her youth? Probably not.

'Anything else?' Belle asked, and looked toward Jules.

'Not a thing.'

'Then if you'll excuse me . . .'

'Of course.'

She walked to the door and turned back with an apology. 'I'm sorry if I've been a pain in the neck.'

'You haven't.'

She opened the door, paused, then walked back to the table and picked up the large loose-leaf charities book. She enclosed it in her arms and returned to the door, speaking to the book.

'I miss him so much.'

Then she was gone, sending back the echo of her heels on the tile floor. Inez waited for her footsteps to fade.

She looked back at Jules. He laughed and made a comic gesture in the fashion of Stan Laurel, lifted his arms, and let them fall at his sides. 'Here we have a table filled with millions of dollars in assets. And she picks up the charities book.' He shook his head.

'Be patient with her, Jules.'

'Do I have a goddamn choice? . . .'

August 28, 1959
Hitchings, Texas

Martha refilled Charlie's and R. C.'s coffee cups, replenished the platter with freshly baked cinnamon rolls, and wondered when everyone had become so grown-up at this kitchen table of hers.

That young woman there was Molly, her pigtails sheared in exchange for a becoming bob. And that young man there was Rufus. With R. C.'s help, both had obtained scholarships to the University of Texas. Now both were quizzing R. C.

mercilessly on what they would find on campus come September. Since both were straight-A students, Martha wasn't too worried. Ezra, eleven, looked on with envy.

'There's always a freshman orientation,' R. C. was saying now. 'Be sure to attend everything because the better informed you are, the easier it will be. Do you understand?'

Both nodded soberly.

Now Charlie looked at his watch. 'If we're going into Amarillo for school clothes, we had better be about it.'

Martha agreed and sent Molly, Rufus, and Ezra to wash up and straighten their rooms. She'd been saving all summer to buy their school wardrobes, and now with R. C. home between semesters, it was going to be an outing for all of the family.

Charlie excused himself to check the air in the tires.

'More coffee?' Martha asked R. C.

'No thank you, I've had more than enough.'

Martha pushed back in her chair and saw an expression on R. C.'s face that she recognized instantly. 'What's on your mind?' she asked, drawing her chair back to the table.

He looked out of the window toward the garage, where Charlie was checking on the tires. 'Derrick Woodall,' he said flatly, and for a moment Martha was lost.

'The private detective,' R. C. explained. 'Remember? I told you about him.'

Martha laughed. 'Over a year ago. Surely you're not still paying him.'

'No, he worked for me for about three months. When I said I could no longer pay him, he said the case interested him, and if it was all right he would like to keep at it for a while longer.' R. C. sipped at his coffee, then studied the table. 'He called me about a month ago.'

'And?'

'Nothing. He said it was one of the most frustrating cases he had ever seen. He backtracked that train at least half a dozen times, and he said it was his opinion that one of two things happened. Either someone took her off the train in

Tulsa while I had gone to get her breakfast, or else she rode the train all the way into Los Angeles. Either way . . .'

He shifted on his chair and shrugged helplessly. 'He said it's just been too long ago. He advised me to forget about her. She might even be dead.'

She reached across the table, wanting terribly to erase that sorrowful expression from his face.

He took her hands and held on tight. 'Some days I catch myself studying every student who passes, every face in my classroom.'

'She's beyond student age now. Twenty-nine.'

'I know, but there are the graduates, women, particularly, who decide to come back to school. It certainly doesn't hurt.'

'Of course not, but you mustn't let it occupy all your life. You should – '

But before she could finish Molly and Rufus reappeared, brushed, polished, combed, and ready to go.

At the same time the little ones, Peter and Maggie, age two, and Danny, now seven, came out, tearing through the kitchen, knowing full well what a trip to Amarillo meant, the fun of a hamburger at a cafe and perhaps a toy if Charlie had change in his pocket, and Charlie always had change in his pocket.

Martha stood and put her arms around R. C. 'Guess it's still all right to hug you even if you are Dr Drusso.'

He kissed her forehead. 'It's mandatory.'

As they started out of the back door, he said, 'Did I tell you the good news? I've been promoted from assistant to associate professor.'

Martha stopped in her tracks. 'Associate professor,' she marveled. 'What exactly does that mean?'

'Well, it means more money, and I won't have to teach so many undergraduate classes.'

'You don't like undergraduates?'

'Let's say they are a challenge. Sometimes their clean slates are just a bit too clean.'

Martha laughed, took his arm, and told the kids to sit flat

in the back of the old pickup. Then she crawled in next to Charlie and R. C.

'Lock the doors!' she said, her customary order before any car trip as though to prevent anyone else from falling out and getting lost.

The kids were singing behind them. 'We're off to see the Wizard, the wonderful Wizard of Oz . . .'

She isn't dead, Martha thought.

She isn't . . .

September 3, 1959
Westwood, California
UCLA

With 'Seventy-six Trombones' playing on the car radio to bolster her spirits, Belle pulled into the student parking lot on the edge of campus, found an empty slot, angled the Ford in, and turned off the ignition. She realized with sinking spirits that parking her car might be the last right thing she would do all day.

She sat for a moment inside the safety of the car and watched a group of coeds giggling as they passed. They looked so young, so confident, in their slim straight skirts and pastel blouses.

Belle felt ancient at twenty-nine. Women her age were having babies, maintaining homes, pursuing a career. Yet here she was, a stack of new school books beside her on the seat, the encouragement and best wishes of everyone including Mac and Billie Rose ringing in her ear, even a new pen and pencil set from Jules tucked inside her purse.

All right, let's go. With dispatch and a large jolt of false courage, she gathered up her books, stepped out of her car, locked the door, and slid her schedule out from the top of her purse.

Yesterday Inez had walked with her all over campus, pointing out the buildings where her classes were to be held. Straight ahead toward the heart of the campus, then turn left, keep going past the Science and Biology Building, then turn right, and there –

'Damn, watch where you're going!'

The collision was sudden. She had failed to see the young black man, arms filled with boxes, coming around the building from the opposite direction.

'I'm sorry,' Belle gasped, and stooped immediately to help restore the lid of a box before the papers blew away. 'I just wasn't watching where – '

'That's all right. First day?'

'Yes.'

'Know the feeling. Of course I'm an old hand. This is my second year.'

She glanced up and smiled at him. He reminded her of Reverend Burton in Little Rock. He was neatly dressed in a dark shirt, blue jeans, and jacket. 'There,' he said as the last lid was restored, the boxes restacked. 'I wanted to distribute them over campus. Your way might even be better than mine.'

'Certainly quicker.' She smiled and looked about for any loose papers. When she looked back, she saw that he had lifted the pyramid of boxes into his arms, thus obscuring his face.

'Here, let me take some.'

'I appreciate it.'

She lifted the top three boxes, shifted her books to the top box, her purse on her shoulder. 'Now where are we going?'

'Right over there,' he said, bobbing his head toward the central plaza, a place where the student traffic was heavy near the Student Union.

'What is all this stuff?' she asked, trailing behind him.

'Information.'

'About what?'

'About the alliance and – '

Before he finished, he spoke to a group of passing students. Belle was impressed. He seemed to know everybody, and everybody seemed to know him. Then he veered to the left and went straight to one of the small wooden kiosks where people were setting up signs for specific organizations.

'Just put 'em there,' he said, indicating the low brick wall behind the kiosks.

Belle looked around. The foot traffic was increasing, people calling out to each other, a sense of comradeship, energy, and youthful passion.

'Hey, you still with me?' Belle looked back and saw the man grinning at her. 'I want to thank you for helping.'

'It was nothing. What are you – '

'We're the Alliance for Free Speech.'

'Is that a problem?'

He looked at her for a moment with a comical and stricken expression. 'Come on, you're old enough to remember McCarthy.'

Belle remembered. 'Can I – is it possible to join?'

'Possible? Hell, that's what I'm here for.'

He shoved a clipboard and pen toward her. 'Just sign on the last number. You sure you're all right?'

'Yes,' she reassured him.

'Listen, you wouldn't want to work with us, would you?'

'I don't understand.'

'Here. Put in a few hours here talking to the students, signing them up if they're willing. We meet once a month, wherever we can find an empty hall, and anybody can say anything they want. It serves a good purpose. We all believe very strongly in what we're doing. And what we're trying to do right now is make everyone aware of what's going on in the South.'

Belle thought a moment. Her last class was over at four. 'I could work this afternoon.'

'Great.'

'From four to about six-thirty?'

'Perfect. That's great. My wife will be here this afternoon. Her name is Drew.'

'Drew.'

'We're late bloomers like yourself. Where are you headed?'

Belle laughed. 'Freshman everything. English, history, business, math – '

'Straight ahead,' he said, and gestured toward the building on his right. 'Don't worry. I can guarantee you won't be a freshman for long.'

She took a few steps away from the kiosk, then turned back. 'What's your name?'

'Mathias Brock.'

'Mathias.'

She turned and took three more steps when he called after her. 'And what's your name?'

'Belle.'

He grinned. 'Well, hello-o-o, Bell-o-o-o.'

She laughed.

'Be here at four, remember?'

'I will.'

She walked toward the English Building with new energy. She felt lighter, younger, more confident.

Maybe this would work out after all . . .

January 10, 1960
UCLA

As president of the Alliance for Free Speech, Belle called the meeting to order and looked out over the crowded hall. Their numbers had grown, over a hundred now as opposed to a mere thirty-five last year.

On the agenda today was a debate. Whom would the league support for president of the United States, John F. Kennedy or Richard Nixon? Belle had had a difficult time finding someone to speak for Nixon, but she'd finally found three young Republicans who now sat to one side of the podium while on the other side sat Mathias Brock, Dr Keith Wilmington, a member of the history faculty, and

Drew Brock. Keith was faculty adviser to the alliance, and Mathias and Drew were sociology majors.

Now, as they made their way through old business, a report from two civil rights workers and a progress report on all civil rights bills pending in Washington, Belle looked out over the faces and realized with a private sense of satisfaction that she knew most of these people by name, and many of them she counted as good friends.

She glanced at her watch. The meeting would run late. Mathias and Drew had invited her to a civil rights meeting at their house in Watts, but she knew Inez would be worried, so she'd try to make it home as early as possible.

Then the civil rights workers were finished and returned to their table, where people could sign up to work if they so desired. Belle had signed up months ago.

She stood on the edge of the platform and looked out over the faces who were taking charge of their world.

'We have met here this evening to hear a debate on the relative merits of Richard M. Nixon and John F. Kennedy. First, speaking for Senator Kennedy will be Mathias Brock . . .'

She smiled as Mathias climbed up onto the platform. As he passed her by, he leaned down, smiled, and muttered, 'Hello-o-o, Bell-o-o-o . . .'

August 12, 1965
Beverly Hills, California

The interesting thing about Jules's wood-paneled conference room was that from the windows, Belle could see the campus towers. Though her body and mind were here, somehow her heart and soul lingered over there.

Since she had graduated on June 7 with an MBA, Phi Beta Kappa, she had sat in on the twice-a-week meetings concerning the management of Cy's estate. Jules had led her at the beginning, but more and more old Jules was sitting back with a self-satisfied smile on his face and merely watching as she challenged this set of figures, then that one, debated those investments, made sound suggestions of her own. The various accountants, stockbrokers, and business advisers were beginning to listen, and while she enjoyed their respect, she still considered the world of business a very limited and two-dimensional one, with the exception of the ease with which one could write an anonymous check for a needy student, a good cause, or to ease a family tragedy. Lately, though, she had encountered Mr Oliver Cranford, accountant, cashier, jerk, and bigot.

She looked over her shoulder from her position by the window. Mr Oliver Cranford was missing. Good riddance. Unfortunately Jules liked him and was at present getting ready to call the meeting to order for him. Now as the other dozen or so men milled contentedly around Jules's always well stocked bar, Belle looked back out of the window toward campus and beyond to where she saw smoke coming from the area around Watts.

There had been trouble there only last night. A young Negro home on leave with too much to drink had been stopped by a policeman in a routine check. There had been a few rocks thrown, some small fires, but today the police chief had called it 'just a night to throw rocks at white policemen.'

Belle had tried all day to phone Mathias and Drew, to no avail. It was her plan after this meeting to drive down and make sure they were all right.

In a curious way, she almost resented her graduation. Last year had been such a pivotal one, things seeming to go from bad to worse, the killing of the three civil rights workers, Goodman, Chaney, and Schwerner, in Mississippi and then the march on Selma, Alabama, to obtain black voting rights.

Every day had brought new challenges, new outrages, new demands. Never had she felt more alive, more involved, more occupied. She might not know where she had come from, but she was beginning to see very clearly the direction in which she was going. Although the vacuum of the past still hurt, still confounded and haunted her, she tried not to dwell on it but to accept what she did not know and what she most likely would never know.

'Penny for your thoughts?'

It was Jules, easing up beside her at the window.

She laughed. 'You don't want to know.'

'I do. In fact, I think I do know.'

'What?'

'You were thinking about the past.'

'Good heavens, does it show?'

'Yes.' Jules put his arm around her. 'I've known you now for almost twenty years, and I've learned to read that expression. You look as though you've lost something and you're trying to remember where you put it. Cy wanted so badly to solve that problem for you.'

'I know. I remember the last detective told us in utter frustration that he could find no information beyond what was already known.'

'Belle, you just discovered at the beginning of your life what most people never realize 'til the end of theirs. It's all a goddamned mystery.'

She hugged him and endeavored to get back on a more reliable track. 'And where is our Mr Cranford?'

Jules shrugged. 'Not like him. I – '

Then there he was, the red-faced, pig-nosed Mr Cranford, the bookkeeper who challenged Belle at every turn, questioned every check, no matter how small or for what cause. Of late Belle had started going straight to Jules over Mr Cranford's head, which of course had outraged him and made him even more contentious.

Now his first words were, 'Goddamn niggers, they're burning down the whole town.' And the laughter at the bar stopped.

'What do you mean?' Belle asked from the window, hearing sirens now, seeing the columns of smoke increase.

'Just what I said,' Cranford barked. 'Every major street downtown is closed by police barricades. Fire trucks all over the place. I heard on the car radio that there were easily seven thousand rioters rampaging along Avalon Boulevard, most armed with sniper rifles, others with Molotov cocktails.'

Belle left her position by the window and glanced at Jules.

'It's a goddamn guerrilla war, is what it is,' Cranford said, still mopping his brow and swallowing great gulps of bourbon from a glass someone had just handed to him. 'If you want my advice, Jules, we'll cancel this meeting and everyone get home as quickly as possible.'

Belle listened to the hysterical man, uncertain how much to believe. Her mind had caught on two words – Avalon Boulevard. Mathias and Drew lived half a block off Avalon on Marquette.

'Jules?'

'I think he's probably right. Let's close up shop for the night and get home. All of you be careful. Belle, can I – '

'No, I'll be fine,' she said, kissed him lightly in passing, then ran down the hall to the elevator ahead of the others. Blessedly one was waiting, and she closed her eyes on the descent and tried to clear her head of everything except what mattered now: to find Mathias and Drew and make certain they were safe.

Out of the parking garage, she headed toward Avalon Boulevard. On the way she encountered fire trucks and police cars, all speeding past her. She lowered the visor against the broiling sun spiked with eye-burning haze and smog and mixed now with the pungent acrid smell of smoke.

This had never happened before. She and all the others had felt that the alliance had made real progress in bringing people together, letting them shout out their frustrations as well as their differences. But clearly not everyone knew about the alliance. Some were taking out their frustration in guns and fires and looting.

'Hey, lady, you out of your goddamn mind?'

The angry shout came from a police officer at a barricade erected about four blocks from Drew and Mathias's house.

'Officer, I have friends who – '

'I don't give a goddamn what you have. If you know what's good for you, you'll turn that car around and head for home, wherever that is. Else I'll arrest you and take you in for your own safety.'

His tone of voice left no margin for debate, nor did his angry face. Reluctantly Belle backed the car around, all the time watching bands of Negroes about three blocks away running from store to store, new fires erupting, hearing sporadic explosions of gunfire.

Alarmed, she drove back to campus, parked, and ran toward the Student Union, where she knew the alliance was meeting tonight. But as she turned the corner, she saw the pavilion in front of the building filled with milling people, a discouraging division she'd never noticed before, blacks on one side, whites on the other.

Then she saw one of Mathias's good friends, Jeremy, and went to meet him. 'Why aren't you inside?'

He said nothing but pointed toward the doors, where she saw a solid line of security guards blocking all entrances.

'I don't understand.'

'Neither do we. Keith is up there now trying to find out what's going on.'

She glanced toward the main door and saw Dr Keith Wilmington arguing with one of the guards.

'Jeremy, have you seen Mathias and Drew?' she asked.

He shook his head. 'Saw him yesterday. He couldn't find Drew. He was mad as hell at something.'

'Are you all right?'

He shrugged. 'Someone burned my house last night, and you know the awful thing? I'm not even sure who did it, crazy white cops or crazy niggers. Hell, it's awful not knowing who to hate.'

He paused, then added, 'Here comes Dr Wilmington,' and Belle followed the direction of his gaze to Keith Wilmington, who was working his way back through the crowd, speaking to a few as he passed, shaking his head.

As he drew near, Belle asked, 'Why won't they let you in?'

'A security risk,' Keith said, 'or so they claim. They say they're acting on orders from the president of the university.'

Belle turned away, annoyed. Of all the times when they needed a forum in which to speak, it was now. And now was the time the school had judged them a security risk.

'Have you seen Mathias?'

'I haven't seen anybody except those cops,' he grumbled, and pointed up toward the security guards standing in front of the Student Union doors, feet spread, arms behind their backs.

'I take that back,' Keith said, suddenly lowering his voice. 'I've seen plenty of FBI crawling around here tonight.' He pointed toward a man on the edge of the group wearing a dark sport coat despite the heat and carrying a small camera.

'Smile,' Keith muttered. 'They've probably taken your picture several times already. Hell, we have got to get these people out of here. They are going to have a record for just standing around here tonight.'

Then an idea occurred to Belle. 'Let me borrow your notebook, Jeremy.' Quickly she took it from him, tore out a single page, then tore that page into smaller sections. On each she wrote the name *The Stables*, followed by simple directions on how to get there.

She handed several slips of paper to Jeremy and several to Keith. 'Do you know where it is?' she asked as both read, then looked at her with matching expressions of incredulity.

'Are you out of your – '

'I live there,' she said, and waited out the second wave of shock and surprise.

Keith put the puzzle pieces together. 'Of course . . .' He smiled. 'Belle Compton. Mrs Cy Compton.'

Jeremy was having more trouble. 'You mean that big-ass place up in Beverly Hills?'

'Can you find it?' Belle asked, sensing the need to move fast.

'You live there?' Jeremy persisted.

'Yes. Now please, pass the word. We'll meet there.'

But all at once, Jeremy laughed. 'Belle-Belle-do-tell,' he chanted in a low voice that alarmed her. 'Why didn't you tell us this before?'

'It never came up,' she said. 'Now please hurry.'

'Well, Belle-Belle-do-tell,' he repeated, and carefully stacked the hastily written maps and folded them as though he were counting money.

Belle glanced toward Keith. He shook his head. 'Go ahead, Jeremy, spread the word,' he urged. 'We need your help.'

'And see if you can find Mathias and Drew,' Belle called after him.

'You go ahead,' Keith said. 'We'll be right behind you.' Then in a considerate afterthought, he added, 'Are you certain this is all right?'

'I'm certain. Hurry now.'

And with that he disappeared into the group, passing out the small slips of paper with the words *The Stables* written on them.

Belle watched for a moment, then ran back to her car. She'd better get there first to alert the security guard and to warn Inez. According to her estimate, there should be about forty-five, perhaps fifty alliance members. She'd open the rotunda where people could sit comfortably on the steps.

It would work. It had to work, and it was good being involved again. Maybe there would be enough voices of reason raised this night that the burning and looting would come to a halt. And the alliance, partially her creation, would be the phoenix that would help Watts to rise from the ashes . . .

It was only at the last minute that Keith Wilmington pulled his Volkswagen into the parking lot of his office building and took the stairs to the second floor three at a time. He didn't exactly like what he was doing, but if ever the old cliché 'Better safe than sorry' applied, it was now. He'd seen the changes on Jeremy's face when he had read the piece of paper that Belle had handed him. He had complete faith in members of the alliance under normal conditions. But these were far from normal conditions.

As he ran down the hall, he saw light coming from the office he shared with R. C. Drusso. He pushed open the door and saw R. C. bent over his notebooks, clearly researching his lectures for the fall.

'You're up and about late,' R. C. murmured, still writing the thought of the moment. 'What's going on?'

Keith smiled. 'You wouldn't believe me if I told you. You better come along.'

'What for?'

'To see a fading piece of what once was the grand old Hollywood.'

'I don't – '

'Have you ever heard of The Stables?'

'The what?'

'The Stables. About forty acres of prime real estate in the heart of Beverly Hills. Cy Compton's old place.'

'What are you going to do there?'

'The alliance is meeting there at the invitation of Mrs Cy Compton.'

'Tonight?'

'This very night. You'd better come.'

'No, I don't think so. I have tons of work to do.'

'Too bad. I think you would like Belle. She's really very interesting. She – '

'Who?'

'Mrs Compton. Belle Compton. She graduated in June, but the alliance is partly her baby. She keeps a close watch. Because of the riot in Watts they wouldn't let us into the Student Union, so she invited us to her home.'

Now he bent over and unlocked his filing cabinet. Blocking R. C.'s view as he drew open the bottom drawer, he took out a small .22-caliber pistol, checked to see if it was loaded, then slipped it into the pocket of his jacket. He was certain he wouldn't have to use it. Still, with a riot in progress and the possibility of encountering hostile gangs, white or black, he might need some protection.

'Sure you won't come?' He looked back at R. C. and noticed a peculiar expression on his face.

'What did you say her name was?'

Losing patience, Keith repeated himself and headed for the door. 'Mrs Compton. Mrs Cy Compton.'

'No, I mean her first name.'

'Belle. If you aren't coming, I've got to hurry. See you later.'

He was to the door and out of it and halfway down the hall when he heard:

'Wait, I'm coming with you . . .'

Belle thought she would arrive first with time to spare, but while she was still four blocks away from The Stables, she looked in the rearview mirror and saw a solid line of cars behind. Some she recognized, some she didn't. Of course there was the possibility that they all weren't with the alliance but just normal Beverly Hills traffic.

Then she turned into the drive and paused at the security gate. 'Lester, let every car in this evening.'

She saw the frown on his face. 'Does Mr Shaeffer . . . ?'

'Mr Shaeffer doesn't live here.'

'Does Miss Cooper – '

'Lester, please. I'll take responsibility.'

'Every car?'

'Yes.'

'Can't you give me tag numbers?'

Fast losing patience, Belle tried to explain, 'We're having a meeting here. I don't know who will come or how many. Just let them pass. Please.'

He shrugged. 'Whatever you say, Mrs Compton.'

She thanked him, started up the long drive, looked in the rearview mirror, and saw the cars following right behind, Lester standing on the curb, his hat off, hands on hips, watching them. She pulled well past the portico to make room for the ones behind her, then left her car and ran to the front door, where Inez was waiting in her robe, having been alerted by Lester.

'Inez . . .' Belle smiled. 'I've invited a meeting here tonight. That's all right, isn't it?'

'Of course,' Inez replied with something less than enthusiasm.

'Then could we turn on the lights, all of them in front as well as in the rotunda?'

'Certainly,' Inez repeated, and glanced out of the door at the cars already jockeying for parking. 'Shall I – what refreshments will you – '

'No, no refreshments will be necessary,' Belle soothed. 'You go on up to your television. I'll handle things from here. We'll meet in the rotunda. There's plenty of room and stairs to sit on. You run along now, and thanks.'

She saw the hesitancy in Inez but was grateful when she retreated back up the steps.

Then the occupants of the first cars spilled in through the door and stopped.

'Wow-ee,' one exclaimed. 'Look at this!'

She knew most of them by face if not by name, greeted them, and told them to make themselves comfortable on the staircase. All eyes, she observed now, were focused on Cy's Italian paintings.

Then there were more at the doors, whites and Negroes this time, all reacting approximately the same at the first glimpse of Cy's dramatic rotunda, a scene capable of giving anyone pause.

'Hey, man, look at this!'

The voice dragged her back, and she saw a young Negro pointing upward at a large bouquet of Oriental lilies arranged in one of Cy's Ming vases. The arrangement sat atop the big round marble table and was itself several feet high. Now she watched the boy scale the table and draw out a stalk of pale yellow lilies, handing them down to a passing girl.

'Flowers for the ladies,' he called out, and proceeded to hand down lilies to anyone who passed by.

Behind her on the rounded staircase she saw that several

people had discovered the possibility of sliding down the steeply descending carved wooden banister and had now turned it into a ride. Nervously she looked toward the door, hoping to catch a glimpse of Keith Wilmington. As faculty adviser he could call them to order and get on with the business of the evening.

Still more were arriving, an almost solid parade coming in through the front door, taking note of where they were, then scattering to the point of greatest interest. For some it was the banister ride, for others it was the paintings. Near the top of the stairs she saw a young boy trying to take a small oil from the wall.

'Please don't do that,' she called up, trying to send her voice over the loud confusion. 'Please leave them so that all can enjoy them.'

The boy hesitated a moment as though listening to conflicting voices inside his head. Then all at once he took the painting from the wall and slid it down the stairs toward a cohort, who caught it, examined it, and made a face at it.

Where was Keith Wilmington? They respected Keith. He'd worked with them for years.

'Mrs Compton, could you tell me where there's a ladies' room? I got to pee real bad.'

She looked down into a young female face. Dear God, she hadn't thought of facilities. Too late she realized there were several things she hadn't thought of.

As she pointed the young girl down the corridor, she smelled the sweetish odor of grass and looked back to see several joints being passed freely around the crowded rotunda. There were far more than forty-five or fifty. Clearly they had picked up some visitors along the way.

Now she saw a second painting being lifted from the wall and called out again, 'Please leave them alone. There is no need to – '

But either the boy didn't hear or wouldn't hear, for now a second painting was ripped from the wall and passed down the line to a young man at the bottom of the steps, who stacked it with the others as though they now belonged to him.

Belle felt her pulse accelerate. She had to regain control. 'Please,' she called out, 'let's come to attention. There is much we have to do.'

She called again and again and saw not one person turn in compliance. It was as if normally well behaved, intelligent students had caught the madness of the night and there was nothing she could do about it . . .

As they pushed open the front door, Keith heard Belle shouting for order and felt inside his pocket for the pistol, doubly glad he had taken the time to stop and pick it up.

R. C. was right behind him, strangely quiet, as he had been on the entire drive to Beverly Hills.

As they stepped through the door, Keith saw a scene of pure chaos, and poor Belle was right at the center of it, still calling for quiet and order.

Keith came up behind her. 'Sorry I'm late.'

'Thank God,' she said, 'I can't – '

He stepped to the center of the rotunda and started calling for attention. At the same time he saw R. C. breaking up smaller groups. Apparently they recognized the authority of a male voice more easily than a female voice, for gradually, begrudgingly, they sat on the stairs. They still passed their joints around freely, but at least they were quieting down. The banister ride was canceled by R. C., who took up a position at the bottom of the stairs. Anyone sliding down would slide right into him.

Keith saw him staring at Belle now and was sorry he had not had time for introductions. Maybe later.

'All right,' he shouted as the last laugh and the last catcall faded from the staircase. 'I scarcely think this is any way to repay our hostess. Do you?' There was the muted grumbling of scolded children.

'We wouldn't have had any place at all to meet if it hadn't been for Belle.'

'How come she gets to live here?' someone shouted.

Keith laughed. 'Well, everyone has to live somewhere.'

'Then I vote we all live here,' the same voice called back, and won for himself a hearty round of whistling and applause.

'I'm afraid it doesn't work like that,' Keith said.

'Then how in the hell does it work?'

He felt himself inadequate to the situation, looked about, and saw Belle standing near the door through which people were still passing. Keith had never seen them before. Obviously word had spread.

'Hey, Wilmington, let's talk about that for a while. How in the hell does it work that folks like her get all this and we get next to nothing? Any one of them pictures' – the speaker, a young Negro, pointed toward a small painting that had been taken from the gallery wall – 'would feed a bunch of us for a long time, or buy books or pay tuition or help with doctor bills. Yet all these folks do is look at 'em.'

Again there was applause, and Keith, growing more alarmed by the minute, realized he lacked even the beginnings of a coherent response. 'I don't believe,' he began, 'that we should concentrate on what makes us different. Rather – '

'Bullshit,' someone muttered from the bottom of the step. 'You all sing the same song. Whitey has to stick together, or else we jigaboos will ride up to your fancy houses and say, "It's our turn now, you hear? Get your white asses out of here 'cause it's our turn."'

Most of the kids were on their feet now, and Keith knew there was only one course of action – to get the meeting over with and disband this tinderbox before it spontaneously combusted and took everything with it.

'All right,' Keith shouted. 'Listen, I want you to – '

Then all at once the group fell silent, their focus on the front door, their faces reflecting shock at something.

As Keith turned he saw R. C. start out of the shadows beneath the rotunda. Then he caught sight of Jeremy helping someone in the front door. Belle hurried to his side, then stopped in the same frozen position as the other students.

It was Mathias, or what was left of Mathias. He appeared to be covered in blood, which was coming from a wound over his forehead. His hand was bleeding as well, and his clothes were torn and soiled.

'Am I late?' he asked. 'I was – detained by a bunch of white bastard cops. I'm looking for my wife. You all know Drew. Well, I can't find her. Anywhere. And it was while I was looking for her that these white – I heard that the meeting was going to be here. I thought Drew might be – I've come for my wife.'

He wavered on his feet. Belle stepped forward, both hands outstretched to help. 'Come on, Mathias. I'll show you where you can lie down. Then I'll call – '

But abruptly he turned about, his face transformed. 'You stay away, bitch,' he muttered.

'Mathias, please, I – '

'Jeremy said this is where you lived. I didn't believe him.'

'What difference does – '

'What difference?' Mathias echoed angrily. 'You must've gotten quite a kick out of the evenings you spent at our house.'

'No – '

'Thinking, Poor jackasses, feeding me their meat loaf and day-old bread while I've got all I need right up here at the top of this fancy hill.'

'Mathias, please, you know better.'

'How am I to know better? You walk with us through some of the worst poverty in this screwed-up country and come back up here every night and wash it off as though it never happened.'

'I don't – '

'And you pretend to be so sympathetic, so understanding, and all the while you're laughing your goddamn head off.'

Keith started to come between them. Nothing was being accomplished. The sight of the injured Mathias had galvanized the group. Everyone was on their feet, and Belle's presence seemed to be causing their resentment to increase.

But just as Keith started toward the door, he saw Belle make one last appeal to Mathias, drawing close enough to touch him on the arm. That single touch seemed to inflame him anew, and he drew back his arm to push her aside and did so with such force that she fell backward, colliding with the heavy oak door, a teeth-jarring blow to the back of her head that caused her to go limp as she collapsed on the floor.

For a moment there was a shocked silence. Then Keith saw the white students moving toward the black students, shouting insults and obscenities. The fistfights started at the top of the staircase and began to work their way down, and as Mathias's loyal lieutenants closed in around him, Keith motioned to R. C.

'Get her out of here,' he ordered, pointing to Belle, who was just beginning to stir.

'Where?'

'Anyplace. Just out of here. Cops are going to be here soon. Hurry up.'

He saw the momentary confusion on R. C.'s face, then saw him pick Belle up in his arms and disappear down a long first-floor corridor.

R. C. had no idea where he was taking her except away from the chaos behind them. He hurried along the dark corridor until he found a small side door that opened up onto the hot night. He kicked open the door and heard sirens in the distance. He looked across the driveway and saw a small building of some sort, nestled in a grove of trees, a dim light coming from muted stained-glass windows.

Now he hurried across the drive and took the walk down to what resembled a private mausoleum. With effort he drew open the heavy door and saw his guess confirmed, a dimly lit place of pale marble and an altar with three urns resting atop.

She stirred in his arms and reached back to rub her head. Carefully he put her down on the top step and hurried back to close the door.

When he looked at her she was sitting up, her head bowed. She was unknotting the pale pink silk scarf about her throat and shaking her head groggily. 'Who are you?'

'I'm a friend of Keith's. I wouldn't do that,' he suggested softly. 'In the event you have a concussion, it would only – '

'I'm fine,' she said in a low voice. Then she bent over and covered her face with her hands.

At last she looked up and finished untying her scarf. She pulled it from around her throat and pressed it against her forehead.

R. C. stood by the door, respectful of the ordeal she had just been through.

'I should be getting back to help Keith,' she said.

He hurried to her side. 'I wouldn't if I were you. Keith was the one who told me to take you to a safe place. I'm not certain if this is safe or not, but it's cool.'

'It's safe.'

'What is it?'

'The family mausoleum.'

'Your family?'

'Not my real one.'

R. C. looked sideways at her. 'I – don't under – '

As she lifted her head to answer, he saw the birthmark, small, in the shape of a bell. At first he couldn't move, felt literally paralyzed. 'I – '

All at once he stood and looked down on her. 'I . . . think I – '

The longer he looked at her, the more clearly he saw her, the little girl with blond hair and blue eyes whom he had put on that train so long ago.

'Are you all right?' she asked.

'No. No, I'm not all right.'

'What is – '

'What's your name?'

'Belle.'

'Belle what?'

'Belle Compton.'

'What was it before that?'

'Belle Burgess.'

He stepped closer. 'And before that?'

She looked startled and tried to answer, but he interrupted.

'No, let me. Drusso. Your name is Belle Drusso – I'm R. C. Drusso. We are not related, but I know the woman who raised us and who gave us her name.'

All at once he started to laugh, and at the same time he reached for her, pulled her up, saw the alarmed expression in her face, and tried to think of something that would put her at ease. But first he had to settle himself, and that was proving to be quite a task.

'I'm sorry,' he gasped. 'I have looked for you for so long, in so many places, in – ' Then he couldn't go on and had to bow his head and wait out incredible emotion.

'Is my name Drusso?' she asked softly. 'How do you know?'

'Because I know you. Because I've known you since you were born.'

Again he started to laugh and at the same time apologized, 'Please forgive me. I've never done this before in my life.' And with that he sat down on the top step, covered his face, and struggled for at least a semblance of control . . .

She watched him. He claimed to know her name. How could he know? Should she believe him?

'What did you say your name was?' she asked, slowly sitting beside him on the step.

He took out a handkerchief and wiped his face. 'R. C. Drusso.'

'How did you . . . get here?'

'I teach history at UCLA. Keith is my officemate. He told me he was coming here, told me your name was Belle. I've looked for a woman named Belle for over thirty years. We thought – '

He looked at her without speaking for such a long time. At first she didn't know whether to believe him or not. But all at once he knelt before her and took her hands in his and said quietly, yet with such conviction, 'I know who you are.'

Then she believed him. She reached out a hand to touch his face, and he took her in his arms, held her close, and whispered over and over again:

'I know who you are . . . '

Dawn found them sitting on the marble floor, side by side, leaning back against the wall, spent as children after a hard day's play, quizzing one another endlessly on certain complexities of each other's stories.

'Then Martha is not my mother?' Belle asked with a degree of disappointment that was difficult to mask.

'No,' R. C. replied, 'but she could tell you about her. She said she helped to deliver you.'

Belle leaned against the wall and closed her eyes. R. C. held her hand and with his thumb caressed the backs of her fingers.

'Then you didn't ride the train all the way to Los Angeles?' he asked, his voice reflecting a weariness that she shared.

'I don't know,' she said honestly. 'My first memory is of a family in San Bernardino.'

He repeated the name and shook his head. 'The numbers of times we were in San Bernardino.'

'Looking for me?'

'Always looking for you. We never gave up, although there were times when – '

As all the frustrations, disappointments, and false leads piled up in his mind, R. C. tightened his grip on her hand. 'I'm so sorry, Belle,' he whispered. 'It was my fault.'

'No,' she protested softly, and leaned closer to him. 'You're the one who found me.'

She rested her head on his shoulder, reveling in the ease she felt with this man she'd only met a few hours ago. But there was more to it than that. There was a recognition, a shared past, and a mutual need that was confirmed in her heart where it mattered most, that this man was the bridge she could cross to find the beginning.

'R. C.?'

'Yes.'

'Could we go home?'

'Yes . . .'

At six o'clock the following evening on a warm, sultry August thirteenth, they started home. R. C. had stayed with Belle all day. They had gone back up to the big house to learn that the riot had been easily put down by The Stables' own security guards, thus avoiding the need to involve the police. Although the damage was extensive, it could be repaired except for two paintings.

Belle had introduced R. C. to Inez, and both, frequently talking at once, had told her the incredible tale of what had happened. Inez called it a miracle. They had wanted to leave immediately for Hitchings, but Inez had wisely suggested a brief rest before such a long drive. As both Belle and R. C. were reluctant to be separated again, R. C. took the guest suite while Belle retired to her rooms.

In truth neither slept, but after a shower and change of clothes, Belle packed a small bag, asked Inez to tell Jules where she was going, and promised that she would return as soon as possible.

They made a stop at R. C.'s apartment, then at his office, where they found Keith, all in one piece and stunned by their revelations of the night.

Belle learned that Mathias had been taken to the hospital and would be all right, and Drew had been located at her cousin's home on the other side of Watts, and the alliance would pay for the damage to The Stables, and they all quite probably would live to fight another day.

With Keith standing on the curb waving good-bye, R. C.

pointed the car out of town on what was possibly the happiest journey of his life. It could also be the most hazardous, for he found it virtually impossible to keep his eyes off her. She was more beautiful than he had ever imagined, and every time he looked at her, he discovered that she was looking at him.

Only one question remained. Who would keep their eyes on the road? . . .

With two exceptions R. C. drove straight through to Hitchings. Once they stopped briefly in San Bernardino so that Belle could show him the Melville house. It was still the Methodist parsonage.

Then she directed him two miles down the road to Harold and Kim Shoda's. The white farmhouse was now something called the Country Mart, with a neon sign and a concrete parking lot out front. In the Country Mart they sold beer and groceries to the people in the housing development that now covered what once had been Harold's farm. After Pearl Harbor, the United States Government had confiscated Japanese property and had sold it to the highest bidder. Belle told R. C. about Lil, about her life here, only a shortened version. More would come later.

They stopped for a sandwich and a cup of coffee, and after that the rhythm of the car had lulled Belle to sleep, her head on his shoulder, her hand resting lightly against his leg, so that he could not move without her knowledge.

In a way R. C. was grateful for her nap. It enabled him to think ahead to Martha, Charlie, and the kids and how best he could tell them. What would their reaction be, particularly Martha's?

Poor Martha . . .

They arrived in Hitchings about six o'clock the following evening. R. C. pulled into the Texaco station and knew that the time had come. He had to call Martha. He had kept putting it off all along the way, thinking that if something should happen, an accident, he could not destroy her hopes again.

But now they were here, a scant fifteen minutes away, and while the attendant filled the car with gas, he walked to the pay phone and with Belle at his side dialed.

She looked up at him. 'Why am I scared?'

He drew her close. 'Why am *I* scared?'

He heard the connection, then Martha's voice: 'Hello?'

'Martha, is that you? This is R. C.'

She laughed warmly. 'R. C., how good to hear from you. How's California?'

R. C. paused and tightened his grip on Belle's hand. 'Martha, I – I'm not in California.'

There was a pause. 'Where are you? Are you well? Is anything wrong?'

'No, no, I assure you. Nothing's wrong.'

'Where are you?'

'Martha, is Charlie there?'

'He's right here. We're just finishing dinner. R. C., what is it?'

He tried to steady his hand on the receiver. 'Martha, I'm coming home.'

'Good, where are – '

'Martha? I have found her.'

A pause. 'Martha? Did you hear? I have found her. I have found Belle.'

He thought he heard a sound on the other end, but he couldn't be certain. 'Martha? Are you there?'

The next voice he heard was Charlie's. 'R. C.? What's going on?'

'Is Martha all right?'

'I don't know. She's just sitting here in the chair crying. What – '

'We're in Hitchings, Charlie. We're coming home. I have found Belle.' Quickly R. C. hung up, though he kept his hand on the receiver.

'What did she – '

R. C. shook his head. 'You'll have to understand. She's

been looking for you since you were three. She's thought of you every day of every week of every month all through those years. It will take time.'

'Come on, R. C., let's go.'

Belle took his hand and led the way back to the car, an expression on her face that suggested that her anticipation and need was at least as great as that of the woman on the other end of the line . . .

At first Charlie thought Martha was having a heart attack. She dropped the phone and sat flat on her chair, her breathing labored.

Then Charlie had found out it was R. C., that he was in Hitchings, and that he was bringing home someone named Belle.

Belle. Charlie had heard the name, though not often. Martha almost never spoke of Belle to him, and he wasn't one to pry. Occasionally in the past he had heard R. C. and Martha talking about Belle, and he'd assumed that it was a child she had lost.

Whoever she was, she was on her way out here, and Martha's face showed no signs of color. Charlie reached up to the top shelf of the cabinet for the good bourbon, poured her a finger, and told her to drink it.

The fumes did the trick, and she looked up with a startled expression. 'He's bringing her home, Charlie,' she murmured. 'Did you hear? R. C. has found – '

Then all at once she was on her feet, clearing the table despite Charlie's efforts to get her to sit still a spell longer. But sitting still wasn't in her plan for the day, and she was every place at once, dumping the dirty dishes in the sink, peering out of the back window, checking on the kids. There were five now, Peter, eight, Maggie, seven, Danny, thirteen, Julie, three, and the baby, John, two weeks, in the crib. The baby had come to them only a couple of weeks ago. Someone had found him in the trash bin behind the five and dime store in Hitchings. Martha was never really happy unless there was a baby in the crib.

He helped take the place of Ezra, who was a freshman at Texas Tech.

Now the baby was asleep, and the others were out back picking strawberries for homemade ice cream.

Watching Martha, Charlie quickly downed the bourbon, sensing he might need the fortification as well, and pitched in to help. The clock on the wall said six thirty-five. Ten more minutes and they would be here.

At a quarter to seven, Charlie stood on the porch, Martha behind the screen door as though she were fearful of stepping all the way out. A few of the children had filled their buckets with strawberries and had drifted around to the front lawn, sensing excitement.

Charlie kept swiveling his head back and forth between the road that led out from Hitchings and poor Martha, who kept thinking of things to do. She drew the apron over her head and smoothed her dress. She pushed her hair back from her face and pinched her cheeks. Charlie had never seen her so agitated.

'Who's coming?' Maggie called up from a sprawled position on the lawn, where she had just completed a fair-to-middling somersault.

'Someone Martha knows,' Charlie answered, figuring that he was the only one capable of answering.

'Who?'

'You just wait and see.' Then he saw the dust, a car coming fast out of Hitchings.

'Martha, they're coming.'

'Charlie,' she replied softly, 'I'm so scared – '

He saw the car, dusty looking, as if they'd driven straight through. Then he saw R. C. waving and at the same time bringing the car to a halt in front of the steps that led up to the porch.

For several moments no one moved, neither R. C. nor his passenger, nor the children, nor Martha, not even Charlie himself. Then he saw the car door on the far side start to open ever so slowly. At the same time Martha stepped out onto the porch.

A young woman appeared, at least the top of her head appeared as she searched the front of the house for what she was looking for.

Martha moved to the top step. Charlie saw her squinting down the walk. She'd forgotten her glasses.

But somehow Charlie suspected that glasses wouldn't make a bit of difference, for she stood at the top step of the porch and watched carefully as the young woman came around the car. Their eyes met and seemed to lock, and as the young woman started up the steps, Martha took one step down. All at once she made a peculiar sound, part laugh, part cry, and then she was running, her arms open. The young woman reached the top of the stairs in time to step into Martha's arms, and they clung to each other, and Charlie heard Martha whispering over and over, 'Belle, Belle . . .'

For several minutes the front yard resembled a garden of statues, no one moving. Finally Charlie saw R. C. crawl wearily out of the car. He saw the children inch closer, Maggie alarmed by the sight of tears. Then at last the two women stepped apart, though they continued to hold on to each other. A curious self-consciousness appeared to set in, Martha at a loss for words for one of the few times in her life.

She started to speak but couldn't and cleared her throat and tried again. 'I'm Martha Drusso. About thirty-two years ago I lost a little girl named Belle. She had blond hair, blue eyes, and right here on the side of her neck there was a small birthmark in the shape of a – '

She never finished, for even as she spoke, the young woman reached up and drew back the collar of her dress.

Well, of course they were hugging again and now laughing. Charlie saw R. C. down at the car leaning against the fender, and he looked plain beat, but he too was grinning. Then Charlie saw Maggie approaching slowly from the yard. In her hand she carried one of Martha's big white daisies. She interrupted the laughing and crying by pulling on Belle's skirt to get her attention.

Belle bent down. 'Hello. Is that for me? Thank you.'

Maggie's daring broke the ice for the others, and within moments they were surrounded by all the kids, each pushing close for special introductions.

Belle and Martha, still holding hands, walked to the porch steps and sat on the lowest one, the better to make their laps available for anyone who wanted to crawl in. Unfortunately all did, and pretty soon the bottom step was a tumbling, giggling confusion of arms, legs, and kisses.

'Are they yours?' Belle asked, obviously enjoying herself.

Martha sat beside her, still wiping at her eyes. 'Not precisely mine. They all started out belonging to someone else. Anyway, I've got them now, and there is nothing I can ever give them that will even equal what they give me every hour of every day.'

Belle listened intently, then leaned over and kissed Martha. For some reason Charlie had the suspicion that there was going to be a lot of that going on for a while. He'd never seen Martha so happily undone.

Finally R. C. managed to get up the steps and stand a few feet away, watching the confusion of children.

Martha looked up at him. 'I have a thousand and one questions.'

'And we have at least as many answers, don't we, Belle?'

But it was still very much the children's hour as one by one each child had to introduce himself, give his or her name and age, and list a couple of unique accomplishments, all of which were properly made over.

It wasn't any more than seven-thirty when Martha slyly announced, 'Bath time, come on, let's go.'

It was an hour earlier than usual, the kids knew it and Martha knew it, but it was obvious she was eager to sit quietly with Belle, figure out the past, and come to grips with all that had happened to both of them.

'Come on,' Martha urged again, gathering her flock to her.

'May I help?' It was Belle, now permanently attached to Maggie, who refused to let go of her hand.

'May you help?' Martha echoed. 'I'm counting on it. Come on, everybody, pick a child. You too, Charlie. The bathtub is that-a-way. Let them do what they can and you do the rest.'

Martha led the way, Julie in hand, followed by Belle with Maggie, followed by R. C. with Peter and Danny, who was old enough to help.

That left Charlie to hold open the doors and fetch a stack of clean towels . . .

About an hour later, with everyone partially soaked from the tub and with the children's room at last quiet, the four of them sat around the big kitchen table, not exactly exhausted, for R. C. could still feel the tension. For some reason he had a pretty good idea that the overhead light in Martha's big kitchen would burn late that night.

'Everyone for coffee?' Martha called from the sink. Not waiting for a reply, she filled the coffeepot and put it on the stove.

Patiently the three of them waited. R. C. kept close watch on Belle, who had grown unusually quiet after the children had gone to bed. She looked tired, and of course she would have to be. With the exception of short naps this would be the third night without solid sleep for both of them. But her quiet now seemed to come from something other than fatigue, a new tension, a new fear.

As R. C. was keeping a close watch on Belle, Belle seemed to be keeping an equally close watch on Martha.

'Martha?'

'I'll be right there, just let me – '

'Did you know my mother?'

The question, stark and unadorned, hung forever on the still air. When after several moments Martha still had not answered, R. C. saw Belle sit up straight on her chair.

'Martha, did you – '

'I did.' Martha's voice seemed dead, without inflection. She was not facing the table, but standing by the sink, looking out of the window at the night.

He saw Belle close her eyes briefly. 'Who – was she?' she asked, her voice scarcely a whisper.

She watched the woman by the sink along with everyone else and saw a curious collapse of her shoulders. Martha held that position for several seconds, then slowly she turned about, lifted her head, and looked straight at Belle. She seemed terrified.

'Will I do?' she asked, and a brief smile crossed her face, though it was quickly canceled as she took a step closer to the table.

'Listen carefully, Charlie,' she said, approaching her chair and holding on to it as though she were in need of its support.

Then she spoke to everyone. 'Charlie and I got cozy once a long time ago. Remember, Charlie, right after graduation? It seemed like a good idea at the time, and it was. We were in love.'

She broke off as though she had embarrassed herself. R. C. listened along with everyone else. He was hearing this for the first time, too.

'I turned up pregnant. I didn't tell you, Charlie, and I know now that was wrong. But I was afraid you would be mad.'

Charlie pushed back in his chair and tried to reach for her hand. But she lifted both in a gentle rebuke. 'No, please, let me finish first.'

He was respectful of her wishes, and she went on.

'I told my mother because I was scared, and that old man overheard us talking and that was that. He threw me out, said he wouldn't have me around embarrassing him and spoiling the family name.'

Charlie left his chair abruptly and walked a distance from the table. 'Anyway, I packed one bag and Mama gave me all her egg money and I hitched a ride into Amarillo and got a bus as far as the money would go, which was Tulsa. I ended up at the Salvation Army Mission, where a man named Captain Meeks took me in and gave me a cot, a meal, and a job.'

She stopped talking and studied her hands. 'I was a large

woman, and it was easy to hide my pregnancy – ' For the first time she broke and bowed her head.

'Well, that Christmas,' she went on, 'I went into labor. I left the mission one night, afraid that if Captain Meeks found out, he'd give me the boot like my father had. I went to the Mayo Hotel, back door. I knew the night porter there. He let me in, and I went down into the basement by the furnace. And a few hours later, here you came.' And she smiled at Belle, who was listening, her hand covering her mouth.

'You were so beautiful,' Martha went on, at last coming around her chair and sitting down as though worn out by her own past. 'I bathed you the best I could and wrapped you in my underslip. I found an old boot box in the corner of the basement, and that was your first cradle.'

She shook her head. 'I don't think I've ever been happier, lying beside that furnace with you in my arms. I rested that night, and then I hid you in the box and hid the box beneath my heavy cape and went back to the mission. Captain Meeks found out, of course, and I told him that I'd helped to deliver you and that your real mother had died. He had let me keep R. C., so I was pretty sure he would let me keep you. And he did.'

Martha looked up to see Belle's reaction and quickly apologized. 'I'm sorry if I . . .'

But Belle said nothing. She stood up from her chair, her eyes on Martha's face, and using the back of other chairs for support, she made her way around the table until she stood before Martha. Slowly she knelt before her, then sat on the floor at her feet, her legs curled to one side, and rested her head in Martha's lap. She said only one word, said it so softly that R. C. scarcely heard, said, 'Mother,' and closed her eyes.

Martha smoothed back Belle's hair in a caressing motion. She looked at R. C., then at Charlie. 'I'm sorry I didn't tell you. I didn't have the heart.' She looked up at the ceiling and continued to caress her daughter in a gentle rhythmic movement.

Poor Charlie. He stopped by Martha's chair, hugged and

kissed her, touched Belle's head, then fled the kitchen for the safe darkness of the back porch, where R. C. heard him blowing his nose over and over again.

The sweet silence was interrupted by Maggie's sharp scream. The child had endless nightmares.

Martha stirred. Belle said, 'Let me go. Please.'

She left the room. A few minutes later Martha and R. C. heard Belle's voice coming from the children's room. 'Come on, Maggie,' she whispered. 'It's all right. Do you see that rocking chair? Come on, I'll sing you a song and we'll rock in that chair until the bad things are gone. Would you like that?'

Head down, R. C. listened and heard the sweetest voice he had ever heard, singing softly, a familiar song usually done in a spirited fashion, now sung as gently and tenderly as a lullaby.

'"Casey would waltz with the strawberry blonde and the band played on . . ."'

R. C. looked up and saw Martha listening, staring straight at him. As the song continued, she leaned forward and reached her hands across the table in his direction, palms up, a clear invitation. He stretched forward until he was touching her hands.

'Thank you,' she whispered.

He put his head down on the table to listen to the voice and feel the peace. Task completed.

A few minutes later Charlie returned, eyes red. He listened to Belle singing, then bent over Martha. 'I love you more than I have ever loved you,' he said simply, and kissed her.

After Maggie's nightmare had been banished, Belle returned. Instead of sitting opposite Martha, she carefully arranged her chair directly between Charlie and Martha.

Then the talking began in earnest: the past relived, the train ride, each talking in turn and out of turn, endless pots of coffee and sandwiches and more coffee and more talk.

When dawn came it was all safely over, all mysteries solved, all questions answered.

All that remained now was to find a way somehow to make up for the lost years. Perhaps it couldn't be done, but R. C. had a pretty fair notion that here were four people very willing to try . . .

As they had taken turns talking all during the night, come morning they took turns napping. But by two o'clock in the afternoon the heat had canceled all sleep, and everyone gathered in the shade of the back porch to watch Charlie spin his magic with the freezer of strawberry ice cream.

Bone weary but happier than she had ever been in her life, Martha never tired of watching Belle. At odd moments she'd catch her eye and the two of them would exchange a glance. Belle always came running to deliver a kiss.

Now Martha watched her in shorts, shirt, and bare feet as she played jump rope with Peter and Maggie. She'd already taught them all the words to 'Casey and the Strawberry Blonde,' and at the least provocation the children would break into song and Belle would join them, her voice silencing the others so that what started out as a group sing always ended up a solo.

Martha's mind was still reeling from everything she'd learned the night before. It would take weeks, months, for her to sort it all out, but Charlie was handling fatherhood very well. He and Belle had taken a long walk before lunch, and both had come back arm in arm, and the first time Belle had called him 'Dad,' Charlie had just about popped his buttons.

Now she saw Belle transfer the jump rope to R. C., and she came breathlessly over to the back steps and sat down. 'I have an idea,' she said.

'What?' Martha asked.

'I think all of you should come back with me to California. The house is so big, isn't it, R. C., and there are swimming pools, tennis courts, horses, and an aviary. Instead of five children we could have fifty, a hundred.'

But even as she spoke Martha smiled and slowly shook her head. 'I don't think so.'

'Why?'

'Because I have what I need here, and I love what I have. I don't need more. Of anything. Least of all now. I have you, and do you know what that makes me? The richest woman in the world.'

'Then I don't want to go back.' Belle sighed.

'You don't have to for a while.'

'Jules will be upset with me. There are always decisions that have to be made. I wish Cy hadn't left it all to me.'

Martha sat on the top step beside her and took her hand. 'Listen, I'm sure Mr Compton knew precisely what he was doing. I'm sure he knew your heart and soul even better than you know them, knew that in time you would use his wealth wisely. And you will, too. Besides, now I have someone to look after you in California. R. C.'

'I want to stay here with you.'

'And I'm not about to let you go. I have an idea,' Martha went on. 'There is one thing I want.'

'Name it.'

'I want you to help me get in touch with everyone you spoke of last night, everyone, leave no one out, that nice Mr Burgess and Billie Rose and Inez and that Mr Schaeffer, what's his name?'

'Jules.'

'Yes, Jules, all of them. Then I want to set up a long picnic table right over there in the shade of those big tall cottonwood trees and I want to cover the table with my best blue-and-white checkered cloth and I want the children to fill fruit jars with daisies and black-eyed susans and line them up and down the center of that table and I'll start frying chicken and Charlie can make his prize potato salad and I want all those people sitting out there at that table, drinking ice-cold lemonade and I want to stand up and thank them for caring for you, for loving you, for watching over you for me. And we'll set a place of honor for Harold and Kim Shoda and remember their goodness. And we'll set a special place for your Cy. Can we do that?'

'Yes . . .'

Charlie called out, 'Ice cream's ready.'

As the children pushed past them on the steps, Martha heard Belle whisper, 'I love you, Mother.'

It took Martha several minutes before she could focus on anything that was going on around her . . .

Belle sat on the porch swing and let her bare feet brush back and forth across the cool floor. She cradled John, held his bottle, and watched as he sucked contentedly.

All around her was everything she had ever dreamed about. Home, family, belonging.

She shifted John in her arms as he drained his bottle. Out on the lawn she watched the children playing tag, the big ones leading, the little ones keeping up as best they could. There was so much love here, so much life, and she was a part of it.

Bottle empty. She put it down and turned John about until she was facing him. She admired his Negro beauty and thought of Mathias and Drew and Jeremy and all the unhappiness she had left behind. She would have to go back sooner or later, but for now she had waited too long for this, had dreamed about it, prayed for it, and now it was here, she was home.

She kissed John, lifted him to her shoulder, and commenced to rub his small back. Maybe this was where she should start, with this infant, with the gift of unconditional love so that when John grew to adulthood he would look about in search of an enemy and find none.

'What are you doing, Belle?'

'Rocking John, Maggie. What are you doing?'

'Watching you. I'm real glad you're home, Belle.'

'So am I, Maggie . . .'

Later that night the front porch was festooned with filled and warm bodies. The children were playing hide-and-seek on the front lawn, Maggie always calling out her hiding place ahead of time for fear of not being found.

Still drying her hands on her apron, Martha stepped out onto the porch in search of a cool breeze. She looked toward the swing and saw Belle rocking John after his bottle. She was nuzzling him and gently rubbing his back.

Charlie sat on his rocker, drawing on his pipe, and R. C. sat on the banister looking up at the stars.

Martha closed her eyes for a brief prayer. It didn't hurt none to let God know that she knew where the credit was due.

Belle placed the baby in his bassinet, then sat back down on the swing. R. C. stretched and yawned, then started down the steps toward the road.

'R. C.?' Belle called out softly. 'Where're you going?'

'Stretch my legs.'

'May I come?'

'Sure.'

Belle left the porch, kissing Martha and Charlie in passing, and caught up with R. C. as he was starting down the steps toward the road.

'Hey, Belle?' Maggie called out. 'Where're you going?'

'Stretch my legs.'

'Can I come?'

'Sure.'

Martha saw Belle and R. C. wait for Maggie, then continued to watch as they turned into the road. She'd never seen R. C. so animated, so alive. He said something. Belle laughed uproariously. R. C. cleverly finagled his way into center position, his arm lightly resting on Belle's shoulder. Now they both were talking a mile a minute.

Martha sat on the top step and continued to watch as R. C. drew Belle yet closer, a protective, loving gesture. Belle's arm was now about his waist while Maggie skipped ahead, kicking up the hot dust of August.

Charlie eased down beside Martha on the top step and watched along with her. 'What do you suppose is going to happen next?' he asked quietly.

Martha grinned, then laughed. She reached for Charlie's hand and kissed it and enclosed it between her own. 'Oh, Charlie, I haven't the faintest idea. But I'll tell you what.'

'What?'

'I can't hardly wait to find out . . .'

Stefan Loose Travel Handbücher

Ursula Spraul-Doring und Richard Doring danken allen Freunden in Thailand, die sie mit Informationen versorgt und unterwegs geholfen haben, vor allem Rene Reinert aus Zürich, Elena aus Krabi, Michael Spjuth von Ko Tao, Jörg Gundlach von Lamai, Thomas Krey aus Phetchaburi. Für exzellente Zusatzrecherche danken wir ganz besonders Klaus Schad aus Chiang Mai, Uwe Löwel aus Mae Sai, Gerlinde Bankemper aus Ko Samui, Monika Schneebeli aus Ko Pha Ngan, Thomas Uhlig und Dit aus Hohenstein-Ernstthal, Kanyarat Tantiviwat aus Bang Sai, Dagmar Minne aus Bremen.

Renate und Stefan Loose danken allen Freunden in Thailand, die sie mit Informationen versorgt und ihnen unterwegs geholfen haben, vor allem Peep Fagrajang und ihren Töchtern Plu, Pla und Paeng aus Bang Yai, Steffen Kochan, Chris und Tan aus Phuket, Apple und Noi aus Kanchanaburi, Armin Hermann aus Sangkhlaburi, Captain Daeng aus Umphang, Uwe Löwel aus Maesai, Klaus Derwanz (†) vom Khao Yai-Nationalpark, Khun Piak von Budget sowie den Mitarbeitern von TAT in Kanchanaburi, Bangkok und Phuket. Besonderen Dank für die Recherche von Pattaya an Volker Klinkmüller aus Chonburi und von Ayutthaya, Sukhothai, Tak und Phitsanulok an die Markands aus Köln.

Zudem bedanken wir uns ganz herzlich bei folgenden Leserbriefschreibern:
Christian Stimming, Bettina Habel, Doreen Tiepke, Marcus Kühn, Sophia Carpetis, Wolfgang Hansen, Tina Sackmann, Christine Falk, Olaf ter Hazeborg, Christa und Henry Heckel, Fabian Brenne, Nina Schulte, Thomas Zorn, Sabine Kunkel, Roland Stuckardt, Klaus Polak, Wolfgang Grimm, Helmut Rieleit, Ron Doering, Ruedi und Ursula Steiner, Anton Schwaighofer, Walter Combosch, Nadine Phlippen, Sonja Ebert und Michaela Raab.

Schreiben Sie uns!
Wir freuen uns über Ergänzungen und Korrekturen, die uns helfen, dieses Buch zu verbessern und aktuell zu halten, am besten per E-Mail. Neue Adressen möglichst in einen Plan einzeichnen. Auch Anregungen, Lob und Kritik sind willkommen.
Besonders hilfreiche Leserbriefe belohnen wir mit einem Freiexemplar aus unserem Verlagsprogramm.

Zuschriften bitte an:
Stefan Loose Travel Handbücher
Zossener Str. 52/2, 10961 Berlin
✉ info@loose-verlag.de